Calling Time
By Adrian Cousins

Also by Adrian Cousins

The Jason Apsley Series

Jason Apsley's Second Chance

Ahead of his Time

Force of Time

Beyond his Time (novella)

Calling Time

Borrowed Time

Deana Demon or Diva Series

It's Payback Time

Death Becomes Them

Dead Goode

Deana – Demon or Diva Series Boxset

The Frank Stone Series

Eye of Time

Blink of her Eye

Before you dive in …

Hello, and thanks for buying this book. This is the fourth part of the Jason Apsley story, which was a trilogy. However, as this is the fourth book, clearly, that is no longer the case. Now it's a tetralogy … apparently. If you've read my Deana series, that will resonate with you. That ghostly diva, with the extensive diction, taught me that new word.

Anyway, if you haven't already, you may want to (and I strongly recommend) read the three preceding books before this one. And perhaps the accompanying novella, *Beyond his Time*.

If you're fully up to speed, then great – dive in. I hope you enjoy Jason's latest time-travel-induced adventure. Before you do, just thought I'd mention that Beth, our hero's seventeen-year-old daughter suffering from a hearty dollop of attitude, can, on the odd occasion, be prone to uttering the odd obscenity – now, as you've made it this far into the series, I'm assuming you can forgive the girl.

Okay, you're good to proceed – oh, but hang on there …

Before you turn the page or swipe left on your Kindle – an action I'm led to believe you would perform on a popular dating app when faced with a creepy bio and picture of a serial killer, not that I've partaken in such activity – dating app or serial killing – but felt it was essential to offer that information for the purposes of clarity – I've laid out below a quick run through of who's who regarding the main characters. It may have been a while since you read *Force of Time* – book three in the trilogy. That's now, apparently, a tetralogy – so you might enjoy a little refresher.

Who's who? A quick reminder …

Jason Apsley – our time-travelling hero. He needs no introduction. Died in 2019, awoke in 1976 – as you do.

Other **Jason** – Ah, him! So, the man our hero replaced in 1976 and subsequently disappeared. If you haven't, although it's not totally necessary to enjoy this book, you might enjoy *Beyond his Time,* which tells his story.

Jenny Apsley – Jason's 'Jessica Rabbit' wife. Not a time-traveller. However, she's a fully paid-up member of the Time Travellers Believers' Club. (TTBC)

Beth Apsley – Jason's bestie from his first life, now his adopted daughter. Biological parents – David Colney and Carol Hall.

Chris Apsley – Beth's half-brother, adopted by Jenny and Jason. Biological parents – Carol Hall and an unknown.

George Sutton – Jason's grandfather from his first life, and now a close friend in his second. George is one of the five members of the TTBC.

Martin Bretton – Also known as Leonardo Bretton, Jason's work colleague from his first life. Martin died six months after Jason in 2019 and time-travelled six months later, arriving in 1977. Technically speaking, Andrew Colney is his biological father following his mother suffering a sexual assault in 1987.

However, due to time-travel, that assault was expunged, so Martin's existence in his and Jason's second life is ... well, I guess, just a time-travelling mystery.

Jess Poole – *Other* Jason's biological daughter. However, due to Jason replacing *other* Jason in 1976, Jess regards Jason and Jenny as her parents. Although she hasn't partaken in such activity, Jess is also a fully paid-up member of the TTBC.

Paul Colney – Nasty bastard. Probably the evilest git on the planet. Died 1977 in a car crash with Martin. Both men time-travelled to 1987. (That's when Martin became Leonardo.) Paul murdered his brother, Patrick, amongst others, before disappearing abroad.

Patrick Colney – Paul Colney's twin, murdered by Paul in 1987. Ex-boyfriend of Jess and father to Faith Poole, Jess's daughter.

David Colney – When a sixteen-year-old schoolboy in 1976, he enjoyed a one-night stand with Carol Hall. Thus becoming Beth's biological father. David abused baby Beth in Jason's first life, resulting in a prison sentence and Beth being raised in a children's home. David became a serial killer in 2015. When Jason time-travelled, he prevented Beth from being abused by David before dropping him to his death from the top of the flats on the Broxworth Estate, thus expunging the rampage of murder that older David embarked on in 2015.

Andrew Colney – The youngest of the four evil Colney boys. Technically, Martin's biological father. Andrew was caught and sentenced in 1987 for a series of sexual assaults. In 1994, he's still enjoying a stay at Her Majesty's pleasure.

Shirley Colney – Criminal matriarch, mother to the four Colney boys. Unbeknown to all until 1987, Shirley and *other* Jason were half-siblings. Shirley died in 1987 when run over by Beryl Brown (née Hall) on the Carrow Road Bridge.

Carol Hall – *Other* Jason's and subsequently Jason's neighbour on the Broxworth Estate. The estranged daughter of Beryl Brown and the biological mother of Beth and Chris. Murdered by Paul Colney in 1976.

Beryl Brown – Beth and Chris's grandmother. The illegitimate daughter of Donald Nears. Due to abuse at the hands of Shirley Colney when in a children's home in the 1940s, Beryl killed Shirley in 1987.

Donald Nears – Ah, our dearly departed Don. Didn't we all love him, eh? *Other* Jason's and subsequently Jason's neighbour on the Broxworth Estate. Due to their friendship, Don became Jason's honorary father. Don died at ninety-one in 1987, moments after joining the TTBC.

DCI French – Frenchie, as we affectionately like to know her. DCI Heather French worked her way through the system to become Fairfield's lead detective. She knows, but can never prove, there's something not quite right about Jason Apsley.

Carlton King – A pupil at Jason's school in 1976. In Martin's first life, he was a close friend of his mother's and became editor of the Fairfield Chronicle, where George once worked. Carlton is an inquisitive, ferret-type investigative journalist in Jason's second life.

Prologue – The Good Life

April 1994

"The good old British weather, eh," Tony muttered, shaking his head.

To ensure the occupants of the beaten-up, ancient-looking camper van couldn't spot his half-hidden position, Tony loitered behind the cover afforded by a large oak a few yards into the dense copse flanking the parking area. He cupped the half-smoked rollie in his mud-splattered hand to avoid the lit end of his cigarette being spotted in the fading early evening twilight.

However, they weren't his only concern. To his right, Tony also spotted a dog walker. Taking care not to be seen, he peeked around the oak, flitting his eyes back and forth from the man clipping the dog on its lead and the couple holed up in the VW.

Despite an unseasonal warm spring, resulting in the Easter holiday reaching temperatures just north of twenty degrees, three days later and, somewhat inevitably, normal service was resumed. Wet, cold, and frigging miserable.

Tony tipped his head back, glanced up and sighed, squinting to avoid the misty drizzle assaulting his eyes. God, he hated this place.

"Not for much longer," he mumbled.

After a few years of living in sunnier climes, which the Costa del Sol offered, a brief trip to Fairfield reminded him why he hadn't missed the damn place. Less than a few weeks back in the UK, he now missed the sun, the birds, the booze, the 'good life' he'd become accustomed to.

Stuff Britain, with its shit weather, crap government, whinging birds, interfering neighbours, TV personalities with over-inflated opinions of themselves, expensive cigarettes, traffic jams, queuing, Eastenders, the Welsh, the Scots, the Irish, Scousers, yada yada yada, the frigging list was endless. Britain was no longer British. Back in the '70s, a man could be a man. Not anymore. As far as Tony was concerned, the dreary place he'd once called home had gone soft.

Anyway, he'd started to leave a trail of destruction, so now was probably the right time to leave. Sod this dump; he was going home. After stealthily taking one last drag on his cigarette, Tony nipped the lit end between his fingers before lobbing the butt beside his mud-caked shovel that lay on the sodden earth.

"Come on, piss off," Tony hissed between gritted teeth.

He shivered as the rainwater snaked down his shoulder-length hair before finding its way inside his collar and down his back. After digging for the best part of an hour, and although building up a decent sweat as the chilly twilight set in, his sodden hoodie now served as a cool pack against his skin.

Tony removed the Bowie knife from his back pocket and twizzled the blade in his hand as his eyes flicked back and forth between the camper van and his rental car parked not twenty or so feet behind. Fortunately, the dog walker had disappeared somewhere along the main road.

The young couple, New Age traveller, eco-warrior, tree-hugging types, didn't appear as if they planned to continue their journey anytime soon. The bearded chap, who flicked his cigarette ash through the quarter-inch gap of his cranked-down window, appeared to be laughing at something the woman had said. When assessing the girl, Tony thought she looked like a hippy student type as she propped her bare feet on the dashboard whilst drinking coffee from a flask. Disappointingly, they didn't appear to be going anywhere soon and had set in for the night.

"Bollocks." Tony sniffed and wiped his dripping nose with the back of his hand, which gripped the seven-inch blade, whilst contemplating his next move.

By the weekend, he would be back in sunnier climes. So, being spotted by the tree-huggers should be of little or no consequence. However, he was still here, and he'd rather not draw unnecessary attention to himself. Tony weighed up his options. The hippy couple would probably fail to remember his rental car if questioned at a future date. He'd been careful, swapping out his car every few days to avoid leaving a traceable trail. However, a man appearing from the edge of the woods carrying a shovel on a cold, wet evening would be memorable.

Tony's choices were limited. He could risk being spotted, which might lead to *the filth* sniffing around the woods and then a news bulletin describing him and his car. A situation he could ill afford before his flight later this week. Or, he could add to the body count and dig two more graves. Although ruddy annoying, collateral damage was sometimes inevitable in his line of work.

Neither option appealed.

Taking into account his joy of inflicting pain and the fact that option two would cover his tracks, that seemed the safer option. However, disappointingly, that would involve more digging in this crap weather, plus being left with a shit-heap of a camper van to dispose of. Despite his predilection to revel in and enjoy torture and murder, Tony thought one grave was enough digging for tonight. He dismissed option two with a sniff and a shake of his head.

Option one, then.

Tony wiped his prints from the shovel, planning on lobbing it into the bushes to avoid arousing too much suspicion when appearing from the woods. With the shovel raised, poised to be tossed, Tony hesitated when spotting movement. The bearded tree-hugger hopped out of his van and jauntily headed towards Tony's position whilst fumbling with his fly.

"Adam, d'you want me to hold it for you?" the woman playfully called out as she cranked down her window.

"I think you'll have a job. It's that bleeding cold out here, I can hardly find it," Adam chuckled, skipping along with his hand rummaging around in his underpants, stopping a foot short of the tree Tony employed as cover.

Tony held his breath.

Adam hooked out his appendage and offered a satisfied sigh to the heavens as he urinated on Tony's boots that poked out from behind a tree.

Psychopath, lunatic, madman, dangerous fucker, just some of the labels which various people had chosen to slap on him throughout his life – even his mother. Fair enough. Murderer and rapist could easily be added to that list. However, apart from his mother, no one had proved those last two. Anyway, Tony had a short fuse, so it wasn't his fault, was it?

Some tree-hugging, bearded knob pissing on his boots after he'd endured a bleeding soaking when digging a ditch to dump his latest victim in was enough to light the blue touch paper. It didn't take much where Tony was concerned.

Just as Adam finished urinating, with a hearty shake of his John-Thomas, Tony stepped around the tree, holding the shovel aloft.

"Oi, you pissed on my boots."

The bearded man, still gripping his exposed appendage, bulged his eyes whilst involuntarily allowing his jaw to sag. As if struggling to focus on two tasks at once, now his focus had moved to gawping at the grinning man who stood before him, Adam halted his penis-waving mid-shake.

Tony swung the shovel's blade in an arc towards Adam's head. The ping that emanated when steel met skull caused the woman to look up and peer through the opened window.

"Adam? Adam, you okay?"

Tony crouched down on his haunches to finish the boot-pisser with his Bowie knife before stepping clear of the trees and striding towards the camper van.

"Adam …" With her hand gripping the half-opened window, the woman paused. "Where's Adam?" She flung open the door and hopped out, giving an exaggerated sigh as her bare feet met the muddy ground.

"Your boyfriend pissed on my boots."

"Hey, who the hell …" again, she paused when noticing the knife held loosely by his side as he made up ground between them.

"Who … where's … oh, God, no," she muttered, now rooted to the spot, fearing what might have happened, or more to the point, what was about to happen.

Tony waved the knife over his shoulder towards Adam's body. "Your boyfriend's bleeding out over there in the trees. If he's not already, I reckon he'll be dead in a few seconds."

The woman swivelled her eyes towards the trees as her brain registered what was going down before preparing to take flight.

Too late.

As she pinwheeled around, Tony barbarously snatched her forearm and hauled her close to him.

"Adam pissed on my boots," he huffed in her face before shooting his eyes downwards. "My boots … they're covered in his frigging piss."

"Who … who," she stammered.

"Me? You're asking who I am, are you, girl?" Keeping a tight grip on her arm, he cupped his hand that gripped the knife around the back of her head. "I'm your frigging worst nightmare."

Part 1

1

October 2015

Message in a Bottle

For the purpose of maintaining an upright position, I white-knuckle gripped the doorframe whilst waiting for the fluorescent strip light to go through its painfully long humming and flickering sequence before it would hopefully illuminate the garage. I should have replaced the light years ago. That particular task, just one of those unfancied jobs on that metaphorical to-do list, always seemed to get relegated to the bottom.

With my free hand, I clutched an envelope containing a letter I'd earlier penned – a one-page letter to my younger self – which, without a doubt, had proved to be the most challenging letter I'd ever written.

Almost to the day, thirty-nine years had elapsed since Jenny and I, along with our two adopted children, moved into our new home on Winchmore Drive. A forever home that, since the development was built in the late '70s, has always been regarded by the residents of Fairfield as a rather select suburb in the unremarkable Hertfordshire market town. And, forty years on, Winchmore Drive maintained that slightly snobby factor about its allotted postcode.

Anyway, as I was saying, thirty-nine years. Which is five years more than the Yorkshire Ripper has so far served after the police felt his collar in January 1981. A lifetime, you could say. Although today was my penultimate day in our forever home, I was leaving with great sadness, not the euphoria of release I presume a 'lifer' would experience. Something I suspected Mr Sutcliffe would never enjoy unless the parole board completely lost their sense of justice.

Of course, during my first few years after time-travelling back to the mid-seventies, I'd devoted a significant amount of time and energy to achieve a cessation of that serial killer's murderous rampage. However, as I soon discovered, knowing the future offered a negligible advantage in being able to change it. Little did I know back then that another serial killer would become more of a concern.

Despite those challenges when attempting to alter time, over the past four decades, Jenny, George, and I, the three founder members of the Time Travellers Believers' Club, achieved some minor successes when attempting to change the future. However, in the main, the future remained rigid and unwilling to veer from its laid down path that history demanded.

Time didn't bend easily.

So, this was it. The final chapter, perhaps. I was moving on to the next phase of my rather extraordinary life. Well, I'd lived two of them. Forty-two years in my first one, which I can't say I hold too many fond memories of, and forty in the second.

The latter being a significant improvement on the first. I'd been a lucky man. Time-travel had provided me with a chance for a second life, which I'd firmly grabbed hold of. Unlike anyone else I'd met, except Martin Bretton and Paul Colney, I lived my eighty-two years over a forty-year period.

Confused? Well, you should try living it. Because, believe you me, reliving the last quarter of the twentieth century and the first fifteen years of the new millennium hasn't been easy.

"Paul Colney," I muttered, before shaking my head and glancing down at the letter wobbling in my trembling hand.

My doctor, a decent sort whose youthful appearance and lingering acne suggested he may have only just escaped puberty, reckoned I displayed the classic signs of stage-four dementia. As I waited for the garage light to spring into life, I considered he may have made an accurate diagnosis. For starters, as I stood hovering in the doorway, I couldn't remember whether I had actually snapped the light on or not.

Often, I struggled to recall my children's names, whether I was married or where we stored the milk. Some days, my memory operated on low-power mode, rendering me in nothing short of a vegetative state. Conversely, on the more lucid days, which were becoming less frequent, I could recall events of my past in surprisingly accurate detail. Today was the latter, easily remembering my first life in 2019 – forty years ago – as if it were yesterday.

The bulb flickered, confirming the damn useless thing was still going through its startup routine – a man could grow a beard or even die waiting. Although, whether a beard was forthcoming, at least it confirmed I had turned the damn thing on. I raised an apathetic eyebrow at my failing brain. Pink blancmange, as I referred to that now useless organ.

Whilst waiting for the dark vista of my double garage to illuminate, my mind drifted to events that were a little easier to recall. For some reason, it settled on the memory of that tosser, Mike, the investment banker chap who lived next door to Beth in that first life that somehow, the second time around, no longer existed.

Time-travel was a confusing thing to get your head around. Anyway, during my first life, back in 2019, when straining my head against the bedroom window of Beth's spare bedroom, I'd embarrassingly ogled at Mike's wife, Amanda, whilst she wallowed topless in their offensively sizeable hot tub. I chuckled, remembering how Beth would refer to her flirtatious neighbour.

"Tits-Out-Amanda," I muttered, smirking at the memory.

Of course, that's before I'd time-travelled to 1976. A time when it's safe to say my character was not the most affable. "Miserable bastard," I muttered. Yes, that just about covered it. Or, as I'd once coined the phrase to describe the man from that now non-existence, Jason Twat Apsley. You see, time-travel provided character development enhancements, which significantly improved the man I once was.

Anyway, Mike and Amanda lived in that house in this life, just as they had when 2015 came around the first time. And, safe to say, Mike was still a tosser. As for Amanda, his Jayne-Mansfield-look-alike-wife, I couldn't comment. In this life, I wasn't the ogling type. And even if I was, in this second life, Beth didn't live next door to the tosser and Tits-Out-Amanda.

I afforded myself a broad smile when thinking of Beth. My adopted daughter, in this life, wasn't a lonely forty-year-old and never became a marketing executive. Instead, my best friend from my first life was married, with a wonderful nine-year-old son, and had followed my wife's career into social care. My daughter didn't enjoy all the material trappings of her first life, which never happened if you get my drift. However, she was far richer in this life – not measured in financial wealth, but in happiness – a quote from my wise counsel and long departed friend, George.

The vast majority of events from my first life happened again in my second. Climate change still threatened our existence; The Clash still disbanded in 1986 – gutted; the twin towers of the World Trade Centre suffered that fateful terrorist attack; Fred West continued his campaign of murder along with burying his victims in the basement of his Gloucester home, and Joe Dolce's *Shaddap Your Face* kept Ultravox's *Vienna* from reaching number one – a travesty.

I attest those five events could not be categorised as having the same gravitas, but you get my drift. Additionally, George Sutton, my close friend, died in 1997. Just as he did in my first life when taking on the role of my grandfather.

That fluorescent bulb, which had amassed an impressive collection of dust and cobwebs during its life sentence of hanging from the roof's rafters, pinged on, illuminating the garage space, which contained what most garages across the country also harboured. Namely, a collection of reasonably useless half-used tins of paint, a battered and dented toolbox, a redundant set of rusting golf clubs, along with a plethora of brown cardboard boxes containing God knows what. However, this garage provided storage space for one item that most garages didn't – a near-mint-condition 1974 yellow Mk3 Ford Cortina.

According to that pubescent doctor I'd become well acquainted with, to accompany the dementia, my physical well-being was also on the slide. He even joked that I was his best customer.

So, over the last year, coinciding with tragically losing Jenny to an aggressive cancer, during my bi-weekly visits to the GP surgery, I discovered that, along with osteoarthritis, I also suffered a fascinating case of pulmonary heart disease. Well, that's what my acne-faced doctor said as he chuckled, stating that he found it amazing I wasn't already six feet under. As I said, he was a pleasant enough chap. However, he seriously needed to work on his bedside manner, which was woefully lacking.

I'd become a keen runner during my fifties and sixties, mainly inspired by an urgent need to hang on to my youth because my wife was twelve years my junior. However, my body now signalled that enough was enough. I'd read that a woman of eighty-eight completed the London Marathon this year, whereas for me, crossing the garage took precision planning and a significant amount of energy.

In one surprisingly swift movement, I threw off the dust cover that protected my vintage car. Apart from being one of the mass-produced saloon cars of the age of glam rock, disco, space-hoppers, and the disturbing emergence of polyester slacks, this particular XL model of a Mk3 Cortina also doubled up as a time machine – apparently.

In this very motor, Martin and I had arrived in 1976 and 1977, respectively. Also, Martin and Paul Colney died in the thing and reappeared ten years later in 1987. Despite being crushed when Martin slammed the bonnet into an oak tree along Coldhams Lane one February night in '77, the police returned it to me in mint condition ten years later. And here it sat, parked in my garage as it had for the past thirty years.

Although I'd never driven it again, scared shitless about the potential issue of time-travelling to some distant era or an even more scary thought of back to 2019 and a return to my first life, I'd often sat in the driver's seat whilst contemplating the ridiculous. Jenny had regularly pestered me to rid ourselves of the hideous thing, as she would say, fearing it could only cause us heartache. Although I agreed with her, I felt the safest place for a time machine was securely locked up in my garage.

After depressing the chrome button, the door hinges gave their familiar squeak as I tentatively pulled open the driver's door and peered inside. Unsurprisingly, the ageing upholstery permeated the interior with a musty smell. My olfactory senses were assaulted by the stale stench of cigarettes and mildew. For one last time, I gingerly shimmied my ageing frame onto the seat and closed the door.

My two adopted children, Beth and Chris, insisted I move in with either of them, suggesting I could spend six months a year at each house. However, they had their lives and families. So, as of tomorrow, I will move into a two-roomed suite at Waverly House, a care home for the elderly. Although I lacked enthusiasm for turning the page and embarking on my life's epilogue, I'd accepted the natural progression towards my final resting place. I'd lost my Jenny, and my adopted children were contented. I was ready for what lay ahead in what I suspected was the not-too-far-distant future.

Chris and Beth planned to handle the transfer of my personal possessions, organise the sale of unwanted items of furniture, and proceed with the house sale. On my strict instructions, the Cortina was to be transferred to Chris's garage on the proviso that it stayed in position and was never driven. A clause in my will stipulated that either Beth or Chris must keep and securely store the car for the remainder of their lives – I had my reasons.

Although I doubted my idea would work, I at least owed it to my younger self to try. This car, which I stored in my garage thirty years ago, had unequivocally possessed time-travel powers – I think. Well, there could be no other explanation, despite the ridiculous notion that a mass-produced saloon car could somehow double up as a TARDIS.

Despite the engine lying dormant for three decades, I silently prayed the Cortina would somehow take my letter back in time. If, and that was a pretty sizable if, successful, my actions could provide my younger self with the information and reason to bend time. From what I learned less than a month ago, lives depended on it. Specifically, one life who'd since time-travelling had become very dear to me.

After pinging open the glove compartment, and despite suspecting the futility of my actions, I glanced at the envelope where I'd penned my name before placing it inside.

"It won't work, will it?" I muttered, before closing the flap and taking a moment to gather my strength to haul myself out of the car. I closed my eyes and offered an audible sigh.

Although I can't explain how my Cortina's time-travelling properties work, they seem to be initiated via a collision or crash. So, placing a letter to my younger self in the past, without crushing the bonnet, suggested my attempts to contact me before 1994 were probably futile.

However, after that meeting a few months ago, I had to do something. Of course, I could attempt time-travel again. One option I'd considered in a moment of madness involved taking the Cortina out for a spin, driving headlong at a tree and killing myself. Although that may ping me through time, wherever I'd end up, I'd still be an eighty-one-year-old man suffering from dementia and a whole host of physical ailments that fascinated my pubescent doctor. I would not be in any fit state to prevent the future, which my letter detailed. Also, my adopted children had forged a life for themselves, so I couldn't justify pinging back in time and thus undoing their lives.

The other option I'd considered, only for a fleeting moment, mind, involved coming clean with my children about that meeting and letting them deal with the issue. However, that would only serve to confirm that I'd completely lost my mind and wouldn't change history.

Altering the past is what *needed* to happen. Of course, changing what had gone before would inevitably change the here and now. For me, well, I was tired. I'd had my life; I was done.

However, I feared what would happen to Beth and Chris in their futures if my younger self changed the past. This dilemma and complicated time-travel conundrum, even for someone possessing a more youthful, sharper brain than mine, were somewhat tricky to comprehend. So, as you can imagine, for me, a senior citizen with failing health, it was a real head spinner.

Anyway, despite the potential complications of my actions, I'd concluded if that letter achieved my aims back in 1994, an alternate timeline would form. Beth and Chris had made good life choices, so I figured they'd do it again just as successfully.

Although entirely futile, and whilst accepting I'd hung up my time-travelling boots, hoping my Cortina could magically send that letter through time remained the best option. My desperate plea to my younger self – a message in a bottle tossed into the sea type scenario, if you like.

For the last time, I hauled my ageing frame out of that yellow Mk3 Cortina. Despite not being the religious type, I offered a brief prayer to whoever might be of the mind to hear my plea to change the past.

With the knowledge recently acquired regarding what happened in 1994, I'd willingly sell my soul to the devil if that would help.

2

1994

Easter Rising

"To sum up. My team is working tirelessly to apprehend the perpetrator of such a heinous crime. As alluded to earlier, I can confirm that we have a thirty-nine-year-old man in custody who is currently helping us with our inquiries. However, at this stage, I am not in a position to offer any further information. I can assure you all that the Hertfordshire Constabulary fully understands the public's concern and will leave no stone unturned to bring the perpetrator to justice."

"What about Gary O'Rourke? The man your officer shot," bellowed one reporter in an attempt to be heard over the indecipherable caterwauling caused by the shouts from the assembled press.

"As I stated a moment ago ..." DCI French paused to allow the room to quieten. "As I stated a moment ago, the wholly regrettable death of Mr O'Rourke is under investigation. However, *this* press briefing is to update you on the investigations into the death of Sandy Rathbone. Of course, along with the investigations into the murder of PC

Darren Tomsett, my colleagues will update you with any further developments when we are in a position to do so."

DCI Heather French concluded her brief statement before brushing some invisible lint from her jacket and rising from her seat. Predictably, the volley of shouts from reporters who'd leapt to their feet and thrust forward their Dictaphones descended the press briefing into chaos. Before Heather could scurry away from the hordes of clicking photographers, Pepé Le Pew, the Divisional Superintendent, who'd joined her for the briefing but, as usual, said nothing, gently placed his hand on her forearm, thus encouraging her to remain seated.

After huffing a revolting waft of his halitosis breath in her direction, causing Heather's eyes to water, the Super held his hand aloft to the members of the press and cameramen, indicating he wished to add something. Despite feeling the need to gag due to the air around her becoming a concentrated mixture of rotting meat marinated in raw sewerage caused by her senior officer's open mouth, which remained pointing in her direction, Heather raised an inquisitive eyebrow. Whilst waiting for the hubbub of shouting pressmen to abate, the DCI wondered what whittling drivel the misogynistic dinosaur, whose breath should be bottled and donated to medical science, was going to offer to the baying members of the local and national press.

A couple of days ago, to the hour, the day before the Easter break, Uniform entered a flat in Dublin House, one of the three brutal grey concrete monolithic towers that made up the Broxworth Estate, after a neighbour had reported a foul smell wafting out of the kitchen extractor.

Apparently, the vile odour was so repugnant it masked the usual smells of stale urine that hung like a heavy fog on all landings across the odious estate. That said, Heather doubted

30

it could be anywhere near as vile as the stench emanating from her senior officer's mouth. Hence, the popular moniker afforded the Divisional Superintendent.

The two officers, unfortunate enough to respond to the call, discovered the decomposing body of a thirty-eight-year-old sex worker, Sandy Rathbone. The less experienced of the two officers, three weeks into his probation period, managed to pebble dash the woman's putrid remains. Whilst the young probation officer chundered over a crime scene, the experienced officer addressed the ever-growing posse of onlookers. Although, as this was the Broxworth, more of a rabble than concerned citizens. All who possessed an unhealthy morbid fascination as they gathered on the landing.

That's the precise point when this murder elevated from what it was – a murder of a local woman – into a news item that had hit not only the air conditioning but the national news.

Heather recalled the report on the BBC's News at Six. After the BBC political correspondent, John Sergeant, eloquently informed the viewers about circulating rumours in the halls of Westminster that the Prime Minister, John Major, faced a potential leadership challenge and Lady Thatcher had waded in to offer her support to the beleaguered PM, Martyn Lewis, the news anchorman, cut to the story emerging from Fairfield.

During Heather's lifetime, the unremarkable Hertfordshire town rarely appeared on the national news. And when it did, the Broxworth Estate was never too far from being the centre of the story.

That experienced officer, now under investigation for misconduct, had taken it upon himself to inform the awaiting rabble that it was only a dead *Tom*, so there was nothing to see. The residents of the Broxworth didn't need much provocation to riot, and the officer's matter-of-fact attitude to the poor woman's death led to a night of rioting.

After a budget-breaking amount of overtime, the deployment of riot shields and a water cannon borrowed from the Met, some semblance of law and order was restored in the wee hours of Good Friday morning. The local council, shops, and insurance companies would be counting the cost for months. Also, fourteen officers were still languishing in Fairfield General, recovering from injuries sustained.

However, that all paled into insignificance when one of their own, PC Darren Tomsett, was fatally stabbed in the ensuing melee by persons unknown. That ill-judged, and frankly misogynistic comment to the rabble of onlookers sparked a riot and ultimately led to the death of a well-loved, young beat officer. To add to the shit storm, a trigger-happy firearms officer had shot dead one of the mob to boot.

Easter in the unremarkable Hertfordshire town of Fairfield had turned into a shit storm.

Heather could easily empathise with the anger resonating across the estate. Not the rioters, most of whom were just rent a mob and probably couldn't give two shits about Sandy Rathbone. However, this whole mess, the death of an officer and the shooting of a rioter, had been a self-inflicted disaster caused by one officer's misogynistic comment about the demise of a young woman.

Although she had the strength of character to channel her efforts into apprehending the killers, she could lynch the suspended officer if given half the chance.

Fortunately for Heather's olfactory receptors, Pepé Le Pew turned away from her as he addressed the press.

"We will take a few questions, as long as they are regarding this case and not pertaining to the unfortunate death of Mr O'Rourke or our fallen officer, PC Tomsett. As DCI French stated, those are separate enquiries currently under investigation by our colleagues in the Met."

Heather shot her senior officer her best I'm-not-amused face. The planned press briefing had only been called in an attempt to dampen down the headlines regarding police incompetence, which correctly suggested had led to the riots. A brief statement with no opportunity for questions would hopefully stop the adverse reporting about the riots and the murder investigation that, so far, had yielded few leads. However, it appeared the Super had hijacked the briefing, which would expose the DCI to a volley of difficult questions. For sure, she knew the Super wouldn't be answering them. Firstly, he wouldn't know the answers; secondly, he was a useless crown-epauletted buffoon.

"Inspector, Inspector," called out Braithwaite, a particularly annoying reporter employed by the Fairfield Chronicle, with whom Heather, unfortunately, had dealings with on a regular basis. Most of their exchanges over the years could be described as being less than cordial.

Heather knew Braithwaite had purposely addressed her as Inspector, not Chief Inspector, just to rile her. However, she would be the bigger person and not rise to the bait.

Pepé Le Pew nodded to Braithwaite as the hubbub in the room simmered down, now momentarily filled with only the sound of camera shutters.

"Inspector," he smirked. "Can you confirm the actions of your officer, who discovered the body of Sandy Rathbone, caused the riots on the Broxworth Estate?"

"No." Heather barked her one-word response, glowering at Braithwaite whilst the objectionable, oppugnant provocateur continued to smirk. Of course, Braithwaite and everyone else knew his statement to be true. However, Heather wasn't going to sit here and confirm the fact.

Braithwaite followed up on Heather's one-word response. "Inspector, would it be fair to say that the Hertfordshire Constabulary CID, led by your good self, is incapable of effectively investigating crime?"

"No, it would not be fair to say," Heather hissed in reply. Although ever the professional, it took all her self-control not to arrest the man. What the charge would be, who knew, but one day, she would get the parasitical git.

"Inspector, I respectfully put it to you, that is the case. You have the murder of Sandy Rathbone. The murder by one of *your* firearms officers of an innocent man, Gary O'Rourke, not to mention the murder of one of your constables." He paused to raise his hand to halt any interruptions from his peers. "Might that not indicate that the Fairfield Police, including yourself, are all incompetent? This is a small town, and through the police's failures to enforce law and order, our communities now live in a state of fear."

"Mr Braithwaite. As my superintendent has stated, this press briefing is regarding the murder of Sandy Rathbone. Regarding the other deaths, as I stated earlier, my colleagues we will be updating you all later today. Also, just for the record, I do not accept your assessment of the policing capability of my team. Thank you. Next question."

Pepé Le Pew pointed to a reporter in the front row. Heather recognised the face but couldn't quite place the name.

"Chief Inspector."

Better, thought Heather.

"Have you and your team looked into the possibility that the perpetrator of Sandy Rathbone's murder could be Paul Colney?"

Twenty-five years had elapsed since Heather French joined the force. She'd battled hard as she fought against the old establishment to climb the greasy pole of success. That dedication and fortitude had paid off, now holding the lofty status of Chief Inspector and the most senior detective in Fairfield. This was her town, and nothing fazed her. Despite that idiot, Braithwaite, and his quip about incompetence, her record in solving crime was second to none. However, this unusually polite reporter's question had dumbfounded her, sideswiping her composure, leaving her with a gaping mouth, resulting in a few camera-wielding parasites to lean forward and capture the shot which would without a doubt hit the front page of the local rag.

"Ehm … sorry. Um … could you repeat the question?" Heather stammered, presuming she must have misheard him because Paul Colney was dead.

A murmuring of soft whispers performed an audible Mexican wave around the room when the members of the assembled press detected the DCI falter. Before they could verbalise their collective glee and thus go for the kill when spotting the officer's vulnerability, the reporter repeated his question.

"I said, have you and your team considered the possibility that the perpetrator of Sandy Rathbone's murder could be Paul Colney?"

Heather blinked a few times as she stared back at him. She hadn't misheard. Every detective had one case that eluded them. A case that kept them awake at night and would haunt their retirement. Heather had one such case from 1987.

She knew one of the detectives on the Eve Stratford case, the Bunny Girl brutally murdered in 1975. Now retired, growing prize roses in his garden in a sleepy village just north of Fairfield, that detective often talked about the devastating effect of failing to catch Eve's killer. Apparently, he'd been quoted saying that he could rarely make it through a whole twenty-four-hour period without being consumed with thoughts about the case and, more to the point, that the evil killer was still at large.

Paul Colney and the string of murders in 1987, including Susan Kane, had the potential to be Heather's version of her retired friend's Eve Stratford. However, the Paul Colney case was far more complicated than the killing of a model nearly twenty years ago.

Pepé Le Pew's nervous cough, shot in her direction, caused by Heather's lack of response to the question, acted like smelling salts, thus hauling the DCI from her reverie. Heather cleared her throat and took a sip of water as she eyed up the reporter who'd asked the question.

"Mr …" she raised an eyebrow.

"King, Carlton King. Formerly of the Fairfield Chronicle and now working freelance. Mainly for the *Today* newspaper and the *News of the World*."

Heather groaned. She could remember him now. Although Mr King hadn't been quite the thorn in her side as Mr Braithwaite remained, she recalled a couple of set-tos when the then young reporter probed for information some years back. Not that she remembered all reporters, past and present, but Carlton King had attended the Eaton City of Fairfield School and, in passing conversation, had mentioned his old teacher, Jason Apsley.

Heather harboured a great dislike for the word 'coincidence'. And that word and Mr Apsley went hand in hand. Some years ago, her team had cause to question the schoolteacher during the investigation into the murder of Susan Kane. Not that he was a suspect, as such. However, his lack of cooperation led to a charge of perverting the course of justice being thrown at the slippery schoolteacher, which was later dropped due to the lack of evidence.

The fact that one of Jason Apsley's old students had cause to ask a ridiculous question about Paul Coney seemed all too much of a coincidence – the word Heather refused to allow her team to utter. To make matters worse, this inquisitive pressman had links to the nationals.

The relatively newish tabloid, the *Today* newspaper, the brainchild of Eddie Shah, wasn't of significant consequence. The failing paper enjoyed a low readership and was reportedly on newspaper death row. However, the *News of the World* was a whole different ball game.

Again, playing for time, she took another sip of water before responding, dreading the potential headlines and accompanying picture, which might end up on the cover of the best-selling Sunday tabloid. It would be just her luck that said picture would share the front page of the trashy publication detailing the story of the latest politician's exposé regarding some sordid affair.

Since the Prime Minister announced the *Back-To-Basics* campaign, Heather mused the fact that there seemed to be a plethora of Westminster sleaze scandals. They poured out of the woodwork with such regularity there appeared to be a politician and associated floozy grabbing the headlines on almost a weekly basis.

There was the Paddy-Pants-Down headlines a couple of years ago, not to mention the revelations of the early eighties when the then incumbent MP for Fairfield, Jemma Stone, had dumped her husband and run off with another MP. That particular headline news served to compound the embarrassment for the local Conservative Party following a scandal a few years earlier involving their candidate for the 1979 election. Brian Gray, a clean-cut local councillor and family man, tipped for future high office in central government, unfortunately, had been papped by a determined, terrier-like photographer when indulging in some extracurricular activities with a well-known drug dealer. Unfortunately for him, due to the Jeremy Thorpe case, which had suffocated the headlines not months before, society had lost its tolerance for such affairs.

Despite accepting that the vast majority served their country with vigour and determination to improve Joe Public's lot, Heather harboured no time for politicians. And to be balanced about her lack of enthusiasm for those in Whitehall, scandals knew no political boundaries. The Paddy-Pants-Down revelation was for a different political party and, when considering the Stonehouse scandal of the '70s, it seemed no political affiliation was immune from such seedy revelations. Anyway, Heather didn't fancy sharing the front page with any of that lot, whatever coloured rosette they sported on their lapels.

The DCI took a deep breath before addressing Mr King with her well-practised I'm-not-intimidated glare.

"Mr King, as you will be fully aware, Paul Colney died in a road traffic accident in 1977. Therefore, his death seventeen years ago would suggest that he could not be involved in the murder of Sandy Rathbone. Also, as stated, there will be a separate briefing regarding the other events later today."

A few sniggers rumbled through the assembled press. Due to his snub of the local paper, Carlton King had alienated some journalist friends over the years.

"Are you sure, Chief Inspector?" Carlton retorted, raising an eyebrow with a smirk he'd borrowed from Braithwaite.

Despite suggesting the ridiculous, Heather detected an air of confidence in the pressman's demeanour.

"Quite sure."

"Alright, if you say so. But can you explain how Paul Colney's twin brother, Patrick Colney, allegedly committed five murders in 1987 after his mutilated body was discovered outside Havervalley Prison?" Carlton turned to his compatriots, soaking up the odd nod of approval.

"I'm sorry, but your question isn't relevant, and furthermore—"

"Oh, I think it is, Chief Inspector," he interrupted. "I suggest to you that Paul Colney committed those murders and is still very much alive. If you were any detective worth your salt, you'd know that Sandy Rathbone is an ex-girlfriend of Paul Colney."

"Thank you, Mr King, for your insights." Heather attempted to shut him down with a raised palm.

"I've recently written a book on the subject. I'm happy to offer you a signed copy if you like?"

For once, Pepé Le Pew came to the rescue. "Err … thanks. Thank you. That's all we have time for today."

Carlton King held Heather's glower whilst the camera shutters continued to click. The general hubbub of chatter mingled with the scraping of chair legs on the worn linoleum flooring of the outdated and somewhat tired Fairfield Police Station's pressroom.

Heather feared that Carlton King could become a problem. He'd made a good point. She knew who Sandy Rathbone had previously been in a relationship with.

More worrying, this nosey investigative journalist had stuck his beak into the unsolved murder of Susan Kane. The unsolved case that would probably become Heather's retirement reoccurring nightmare.

In 1987, Heather and her team identified Patrick Colney as the man responsible for the arson attack on a bail hostel and the Black Boy's Public House, killing five. However, despite many eyewitnesses and irrefutable evidence of his guilt, Patrick's mutilated body had been discovered only yards from the prison he'd just been released from. The pathologist report unequivocally stated that Patrick had already departed this world before the arson attack on the pub and a day before he signed into that hostel when released from prison.

At the time, their investigation was in turmoil. They had a dead man wandering around Fairfield, setting fires and murdering folk.

To add to this conundrum, Heather and her team secured many eyewitness accounts placing Patrick at Susan Kane's flat the day she died. However, Patrick was still languishing at Her Majesty's pleasure at the time of her death. It didn't take a great deal of detective work to realise, despite the eyewitness accounts, that Patrick Colney hadn't murdered those six people.

The obvious answer was the crimes were committed by a look-alike imposter. Paul Colney was Patrick's identical twin. However, as Heather had just reminded that investigative journalist, Paul Colney died ten years prior when sticking his head through the windscreen of a yellow Mk3 Cortina and bleeding to death when skewered by a windscreen wiper blade.

If that wasn't enough to cause synchronise head-scratching in the dilapidated and under-funded CID offices of Fairfield nick, they also secured many eyewitness accounts that three days after the arson attack, either the dead Patrick or Paul boarded a fishing boat at Brightlingsea on the Essex coast when presumably fleeing to the Continent.

Dead men don't go around murdering people. With no leads, a lack of resources, and an attempt to bury the embarrassment, the 'suits' hurriedly wound down the case. Seven years on, those six murders were consigned to history. Unsolved cases with no leads and no resources to warrant further investigation.

However, something niggled at the back of Heather's inquisitive mind. To add to their workload, they also had a misper case. Claire Bragg, a resident of the Broxworth Estate, had been missing for nearly a week. The flat in question being 121 Belfast House. The very same flat that a certain schoolteacher had rented twenty years ago. Perhaps it was time for another chat with a certain Mr Apsley and anyone associated with him. Regardless of how tenuous those links might be, Jason Apsley's name always seemed to pop its head above the parapet when it was most unwelcome.

3

1994 ... A few days earlier

Definitely Maybe

"Come on, Gramps, make a wish," Faith whispered in my ear as I bent forward and sucked in a breath.

I exhaled, swivelled my head, and raised an eyebrow at her.

"Gramps?"

"Uh huh, you're officially old. So yes, I'm afraid it's Gramps all the way from now on."

"Christ," I muttered. "Gramps!"

"Come on," came the chorus as I sucked in another lungful and prepared to blow out the six candles that adorned the top of my birthday cake. A culinary masterpiece Jenny had slaved away producing when on one of her famous marathon 'baking Saturdays' which turned the kitchen into something of a flour storm.

Each candle denoted a decade. Two of which I'd enjoyed in this life and four in my previous. Apart from the difficult times in 1976 and 1987, the two out-trumped the four by some considerable distance.

The last time I'd celebrated a birthday in 1994 was my seventeenth. To say that felt like a lifetime ago would be an understatement because, technically, it was two lifetimes ago.

That birthday had been a muted affair, celebrated with my brother, my ageing grandparents, and a cake of significantly less opulence. Ivy, my grandmother in that life, could knock up an epic Sunday dinner. However, Mary Berry would declare her sponges as one of those 'soggy bottom' failures if Ivy had lived that long to become a contestant on *The Great British Bake Off*. Although loosely termed as reality TV, and a show Jenny looked forward to watching when she retired, true fly-on-the-wall shows such as Big Brother, with Nasty Nick Bateman's antics and Jade Goody's striptease, were some years away from sullying our evening's entertainment.

Jenny struggled to understand the concept of the show when I'd attempted to describe it. Who would want to watch ordinary people locked in a house, she'd said?

She made a fair point. That said, when I described the 'Bake Off' programme, she thought watching people cook sounded terrific.

Hmmm.

So, one week before my grandmother had presented her 'soggy bottom' adorned with seventeen candles – that offers up a disturbing thought – a few mates and I attended an Oasis gig at the 100 Club in Soho.

We'd lived in that era when blagging your way in and claiming to be older than you were was still possible. I knew that would soon change as the 'nanny state' became even more dictatorial through the millennium.

Back in my old life, when a forty-year-old miserable bugger, I remember moaning about the UK's meteoric rise in the NSI,

Nanny State Index, as successive governments deemed it necessary to regulate anything that might be construed as harmful. That said, now an ex-smoker, I'd become one of those over-the-top moaners about anyone who lit up within a hundred miles of me – that exaggerated hand-waving and choking action suggesting the perpetrator was liable to cause me great harm. I accept that's a bit rich based on my forty years of smoking.

So, where was I? Ah, yes, Oasis. The brothers played that club again, just as they had in my first life. However, although not my favourite band, Jenny, not benefiting from the experience of time-travel, thought the Mancunian brothers' rock-cum-Britpop style was akin to the rest of my musical taste, as in bloody awful.

Fair enough. You see, for Jenny, born in 1946, her era was more the Fab Four, then on to Donny Osmond and David Cassidy. Whereas for me, technically born in 1977 and my teenage years of the early '90s, The Beatles were the love of the generation before me. Of course, being twelve years younger than my good self, Jenny was born at the end of *The Silent Generation*, whereas I was a product of *Generation X*.

Technically, Jenny was born thirty-one years before me, although I was twelve years her senior. You should try time-travel – what a head spinner.

Apart from the five members of the Time Travellers Believer's club (TTBC), pretty much everyone I knew found it somewhat bemusing, almost comical, that me, aged sixty, enjoyed the same music as my twenty-three-year-old son. Singing Blur's *Park Life* in the shower was okay. However, I ensured I was careful not to be heard singing future songs around my two adopted children, who still had no idea about my true identity or where I'd come from.

Of course, Beth and Chris found it cringeworthy that my taste in music was similar to theirs. Despite the cramping of their style, and as an early birthday surprise, they treated me to that gig at The 100 Club to see Oasis … again.

I've experienced this odd feeling on many occasions since time-travelling from 2019 to 1976. However, whilst the brothers rather aptly bashed out *Live Forever,* I couldn't help wondering if Chris had been there the first time around. This time, Beth was my daughter. The first time, when my best friend, she'd flirted with the doorman to ensure those of us in the group who were underage managed to gain entry.

Of course, I wouldn't see myself there because, in my second life, I wasn't born. Regarding Beth, well, that first existence had been eradicated when I time-travelled. For the last two decades, I've researched time-travel to the nth degree, a hobby if you like. Although time-travel being the stuff of science fiction and shouldn't be possible, I was living proof that it was. The only explanation I could conjure up for Beth, my daughter, and Beth, my friend, not co-existing was the concept of alternative worlds or closed timeline curves. However, that head-screwing thought that a week before my seventeenth birthday, I could have rubbed shoulders with my adopted son whilst Oasis banged out their six-song set to a select audience caused my brain to ache.

As instructed by my seventeen-year-old granddaughter, I made a wish and puffed out the candles. Of course, technically, Faith was *other* Jason's granddaughter. Her mother, Jess, was *his* daughter. But since replacing the poor fellow in 1976, they'd become my family. *Other* Jason still hadn't materialised, and I'd concluded he wouldn't until my death. Where was he right now? Well, who knew? Perhaps languishing in suspended animation or some form of human hibernation. One thing is for sure, if he ever showed up in my lifetime, that really would set the cat amongst the pigeons.

Not that I believed in the power of a wish, but my birthday prayer was the same as it had always been for the last two decades – no more time-travel.

When flanked by my adopted daughter and granddaughter, Beth with her arm around me and Faith planting a kiss on my cheek, Jenny snapped away with her new Canon Sureshot camera, capturing the moment.

My wife had secured herself a camera with a built-in flash. With this upgraded gismo, she no longer worried about wasting the flashbulbs, resulting in her trigger finger on overdrive. We were a couple of years from digital cameras becoming mainstream. Anyway, Jenny enjoyed receiving her snaps in the post after she'd sent the 35mm films off to be developed in those *Truprint* envelopes. Come the emergence of the iPhone, Facebook, and Instagram, I had Jenny pegged as a habitual user of social media.

Fortunately, we were still at least a decade from those two events. So, I could make it to my allotted three-score-years-and-ten before my wife, children, and the rest of the world's inhabitants become social media obsessed. A future time when FOMO caused many to feel the need to devote their lives to scrolling.

Despite mobile phones becoming popular, they were still of a size that was uncomfortable to slot into your pocket. Not of the Dom Joly size, but big enough for passers-by to wonder if you were pleased to see them.

My son, Chris, seemed chuffed with his Mercury one2one mobile with its green light-up buttons, even though the networks, more often than not, were on the blink. His phone was more of a status symbol than of any use, bearing in mind that none of his mates had one, rendering the thing pointless because he had no one to call.

Although Beth and Faith had remained close through their teenage years, after their joint obsession with Bananarama, both girls had trodden separate paths in forming their style.

My seventeen-year-old adopted daughter was growing out of her Madonna phase. Similar to how I remember when we were both that age in my first life. Beth now favoured a more understated waif-like style as she attempted to replicate the Kate Moss look. The model whose career had just gone supernova with her minimalist aesthetic. My daughter Beth rarely covered her navel.

As for Faith, well, she was firmly rooted in the '70s retro-hippy style. I guess she took her influence from her mother, Jess. Who, twenty years on, still dressed in flowing maxi dresses and all things tie-dyed.

"Chris, there's a couple of bottles of Asti in the fridge. Be a darling and grab them for me," Jenny called out above the hubbub.

"Okay," Chris replied, rifling through the cupboards to grab some plates, leaving his mother to snap away when over-indexing on capturing the cake-cutting ceremony.

"Dad, you're making a right pig's ear of that," chuckled Beth, as I attempted to slice through Jenny's sponge cake. "Go on, help Chris and leave it to me," she giggled, wiggling her hips and nudging me out of the way.

"Darling, you've still got one more present to open," my wife announced whilst capturing a few more shots for posterity.

Those who were dearest to me congregated in the kitchen on this surprisingly warm March day. My birthday could conjure up all spectrums of the weather, from snow blizzards to warm sunny days topping out above twenty degrees. Today was one of the latter. Four days after changing the clocks to British summertime, we all enjoyed the spring afternoon with cake and bubbles following my birthday celebratory lunch.

My son-in-law, Colin, quietly entertained George and Ivy, who, now both octogenarians, could find the loud chatter produced by the rest of the younger members of our family quite exhausting. Although different in style, Beth and Faith could machine-gun their youthful enthusiasm at such a rate it could make your ears bleed. Chris allowed the girls to hold centre stage whilst he and his long-term girlfriend, Megan, quietly cooed at each other.

Young love; which in a sense was a relief after that scary night when we discovered our boy had started dating my fifteen-year-old ex-wife from my first life. That night back in 1990, the night the remainder of the Carrow Bridge collapsed during the 'Burn's Night' storm, I'd once again had to face my old in-laws when Jenny had insisted that we drop Lisa home and 'have a word with her parents', as she put it. Safe to say, the conversation with Mr and Mrs Crowther, as were all in my first life, was as enjoyable as sticking needles in your eyeballs.

Despite my protestations about their ages, Chris had confided in Jenny that he intended to ask Megan to marry him. I guess you could say they were a perfect match, the Ken and Barbie, or to be on trend, Grant and Hurley. That said, I hoped Chris wouldn't partake in a little extra fun with his version of Divine Brown. No, I'm sure he wouldn't. Perhaps they'd be more like Posh and Becks, who I presumed would still get it together a few years from now. Assuming the Spice Girls still formed and David continues on his path to become a footballing icon.

Knowing the future and always keen to keep abreast of the news and events, Jenny and I regularly updated our 'yearbooks'. Those tatty school exercise books in which we recorded the future as best I could remember. Mr Beckham debuted for Manchester United a couple of seasons back as part of the 'Class of 92' and appeared on track with his stupendous career. A career he needed to repeat so he could score that free kick against Greece in 2001.

Incidentally, I'd made a note about contacting him in 1998 to ask if he could see his way clear to not to kick Diego Simeone during the World Cup match against Argentina, avoid receiving a red card, and perhaps then we could have at last won a bloody penalty shootout.

As for Posh, well, I was aware a girl band called *Touch* had just been formed and presumed the Spice Girls would soon evolve. However, unlike the need for David's career to blossom and not wanting to seem overly uncharitable about it, I couldn't have given two shits if Victoria followed the same path she had in my first life. When you're a lifelong fan of The Clash, something my family found rather odd for a now sixty-year-old, the Spice Girls didn't cut it for me.

Anyway, back to my gathering. Of course, *other* Jason's daughter, Jess, was with us, enjoying cake and bubbles. Along with Beryl, Chris's and Beth's maternal grandmother, and her husband, the now-retired detective Steven 'Paddington' Brown. My older brother was the only missing member of my somewhat strange family. He, at twenty-two in this life, was away at Durham University, just as he was in my first life.

Incidentally, that was still a super tough relationship. I struggled to shake off the memory of him as my older, somewhat annoying brother. However, as far as he was concerned, I was just his old schoolteacher and a close friend of his grandparents, George and Ivy, who were my grandparents in my first life but not now. I guess I would still be their grandson if I was born in 1977, as I was the first time. However, that wasn't possible due to my parents' death shifting from 1984 to 1976. So, as I say, my brother from my first life and I, as was the case in my second life, weren't close. Still with me? I know, it's a head fuck.

"Come on, darling, open it." Jenny hefted the large, wrapped box onto the breakfast bar.

"What is it?"

"Open it, silly," she smirked before sipping her Asti.

"I reckon it's a pair of tartan slippers," chuckled Chris.

I shot him a look, which my son reciprocated with a placating hand gesture and a smirk.

"Well, you are sixty, so I reckon it's time you had a pair."

I nodded a tight smile reply, which my son instantly picked up upon, reading my mind. Chris knew the mention of tartan slippers pulled back memories of Don, my honorary father, and his great-grandfather, as we discovered in 1987.

Chris rapped his knuckles on the counter, effectively halting the chatter, including the girls, thus gaining everyone's attention.

"Listen up, everyone. Before Dad opens his present from Mum, I would like you all to raise a glass." He paused, waiting for all to comply. "To Don, always in our hearts and never forgotten."

"To Don," a chorus rang out.

I grabbed my son's elbow. "Thank you," I mouthed. Don, who we'd lost seven years ago, and along with George, had smoothed the path for me when I'd time-travelled and landed in 1976. I missed him every day since.

"Come on, you soppy old git, open that present," Chris chuckled.

"Okay, okay," I mumbled, ripping away the paper to reveal a brown box with the unmistaken IBM stamped in blue lettering across the top. "Oh, my God. Jenny, this must have cost you a fortune?"

"It's your sixtieth, darling. It's a special birthday," she cooed.

Although not from the future, but a founder member of the Time Travelers Believers' Club, Jenny knew the laptop in this box was, for me, archaic. Of course, she couldn't comprehend the MAC book I'd left in 2019. That said, she knew I'd been itching to get my hands on a laptop. I'd eagerly awaited the release of this model – an IBM ThinkPad with MS-DOS operating system, Windows 3, and an impressive 4MB memory – which in my day would be regarded as a bloody dinosaur of a machine. However, in 1994, the ancient lump was the best available.

According to the media, technological advances were happening at a supersonic pace. However, for me, waiting for stuff to be developed was like waiting for a VHS tape to rewind – painfully slow. On that note, this was a practice we regularly performed before returning a rented film from Blockbusters to avoid being fined.

"Lad, what you got there then?" piped up George, as he placed his champagne flute down. Apart from pretending to sip bubbles when toasting Don, none of the Italian sparkling bubbles had passed his lips. George was a pint of mild type of man, not fancy sparkling wine.

"It's a laptop."

"Course it is," he chuckled.

"George, it's a computer," chimed in Chris.

"I gathered that, lad. Now, I expect your father will expertly advise me otherwise, but apart from sending men into space, no good will come from computers."

"Oh, George, you philistine. They're everywhere now," Jenny chipped in. "All our records are being computerised. Not that I can work the ruddy machine. Nothing wrong with a bank of filing cabinets if you ask me."

"Well said, Jenny lass."

"Oh, Mum, now *you* sound like an old fuddy-duddy," chuckled Beth.

"Well, I love it," I announced, hugging the box.

"What about this one? It came in the post this morning," Beth announced whilst waving around a padded envelope before placing it in front of me. "Bit odd if you ask me. Who's it from?"

I glanced at the handwritten address before a chink of fear crept in through the gaps in my joyful birthday persona when reading the message on the reverse.

Happy sixtieth Birthday Mr Apsley

Thought you might enjoy this!

We both know dead men can't talk – or can they?

As I hesitated, all twelve attendees of my birthday soiree focused on the back of that envelope. For eight people in the room, it represented an extremely peculiar message that made no sense. For the members of the TTBC, namely Jess, George, Jenny and me, it spelt trouble.

Jenny's grip on my arm tightened. Jess audibly sucked in a breath of air, and George, in true George style, started playing a symphony in his pocket as he jangled his loose change.

"What does 'dead men can't talk' mean?" quizzed Chris, as he glanced around the group.

The other seven, who were clueless to the meaning, all shrugged. Jenny, Jess, George and I, all simultaneously and somewhat nervously, cleared our throats. It appeared that someone else who was not in this room knew something of the events of a decade ago. That rather odd happening in the late 1980s when the previously dead Patrick Colney had somehow committed six murders. A conundrum, leaving the police in a state of bewilderment.

Of course, we knew those murders were committed by his time-travelling brother, Paul Colney, who disappeared on a boat from Brightlingsea in 1987.

Apart from the four of us in this room who knew the facts about what happened back then, there were two others. Martin, who I occasionally enjoyed a call with as he soaked up the Spanish sun whilst enjoying the 'good life', as he put it. And, of course, that sadistic, murdering, rapist bastard himself, Paul Colney. Now, although the despicable git had probably worked out that he'd time-travelled after dying in my yellow Cortina in 1977 and awakening ten years later, I doubted he would be sending me a package with a cryptic clue penned on the back.

With eleven pairs of eyes upon me, I ripped open the packet and extracted a book. As if it had suddenly burst into flames, I dropped the hardback onto the breakfast bar, causing all eyes to swivel downwards and lock onto the cover depicting a photo of two brothers.

Not Liam and Noel Gallagher, but Patrick and Paul Colney.

4

The Turning of the Screw

"Ye gods and little cod fishes," announced George.

"George?" asked Ivy, clearly clocking the shock etched across her husband's face. I suspect now wondering why he appeared so concerned by a picture of two, as far as she was concerned, dead criminals.

Ivy, my grandmother in my first life, was a no-nonsense type of woman who suffered no fools. For that very reason, we'd never issued her with an application form to join the TTBC. Ivy was far too level-headed to get wrapped up in any of that silly stuff – if only she knew.

"That's Patrick …" Colin's voice trailed away as he slowly shook his head and closed his eyes.

In a hissed whisper, I read the title—

The Ghosts of Evil

The explosive account of post-war Fairfield's most notorious criminal family. Are the Colney Twins alive?

by Carlton King

No one said a word. Jenny's grip on my arm tightened to that akin to a blood pressure pump on speed. George's pocketed-loose-change jangling routine started up again, now on the second movement of whatever symphony he was playing. Jess buried her head in her hands.

"Who's Carlton King?" blurted Beth.

"He's an investigative journalist, lass. He worked up at the Chronicle before moving to one of the nationals a couple of years back," announced George, halting his symphony mid-movement.

I shot him a look. Although a rare occurrence, we both knew that time had bent, altered if you like, from my first life. Carlton King should be about to become the editor of the Fairfield Chronicle. However, in this life, he'd become an investigative journalist who appeared to be digging into recent history and unearthing some concerning information that should stay firmly buried in the past.

Which past? Well, good question.

As was 1987, I feared 1994 would become my second annus horribilis.

"Bollocks," I muttered.

Everyone, apart from Ivy, who tutted a response, remained silent after I'd uttered my favourite word, which I employed in most unfavourable situations. The radio, playing on a low volume and thus just background noise that previously couldn't be heard above the laughter and general chatter, filled the soundscape.

Enigma sang that haunting tune, *Return to Innocence*. A song I'd forgotten about from my first life and now afforded the opportunity to enjoy again after its release a few weeks back.

The irony wasn't lost on me regarding the fact that the lyrics were about trusting your instincts, and truths can be found by returning to a state of innocence. As I pondered the book cover, specifically that line – *Are the Colney Twins alive?* – it felt as if that higher power that sent me reeling back in time had now chosen this moment to play that haunting melody to focus my mind.

Seven years had elapsed since Paul Colney time-travelled from 1977 to 1987, murdered his brother, Patrick, stole his identity and then disappeared to God knows where. I knew back then that someday in the future, our paths would cross again.

Now, my ex-student, that thicko, Carlton King, was overturning rocks. If he persisted, I feared he'd eventually flip over the stone where that evil bastard Paul Colney lay hidden.

I shuddered at the thought as if that fiendish vermin of a man were here in the room with me.

"Dad? You okay? You've gone all pale. Mum? What's going on?"

"Nothing," came the chorus from George, Jenny, and Jess in answer to Beth's questions. Their quick denial of anything untoward served as confirmation of the exact opposite, and all was not well. Like me, I suspected they harboured similar concerns.

"Beth, I'm fine. You don't need to worry. Both men *are* dead," I lied, concerned for my daughter, who knew these two evil men pictured on the book's front cover were her biological uncles. The brothers of the sixteen-year-old David Colney, her biological father, who I'd dropped to his death in 1976. That act prevented him from becoming a serial killer in the next millennium, as he had in my first life.

"Well, I have no idea what that author's on about," chimed in Steven. "I was on that case, as you know. And I can tell you for a fact that Patrick Colney is dead because we identified him from dental records. As for his brother, Paul, I seem to recall he died in a road traffic accident in the '70s. There was something odd about that, though. When we discovered Patrick's body, the car Paul Colney died in turned up again."

Jess and I exchanged a look. Both of us were in that car when Paul Colney died in 1977. Although my children were aware of my old Cortina, they had no idea it was the same car now being discussed.

"Err … what d'you mean his car turned up again?" quizzed Chris.

"Oh, well, it was a right old strange affair …" the retired detective paused and shot me a look. Although oblivious regarding time-travel, he knew about my involvement in that case due to being arrested for perverting the course of justice.

The tiniest shake of my head was enough to halt him from adding further information which my children were unaware of.

"Yes, but that case regarding Patrick was never solved, was it?" Colin interjected, grabbing hold of his wife's hand as he continued. "Those murders in '87 happened after Patrick was released from prison. Someone bludgeoned him to death before he reportedly killed that woman on the Broxworth Estate and set fire to his bail hostel."

Although Colin was also entirely in the dark regarding time-travel, he was always sensitive when mentioning Patrick Colney, Faith's biological father, Jess's ex-boyfriend. As for me, I was just relieved he'd moved off the subject of my Cortina before Steven had the chance to tell the story of my car miraculously re-materialising in mint condition after my time-travelling buddy, Martin, had crushed the bonnet into an oak tree ten years earlier.

"True, but that couldn't happen because we knew Patrick was dead before those murders occurred."

Jenny's grip on my arm became vice-like. George shot me a look, and I detected Jess muttering what I presumed was a silent prayer whilst Colin and Steven continued to discuss the impossible.

"Well, what did happen, then? Who bludgeoned that woman to death, and who was responsible for the fire?"

"We never found out. Course, my old Guvnor, DCI French, had us lot running around in circles trying to figure out how a dead man went on a killing spree like the Ghost of Mr Quint."

"Who?"

"Peter Quint. The valet of Bly."

"Who's he? Did you investigate him?"

"No," chuckled Steven. "The Ghost of Peter Quint, from the novella by Henry James, *The Turning of the Screw*."

"You've lost me, that I can say. What on earth has a Victorian novelist got to do with that rubbish?" Ivy blurted, pointing at the book, which ominously lay on the breakfast bar like some grimoire containing evil spirits.

With no answers forthcoming, she glanced up at a nervous-looking George, I guess suspecting her husband wasn't being full and frank about his concerns regarding the Colney twins.

"Nothing," I threw in, followed by a whiny chuckle. "Nothing," I repeated, keen for this conversation to move off the subject of the nefarious brothers, which could only lead to a discussion about murdering ghosts or, God forbid, time-travel.

"That Carlton King was one of your old students, wasn't he, darling? I suspect he sent you the book to show you how well he's done … you know, becoming an author." Jenny snatched up the book and flipped open the cover.

"Absolutely. That will be it. I suspect the story is a load of old bolloc—" I stopped myself just in time before uttering my favourite word when remembering my audience. Ivy was most certainly not one for profanities – uttering or hearing. In my previous life, when her grandson, the amount of fines I paid for swearing during my teenage years could have serviced the national debt of many an economic-stricken country.

I cleared my throat and continued. "It will be full of journalistic twaddle. Anyway, anyone for another slice of cake? Top up of Asti?" I held the bottle aloft, raising my eyebrows as I waved it back and forth, only receiving solemn shakes of their heads. It seems the book that Jenny now flicked through had spoilt the party.

"Yes, you're right, darling. I suspect this book is all sensationalist codswallop and full of his silly, unfounded speculations. Probably just hoping to make a killing with the catchy title." Jenny paused as she frowned at the first page, reading the one sentence aloud—

The irrefutable truth that Paul Colney is alive

"As I said. All codswallop. Dead criminals are dead, not roaming around like one of Steven's literary ghosts." Jenny wagged a finger at Steven and took a breath before continuing her rant, presumably designed to deflect the conversation away from where the four members of the TTBC feared this was heading following my failed attempt by way of offering cake and bubbles. "Journalists are always writing books about criminals and unsolved cases. I suspect the shops will be full of books from investigative journalists claiming to have unearthed the key evidence that proves who shot Jill Dando."

A brief moment of silence ominously hovered as all furrowed their brows and stared at my wife as she looked up from where she'd been studying the cover.

"Sorry, did I say something strange?"

I bulged my eyes at Jenny, willing her to cover up her time-travel-induced cock-up, something only I would typically be accused of. Only yesterday, during our March meeting of the TTBC, held at our headquarters, namely the window seat in The Three Horseshoes Pub, we discussed this decade's future events. The murder of Jill Dando had come up in conversation. Although I didn't know the exact year, I guessed it occurred in the late '90s.

"Do what?" blurted Chris.

"Pardon. Christopher. The word is pardon. Not what." Jenny chastised our son, I suspect to grab a moment to think rather than annoyance regarding Chris's chosen vocabulary.

"Okay! Pardon, Mother—"

"Isn't she that newsreader woman who also presents the *Holiday* programme?" chimed in Megan. "My dad always says she's a bit of alright. When did she get shot, then?"

"I always preferred it when Cliff Michelmore and Fyfe Robertson presented the show. All those young women flaunting flesh in their skimpy low-cut tops and those bikinis on the television these days is so unnecessary." Ivy threw in, oblivious to Megan's question.

"I have to say I always thought Joan Bakewell was rather good at it," added George.

"Thinking man's crumpet. That's what they call her," chuckled Steven, his face dropping when receiving a rather acerbic glare from his wife, Beryl.

Ivy shot George a look. "So that's why you never watch it now, is it? Your thinking man's piece of crumpet is no longer presenting the show," she tutted. "That explains your sudden interest in that documentary series, *The Heart of the Matter*, eh?"

"Hang on," blurted Colin. "Sorry, Ivy," he nodded in her direction as an apology for interrupting before waving his finger at Jenny. "You said Jill Dando was shot? When? Where? Was this on today's news?"

Looking pleased with the interruption, George cleared his throat. Rather than respond to Ivy, who still held her eyebrows aloft, he resumed his symphonic coin-jangling routine.

"You meant Bruce Lee, didn't you?" suggested Jess.

"No, Mum said Jill Dando." Chris side-eyed Jess before turning to his mother and opening his palms. "Didn't you?"

"I think your mother was thinking of John Lennon." I threw in, desperately trying to defuse this ridiculous conversation and deflect it away from a future murder. Although the TV presenter's future death had hit the TTBC's agenda, like most impending tragedies, we'd conjured up bugger-all plans about how to prevent it.

Beth shot a look at Chris and then back at me. "What's going on? I know that look. That's your 'don't tell the kids' look."

"Beth, your mum was referring to Marvin Gaye. It's easy to get mixed up."

"What?"

"It's pardon, Beth."

Ignoring her mother's correction, Beth side-eyed her brother before challenging Jess. "Mixed up? You said Bruce Lee and now changed your mind to Marvin Gaye.

Anyway, how can you get Jill Dando and Marvin Gaye mixed up? They don't exactly look like each other, do they?"

"J. R.," chimed in George, halting his coin jangling. "Jenny lass was referring to all the theories about who shot J.R."

I groaned in despair at how this conversation seemed to morph from the ridiculous to a full-on comedy of errors with the members of the TTBC, including myself, throwing in random names of celebs who died from gunshots. And now George had added bloody J.R.

"It's time we went home, you silly old fool. Too much sugar and that fizzy wine has gone to your head. J.R., indeed!" Ivy barked.

After my parents died in 1984, that's in my first life, before their deaths were cruelly moved to 1976 in my second life, as a distraught little seven-year-old, Ivy had pretty much single-handedly raised me and my brother. George was a man of great wisdom, but the day-to-day task of raising two small boys had fallen on my grandmother. The love and comfort she showered upon my brother and me was immeasurable – biblical proportions, you could say, although in a good way. However, at a little over five feet tall, Ivy could quickly become ferocious when she wanted to bare her teeth. Something her six-foot-one husband had just been on the receiving end of.

George knew when to obey.

"Right, lad. Ivy and I will be off now. Let you young'uns dance the night away, or whatever it is you do these days," he chuckled, attempting to lighten the mood.

As we all funnelled out of the kitchen towards the hall, with Beryl, Steven, Colin and Jess also deciding to make a move, I noticed Beth and Chris conducting a hissed conversation. George's frankly harebrained suggestion that Jenny had inadvertently said Jill Dando, when meaning J.R. Ewing, was enough to deflect the group's conversation. However, it was clear that our adopted children were not of a mind to let it go. After a round of air-cheek kissing and goodbyes, with Jenny and I accepting an offer of a late supper at Jess's, we all syphoned our way back to the kitchen.

Whilst Jenny set about clearing away glasses and plates, I detected my son was preparing to push for answers. When ignoring his girlfriend's glare, which suggested she felt somewhat awkward, Chris side-eyed Beth, who nodded.

"Mum, Dad, can we …" he paused when Megan grabbed his hand.

"What?" Although I knew his intentions where Megan was concerned, I surmised this wouldn't be a conversation about their planned nuptials.

"Well … the Colneys, and that." Chris nodded to the book which lay, almost as if holding court, on the breakfast bar. "Ignoring Mum's claim that she got mixed up with who's been shot, you both appear concerned about—"

"They are dead, aren't they?" interrupted Beth, animatedly waving her arms around like only Beth could. "Paul, Patrick and their evil mother, Shirley, are definitely dead and never coming back to haunt us?"

Jenny, plates and glasses in hand, bowed her head at the sink with her face turned away from Chris and Beth, who looked at each other again. The fear on my daughter's face ripping holes in my heart.

63

Seven years ago in 1987, that annus horribilis year when Paul Colney time-travelled from 1977, his sadistic, twisted mother had tried to kidnap Beth and Faith. Of course, that odd twist of fate when Beryl crushed Shirley to death on the Carrow Road Bridge put an end to *Cruella de Vil's* evil plans. Although only ten at the time, I knew the fear of what might have happened if her grandmother hadn't killed Shirley would haunt my daughter forever.

Eighteen years ago, the month preceding my time-travel to 1976, I'd billeted at Beth's house after divorcing Lisa. In that life, Beth was a ball-busting Miranda Priestly type character of the marketing world. Although not the devil, she wore Prada and scared most men shitless. In this life, as a product of nurture, and although high-spirited, she wasn't the cold-hearted bitch of her previous existence. The terror etched on her face as her question hung in the air confirmed that Beth would never forget her heinous paternal grandmother.

Of course, Shirley and Patrick were dead. Apart from the members of the TTBC who knew differently, so was Paul. As far as I was aware, only three people had time-travelled in my 1974 yellow Ford Cortina – which I'd safely secured in a lock-up to prevent any further transtemporal travel – my old work colleague, Martin Bretton, my good self, and that bastard Paul Colney. Although I wanted to reassure Beth that her biological father's relatives could never cause her harm, that would involve lying.

Fake news, a term that Donald Trump liked to trot out in my old life, was something I'd become skilled at. I could spin the truth to such a level that politicians would be in awe of. Well, being a time-traveller required lying skills. Not to the 'Stonehouse', 'Watergate' or the recent 'Arms-to-Iraq' level, which I knew would soon wallop in a final nail in the coffin lid of John Major's government, but lies that could cover up time-travel. However, lying to my adopted children was difficult. When they were younger, they either didn't know any better, or I just used bribery as a tool to wriggle out of a tight spot. Now they were young adults, they weren't so gullible.

"Well ..." I paused as I rolled my head around and scrunched my shoulders. "You don't need to worry—"

"They're dead!" boomed Jenny, before dropping the plates in the sink, spinning around, and repeatedly chopping her hand on the draining board to force home her point. "They're dead, and that's the end of it! I'll not have their ruddy names mentioned in my house again, d'you hear?"

If only that was the truth.

5

Carrott Confidential

My wife wasn't known for losing her temper. However, it's fair to say that the 'They're dead' incident put a bit of a dampener on the prospects of any continuation of my sixtieth birthday celebrations. All balloons were burst, literally and metaphorically. The party atmosphere, along with the half-drunk bottles of Asti Spumante, had lost its fizz.

Chris and Megan shot off to who knows where. Closely followed by Beth, who said she planned to meet up with friends, which I knew meant her secret boyfriend, whose identity I was keen to discover.

Although my daughter thought she had the wool pulled firmly over my eyes, I was damn sure a boy, or man for that matter, had weaselled his way into my daughter's life. I just hoped he hadn't weaselled his hands, or worse, into somewhere he shouldn't.

Hmmm.

Okay, Beth was a high-spirited, stunning seventeen-year-old. I wasn't deluded enough to believe she hadn't already dabbled. Well, you know, with boys if you get my drift. However, as her father, and being fully aware of the kind of desires that were uppermost in young men's minds, I just wanted to know who my daughter was seeing – fair enough? Well, I thought so.

Jenny reckoned I was worrying too much and unnecessarily overplaying the protective father card. Beth's a sensible girl, she'd said. That's as maybe, but I'd been a young man once and seem to recall my rampant desires during the latter stages of puberty. Not that there had been many opportunities forthcoming when in my teens, probably due to the vast majority of young ladies struggling to find my endearing qualities. To be fair to those girls, I think I kept them well hidden – even from myself.

Also, although Beth, in this life, differed from the girl I knew in my old life, I couldn't shake the thought that nature would win over nurture. If my daughter was anything like that Beth, who'd been my best friend in my first life, then it wasn't the young men's desires that I needed to worry about. Back in the early '90s, the first time around, Beth was … well, let's just say she liked the boys, and they liked her.

My fears for my daughter came to fruition just a few minutes after we arrived home from a pleasant evening at Jess's. There I was, settled into watching *The Detectives*, a show I'd set up our JVC video recorder to tape earlier that evening. Although I could vaguely remember the Jasper Carrott and Robert Powell spoof police show from my first life, at seventeen, I hadn't appreciated the humour. Now, the second time around, I appreciated all things Jasper Carrott. Anyway, as I chuckled at their bumbling antics, I heard the back door creak open.

After snatching up the remote, I paused the tape. I cocked my ear whilst attempting to listen as my mind raked through the possibilities of who may have sneaked in. The TV screen depicted a shaky image as the VCR's tracking shot white lines across the paused frame of a surprised-looking Jasper. The comedian and I now sporting similar expressions. When hopping up to investigate, silently berating myself for not securing the back door following the day's events, I crept towards the lounge door before peering into the hall. I spotted my daughter tip-toeing along the hall, sneaking along like a cat burglar attempting to skulk in unnoticed.

I snapped on the hall light.

"Bollocks," she hissed, scraping her sodden muddy hair away from her face.

"Bollocks, indeed, young lady!" My barked response alerting Jenny to our daughter's somewhat bedraggled appearance, when exiting the downstairs toilet.

Beth grinned, shooting glances back and forth between Jenny and me.

"Hi."

"My giddy aunt. Where the hell have you been?" Jenny boomed, thumping her hands on her hips, that trademark stance my wife liked to employ when indicating she was not best pleased.

"Err … um."

"Well?"

"Out … I've been out."

"Don't get smart with me. I'm well aware of that. Where've you been? And with who? And why on earth are you covered head to toe in mud?"

Beth bowed her head, causing her slatternly matted hair to flop forward as she tugged at the thighs of her sodden jeans. "I … fell over in a puddle," she mumbled.

"Christ, girl, it must have been a ruddy sinkhole looking at the state of you!"

"It was big … and muddy."

Jenny barrelled past me, halting an inch from our daughter's down-turned head. "Look up … I said look up."

Beth slowly raised her head, shooting me a pleading look as she peered over Jenny's shoulder.

"Don't give your father those doe-eyes. Open your mouth."

"Dad?"

"Mouth. Open!"

Beth complied, sucking in air and holding her breath as Jenny nudged closer and sniffed.

"I can smell drink and cigarettes on you, young lady."

Unable to hold her breath any longer, Beth exhaled in an exaggerated huff due to presumably accepting that she'd been rumbled. Although not quite in the Kevin and Perry style, comedy sketches I thought would soon land on our TV screens, Beth's shoulders sagged in defeat.

Jenny and I considered ourselves somewhat fortunate to have made it this far down the parenting road without suffering regular bouts of Harry Enfield's Kevin-styled teenage attitude from either Beth or Chris. That said, I had a sneaking suspicion we were about to be treated to some 'attitude' from our daughter.

"Come on, where've you been? You're not eighteen yet, so you shouldn't be in pubs at your age." Jenny turned to me. "She's been drinking!"

"I heard."

Jenny swivelled around and wagged an accusing finger in our daughter's face. "Come on, spit it out. Who've you been with? Not that Melanie, girl, I hope. She's a bad influence."

"You used to like Melanie," Beth whined.

"When she was ten. She was a lovely girl back then. Her poor parents, that's all I can say. That damn girl has built herself a reputation that Lilo Lil would be proud of."

"Who?"

"The girls a tart! Nothing but a hussy hanging around men like a bitch on heat!"

"She's not—"

"Don't answer me back, young lady," Jenny again wagged her index finger in Beth's face before swivelling on her heels and jabbing it in my direction. "Well? Are you going to say something, or are you intent on just standing there with your mouth open?"

"Okay … let's all calm down—"

"Don't you calm down me. And don't you *dare* make excuses for her."

I opened my mouth but abruptly closed it when nothing sensible popped into my mind as a way of responding. Jenny offered an exaggerated tut in my direction before glowering at our daughter. "Well? I'm waiting."

Beth huffed, offering an eye roll. "D'oh! Just out … I've just been out. I had a couple of drinks, that's all. It's no big deal."

"Where?" Jenny barked, holding her accusing finger inches from our daughter's hard-done-by expression.

"Just down the Woolpack with a few friends from college," she whispered. "Not Melanie, though," stated with more conviction, as if this added information would soften the blow.

"That place! Smoking and drinking?"

Beth nodded. "I'm nearly eighteen! None of my friends get treated like a child."

"You *are* a child!"

"I'm a woman!" shrilled Beth.

Shocked at the ferocity of our daughter's retort, Jenny hopped backwards.

"I'm a woman, not a little girl," Beth stated in a more adult tone before wincing when concerned she'd offered unnecessary information.

Although my wife frowned when attempting to read between the lines of Beth's announcement regarding her transition to womanhood, I'd definitely worked out what she was suggesting. My fears about what sort of activities my daughter might get up to with boys had been fully realised.

Jenny shot me a look, then glanced back at Beth, who now chewed her lip. "Beth, are you telling us that you've … you …" Jenny paused and nodded towards Beth's midriff area. "You've … err—"

"You mean, am I still a virgin?"

Jenny swallowed hard, the sound loud enough for all to hear.

"Course I'm not. Blimey, I'm not a nun."

It appeared to be Jenny's turn to open and close her mouth without uttering a response.

Back in my old life, when at school together, Beth had confided in me she'd lost her virginity at the tender age of fifteen to a lad in the sixth form. That said, there had been nothing tender about my close friend. At that point in her life, just before leaving that children's home, the Beth I once knew had blossomed from a scrawny kid to a badass teen who could rival any female heroine that the Marvel franchise would conjure up in the future. Apparently, this three-minute wonder took place one lunchtime behind the sports hall. I remember thinking I hadn't even kissed a girl by then. First base, the kids called it in my old life. At fifteen, Beth had made it all the way to fourth base, skipping the first three.

"Jason, say something."

"Err …"

Beth, probably regretting offering this information, jumped in. "Look, it was only once, and that was ages ago … it doesn't matter."

"What d'you mean, ages ago?" Jenny barked, returning to her favoured stance of hands thrust on hips.

"Months … months ago … sort of. I'm not pregnant!" Beth whisked her top up to expose her almost concave stomach, inadvertently revealing her bra.

"Beth!" I boomed, holding my hand up and turning away.

"Oh, sorry, Dad. I was just showing you that I'm not up the duff. He wore a condom, and I'm on the pill."

Still sporting that gobsmacked expression, Jenny raised her hand as if asking for permission to speak. "You're … you're on the pill?"

"Uh-huh."

"Jason, our daughter's on the pill."

"I heard," I muttered.

"Say something. Do something."

"Like what?"

"I don't know, but our little girl ... she's ..." Jenny paused. "You can't be having ... doing that. You're too young!"

"I could get married; you only have to be sixteen."

"Married!" shrilled Jenny, enough to cause my ears to bleed. "You're not going to get married!"

"No! Mum, don't be so ridiculous. I'm just saying I *could* get married or join the army at my age. I'm not too young."

"Army ... Jason, she's going to join the bloody army!"

"Oh, Mum. I'm not joining the army. I'm just saying."

"Who was it? This ... him," Jenny released her right hand and waved it at Beth's tummy. "This boy, who is he?"

"No one; it doesn't matter."

"I think it damn well does! Who is he?"

"Mum, I'm not seeing him anymore. It doesn't matter."

Jenny glanced at me, raising her eyebrows.

"What?" I shrugged.

"Jason! Have you been listening?" After a few seconds, with no verbal response from me, Jenny turned back to face Beth. "And how did you end up in this state?" Jenny's tone now a smidge less rancorous. My wife gesticulated her hands up and down, indicating Beth's bedraggled appearance.

"I fell over in a puddle in ..." Beth paused, appearing to decide not to divulge the location of said puddle or sinkhole as Jenny had suggested.

"Where?"

Beth closed her eyes and took a deep breath.

"Where? God damn it."

"Near the old Belton's electronics factory."

"Oh, my God! Not Lovers' Lane?"

Beth nodded. "I didn't do anything, though."

"Beth," I waved my hand downwards, suggesting she could lower her t-shirt, indicating there was no need to keep her bare stomach exposed.

"Oh, sorry."

The information that our daughter had lost her innocence and spent the evening rolling around in the mud at Fairfield's premier dogging venue appeared to have rendered my wife a smidge lost for words. Before this turned into an all-out mother-and-daughter war, a state of hostilities that since Beth turned sixteen had become an all-too-regular occurrence, I thought I'd better play peacemaker.

"Beth, I think you better get up to the bathroom and sort yourself out. We'll talk about this in the morning."

"Talk about what? There's nothing to talk about."

"If you're seeing boys, then there's plenty to discuss, I can assure you."

"Oh, this is so embarrassing! I'm not telling you anything!"

When I thought of Beth from my old life and how she was super keen to provide that blow-by-blow account of her exploits behind the sports hall, a wry smile briefly skated across my face. That conversation took place a few years ago – although, technically, was over forty years ago – but I could still remember it as if it was yesterday.

"Well, we'll see. But you and your mother need to have a little chat. However, I think that can wait until the morning, don't you?"

"A chat? It's a bit late for that kind of conversation."

Jenny tutted and dismissively shook her head. "I'm so disappointed."

"Oh, so it was okay for Chris to knob half the girls in college. I have one fling with some bloke, and we need to have 'a chat'," Beth performed the bunny ears quote when raising her hands in the air. That act caused the jacket slung around her shoulders to slip to the tiled floor.

"Chris is older than you."

"Err … are you that deluded?"

"I beg your pardon!" blurted Jenny, stepping forward again after remaining silent for a moment.

"Chris! Before he and Megan became all gooey-eyed, he'd regularly bring back girls when you were away on holiday."

Jenny shot me a quizzical look.

Beth bashed on. "When you went to Paris for that weekend a few years ago. Chris was supposed to be babysitting me, you remember? Although I was fifteen, so frig knows why you thought I needed babysitting."

Jenny and I offered no response. Instead, we waited for our mud-wrestling daughter to throw her brother under the bus.

"He brought back three girls, and they stayed in bed for the entire weekend. I had to make my own dinner and tea whilst he enjoyed group sex in your bed!"

"My bed! With three girls."

"Yup," Beth joyfully announced, delighted to have deflected her mother's mind away from her dallying down Lovers' Lane with whoever. A boy that my seventeen-year-old daughter appeared intent on keeping his identity undisclosed.

"What girls?"

Beth shrugged. "That Lisa girl he was seeing and two others."

"Lisa?" I quizzed. "Lisa Crowther?"

"Yeah, that's her. If you think Melanie has built herself a reputation, she's got nothing on that Lisa. Chris is well-shot of that one, I can tell you."

Jenny and I exchanged a knowing glance before my wife fell comatose as her jaw sagged a smidge further towards the floor. I guess when you think about the information just received, it was a bit of a head spinner.

Lisa Crowther was the woman I married in 2006 and divorced in 2018 after discovering she'd been enjoying multiple affairs; one such fling with my work colleague, Martin. Unwelcome information that came to light after we'd both time-travelled in 2019 back to the late '70s. In some weird twist of fate, in this life, she'd become our adopted son's girlfriend. Then, she'd enjoyed a gang-bang in our bed with two other girls and Chris whilst Jenny and I embarked on a long weekend away to sample the delights of the Parisian romantic ambience. Although, during our failed marriage, my ex-wife had regularly dabbled in extracurricular activities, she'd never once suggested a foursome with a couple of girlfriends. I think I'd remember that. Although Lisa Crowther was no Elle Macpherson, it appeared my son had already savoured an erotic session with three sirens.

"Three girls … three girls and just Chris?" I asked.

"Uh-huh." Beth nodded.

"All weekend?"

"Yep. I even had to help wash the sheets because he didn't know how the washing machine worked."

"Wow." I grinned, raising an eyebrow, thinking that my son, at about nineteen or twenty, had enjoyed a fantasy that most blokes would never get the opportunity to play out in real life.

"Jason!" Jenny barked, probably because of the salacious smirk now plastered across my face.

"Oh, sorry," I somewhat nervously grinned, as Jenny's retort hauled me out of my reverie.

Jenny huffed, shooting me a disapproving glare before addressing Beth. "Like your father said, I suggest you get upstairs and clean yourself up." Jenny pointed to the leather jacket on the floor. "Whose is that?"

Beth glanced down at the man's jacket that lay in a crumpled heap. "Oh, a man gave me a lift home and offered me his jacket after I fell in the puddle."

"A man? What man?"

Beth glanced up at me. "Just some bloke. It was well weird, though. He looked and sounded just like you. Younger, but he could have been your twin."

6

Official Secrets

"Twin?" Jenny and I blurted in unison.

"Well, yeah, sort of. He was a bit of a weirdo but looked like you."

"Weirdo?" we both barked.

Beth raised her hands. "Oh, not like that ... he didn't try anything?"

"I should hope not! What d'you mean he looked like your father?"

"Well, he did," Beth shrugged. "Younger, of course. But had your big ears, same eyes, face, features, everything." Beth gesticulated with both hands, pointing out my features as she rattled through her list. "He had a goatee beard thingy, but other than that, he was identical."

Jenny shot me a look before turning back to machine-gun her questions at Beth. "Did he say anything? Who was he? What's his name, eh? Come on, spit it out. You're in enough trouble already, so you might as well come out with it."

"I don't know! Stop having a go at me. I don't know who he was, his name or anything. I was down Lovers' Lane when me and Craig—"

"Who's Craig?" I interrupted. Any male name associated with my daughter instantly loaded up the questions I was ready to fire off in her direction. After Beth's admittance regarding the passing of her maiden status, those questions regarding her male acquaintances morphed from fear about where they wanted to put their hands and other appendages to concerns about their suitability as long-term boyfriend material.

Beth shook her head. "I'm going to bed."

"Oh, no, you don't," Jenny announced, almost simultaneously slapping her hands on the bannister and wall opposite. My wife's aggressive stance blocked our daughter's escape route as she attempted to make for the stairs.

"Oh, what now?" Beth whined.

"Answer your father. Who's this Craig?"

Beth huffed and shook her head.

"Don't you shake your head at me. I want to know who these men are that you seem intent on gallivanting around with like some trollop."

"Oh, come on. This is so unfair!" Beth whinged. "It's private. I don't have to tell you everything."

"Just because you think you're all grown up now you've allowed some man to deflower you, that doesn't give you the right to talk to us, your parents, like that."

"What," Beth chuckled. "Deflower! What the hell does that mean?"

"You know damn well what it means."

"I know! So, I let some bloke pop my cherry. Big–bloody–deal. Newsflash, everyone, Beth Apsley is no longer a virgin. Amazeballs!"

"Oh, for God—"

"Hang on," I interrupted when grabbing my wife's arm, thus effectively stopping Jenny from launching into another retort regarding our daughter's life choices. "What did you just say?"

As I removed Jenny's grip on the bannister and stepped forward, Beth glanced away from her mother to look at me. If I could see into my daughter's mind, I suspect I'd witness a mass of electronic pulses and neurons zipping back and forth as they attempted to pinpoint the exact word or phrase that had caused my question. After an elongated pause, Beth uttered her favourite word, followed up with that perfected shrug. Expertly conveying her 'I don't give a shit' attitude.

"What?"

"What did you just say?" I repeated, tightening my grip on Jenny's arm, sensing she was about to cut in.

"Dad, I'm sorry. I'm not a virgin—"

"Not that. You said a word. What did you say?"

"Oh, I don't know. Why? What's some word I can't remember saying got to do with anything?"

"Beginning with A … you said a word beginning with the letter A."

Beth's facial muscles twitched imperceptibly. That tiny act indicated her change of attitude from the hard-done-by teenager to that of concern.

"Beth?"

"Amazeballs," she muttered before repeating herself with a little more conviction. "Amazeballs."

"What made you say that? That word?"

"Jason—"

"Hang on," I threw at Jenny whilst keeping my focus on Beth, awaiting her answer.

Eighteen years had passed since time-travelling. Akin to a spy satellite, my big ears expertly tuned into picking up anything that wasn't quite right or didn't fit the era I was now living in. Although Martin, that evil git Paul Colney, and I had experienced time-travel, I was always alert to picking up any snippet of information that might suggest there were more of us types roaming the earth. The odds that we three, originating from this unremarkable Hertfordshire town of Fairfield, were the only time-travellers on the planet were, I suspected, on the low side.

Like any good analyst at GCHQ, when listening in on conversations and picking up on words such as 'bomb' or 'suicide vest', the word 'Amazeballs' caught my attention. Amazeballs was not a word for this era – it stood out and was as comfortable in 1994 as a vegan would be in an abattoir – somehow, that word had time-travelled. My concern now centred around whose voice my daughter had heard to pick up that out-of-place word.

"Beth?" I pushed when no reply appeared forthcoming.

She offered her well-practised shrug. "That bloke said it. I thought it was cool."

"Cool?"

"Yeah."

"This chap who gave you his jacket, who's apparently the spit of me, said amazeballs?"

"Yeah … what's the big deal?"

"Beth, where is that man now?"

"Dad?"

"Beth! Answer the bloody question," I barked, causing my daughter to flinch in surprise.

Although no parent likes to admit it, but we all have a favourite child. The one you just seem to forge a closer relationship with and perhaps possess a deeper affinity to. Whether in my family, the reason was due to Beth and I previously being best buddies or because of the classic father-daughter relationship, who knew?

Chris was a Mummy's boy – well, that's before the four-in-a-bed information came to light – and Beth was definitely a Daddy's girl.

As a consequence of that father-daughter relationship, it would be considered rare to hear me raise my voice at my daughter. However, right now, with my mind performing a triple Salchow, let alone reverse somersaults, with the amygdala posing the fight-or-flight question and thus closing down all other rational thoughts, I considered the impossible – *other* Jason.

When spotting our daughter's shocked expression, Jenny laid her hand on my chest and gently encouraged me to step back before taking hold of Beth's hand, giving it a motherly rub.

"Beth," she whispered. "Your father and I need to know who the man is that gave you that jacket." Jenny nodded to the abandoned leather garment that remained crumpled on the floor. "We're disappointed about … well, you know, but this is important." Jenny glanced at me. That tiny act conveyed that my wife had joined the dots and now, like me, feared the worst.

The potential impact of *other* Jason re-materialising after I'd taken his place in 1976 held a prominent position in my thoughts for all of those eighteen years. For sure, as the years rolled by, that concern had sometimes slipped onto the back burner. However, those worries were again front and centre, consuming me. If *other* Jason was back, what did that mean? We weren't the same person, despite our apparent doppelgänger appearance, but could we co-exist in the same time? What would happen if we met? What would the effect be on the space-time continuum? Whatever the hell that was. Despite my anorak-styled obsession with time-travel, I struggled to understand Einstein's theories. My inability to grasp the Special Theory of Relativity didn't negate my concerns regarding the potential effects of him co-existing with me. Based on the fact that we were essentially different people, I think, should I be concerned?

Too many questions.

"He likes coffee; I like tea," I vacantly muttered, remembering that first day I arrived in 1976 when discovering the man I'd replaced wasn't a coffee freak.

"Dad?" Beth quizzed, probably wondering if my deranged mutterings about hot beverages, coupled with my less-than-friendly demeanour, demonstrated that her father had lost his mind.

"Nothing," I said when Beth nudged me with her free hand. I guess my daughter was wondering why her father's thoughts appeared to have floated off-piste.

That deviation, when my inner voice suggested *other* Jason, sent my mind brown-water rafting along diarrhoea river towards a shitty end. A place where I never wanted to go – like swimming off Amity Island, but worse.

"Go and get cleaned up. We'll talk tomorrow," Jenny offered our bemused daughter an encouraging nod to the stairs.

"Is Dad alright? He looks a bit strange?"

Jenny nodded. "Go on, up you go."

"Is it the … you know, popping of my cherry thing?"

"Beth … we'll talk about that tomorrow. Please, up you go. I need to talk to your father."

"What about my bollocking?"

"Go!" Jenny hissed.

"Oh, alright, whatever," Beth mumbled as she pushed past me before halting on the fourth rung of the stairs and peering down at us. "You know, he said something really odd. Something about my husband in the future. He reckoned I'm going to marry a lawyer called Phil."

Jenny and I gradually swivelled our heads upwards.

"The future?" I quizzed.

"Yeah. Frigging nutter. I wouldn't be pretentious enough to marry some knobby lawyer. I'm going to marry George Michael. Night. Love you!" Beth blew a kiss and bolted up the stairs.

"I doubt that," I mumbled.

"Yes, well, that just goes to show how immature Beth still is, despite the revelation that she's allowed some boy to …" Jenny tutted. "I'm not going to say it. You know what I'm talking about. I must say, I'll be delighted if she married a lawyer rather than fantasising about pop stars."

"No, you're right. Anyway, I don't think George Michael would be attracted to Beth."

My wife shot me a look after I'd retrieved the leather jacket from its crumpled-heap position before we padded towards the kitchen.

"Odd thing to say. Our daughter might have some unsavoury heritage, and I know I'm biased, but I imagine she has to fight off the attentions of many boys."

"No, that's not—"

"Just a damn pity she didn't fight them all off!"

I decided not to explain why said pop star wouldn't be attracted to our daughter. Exactly when George Michael came out and shattered many a girl's dreams, I couldn't remember. Anyway, rather than enlighten Jenny, I needed to haul the conversation back to the subject, which I knew we both were probably too scared to broach.

"Jen?" I raised my eyebrows at her whilst laying the jacket on a bar stool.

She offered a slight nod in my direction, confirming she was ready to discuss what we both feared before flicking on the kettle.

"You want a coffee?"

"No, I'll be awake all night. Now I'm sixty, I've probably reached the age that means I'll need to start visiting the toilet in the middle of the night."

"Not the best end to your birthday, what with that damn book as well. I've got this horrible feeling." She paused and turned to look at me. The expression of terror akin to contemplating a spot of lunch with Hannibal Lecter. "It's all going to start again," Jenny paused again, grabbing a couple of mugs from the cupboard before swivelling her head at me. "Is it?"

After scrubbing my hand across my face, I rested my elbows on the breakfast bar and cupped my chin in both hands. I wanted to reassure my wife that the calamitous chaos of seven years ago wouldn't resurface. However, I harboured a nagging concern that I couldn't offer that assurance.

"Darling? D'you think the owner of that jacket is *other* Jason?"

"Jen, something's not right. *Other* Jason should be stuck in the past. Y'know, when I took his place in 1976. The trouble is, that bloke who Beth met tonight must have come from the future."

7

Who's Heisenberg?

With the kettle poised in mid-air, ready to pour the boiling liquid, Jenny froze. My wife appeared stupefied, as if time itself had taken a breather, hit the snooze button and paused. I guess my comment regarding *other* Jason's potential arrival from the future had the effect of sending her mind off on some rabid journey, resulting in her thoughts to scoot around and consider the baffling possibilities of time-travel.

As I prised the kettle from her hand, concerned she was about to pour boiling water anywhere but into a mug, Jenny broke from her trance and bug-eyed me.

"Future?"

"Without a doubt." I nodded whilst making her coffee.

"But why? What makes you think …" Jenny paused when remembering Beth's words. "That word. What was it?"

"Amazeballs."

"Never heard that before. What does it mean?"

"That's my point. That word is from the future. I don't know when, but definitely not from now. It's the sort of stupid word that people liberally threw on Twitter when commenting on some bollocks that some other idiot has posted. It sort of means amazing.

"Twitter?"

I side-eyed her as I ran the spoon around her mug, creating a coffee whirlpool. "You remember that stuff I said about social media, which controls our lives in the next century?"

"Oh, yes. What was it? Bookfacing, I think you called it?"

"Facebook," I chuckled. "Yeah. There's lots of them … platforms, they're called. Twitter is just another one, that's all," I replied, nipping across the kitchen and closing the door. Although I could hear the shower running as my daughter expertly emptied the hot water tank, a skill she seemed to have mastered, the last thing I needed tonight was Beth earwigging our conversation regarding time-travel.

In the interest of not exposing my true origin to our children, Jenny and I rarely discussed such matters when either Beth or Chris were home. However, tonight was a potential crisis situation, with the kitchen doubling up as our COBR to hold an impromptu TTBC meeting with the CEO and COO present. For sure, I'd have to update the other two members, George and Jess, first thing in the morning. Also, although now living the 'good life', therefore only an honorary member, I would need to bring Martin up to speed when on our monthly catch-up call.

Whilst gripping her mug in both hands, Jenny sipped her coffee, presumably trying to work out what this all meant.

As I said, the study of time-travel had become a hobby. In fact, you could accuse me of being slightly obsessed with the subject. Well, after my transtemporal experience in that mass-produced saloon car, who could blame me for spending an inordinate amount of my free time researching the ridiculous?

With the exception of three living souls – including Paul Colney, who I doubted possessed a soul – everyone knew time-travel was physically impossible. The stuff of science fiction, *Doctor Who, Back to the Future,* and *Bill and Ted's Excellent Adventure.* What the hell H.G. Wells would make of the latter, where those two idiots manage to kidnap a plethora of historical figures, would be interesting to know. However, comic capers aside, and whether you believed in alternative worlds, closed timeline curves, the theory of relativity, Niven's Law, or Novikov's recent theorising about paradoxes, time-travel shouldn't be possible.

But here I was.

Also, I feared the man I replaced in 1976 had landed at some point in the future and then scooted back through time to 1994. If that 1974 yellow Mk3 Cortina, secured in a lock-up on the Bowthorpe Estate, was a time machine, then it appeared I wasn't the only Jason Apsley in existence. I pondered the possibility that The Ford Motor Company had diversified its production lines to produce time machines for their more discerning customers.

Hmmm … maybe not.

However, a man who apparently looked like a younger me had met my daughter. No, my adopted daughter, my previous best friend. Who, if this man was who I thought he was, would be Beth's great-uncle based on the fact that Shirley Colney, Beth's paternal grandmother, was apparently the half-sister of *other* Jason. Well, that's according to Don, my honorary father, who was actually Beth's and Christopher's maternal great-grandfather due to an affair he enjoyed before the war that produced Beryl, my children's grandmother. Who's the woman who killed Shirley Colney, the mother of that evil bastard Paul Colney, whose current location, so far, remained unknown.

Lost? Me too!

Although technically, I wasn't part of this family tree, when I time-travelled and took *other* Jason's place, I'd parachuted into the most complicated of extended families.

After aimlessly conducting an in-depth study of the floor tiles, Jenny raised her head and pointed her coffee mug in my direction as I perched on a bar stool. "You think *other* Jason time-travelled forward to some point in the future, and then back to now … 1994?"

I nodded, then shrugged.

"But we thought *he* would only materialise when you die … y'know, you said something about he would come back when you've gone."

With my hands still clamped around my face, I glanced up at Jenny and raised a questioning eyebrow.

"Oh, no … you don't think?"

Jenny slammed her cup on the draining board and scooted around the breakfast bar before flinging her arms around me. My wife cuddled me like she would the kids when they were younger after they'd suffered a paper cut or some other catastrophe like an argument with their bestie. Jenny had taken to motherhood like an eco-warrior at a tree-hugging convention. Due to her enthusiasm for the role, my wife was prone to displaying overprotective tendencies where our adopted children were concerned. After disentangling myself from her grip, I took her hands in mine.

"Jen, I'm still here. I'm not dead. If Beth did happen to stumble upon *other* Jason tonight, then my theory that he would only appear when I'm dead was clearly all bollocks."

Jenny released one hand from mine and laid it on her chest before tipping her head back and closing her eyes. "Oh, you're right. Thank ... thank God for that." Her quivering lilt appeared to instruct her tear ducts to moisten, which she abated by pressing the heel of her palm to her left eye socket.

After dragging her raised hand back into mine, she tipped her head down and sniffed, offering her best 'I'm alright, although I'm not' smile.

"We don't actually know it's him. Do we? I mean, this bloke could be someone who just happened to look like me."

"It's a bit of a coincidence, though."

"Yeah, agreed."

"That word. When did it become a word?"

I sucked in a deep breath and pursed my lips after exhaling. "I don't know. If I had to guess, I'd say some time twenty years from now."

"Could you be wrong? Could that word be around now, and you've not heard it before?"

"Jen, I'm a schoolteacher. If that word was already in use, you can guarantee that marauding troop of delinquents who I try to instil some modicum of education would utter it every five minutes instead of sick or wicked. Or cool, as our daughter would say."

"So, this bloke, who's the spit of you, said amaze ... what was it?"

"Amazeballs."

"Yes, okay. So that confirms he's come from the future ... sometime after 2010?"

"Yeah, there or thereabouts. Thing is, if it's him, how did he end up in the future ..." I paused. No sooner had I uttered those words the metaphorical penny not only dropped but plummeted. As if released from the viewing platform of The Shard – or One Canada Square in Canary Wharf for this era – that penny had plunged from a great height. It wasn't rocket science. *Other* Jason time-travelled in 1976 and landed the moment I kicked the bucket for the second time.

In 2019, after ploughing my company Beemer into that white van in Cockfosters High Street, I presumably died and ended up in 1976. What I'd always believed was the man who I replaced would materialise the moment I died again. Hopefully, my second death would be due to old age and not as a result of an impromptu road traffic accident.

The question was, how much time did I have left? It appeared that my life path, this time around, would be determined as to when that stupid word became popular in the English language. I deduced I may not make it to become an octogenarian, which was quite a sobering thought.

"Darling? What's the matter?" Jenny wiggled my hand to break my reverie.

My mind settled on the scene from *Breaking Bad.* Specifically, when Walter White receives the diagnosis, suggesting the poor chap only has two years to live. If my assumption panned out to be correct, I could look forward to significantly more than two more years. Contemplating my demise as if some consultant had calmly delivered the news of my impending death put a bit of a dampener on my already melancholy mood.

'Mr Apsley, I'm sorry to inform you, but you don't have long left.'

'How long?'

'Well, I can't be certain on timings, but a time-traveller will take your life in about ten or fifteen years … give or take.'

Fair enough, I'd taken *other* Jason's life eighteen years ago, so I guess I had no room to complain. The spooky resemblance between Walter and me had set my mind racing. The character and I knew time was limited. Also, we were both schoolteachers specialising in educating the mostly disinterested youth on the finer points of chemistry. That said, I couldn't see myself starting up a methamphetamine lab in my lock-up, even though I possessed the skills and knowledge to do so.

"Darling, what is it? What's the matter?" Jenny repeated when noticing I seemed to have slipped back into some kind of odd stupor.

"Nothing," I lied. This wasn't the moment to inform my wife that I predicted my demise. "If it is him, then somehow he's found a way to time-travel."

"What d'you mean? You've time-travelled."

"Yes, but only the once."

"Martin time-travelled twice."

"Good point, he did. But that was in that car. My Cortina."

"Oh, God, that thing. I really don't know why you don't scrap it. Crush the damn thing."

"I have a feeling my old car won't stay crushed. As we both know, it seems to find a way to un-crush itself."

"Yes, but—"

"No, Jen. The safest place for that thing is under lock and key, so I know exactly where it is."

"Alright, if you're sure. So, you think this *other* Jason has a car like that one, too?"

"I don't know. I mean, I presume Ford didn't mass-produce time machines. Anyway, to time-travel in that car, you need to die."

"Perhaps he has. What if he landed in whatever year in the future, heard that word, amazeballs, died in his time machine and travelled to 1994 where he met Beth, gave her a lift home, and inadvertently mentioned that word which Beth picked up on?"

I shook my head after stifling a snorted laugh. "That's the sort of drivel one of my students might come up with to explain why they haven't completed their homework."

"That's as maybe, but what other explanation do you have to explain how our daughter met a man who's the spit of you from twenty years ago who just happens to utter words from the future?"

She made a good point.

"Hmmm, fair enough. Let's say it was him. D'you reckon he knows who Beth is? Or was it just a coincidence that she bumped in to him down Lovers' Lane?"

"Oh, don't mention … what on earth was she doing down there in the first place?"

I raised my eyebrow.

"I'd rather not think about that."

"Well, as much as I don't want to imagine it, but I guess our girl is growing up fast. She and this Craig boy were doing what teenagers do."

"Christ," Jenny muttered, before offering a disapproving tut when presumably imagining our daughter performing some lewd act.

"Your point, though. What was *other* Jason doing there?"

"Darling, I have no idea, but our girl needs to answer some questions."

"Not tonight."

"No, you're probably right." Jenny nodded at the jacket. "If he dropped her home, he might come back for that."

"Oh … of course." I plucked it up and held it out. "Looks expensive, although a bit retro."

"Indiana Jones."

"Nah, more Tyler Durden in the *Fight Club*."

"Who?"

"Brad Pitt. Y'know, that action thriller film."

Jenny pulled a face and shook her head.

"Oh, maybe that's still to come. I remember watching it, but I suppose that could have been in my first life."

"To be honest, darling, it looks like something David Soul would wear."

I shot her a look. "Christ, I said retro." I grabbed the wide lapel, waving it at Jenny. "Either this bloke has had this hanging in his wardrobe for over twenty years and decided tonight was the night to dust it off and give it another runout, or the owner just took a trip from the 1970s."

As Jenny grabbed the jacket, a folded single sheet of paper slipped from the inside pocket and floated to the ground. As it came to rest on the tiled floor, the top line of the letter became visible.

Dear Jason

Before either of us could make a grab for it, the back door swung open with such force I half expected the hinges to give way. Either Michael Standing's character had set a too-big a charge, leaving me wondering if I should quote Michael Caine. Or a herd of marauding elephants had escaped Whipsnade Zoo and decided to barrel through our back door when sniffing out Jenny's cheese plant. Said foliage, which at over four feet wide and tall, was in danger of engulfing the vast majority of the hallway.

It wasn't the cast of the *Italian Job* or a charging trunk-to-tail line of pachyderm.

Something told me my fears about my future were about to become realised. My sixtieth birthday just kept giving.

8

The Carnival is Over

"Bloody hell! What's going on? Are you alright?"

"I haven't got long. I'm on my way to pick Faith up from a friend's over in Luton, but something's happened." Jess closed the backdoor, which, after she'd ripped it open, I was surprised still slotted snugly into its frame.

As my daughter hovered by the door, my eyes oscillated from her and the letter that tantalisingly bore my name at the top.

"Jess?"

Jenny scooted across to her, taking her hand before leading my stunned-looking daughter towards the breakfast bar. I retrieved the letter from where it lay enticingly, or ominously, depending on the content, on the tiled floor.

On the subject of complicated family trees, you could say that Jess added a pinch of extra spice to my genealogy. Although the rest of the world assumed Jess to be my biological daughter, the five members of the TTBC knew differently. Jess and I shared no heredity because she was technically *other* Jason's daughter, and subsequently, Faith was *his* granddaughter. That all said, Jenny and I loved them both as if they were our own.

To add to this head-spinning conundrum, although I was, for all intents and purposes, born in 1934, I actually came into this world in 1977. And despite Jess being born in 1956, twenty-one years before me, I was twenty-one years older than her.

Time-travel is super complicated.

"Is Faith alright? Colin? Nothing's happened to Colin, has it? Oh my God, he's not back, is he?" Jenny machine-gunned, still holding Jess's hand whilst peering into her eyes.

"Who?"

"Paul—bloody—Colney, that's who."

"Oh, no."

"Oh … just after that bloody book arriving today, I seem to have that evil fuckhead shyster lodged in my brain."

"Jess, what's going on?" I asked, plonking the letter on the breakfast bar. "It's nearly eleven." I tapped my watch whilst raising a quizzical eyebrow at my wife.

By her standards, I was somewhat surprised regarding the volley of invectives that just poured from Jenny's mouth. Jenny shrugged back at me before I turned to Jess.

"What's so important that you need to come over at this time of night?"

"Dad, I'm sorry. I know it's late, but I saw the lights on and assumed you were still up."

"No, you know that's not what I mean. What the bollocks has happened?" Jenny and I shot each other a look. I could tell Jenny's thoughts were in line with mine. Which, after discussing the events of the evening thus far, probably meant

Jess was about to offer some revelation about another time-traveller. Who, I suspected, would be *other* Jason.

God help me.

"Dad," Jess paused whilst chewing her lip and glancing between Jenny and me. "Dad, I think I may have just seen my father."

Apart from the humming of the fridge and the flushing noise of the soil pipe draining away Beth's shower water, an air of silent calmness took hold. Still holding Jess's hands, Jenny cleared her throat and glanced around towards me as I pursed my lips while bug-eyeing my daughter. Upon hearing water sluicing through the soil stack pipe, Jess broke the silence.

"Shit, is Beth home?"

"Yeah, as you can hear, she's emptying the hot water tank."

"Why? You got a plumbing issue?"

"No," I chuckled. Despite the seriousness of the situation, a vision of Beth wearing a blue boiler suit whilst wielding a wrench held a certain amusement factor to it. My seventeen-year-old daughter was a girlie girl, and there was nothing tomboy about her whatsoever.

"Let's just say, due to her mud-wrestling exploits, she's taking a long shower."

"Mud wrestling?"

"We'll come to that in a moment." Jenny wiggled Jess's hands. "Where did you see him? Did you speak? Did he see you? It *was* him, I take it?"

"You don't seem surprised. I thought … oh, did you know he's here?"

Jenny grimaced at me, indicating I should take up the story regarding Beth's encounter with a man who'd lost his jacket.

After enlightening Jess with a quick run-through of Beth's adventures – although omitting the particulars regarding Beth's 'popped cherry' announcement due to that being a subject for another day – I probed Jess on what she'd seen.

"So, come on, spill the beans. Where did you see him?"

Jess ignored the question, seemingly more interested in my other daughter's antics. "Lovers' Lane. Beth was with some boy in Lovers' Lane?"

"Oh, don't ask. It seems that Beth has been seeing some boy called Craig," Jenny bristled.

"And she was," Jess paused to offer a perfected Kenneth Williams styled ooh. "Beth was having a bit of how's-your-father down that creepy place with all those doggers."

"Doggers?" Jenny furrowed her brow and leaned back.

"That's where they all congregate, isn't it?"

"Who? Who are doggers?"

"Jenny, you know, dogging! Doggers having sex."

"Dogs having sex?"

"No! You know, those groups that like to, you know … through a car window."

"How on earth do you have sex through—"

"Jen, I'll explain later," I interrupted, fearing my wife would need a diagram to understand.

Although we'd enjoyed alfresco nookie on the terrace of a Spanish villa when the kids were young, risqué sexual activities weren't something Jenny or I were that cognisant of. Despite both being slightly sozzled after too many G&Ts, which resulted in relaxing our inhibitions in the first place, Jenny worried about being seen. Perhaps someone on the headland four miles away might spot us if they happened to be traipsing across the dangerous rocky ridge in the dead of night with a pair of night vision goggles slung around their neck just on the off chance that they might spot a couple copulating on the other side of the bay. My wife, despite a tendency to be cautious, always enjoyed an overactive imagination.

Jenny was no prude. Although twelve years my junior, she was born at the end of the Second World War. So, technically, thirty-one years my senior and the product of a very different generation. You could say my wife hadn't partaken in the 'free love' antics of the '60s, despite by all accounts that her parents like to dabble in a spot of suburban '70s-styled swinger action. Information that her mother, Frances, let slip one drunken evening some years back. Fortunately, my mother-in-law's admission didn't fall on Jenny's ears.

Presumably sensing what Jess was talking about, without the need for visual aids, Jenny nodded and took up the probing for information.

"You've never met your real father, so what leads you to conclude it was him?"

Jess huffed, letting her breath out in a long exhalation in preparation to tell her story.

"Colin was planning to pick up Faith but was watching *Sportsnight* when she rang. Des Lynam was banging on about the cricket. Means nothing to me, but Colin wanted to watch the test highlights, so I said I'd go. When I opened the car door, he appeared in the driveway and called out my name."

"Jason, your father? *Other* Jason."

Jess nodded. "Dad, it was him. Of course, I jumped out of my skin because it was like seeing you from when we first met. It was frigging creepy as hell. Just as if you from the mid-seventies had just waltzed up the driveway."

"He looked like me from back in '76?"

"Identical, the resemblance is uncanny … face and build, that is. His hair was long, and he had a goatee beard thing going on, but other than that, yes, identical. I thought it odd he was only in a t-shirt. I know it's been a nice day, but it's chilly tonight, and I could see he was shivering."

Jenny and I glanced at the jacket that lay on the breakfast bar. Although I'd given Jess a quick run-through of the events of Beth's evening, I'd not mentioned the jacket.

"Christ. What the hell did you do?" Jenny chimed in.

"Well, as you can imagine, I just gawped at him. I think I said his name because I remember him nodding and saying he was my real father."

"Did he say where he's been?"

"No, he ran off down the road when Colin came to the door to ask me to pick up some milk on my way home."

"Did Colin see him?"

"No." Jess shook her head. "I don't think so. When Colin closed the front door, I turned around, and Jason, that's him, *other* Jason, had ducked down behind my car."

"Then he ran off?"

"Yeah …" Jess paused, her eyes shooting back and forth between us.

"What?" Jenny questioned when sensing Jess was holding back.

"He told me he'd come from the future—"

"And?" I exasperatedly threw my arms up.

"Dad, he said the weirdest thing—"

"Stranger than claiming he'd come from the future?"

"Well, yes, Mum, I see your point."

Although Jenny wasn't her mother, and their ages were less than ten years apart, Jenny had always taken on that role since Jess discovered me back in '77. Jess would alternate calling my wife Jenny or Mum, depending on the conversation. In moments of anxiety or high stress, Jess always called Jenny Mum. My wife employed that well-practised maternal comforting trait of rubbing the back of Jess's hand as we awaited to hear what my namesake had said.

"I'm worried. He said I must stay home, lock the doors and not venture out on the 6th of April … next Wednesday."

"Why?"

"I don't know. That's when he ran off."

"Where … where'd he go?"

"Dad, I don't know."

Whilst Jenny continued her Blofeld-cat-stroking-routing on the back of Jess's hand, I took a moment to think. I'd surmised earlier that *other* Jason must have landed in the year of my second death. His statement to Jess, claiming to come from the future, confirmed what we'd already concluded. Although I'd regret asking this, the answer might indicate how long I had left.

Dreading the answer, I took a couple of deep breaths to prepare myself. "Jess, did he say when in the future? What year he'd time-travelled from?"

Jess shook her head, causing her long brunette hair to sway. "No."

Apart from the regular morphing through a rainbow of different colours, my daughter had always maintained a long, free-flowing hairstyle sporting a straight fringe. The Judith

Durham or Mary Hopkin look, if you like. Jess resisted the 'feathered look' of the late '70s, the perms and 'big hair' of the '80s and the 'choppy layered' look of the '90s. The latter, I was aware, would be known as the 'Rachel' due to Jennifer Aniston's character in Friends. A style my ex-wife attempted to model herself on sometime in the new millennium. An attempt which, in my opinion, failed spectacularly.

And, yes, whilst we're on the subject of confusing time-travel, that's Lisa, my ex-wife, who in this life had enjoyed a frolic in my bed, this time with two other young ladies and my son, not me. I'm sixty, and Lisa was barely twenty, so that would be a non-starter in this life, let alone considered somewhat perverted.

Anyway, it seems that I'm none the wiser about discovering the date of my second demise. For now, the 'Carnival' of my life was still in full swing and wouldn't be over until some knob popularised that word 'amazeballs'.

"Darling." I glanced up at Jenny as she paused. "*Other* Jason has been to the future and discovered something will happen next week. But why would he instruct Jess to stay inside with the doors and windows shut?"

Confused as she was, I offered a shrug.

"Does something happen this year? I don't remember you saying anything about a nuclear attack or some swarm of killer wasps plaguing the country."

See what I mean? My wife harboured one hell of a vivid imagination. My mind momentarily flickered to the film *The Swarm*. Although boasting an all-star cast, in this life as well as my last, the film was widely considered cinematography's greatest flop.

When noticing my wife's raised eyebrow as she impatiently awaited my answer, I shoved the vision of killer bees to one side and rejoined the conversation.

"Perhaps time has changed. Some tiny effect has rippled out, and now the future I lived through the first time will dramatically alter," I suggested, thinking on my feet.

"Killer wasps!" Jess exclaimed, a delayed reaction to Jenny's suggestion.

Jess was one of those people who performed a demented dance of flailing hands when within a hundred yards of a common wasp. Once, a hornet became entangled in her hair while on a picnic. The ensuing thrashing about made Kate Bush's antics when performing *Wuthering Heights* on *Top of the Pops* appear almost inert.

"What about Saddam Hussein? In our 'yearbooks', we have the Iraq War starting in the next century. I remember you saying that he's executed. What if that's changed? Last year, Iraq tried to assassinate George Bush, didn't they? Perhaps they have amassed a stockpile of nuclear weapons and plan to bomb us all?"

"Jen—"

"Jason, we need to alert the government. Next week, that nutter will start indiscriminately blowing up the bloody world. All because we forced him out of Kuwait a couple of years back during the Gulf War."

"Jen! Calm down," I hissed, concerned about raised voices and the fact that the waste stack no longer produced any flushing sounds, thus suggesting our daughter had vacated the shower after probably leaving the bathroom resembling a Turkish sauna. "You're assuming that *other* Jason knows about an event that affects the entire world."

105

"And?"

"What if it's not that?"

"Dad?" quizzed Jess as they both waited for me to explain.

Since George persuaded my wife that I'd time-travelled, Jenny and I had for many years kept a stack of 'yearbooks', as we called them, that formed part of the monthly agenda for the TTBC.

Those books, essentially a bunch of exercise books in which Jenny captured the future events, we used as a reference when planning to stop future disasters. So far, we've achieved less than a woeful success rate because time has a way of repeating itself despite all our best endeavours. My attempts to stop the Yorkshire Ripper being a case in point. That said, regarding smaller events that directly affected our futures, there were some successes to boast about. One such event being when I killed Beth's father, David Colney, thus preventing him from becoming a serial killer in the future.

Also, keeping a record of the future, along with my details of Formula One racing results, helped to ensure we placed modest but accurate bets. This strategy ensured we maintained a lifestyle that was more than comfortable whilst ensuring we didn't draw attention to ourselves – Biff Tannen style.

"What if *other* Jason knew of something that will only happen to us or just Jess?"

"Like what?"

I swallowed hard, not wishing to verbalise my suggestion. If what was rolling around my head were about to come to fruition, then that dystopian future that Jenny feared might take place if Saddam Hussein had his hand hovering over the nuclear button or a plague of rabid killer wasps were about to descend, paled into insignificance.

Jenny grabbed Jess's hand and thrust them up to her chest. "Oh, no, you're thinking someone will hurt Jess!"

Paradoxically, I considered harm to my daughter worse than obliteration from a nuclear strike.

"Blimey, what's all the shouting?" Beth boomed as she barrelled into the kitchen, sending the door flying as she barefoot padded towards the fridge. "Oh, hi, Jess. To what do we owe the pleasure?" she sarcastically asked before grabbing a carton of orange juice from the door and slugging back a few gulps.

"Beth! Use a glass."

Our daughter belched and grinned.

"Beth! We have visitors."

"Where?" Beth crouched and dramatically glanced around with her open palm placed above her eyes as she mockingly scoured the kitchen.

"Oh, Beth!"

"Sorry, Mum," she giggled and waved the carton at Jess. "You alright? You look, I dunno, pissed off." Beth took another swig of juice as the three of us watched the bath-towel-wrapped Beth as she upended the carton to glug down the remainder. When no one spoke, she side-eyed us before lowering the carton and uttering her favourite word. "What?"

"It's pardon. Not what."

"Yeah, whatever."

"And please don't walk around the house naked!"

Beth performed a hiccup, braying laugh as she bent double, allowing the towel wrapped around her hair to slide away and drop to the floor.

"Oh, Mum! I've got a towel on. I'm hardly parading around like some erotic pole dancer, am I?"

"Yes, but you're at that age ... oh, forget it. Too bloody late now, I guess."

I raised an eyebrow at Jenny, who presumably was thinking about our daughter's earlier revelation that she'd already made the leap from childhood to womanhood.

"So, you okay? The Gestapo here giving you the third degree?" Beth waved the empty carton at Jess, who appeared lost in her thoughts about what great catastrophe would bestow her precisely seven days from now. "Hey, big sis, don't let the bastards grind you down. That's what I say."

"Beth!"

"Oh, what's this?"

"Oh, no, you don't," I reached out to grab the folded sheet of paper I'd laid on the breakfast bar.

Beth hopped away and giggled. "Uh-uh, I want to see what it says."

"Beth ... no, that's private." I made another lunge, but my errant seventeen-year-old daughter, who benefited from a nimble posture and greater fleet of foot than I, despite my routine of morning jogs around the park, avoided my flailing hand.

Knowing Beth from my first life – and despite her childhood this time being a loving experience with two parents who doted upon her, as opposed to being raised in a loveless children's home – her boisterous and sometimes wayward traits that nature had supplied from her biological parents would come to the fore.

As a result of her leaping and general foolery, Beth's towel loosened from her cleavage, resulting in my half-naked daughter clamping the loosened towel to her chest with one hand as she leaned against the cooker and held the paper in the other. No father should see his daughter in a state of undress, so I glanced away and averted my eyes just at the point her face became ashen.

"Dad?"

For sure, the tremor I detected in her voice as Jess hopped across to cover her up wasn't because of the verbal lambasting her mother was now dishing out for either standing half-naked in the kitchen, her earlier declaration of being deflowered or reading that note which was clearly addressed to me but born out of what that letter contained.

With Jess barrelling through the door earlier, I hadn't had a chance to read it, and the details my daughter had just consumed were more than a smidge worrying.

I considered, as the melee of shouting ensued, that I may have to enrol my daughter, my previous best friend, into the Time Travellers Believers' Club.

"Bollocks," I mumbled.

Perhaps the 'carnival' was over because I very much doubted my daughter would ever swallow that story.

9

Dead Man Walking

"She's decent," Jenny announced, after Jess had corrected my daughter's wardrobe malfunction, thus allowing me to turn around and face her. With her damp, matted hair slapped to the side of her face, she reminded me of Beth from my first life. Beth had been the sister I never had, with me taking on the role of her brother due to her delinquent older half-brother languishing in prison.

Time-travel offers miraculous opportunities to improve someone's lot. That degenerate half-brother was now my adopted son. Now forging a successful career in the civil service instead of his previous existence of languishing in various borstals and prisons. It's safe to say, with my knowledge of what had gone before, or never, if that previous existence is expunged, my wife and I were super proud.

"Dad, what the hell is this?" she waved the one page in the air. Whether her demeanour was born out of fury or confusion, I couldn't tell. However, tears appeared to be on the horizon.

Jenny snatched the letter from her grip.

"Beth, I don't know. I haven't had a chance to read it."

"Who wrote it?"

"I don't know," I glanced at Jenny as she squinted whilst scanning the letter.

"Where'd it come from?"

I pointed to the leather jacket that lay on the breakfast bar. "The inside pocket of that jacket."

"Is that his jacket?" Jess blurted, whilst waving an accusing finger at the inert item.

I nodded.

Jenny held her arm aloft, effectively halting the father-daughter exchange before poignantly nodding at me.

"I'm not sure Beth should be in the room for this conversation."

"Wha … I'm not going anywhere! I want to know why that letter states that Chris and I don't know who you are?" As Beth screamed her statement, ending on a crescendo, the tears rolled.

I stepped forward, that natural action of wanting to hug my distressed daughter. However, a shake of the head from Jess halted my advance. Presumably sensing she was best placed to offer comfort, Jess wrapped a succouring arm around Beth's shoulders and pulled her close.

"It's too late to exclude her now," I mumbled.

"Jason!"

I exasperatedly waved my hand at my two daughters, who remained tightly embraced as I replied to my wife's bark. "She's read whatever it says."

Jenny offered a resigned nod. "It's in your handwriting," she stated, raising a quizzical eyebrow before reaching for a pair of her many reading glasses from the windowsill.

111

I furrowed my brow, wondering why *other* Jason, who I knew from letters and notes discovered in that flat on the Broxworth Estate owned the same handwriting as me, would write a letter to the man who took his place all those years ago.

"You ready?"

"Yeah, let's hear it."

"It's dated October 2015." Jenny peered over her spectacles at me and then at our two daughters, who remained in a tight embrace.

"2015?" I mumbled.

Jenny turned back to me and nodded.

"Okay," I shrugged as Jenny held my stare like a schoolmarm peering at me over the top of her glasses.

Jenny cleared her throat and read aloud.

My mind raced. If this letter was penned by *other* Jason, written when he time-travelled to the future, that could only mean that sometime in the month of October 2015 was presumably when I'll depart this world for the second time.

I will die at the age of eighty-one. Okay, not a bad innings, I guess, and it was good to know I wasn't about to get run over by a wayward bus or suffer an impromptu heart attack. Although I wasn't a fully paid-up member of ASH, I had managed to kick the habit that had ravished my lungs for thirty-odd years. However, I accepted the effects of smoking could induce a heart attack at a young age. So, despite now feeling like one of those tormented souls waiting on death row as they watched the days tick by to their execution date, with my history of smoking, I guess I should be grateful to make it past eighty.

Nevertheless, how would I feel as that month, twenty-one years and eight months in the future, grew ever closer? Would I develop death row syndrome? I'd watched a documentary about it some years ago, *Panorama*, *Everyman*, *World in Action*, or *The South Bank Show,* one of those. However, I doubt it could have been the latter because Melvyn Bragg would probably not report on the plight of America's most evil killers. No, that Sunday night programme was more high art, most of which was way above my head and slightly more cultured than anything Banksy could muster up. That said, by the next millennium, that 'highbrow art' would only be worth a smidgen compared to that street artist's work.

For some unbeknown reason, as Jenny started reading, my mind played the tune to that late-night Sunday arts programme. A variation of Paganini's 24th Caprice, I believe. The open visuals, specifically the image of Michelangelo's Sistine Chapel painting of the hand of God giving life to Adam, consumed my thoughts. Someone or something gave me life, and now *other* Jason would take it away.

"Darling? Did you hear me?"

I shook away my vision of Michelangelo's artistry and peered up at Jenny, who continued to perform her schoolmarm impression.

"Sorry, start again."

Jenny, again, cleared her throat and read aloud—

Dear Jason.

This is a somewhat odd letter to write. Penning a letter to my younger self is quite a tricky thing to do. Also, whether you'll actually receive this, well, who knows? However, you and I (although we are the same person) both know that strange things happen in that Cortina.

113

Anyway, to be honest with you, this is now my eleventh attempt at writing this damn letter. My other attempts have all gone the way of the shredder.

Anyway, let's move on from the ramblings of an old man. There is, of course, an enormous risk in penning this letter. If it were to fall into the hands of the wrong person, that could cause difficulties, to say the least. Chris and Beth still don't know who I am and where I come from, and as I enter my ninth decade, I'm still uncertain whether I will ever tell them.

For obvious reasons, I've not detailed future events because you already know them. However, certain information has come to the fore, and this is the reason for trying to contact you in the past.

You will remember the 12th August 2019, and specifically the news item on the radio as you (I) drove to work. I've not detailed them in this letter for the reason stated, but what was reported that day has happened again. I bent time in 1976, but as we know, time has a habit of pulling back to the laid-down path the future demands.

Now, whether that Cortina, still parked in our garage, can transport this letter through time – again, who knows? Also, if by chance this happens, I have no idea if you will receive this in time to act – but if you do – act, you must. Your daughter's life depends upon it.

As we both know, time-travel is exclusive to just the three of us. April 1994, be ready to act. One of those time-travellers will re-emerge under a pseudonym – you know what to do.

'Other' Jason still hasn't surfaced. Of course, as we both fear, I suspect he will after my death. Jess holds the key to ensure that, if this happens, 'other' Jason can continue where you and I've left off. However, unfortunately, I never got the opportunity to prepare her for that day. I'm aware that this letter may seem vague, but as we share the same mind, I'm hoping you can read between the lines.

As we both know, we're not the praying type, but I sincerely hope by sending this letter, you can bend time and thus allow Jess to prepare.

Good luck to you (me).

Jason.

"What the … bollocks …" my voice trailed away as my jaw sagged. *Other* Jason hadn't written the letter. Instead, I, at the age of eighty-one, had written to me. My mind was on overdrive. I was still alive in October 2015, so how long did I live for? Good news: I was no longer on death row. My Cortina was in a lock-up, not parked in the garage. So, when did I move it, and why?

That radio report on the 12th of August 2019 was about the serial killer David Colney. I killed the then sixteen-year-old David Colney when I let him drop to his death from the roof of Belfast House in 1976. How could time have bent back? And what was that about my daughter in danger? Was that Beth or Jess? Also, how had other Jason got hold of that letter, and had my older self met up with the man who gave Beth his jacket?

A cornucopia of unfathomable questions.

"Dad?" Beth's whimper broke the deadlock.

"I need to fetch Faith. She'll be wondering where the hell I've got to."

Jenny and I exchanged a glance. *Other* Jason and eighty-one-year-old me had warned that something terrible would happen to Jess. However, as both warnings were specific about the date, I guess she was safe for now. Knowing she needed to collect Faith, Jenny and I nodded at Jess.

"Colin has a late one tomorrow. I'll come around at about five?"

"What about Faith?" Jenny asked, whilst removing her glasses.

"She's got rehearsals tomorrow, so she won't be back until late."

As our exchange continued, Beth's bug eyes shot between the three of us like a nervous lizard when on high alert, wary of a predator in close proximity.

"Alright," I nodded. "Text me you've got home safely."

Jess raised an eyebrow.

I waved my hand as if to wipe away my misspeak. "Sorry, that's the future. Very soon, I might add."

Beth swivelled her head towards me, still bug-eyed, now adding a gaping mouth to the look.

Of course, in a few seconds, we would have to deal with the issue of divulging my true identity to Beth. However, whilst my larger-than-life seventeen-year-old daughter was unusually taciturn, this was the opportunity to ensure Jenny, Jess, and I were on the same page regarding the need for an urgent TTBC meeting.

"Jess, go and get Faith. I'll ring George first thing, and we'll reconvene at the pub at five-thirty tomorrow."

Jess offered Beth a tight smile as she rubbed her shoulder. "It will be alright. All I can say is … believe your father. Your mum and dad are the most wonderful people on the planet. Never forget that."

Beth, still in a state of bewilderment, swivelled her eyes towards Jess. Other than that slight movement, she didn't appear ready to offer any response.

Jenny and I hugged Jess before my wife scooted off to the hallway. I hung my head, unable to look at Beth. Of course, seven years ago, we'd had to convince Jess who I really was. That hadn't been too difficult based on the fact she'd experienced those encounters with Martin and Paul Colney, who she'd believed had died ten years prior. Real live walking and talking ghosts have a tendency to help nudge the mind into believing the ridiculous.

Chris and Megan rented a studio flat in town. So, tonight, I wouldn't have both children to convince I'd time-travelled from the future. However, that didn't make the prospect of what the next few hours looked like any easier.

Jenny bustled back into the kitchen clutching a dressing gown, which she wrapped around Beth's shoulders as she guided her to a bar stool. After settling our comatose daughter onto the seat, Jenny planted an elongated kiss on her crown before grabbing three glasses from the cupboard and selecting a bottle of white wine from the wine cooler.

Beth and I locked eyes.

Jenny placed the glasses on the breakfast bar and winced as she applied pressure to the screw cap before unscrewing it and lobbing it towards the sink. I guess my wife was expecting the three of us to finish the bottle.

Although we disapproved of Beth's drinking, we introduced our children to wine with meals from an early age. Apparently, learning how to respect alcohol from a young age prevented the binge-type relationship that many older teens suffered. The TV was full of programmes depicting drunken teenagers splayed out in a state of undress outside some Magaluf bar. Frances and John, my in-laws, believed an early introduction to wine to be the right course to take when raising children. Look at the French, she'd said. 'You don't see many Parisian mademoiselles sloshed and unconscious, with their tiny skirts up around their armpits when they stumble out of a nightclub during the witching hours, do you?'

I guess she made a good point. That said, John and Frances were piss-heads, so maybe not.

Jenny glugged a full glass before refilling hers and the other two glasses. She slid one towards Beth. "Drink it."

Beth glanced at her mother. "What?"

"Beth, drink it. You're going to need it."

I padded over and slithered onto a bar stool opposite Beth, watching her as she necked the wine as per her mother's instruction.

Jenny grabbed the letter and placed it in front of me. My eyes drifted downward to the handwritten note. Definitely my handwriting, although a little shaky.

"The Ys give it away."

I swivelled my eyes towards Jenny as she refilled Beth's glass.

"Sorry?"

Jenny offered her best I-love-you-and-don't-you-forget-it smile to Beth as she poured the wine before tapping the page in front of me.

"The handwriting is a little erratic, but the Ys confirm you wrote it. You always do that funny squiggle where your pen leaps up when you write the letter Y."

Beth scraped the letter across the counter before lifting it in the air so she could read whilst glugging her second glass, which my wife reciprocated. The bottle was already empty, and we hadn't even broached the subject of time-travel.

Beth petulantly lobbed the note back towards me and slammed her empty glass onto the worktop. "So, Dad, who the fuck are you?" she sardonically questioned.

Her steel-cold eyes, the lip curl, and the tone were all the traits of the Beth I once knew back in the future. That Beth was a ball-breaking, no-nonsense hard bitch. Knowing what I was potentially facing, I needed some fortitude to get through the next few hours unscathed. In one swift movement, I snatched up my glass and guzzled the contents.

10

I Have a Dream

"Beth!"

"What?"

"Don't use that kind of language to your father!"

"Why the fuck not?"

"Beth, stop it."

"No! I can't say fuck, but you two can keep secrets from Chris and me about who the frigging hell our parents really are."

"Woah. Hang on."

Both women shot me a look. Neither were expressions that could be termed endearing. But hey, this was a super stressful situation.

The phone shrilled, causing all three of us to look at the wall where it hung. I raised my palm, indicating we should ignore it. At this point, I felt we had bigger fish to fry than some automated cold call, a phenomenon that appeared to be on the increase.

"Beth, I'm going to ask you to suspend your beliefs. So, let's just say anything goes for tonight. If you want to verbally abuse your mother and me, call me wanker, your mother a bitch—"

"Jason!"

I raised my palm to halt Jenny's protestations. "Hear me out." Leaving Jenny sporting a sagging jaw, I turned and wagged a finger at our daughter. "So, you throw any obscenities you like, scream, shout, cry, whatever. However, that's on the proviso that you accept two conditions." I waited for Beth to nod before continuing. "First, you don't assume licence to say anything like that to your mother or me ever again. Second, you open your mind, hear us out and don't storm off in a strop."

Beth opened her mouth to protest about the accusation that she could occasionally throw a strop but thought better of it and promptly closed it again.

"Although, can we not use the 'C' word? I find it so vulgar and unnecessary."

"And the 'B' word, thank you very much. I'm not a dog. I'm your mother, who just happens to love you more than you can ever imagine."

Beth offered Jenny her perfect yeah-whatever type shrug.

"So, do we have a concordat?"

"Thought you were supposed to be a schoolteacher?"

"I am … but," I paused, trying to work out how to tell my daughter that, in twenty years from now, I was a forty-year-old marketing executive for a sheet metal fabrication company. "Beth, as mad as this sounds, in the future, when I was younger, I wasn't a schoolteacher."

"No, I meant I thought you were supposed to be educated. Concordat, although meaning an agreement, which is what you presumably were asking me, is a word that would normally be used in relation to describe a convention between the Holy See and a sovereign state regarding the Catholic Church and all matters pertaining to it."

I glanced at Jenny, who offered a roll of the eyes and a shrugged response.

"The point I'm making is you're supposed to be the schoolteacher, so I would have thought you would have chosen the right word. Instead of concordat, the word agreement would have sufficed. And yes, I agree to the terms, you wanker."

"Beth!"

"Uh-uh," Beth dramatically shook her head from side to side, causing her damp blonde hair to swish around before coming to rest and partially covering her face. "Dad said I can call him a wanker tonight."

"Christ," I muttered. "I need another drink … you'd better make it a large one."

Beth snatched up the now crumpled note, slapping the page with her free hand. "What do you mean by the future? Why have you written a stupid letter to yourself and dated the bloody thing 2015?"

On top of what I suspect would have been a few Bacardi and Cokes in the Woolpack Pub, two glasses of wine appeared to have provided Beth with an air of bolshiness. However, as she awaited my answer, I spotted her chin wobble. My little girl was doing her level best to hold it all together but, I feared the floodgates were about to fail and, her tears would soon roll.

If we could zip back ten minutes in time, perhaps I could have grabbed that letter before Beth, or we could have played it differently and claimed it was some joke.

However, notwithstanding my ability to time-travel forty-three years into the past, a ten-minute scoot back in time was beyond me.

Jenny repeated the wincing face routine as she unscrewed the top of the second bottle. She lobbed the cap in the general direction of where the first one landed and topped up my wine. After placing the bottle on the counter, appearing deep in thought, she grabbed Beth's free hand. Whilst continuing to perform that motherly, comforting act of stroking our daughter's hand, Jenny gently shifted some wayward strands of hair away from Beth's eyes.

My girl was about to crack.

"Let's start with what you already know. Your father and I adopted you and Chris in 1977 after your mother, Carol … well, we know … she left this world."

Don and I had always suspected that Paul Colney murdered Carol with an overdose. Information that both he and I decided to take to our graves. We could never prove it, and even if we could, that wouldn't have saved that poor tortured woman's life. As I know from my first life, Carol didn't protect her children, leading to Beth being abused by her father. My time-travelling escapade had expunged that nasty piece of history, so Beth never had to suffer. Also, a string of women in the early 2000s avoided their horrific, painful death at the strangling hands of a serial killer. Whilst I mused about time-travel, Jenny continued.

"Your father and I love you, which I know you know, even though you like to call us the Gestapo."

Beth smirked. Despite that scornful facial expression, I noticed our daughter tighten her finger grip around Jenny's hand. That involuntary show of affection in direct contrast to the deadpan face she now tried to adopt.

Teenagers' and parents' relationships were a battle of wills.

"I met your father in 1976. At the time, Carol was one of my cases, and I was concerned about your mother's ability to raise Chris. Also, with you coming along, it was my job to protect vulnerable children from potentially dangerous situations." Jenny glanced at me and accepted my encouraging nod. "Your Dad was living in the next flat to Carol."

"I know … you've told me how you met."

"Okay. So, do you remember Dad's friend, Martin?"

Beth stuck out her bottom lip and shook her head.

"She was too young," I chimed in.

Jenny nodded. "What about Leonardo? He stayed with us back in the '80s."

"Oh, yeah, him. That weirdo who came from South Africa? That's when he and Dad got arrested for perverting the course of justice, and Granny Beryl killed my other grandmother, Shirley Colney, just before she planned to kidnap me and Faith."

The way Beth trotted out, rather matter-of-factly, the events of that year, she made it sound all so normal. However, there was nothing straightforward about the family I'd parachuted into. There was the maternal grandmother murdering the paternal grandmother, for starters. Despite my schoolteacher credentials, I wasn't aware of an allotted 'cide' word for that particular type of killing. Perhaps, Blue-rinse on Blue-rinse or *granniecide*, who knew?

Jenny continued. "Yes. Well, you see, Leonardo was … is, I should say, actually Martin. The same man who died in 1977 with Paul Colney. When Martin time-travelled to 1987, he used the pseudonym Leonardo and claimed to be Martin's brother. You see, Martin was already buried in 1977, so couldn't be

Martin again. Of course, Martin time-travelled twice. The first time being in 2019, back to 1977, six months after your father.

Beth shot me a look.

I offered a slight wince, knowing how what Jenny had said would have sounded to anyone with half a brain. Clearly, after Beth's 'concordat' comment, my daughter possessed significantly more than half.

"Jesus, frigging hell, Mum. Have you found my stash of weed? I don't smoke much, and it's not really strong, but you sound as if you're skunked up on some wacko trip."

Jenny shot me a look. "Jason! Did you hear? Our girl is not only drinking, smoking, messing around with boys, but she's a ruddy druggie too!"

"Mum!"

"Jason, say something!"

I groaned before puffing out my cheeks.

"Oh, God, don't tell me you knew?" Jenny thrust her hands on her hips as she glowered at me.

"I might have … sort of known, if you like."

"I don't ruddy like."

"Jen, I didn't mean—"

"Oh, great! So, what else do you know that I, as her mother, seem to be out of the loop on? I suppose you know about all her little trips down Lovers' Lane, too?"

"No, Jen—"

"Just that she's a drug addict, then? Well, that's okay then, I suppose. No drama here … no need to worry. Beth's a drug addict, but that's okay!"

"Oh, come on!" Beth threw her hands in the air.

"Jen, we need to stay on track."

My wife huffed, realising I was right.

"Jen, d'you want to get a handful of those exercise books? They convinced Jess, so it might work on Beth, too?"

"Books?"

Ignoring Beth's question, Jenny scooted out of the kitchen. "I'll go and get them, shall I? You two can whisper more secrets to each other whilst I'm out of the room," she hollered over her shoulder before thrusting open my office door. By the sounds of the force employed, it would be the second door I needed to assess the state of the hinges.

"Dad, what books?"

"Beth, we had an agreement. For tonight, you adopt an open mind, yes?"

Beth blew a raspberry and rolled her eyes. "Yeah, I know, but really? You want me to believe you're Marty McFly?"

I placatingly raised my palms. "I know. So, just for me, pin your ears back and let me run through some stuff. Then your mother and I will show you these books." I nodded to the dog-eared heap of yellow exercise books that Jenny somewhat unceremoniously lobbed onto the breakfast bar before aggressively folding her arms.

"Jen, please."

My wife snorted through her nostrils. "Alright. I got this year's and a few for the next century." She nodded at the books splayed out in front of us.

"Good."

Beth reached for the books.

"Hang on." I batted away her hand. "Hear me out first. So, in 2019, during my first life, you and I were best mates …"

126

A further round of wine top-ups from Jenny, and a little short of thirty minutes later, I'd completed my précis of lives one and two thus far. My synopsis contained all the main points and was delivered in my well-practised schoolteacher style. However, I guess I lost Beth during the first sentence when I'd claimed we used to be the same age and best mates in some alternate universe that I presumed no longer existed. Fortunately, despite Beth's repeated attempts to break our agreement, when storming off, only to return when I reminded her of our concordat, I made it to the end of my spiel.

Fair enough, this was always going to be a tough sell.

Hey, but history shows it is possible to convince people of the impossible. There's Churchill's *Finest Hour* speech, where he mobilised the English language and convinced the country there was still hope after the fall of France. There was Martin Luther King Jr.'s speech, *I Have a Dream*, which influenced the US Federal Government to take direct action to realise racial equality. And, of course, there was Buzz Lightyear's impassioned and inspirational talk to the other toys when they were less than convinced about their ability to rescue Woody from Al's Toy Barn. Okay, maybe the last example didn't quite hold the same gravitas. Nevertheless, all are high in the tough sell category of inspirational speeches. I just had to push on and continue to employ my best Lightyear-esque techniques to convince my daughter of my true identity.

So far I thought Buzz would be proud of my efforts. I imagined in my mind's eye the Space Ranger and me offering each other a fist bump.

"Is that it? You done?"

I nodded, trying to read my daughter's thoughts.

"Jesus, Dad. What the frig's the matter with you? Fuck me, I've heard some bollocks, but you've bloody lost it!" Beth shot

127

Jenny a look before stabbing a finger at me. "Christ, Dad, you sound like that frigging nutter on Wogan. David Icke, sitting there in his blue shell suit, claiming to be the son of God. They reckon he's a nutter, but you sound ten times worse!"

Fair enough.

Hmmm, maybe my Churchillian persona needed some work.

However, with the benefit of knowing the future, I knew some of what David Icke claimed about the controlling media held a certain 'truth' when you consider the term 'fake news'. Now, hang on there, I'm not saying I'm a conspiracy theorist, as Mr Icke also always stated he wasn't. But here's the thing. Time, and the passage of time, can change perceptions. What we know now, as in 1994, could and most probably would appear very different in the future.

If nothing else, time was a great teacher.

Anyway, one thing I don't think Mr Icke claimed was that he'd time-travelled. So, my claims were on a whole new level to what he'd spouted on the Wogan show a couple of years back. My daughter, without the knowledge of what time can provide, was well within her right mind to believe her father was a complete nut job.

Jenny shoved the exercise books across the breakfast bar. "Beth, sweety. Look at these. Your dad and I have recorded everything he can remember that's happened from 1977 through to 2019. Everything your father said would happen has." Jenny grabbed this year's book and thumbed through the pages before slapping the book in front of Beth, tapping her finger on the page. "Look, we've written—"

"No!" Beth hopped off her stool and stumbled backwards.

"Oh, Beth," I whined, leaping forward.

"Stay back, both of you." She made a sign of the cross with her fingers as she backed away.

If the situation wasn't so serious, I might have laughed. However, it seemed our daughter had decided we were the disciples of the antichrist, or at the very least, vampires. As the three of us held our ground, and for the second time tonight, the back door flew open.

"What the?" Jenny and I exclaimed in unison.

11

The Desert Fox

Akin to many a comic farce on stage and screen, as my sixtieth birthday drew to a close, our kitchen seemed to fill up with new characters to take this evening's events from the sublime to the ridiculous. All that was missing from our *Carry On* type caper was a live audience to applaud the new arrival.

Beth maintained her position, only swivelling her eyes to see who'd joined the party.

The new arrival knitted his brows as he assessed Beth's rather odd stance. "Oh, bit late for playing charades, ain't it?" He wagged a finger at Beth. "Don't tell me, Dracula. Did I guess right, lass?"

"George, it's nearly midnight!" Jenny fired back.

"Ah, well, yes, lass, I tried to phone but couldn't get through."

I glanced at Beth, who held her stance but edged towards the kitchen doorway. "Well, you see, it's been what you might call a somewhat difficult evening."

"George, what's the matter?"

"Well, lass, something's happened." He nodded to Beth, indicating this wasn't for her ears. Which, in some way, was a relief knowing nothing had happened to Ivy. George's late-night urgent flit across town presumably concerned the members of the TTBC. Although, after the events thus far, that wasn't a good omen either.

"What?" Jenny fired back.

George nodded to Beth. "Lass, are you alright?"

My daughter, still with her fingers forming that cross, didn't respond.

George raised an eyebrow at her non-response before answering my wife's question, although directing the answer at me. "Ehm … lad, this is—"

"TTBC business?" I interrupted.

"Correct, lad. What about the lass, here?" George questioned, surreptitiously nodding towards Beth.

"I'm afraid it's too late. The cat is out of the bag, so to speak. Beth has found out."

"Ooh heck. I take it by the look on the lass's face, she didn't take it well. Either that or you accidentally threw in that you're a vampire, too?" he chuckled, which quickly dissipated when clocking the atmosphere appeared to lack humour.

"Uncle George, you believe all this crap, too?" Beth fired back.

"Why don't you uncross your fingers and take a load off? Come on, park your bottom on a stool, and we'll have a little chat," George responded before turning to Jenny. "Is the kettle on, lass? I'm parched. I had to drop Ivy over at her sister's in Aylesbury because she had another one of her turns. My good lady thought she'd stay over for a couple of days. I ain't had a cuppa since I left here this afternoon."

George eased himself onto the bar stool whilst Jenny made tea as instructed. Although now in his eighties, my good friend and previous grandfather maintained a spritely spring to his step. Something I recall had long since departed when in my first life. George had always insisted he must never know when his time was up. After what had transpired this evening and that feeling of being on death row, I could understand his logic. If history repeated itself, I would lose George from my life within three years.

"Amy Elisabeth, come on, I want to talk to you." George patted the stool beside him whilst extracting his wallet from his jacket pocket.

My daughter, accepting her parents weren't suffering from vampiric tendencies, dropped her stance, huffed and obeyed. George, in both of my lives, afforded an air of calm rationale about him. Simple honesty, if you like, affording him the capability to defuse even the trickiest of situations. After the Camilla Gate scandal of last year, something that completely passed me by the first time around, and the worsening relationship of the Wales's marriage, the Crown could do worse than asking George to mediate. He was that good.

"So, you believe this shi … rubbish … Mum and Dad are spouting?" Despite my licence offered earlier, which gave Beth free rein to utter any obscenity she felt befitted the situation, at least she had the presence of mind to temper her vocabulary in front of George.

"I believe … and know for a fact." George opened his wallet and thumbed out a wad of paper slips bound by an elastic band. "I've kept these as a memento." He waved the wad at Beth, who now appeared calm. She patiently waited as George laid out the betting slips in front of her as if they were playing cards and he was setting up a game of patience. George glanced up at me. "Lad, I'll have that betting book of yours if you please."

"Formula One, or just general betting?"

"General betting, please, lad." He replied without looking up as he focused on handing each slip to Beth and, in turn, pointing to where he required her to place it further along the breakfast bar. In that instant, the dynamics shifted from Beth's centre-stage teenage rants to her and George appearing to calmly play a game. With Beth wrapped in her dressing gown, if she wasn't a seventeen-year-old woman, the scene could easily be a grandfather entertaining his granddaughter before bedtime. All that was missing was a glass of milk and perhaps a cookie for my daughter before her grandfather tucked her in and read the little girl a bedtime story.

When I returned from my office with said exercise book, they'd laid out a line of slips. George grabbed the book and thumbed through the pages before offering it to Beth. My now obedient daughter held the book open, awaiting instructions.

"Right lass. I need to talk to your parents. So, while I do that, you sit there and compare these winning slips to that book. You can see the bookies have stamped 'paid' on the slips, confirming they were winners. Take each one, the date the bet was placed, and compare it to your father's predictions. Now, I know you're not a huge sports fan, but you like a bit of tennis, that much I do know. So, start with that one." George stabbed one of his sausage-sized fingers on a slip, which Beth reached for before reading aloud.

"Bet placed 24th May 1985. Boris Becker to win Wimbledon in 1985. Twenty pounds placed at four-hundred-to-one. Winnings … eight grand! Eight frigging grand!" Beth glanced up at George. "Is this a fake?"

"Lass, would I have a bookie's stamp to mark on each slip? And would I have a stash of fake slips in my wallet?"

"Well, no, I s'pose not."

"Becker won the juniors tournament in Birmingham that year. That's when your dad suggested we place the bet. If we'd have placed the bet years before, we could have scooped a fair bit more than eight thousand."

"Why didn't you?"

"Beth."

My daughter shot me a look as I interrupted. The curl of her lip suggested I wasn't to be afforded the same courtesies she'd offered George.

I bashed on. "I have to be careful. We can't very well go waltzing into the bookies and place bets on something that will take place years in the future. That would not only draw attention to ourselves, but the bookies probably wouldn't take the bet. Timing is key. With Becker winning the juniors championship a month or so before Wimbledon, that meant we were offered good odds. And, because of the timing, the bet didn't seem too outlandish."

"I bought that nice new Vauxhall Vectra with the winnings. I told Ivy I'd come up on the premium bonds. Actually, my good lady thinks we've had a run of good luck with good old ERNIE. She's been telling all her friends at bingo to invest in National Savings," he chuckled.

"There's your tea, George. Now, what's happened?"

"Thanks, lass." George grabbed the mug and took a noisy slurp before patting Beth's hand to break her trance. "Now, you go through those slips and compare to that book, as I told you. I think you'll find it might help you understand that either your father is an astrologer like those fortune tellers or he has come from the future. Which, young lady, he most certainly has."

Beth gawped back at George.

"Go on then," he encouraged, before taking a gulp of tea and smacking his lips. "Smashing brew, lass."

Beth shook her head, releasing the trance before plucking up the next betting slip. It was a good one – a bet placed in 1979 for Trevor Brooking to score in the 1980 Cup Final. Of course, he was Sir Trevor Brooking, but I wasn't sure when the Queen performed the accolade ceremony and dubbed the sword upon his shoulders. So, for now, mine and George's football hero was just plain old Trevor.

"George!" Jenny exasperatedly raised her hands.

"Right. So, as I was saying, I dropped Ivy over at her sister's. Eva only keeps a small single in the spare room, and the days of squeezing into one of those with my good lady are long gone. So, I said I'd head home and pick her up in a day or two. Anyway, I need to get up the allotment early tomorrow. I need to catch that damn rabbit. The little blighter's making a mess of me broad beans."

"Christ," I muttered.

Not hearing my frustrations, George took a sip of tea and continued. "Little bugger. Nearly had the furry feller last week. I said to Ivy, he'll make a nice stew when I get me hands on him."

George took another gulp of tea. As he held his mug to his lips, he crinkled his eyes when spotting our gritted teeth expressions. "Ah, I'm off track."

I nodded.

Jenny bit her lip.

"So, there I was, trundling down the High Street, when I pulled up at the lights. You know that new set the idiots at the council have stuck halfway down where the Green Shield Stamp shop used to be. Think it's one of those video rental shops now. What'd they call it, Ballbusters?"

"I think you mean Blockbusters." I shot Beth a look, expecting a quipped comment in response to George's faux pas. However, she appeared engrossed in her allotted exercise, holding a slip in one hand whilst raking through the pages of my betting book.

"That's it, lad. Ballbusters," he chuckled. "That was my old sergeant major. Bert–ballbuster–Bullard. Nasty bloke, I can tell you. Classic case of what they now call short-man syndrome. When we were stationed in Tripoli in '42, giving that scoundrel Rommel a good bashing, old Bert-Ballbuster-Bullard—"

"George," barked Jenny.

"Ah, sorry, lass. So, there I was, waiting for the lights to change. You'll never guess what car were parked on the hill not twenty feet away."

"Amazeballs! You won a grand on *Lunchbox* Christie at the 1992 Olympics."

"Beth! Please, that's so rude."

"Oh, give over, Mum. The man's got the biggest one I've ever seen."

Jenny's jaw sagged.

"What's that, lass?"

"George, please don't ask," I interrupted, noticing my daughter grabbing another slip whilst struggling to contain her laughter. At least she wasn't scowling and making a cross symbol to ward off vampires. "So, what car did you see in the High Street?"

"Your Cortina, lad. There it was, plain as day. Now, I thought it unlikely you would have driven it. You know, knowing what happens in that thing. Anyway, I pulled in just a few yards ahead. I was about to hop out and investigate when the strangest of things happened …" he paused. Whether to add drama or waiting for us to ask, I couldn't tell. Anyway, it appeared my wife's patience had run out.

"What? Come on, George, spit it out!"

"Alright, lass, I'm getting there."

Jenny huffed and nodded an apology.

I held my breath.

"Well, as I said, I was about to get out and have a shufty when I stopped myself because I spotted *you* running down the High Street."

"Me?"

"Yes, lad. Although … it wasn't you. I think it was *him*."

12

What's Up, Doc

Notwithstanding Beth's claims that she'd accepted a lift home from a man who looked like me from twenty years ago, after she'd presumably been doing something lewd with that Craig's lunchbox in the secluded area of Lovers' Lane, my subconscious had tried to rebuff the idea that *other* Jason had actually arrived in 1994.

Of course, that letter, shakily penned by the eighty-one-year-old version of me, had made it back from 2015 via that man's jacket pocket. I guess I'd tried to conjure up an alternative reason to how that happened, rather than accept that *other* Jason and my older self had presumably met up for a coffee and chinwag in the future. That future would have to be post 2015 because my older self had stated in that letter that *other* Jason still hadn't materialised at that point.

However, George had spotted me, albeit a younger version, only half an hour before when clambering into the driver's seat of my time-travelling Cortina. Which, I should point out, should be secured in my lock-up on the Bowthorpe Estate.

Now, before my mind, and yours, for that matter, spontaneously implodes when ruminating about the various time-travel conundrums that potentially were in play, there's the consideration regarding that yellow car. Was *my* Cortina, the one I landed in back in 1976, previously owned by *other* Jason, still secured in my lock-up? Or did it have a clone now driving around town with *him* at the wheel? Or was it the same car, taken from the future, pinged back to now, and therefore wasn't in my lock-up?

None of this sounded good.

Also, my brain hurt.

And, not forgetting the bleeding great elephant in the room. Namely, that letter which remained on the breakfast bar.

We'd spent our late evening guzzling a particularly fruity Californian Sauvignon Blanc whilst trying to convince Beth that I'm a time-traveller. Then, followed that up with listening to George's tales of his war efforts when he dished out a good-old Tommy-styled bashing to the Desert Fox, along with his battle of wits with a broad-bean-ravaging Bugs Bunny.

So, that 'elephant in the room' remained undiscussed.

Beth waved what appeared to be a betting slip that George had scooped a hearty win when wagering Martina Navratilova would win Wimbledon in 1978. I can't remember the odds they offered him a year before the tournament. However, I recall it was the last time he placed a bet on the Praguer due to her becoming the bookies' favourite for many a year to come. My daughter used the betting slip as a pointer as she alternated the direction of her thrusting arm when deciding who to address. She settled on me.

"Dad, I should have mentioned earlier. That bloke who gave me a lift was driving a car like yours. Y'know, that old thing you keep in your lock-up."

"What's that you say, lass?" George asked my daughter as he waved his empty mug in Jenny's general direction.

139

Jenny huffed and grabbed the mug from his hand. "I take it I'm tea lady tonight, then?"

"Best tea lady north of the river, lass. That you are."

"Which river?" Jenny asked, whilst flicking the kettle on.

"Any river," George threw back, keeping his focus on Beth. "What was that about a man driving your father's car?"

"I was in Lo—"

"Beth," I interrupted. "George only needs to know the tail end of that story."

George was a man of the world, and I dare say in his day, he and a few ladies may have dabbled on the wrong side of the blanket in between giving Rommel what for in the desert. However, I didn't think he needed to hear about our daughter's exploits down Lovers' Lane.

Beth offered me a smirk, poking the tip of her tongue out and allowing it to rest on her upper lip. Throughout the years, our relationship has always been a difficult one for me to balance. She was my adopted daughter. However, she used to be my best mate. The wicked facial expression now offered would have made me laugh in my previous life. However, when donning my 'Dad hat', I struggled with her expression, which suggested my seventeen-year-old little girl had performed lewd acts with this Craig chap in Lovers' Lane.

Before I could decide on an appropriate response, Beth dropped the lascivious smirk and addressed George. "I went out with a … few friends—"

"Drinking and smoking!" Jenny barked, placing George's steaming mug of tea beside him.

"Yes, Mum, drinking and smoking. Doing what every teenage girl does. Having a good time. It's the '90s, for God

140

sake. It's not my fault you were brought up in the bloody dark ages."

"Lass, mind your P's and Q's. No need for obscenities if you don't mind."

"You should have heard her earlier." Only Jenny heard my mumble because Beth continued.

"Sorry, Uncle George. So, as I said. I was out with friends and then got separated on our way home and fell into a puddle."

"Fell in a puddle?" George raised an eyebrow as he held his mug to his lips.

"Err … yeah, sort of. Anyway, this bloke offered me a lift home."

"A stranger, lass?"

"Yeah—"

"Listen to me." George placed his mug down and grabbed Beth's hand. "Now, lass, I'm not your father, and I have no place in saying this. However, you listen to me. The world is full of men who have mucky thoughts."

"Mucky thoughts?"

"Yes, lass. The sort who buy those top-shelf debauched magazines and then get fanciful ideas about women."

"Wait 'til you see Pornhub," I muttered. Fortunately, again, only Jenny heard my mumblings. I thought I should intervene because, as per usual, George appeared to be sending the conversation off-piste. However, like any parent-teenager relationship that involves rebellion, I decided to let the conversation flow because Beth might take some of George's sound advice, which may keep her safe in the future.

"I don't know what you mean, Uncle George." Beth adopted a deadpan, butter-wouldn't-melt expression. Innocence personified, you could say. If only George knew.

"Oh … what I'm trying to say. Hmmm … tricky subject this," he mumbled.

"Uncle George?" Beth's reapplied suggestive smirk confirmed my daughter revelled in hearing George's woeful attempt to explain a tricky subject. George was oblivious.

"Yes, I'm sure you don't, a nice young lass like you. What I'm trying to say … I don't think you should get into strange men's cars. You don't know what they might be thinking. Some men have …" he paused, presumably trying to conjure up the appropriate phrase.

"Unhealthy desires," I chimed in.

George clicked his fingers. "That's it, lad. Your father's got it, unhealthy desires."

"Oh, Dad, have you got unhealthy desires?" Beth quipped, offering me a wink.

I rolled my eyes.

"Oh, no, lass. I mean, your father has said what I was trying to say. Some men have the wrong thoughts."

Beth nodded at George. "I know. I was just screwing with you."

George's wide-eyed expression suggested he was horrified.

"She means yanking your chain."

Jenny tutted, dismissively shaking her head whilst folding her arms.

"Oh, right, lad." George, presumably satisfied that Beth hadn't uttered something rude, plucked up his tea, thus allowing Beth to finish the story.

"So, this man who gave me a lift home." Beth leaned in and dropped her voice a couple of octaves. "The man who didn't show me his lunchbox or any unhealthy desires," she smirked, leaned back, and continued. "He was the spitting image of Dad from years ago. He reckoned he knew Jess. Well, he *used* to know her and was driving a yellow Cortina just like that crap heap Dad keeps in his lock-up."

George shot Jenny and me a look, only dropping his eyes when my wife handed him the letter to read. Whilst leaving George to peruse my future written word, I locked eyes with Beth.

"What d'you think?" I asked, nodding to the heap of betting slips and my betting prediction book.

My question wiped away all of Beth's teenage antics. What was rolling around her head, I couldn't predict. My daughter hesitated, keeping me guessing for what seemed like a lifetime. Whilst awaiting her response, I glanced up at the kitchen clock. Half past midnight. My birthday was officially over, and I'd entered my sixty-first year. I feared what it might offer. I halted an involuntary yawn, pleased we were in the middle of the Easter holidays and didn't need to get up for school in the morning.

"Last year, Melanie confided in me—"

"That trollop."

Beth ignored her mother's interruption and continued. "She said her parents told her that a few years ago, her father had an affair, and she has a little step-sister—"

"Like father, like daughter. No wonder the girl puts it about. It's in her genes."

"Mum."

143

"Carry on." Jenny released her defensive arm fold and flicked the air with her right hand whilst chewing a metaphorical wasps' nest.

"Mel said it blew her life apart. Everything she thought she knew about her parents, well, her dad, had been obliterated. I think that's why she is like she is. You're right, Mum. Mel shag …" Beth paused and glanced at George, then changed the word she planned to utter. "Mel goes with lots of boys."

Jenny tutted.

"You're not telling me something like that, but you actually want me to believe you're a frig … a time-traveller?"

"What about that lot?" I waved my hand over the myriad of betting slips strewn across the breakfast bar.

Beth shrugged. "I dunno." My daughter swivelled her eyes back and forth from Jenny and me as she tried to make sense of what we were claiming.

I guess her expression could be that of earnest personification. Fair enough, we were at the tipping point, the precipice, if you like, in our parent-daughter relationship. Would she leap with us? Or perhaps reject our claims and slide off the rails, similar to her friend Mel? I feared we may have pushed our daughter away, and thus she'll end up joining Mel on her shagathon through the male population of Fairfield College.

Jenny grabbed the 1994 book and raked through the pages. With the page open at March, she waved the book in my face.

"Brilliant," I muttered.

This particular entry, which Jenny had penned many years ago, was dated the 31st of March. As we'd now passed midnight, that was today. Although not an international event from history, and certainly not something to place a bet on at the bookies, it would surely help Beth believe and thus become the sixth fully paid-up member of the TTBC.

The day after my seventeenth birthday, like many days at that age, my mind had been a bit on the foggy side due to consuming copious amounts of alcohol the previous evening in the pub when celebrating with a bunch of mates. However, when Jenny and I started recording future events in our 'yearbooks', this event was easy to remember because it happened the day after my birthday.

Jenny shimmied onto the stool and laid the open page in front of Beth. "Sweetheart. I wrote this down about six or seven years ago. This will happen tomorrow, and that will help you understand your father is who he says he is."

Beth furrowed her brow and read the paragraph.

"Oh, ye Gods and little cod fishes. Is this what I think it is?"

Leaving my daughter and Jenny to pore over Jenny's written word. I glanced at a perplexed-looking George.

"A letter I wrote in 2015."

"How the blazes?"

Keeping to the facts, without any waffle, I brought George up to speed regarding how a letter I penned in 2015 ended up on our breakfast bar in 1994. I say facts, but *other* Jason providing the time-travel transportation for the letter could be the only logical conclusion. That said, as I relayed the events of the evening thus far, I suspected logic had flown the cage.

"Lad, what's this bit about your daughter's life depends on it?" George glanced at Beth.

"I think I, well, older me, was referring to Jess."

"Something's going to happen to her?" It wasn't a question but more of a verbalising of what was running through his mind.

"I'm going to bed," Beth announced as she hopped up from her stool. "Jesus, you're all frigging nutters!" she threw over her shoulder as she stomped out of the kitchen, slamming the door behind her.

"Christ, what happened?" I fired at Jenny.

"Any more tea in the pot, lass?"

Part 2

13

Summer 2015

A New Hope

Some would describe it as a thankless task. Well, that's how most would see Simon's employment. But, hey, that was society's view in the twenty-first century. Simon was only one man, and he alone couldn't change the world. However, offering pastoral and religious guidance could not be considered pointless, and Simon knew he could, in some small way, impact the lives of a few who'd taken the wrong path.

After finishing his degree, Simon harboured many thoughts and ideas about his life path. Not for one crazy moment did he imagine fulfilling this role. However, after volunteering last summer, the opportunity arose. And despite being advised that he would be a shoo-in, so strongly encouraged to apply, he harboured serious reservations. Externally, Simon made all the right noises but internally dismissed the offer. Nevertheless, after a few weeks, God changed his heart and mind, and the opportunity became his life calling.

Chaplaincy offered the chance to discuss many issues with those seeking spiritual guidance and opportunities to help those with troubled minds find the right path through their damaged emotional maze.

Of course, forgiveness is a core part of chaplaincy. Simon found the Holy Spirit very faithful in allowing forgiveness for all, including the wretched men he attempted to guide on a daily basis. Although he offered his services freely and would regularly approach those in need, Simon was forever mindful that he only touched a small percentage. By the very nature of the men with whom he interacted, most rebuffed his offer of help and support. Which was disappointing, although to be expected.

Today, he'd received a request from a prisoner in A Wing. This area of Havervalley Prison being the only area where the officers restricted Simon from mingling freely with the inmates. Those incarcerated in A Wing were an eclectic mixture of 'lifers' and those whom the authorities deemed as volatile. So, not a safe environment for a prison chaplain. Even the well-seasoned prison officers entered this area wearing stab vests and a grimace.

John Curtis, a fifty-one-year-old lifer, had never previously requested time with Simon. Although John kept himself to himself, so not classed as volatile, the prison officers were dubious about the prisoner's unusual request. So much so that the meeting was to be held in the prison chapel with two guards present. Simon wasn't concerned. He knew God had great plans for him and would never place him in a situation where he could be in danger.

With a copy of the Bible and a pamphlet about forgiveness clasped in his hand, the twenty-seven-year-old chaplain followed two officers through to the chapel where they'd earlier shepherded and deposited under guard, John Curtis.

Much to the chaplain's escorts' dismay, Simon requested that John not be handcuffed in a house of God.

Spike Townsend, one of the senior officers, held the chapel door open for Simon before laying a hand on the chaplain's forearm.

"There're two officers in here with him."

Simon offered an understanding nod.

"You don't have to see him, you know."

"I do. It's my duty."

"Your funeral, vicar."

Simon chose not to correct Spike on the inaccurate title. "God will listen to any man who wishes to speak with him. I must offer John that chance to have his say."

"Well, if you've got a direct line to him up there …" Spike paused and nodded to the ceiling. "Then, if I were you, I'd give him the heads up that there's some evil shits who can't be helped. John Curtis is a murdering scumbag who deserves to die. Bastards like him are going to hell, irrespective of what bull he comes out with."

Simon offered his well-practised, non-judgemental smile. God would be the judge of John's character. If the prisoner now sought forgiveness for his crimes, then, as far as Simon was concerned, no prison officer was in a position to second guess the Lord's decision.

The prison chaplain had diligently completed his homework. On Christmas Eve last year, after a series of tests during a secure trip to Fairfield General, an eminent, brave oncologist diagnosed and informed John Curtis about the aggressive lung cancer that had also spread to his pancreas and liver. A present from Santa, Spike had announced when hearing the news. Simon knew the officers cruelly sang the Mariah Carey song in John's earshot, only replacing the 'you' with 'cancer'.

At the time, Simon requested to speak with John when hearing the prisoner had refused treatment. Despite the prognosis suggesting John would not see next Christmas, Simon wished to understand the man's decision and perhaps offer spiritual guidance. However, eight months ago, John refused the meeting request, which, of course, was his right to do so.

At the turn of the millennium, John Curtis had been transferred from a Spanish prison at the behest of the Spanish authorities. Presumably, the request was due to John being a British National, and they probably thought British taxpayers should pay for his keep rather than the hard-working Spaniards. Also, John's crimes were Brit on Brit. So, Spain had no desire to continue incarcerating a British man who'd raped and murdered three British holidaymakers over a two-year period sometime back in the late nineties.

Disappointingly, John Curtis had always protested his innocence despite the DNA evidence and the fact that the boyfriend of his last victim caught him in the act. Perhaps today could be the start of John's road to redemption when he would confide in the chaplain and confess his sins. Well, that's what Simon prayed.

John Curtis perched on a chair in the front row. His legs outstretched and crossed at the ankles, with his arms splayed wide whilst gripping the backs of the adjoining chairs. He offered Simon a tombstone-toothed grin as the chaplain nervously settled sideways on a chair two seats away.

"Hello, John. We haven't met before. I'm—"

"Where do we go when we die?" John barked his interruption. So much so, Simon flinched. The snorted laugh from the prisoner suggested amusement at seeing the man quiver. "Bit jumpy, ain't you?"

"Err … sorry, I was just introducing myself. Perhaps you'd like me to talk through the services I offer and how I might help you."

"Yeah, whatever. Look, you're one of those Bible-bashing gits, right?" John nodded to the Bible positioned on Simon's lap, covered by his palms.

"I'm the prison chaplain."

"Yeah, so you know the answer, then?"

"As in, where do our souls go when our bodies leave this world? That's what you are asking?"

"Yeah." John sniffed before using the sleeve of his regulation grey prison sweatshirt to wipe the end of his nose.

"John, if you're seeking forgiveness, then now is the time to admit before God your crimes."

John snorted a response, breaking eye contact to look at the impassive officer not five feet away. "You wanna step away, mate? This is private."

Simon nodded to the officer, who'd raised a questioning eyebrow at him.

"Yeah, go on, give us some space," John sneered as the officer shuffled back a pace.

"John, do you repent? Do you accept what you have done and seek forgiveness before God?"

John shifted his legs back and swivelled in his chair to whisper. "Say I do. What will happen to me when I die?"

"Spiritually?"

"Yeah," he nodded. "I s'pose they'll just burn my body."

"And you repent and are penitent before God?"

"Yeah, go on then."

Simon sighed. It wasn't quite what he wanted to hear, but accepted it was a start. "John, as a Christian, I believe death is not the end of our existence. There will be a day of judgement when we face God, where we will explain our life's choices. If you repent now and beg for forgiveness, God will hear you. It's not too late."

"What about … coming back? What is it, reincarnation?"

"No, John. There are other faiths that believe in reincarnation, but that is not the Christian belief."

"What faiths?"

"Many. Buddhism, for one."

"What if I ask Buddhism for forgiveness? Will they reincarnate me?"

"John … why are you asking about this? Do you want to repent?"

"Look, vicar, do Buddhists come back after they die? Sort of start again, like time-travel?"

Despite the chaplain's relative lack of experience, the prisoner's questions suggested he wasn't ready to repent. It appeared, due to now facing imminent death, the deluded prisoner clutched at straws in a pointless attempt to avoid the inevitable. Notwithstanding the futility of continuing the meeting, Simon wanted to take this opportunity to help John understand.

"John, no faith, or belief, believe in time-travel. Christianity is based on the belief of the teachings of Jesus Christ, the son of God, who created Heaven, Earth and the Universe. Time-travel does not exist apart from in the minds of novelists and filmmakers. It's fantasy, not a religion or faith."

"Jediism? You know, Jedi Knights."

Being a lifelong Star Wars super fan, with an extensive collection of Lego presented in glass cases in his two-bed maisonette, Simon knew what John was referring to. His latest project, the Death Star, an unopened product he paid a little over five hundred pounds for from eBay, he'd started to build a couple of weeks ago. Much to his partner's dismay, their dining table doubled up as his command centre to erect his creation. However, despite many believers and followers, Simon was more than a little taken aback by the prisoner's suggestion that Jediism could be classed as a religion.

When clocking Simon's focus had shifted, John edged closer. "Well, vicar, what about Jediism, then? Those Jedi Knights believe in its mystical powers, don't they? Perhaps a belief in this Jediism might include time-travel?"

"John, the belief in Jediism is loosely based around Buddhism and Daoism. However, it's a storyline created by George Lucas for the films. It's not real. And, anyway, the beliefs of Jediism are about truth, knowledge and justice, not travelling through time."

"Yeah, whatever, but those Jedis used the power of the Force."

"No, John," Simon dismissively shook his head, disappointed that John's request to see him was born out of the prisoner's fantasies rather than a desire to atone.

John sniffed again and retook his relaxed position of legs out and arms splayed wide across the back of the chairs. "Alright. I'll repent. I'll admit to my crimes and tell God what I've done."

"John, do you take Jesus Christ into your heart?"

"Yeah."

"John, let us pray together. Repeat after me."

Simon recited the Lord's Prayer, encouraging every few words for John to repeat after him. Although John stumbled on a few, he managed to make it through to the end.

"What happens now? Will I see God when I die?"

"I want you to take these. The Bible and this pamphlet. These will help you understand forgiveness. Start reading them tonight, and we shall meet again next week. I will help you understand how to embrace the faith and allow Jesus into your heart." Simon placed both the Bible and leaflet on the chair between them.

With a jittering head, John pursed his lips and glanced up from where he'd been glaring at the carpet-tiled floor.

"Can you do me a favour?"

Simon raised an eyebrow.

"Look, I'll have a butchers at these ... open my heart and all that—"

"And admit your guilt, John. The families of your victims deserve to know that you admit to the crimes to which you are guilty of committing."

"Yeah, and that," John dismissively waved his hand.

Simon took that gesture to indicate that John lacked sincerity about his desire to repent. Despite that, the prisoner had asked for help, and it was his duty before God to assist wherever he could.

"Alright, John. How can I help?"

"I'm going to die soon. I don't have any family, no kids and that." John shifted back in his seat and turned to face Simon. "I want to have a visitor. You know, like all the other inmates do."

Simon nodded. "We have many volunteers who can come and sit with you during visiting times. They can chat with you and, although you don't have long left, you'll get to know them. Is that something you'd like me to set up?"

"I want to see one man. Can you get him here to visit me?"

"If this person hasn't visited you before, why would they now?"

"Reasons. Can you ask him?"

"Yes, probably. However, if this man refuses, that will be the end of it."

John nodded.

Simon extracted a notebook from his jacket pocket, clicking on the Parker pen. "Who is he?"

"Name's Jason Apsley. He used to be a schoolteacher at the Eaton School in Fairfield. He's retired now, but if you mention that I know where Paul Colney is, I reckon the man will want to see me."

Simon narrowed his eyes at the prisoner, pen still poised on the paper. "John, I'm not here to pass messages out of the prison."

"Vicar. I'll repent. I'll admit my crimes before your God." He leaned forward, causing Simon to jolt his head back and both guards to step forward. "A dying man's request is all I want in return. Before I die, I need to talk to Jason Apsley."

14

1994

Cool Britannia

Despite Jenny and I making regular forays up to Beth's bedroom, offering a tentative tap on her door to see if she was awake, midday had come and gone before our daughter surfaced.

After Beth stormed off in a huff, George left soon after, following another well-steeped cuppa. Jenny and I had lain awake most of the night trying to decipher the letter my older self had written twenty-one years in the future.

Eighty-one-year-old me had stated I should be able to read between the lines, which, to a point, I could, but just wished he, or is that me, had spelt it out in plain English.

Okay, so other Jason, if that's who he was, after giving Beth a lift home in his or my Cortina, another concern I would need to investigate, had offered Jess a prenotion of some impending doom before scuttling off to God knows where. So, it is reasonable to assume that the daughter referred to in the letter was Jess and not Beth.

Jess endured some tough times in her younger years and could be described as benefiting from a stoic persona. However, despite Jess's ability to cope with tricky situations, the letter suggested an imminent threat to her life.

My older self stated a repeat of the news item reported on the 12th of August 2019. That would suggest murder, specifically a serial killer. Although now nearly twenty years and another life since hearing that news item, I could easily recall that radio report regarding a fifty-nine-year-old David Colney wanted in connection to a string of murders. However, that evil bastard who just happened to be Beth's father was dead because I watched him plummet from the roof of Belfast House in '76. So, unless he'd miraculously become part of the walking dead, David couldn't be embarking on a serial killing campaign as he'd enjoyed in my first life.

Andrew Colney, the youngest of the four Colney boys, convicted of rape in 1987, was still enjoying life at Her Majesty's pleasure. Patrick Colney died in 1987 when his dead twin brother pulverised his head and cremated his body with the aid of the contents of a jerry can full of Esso's finest four-star on a piece of waste ground that same year.

As for Paul Colney, one of three time-travellers, he disappeared on that boat across to the Continent the same year as those other events. Although dying in 1977 and reappearing in 1987 after time-travelling in my Cortina, Jenny and I could only assume that nefarious tosser was still at large … somewhere. Despite keeping my ear to the ground on all matters Colney, his current location remained unknown. That letter stated the return of a time-traveller. So, I presumed older me was referring to Paul Colney and not suggesting Martin had decided to go rogue.

Safe to say, that thought put a bit of a dampener on our moods as we attempted to sleep through the witching hours. Also, terrorising my mind as I lay awake staring up at an incywincy spider performing a pointless circling path across the ceiling whilst presumably trying to locate the water spout, April was now only one day away. Although older me hadn't been specific on the actual day in April when some heinous act would take Jess's life, that warning from *other Jason* had explicitly stated the 6th. In less than twenty-four hours, we would face six days of terror as we attempted to prevent the unknown horror facing Jess.

Although Beth had now surfaced, it's fair to say all was not cordial in the Apsley household. A knife wouldn't suffice. No, I doubted even a chainsaw could slice through the atmosphere in our kitchen as Jenny and I awkwardly hovered whilst watching our daughter noisily gobble down a bowl of Alpen.

The portable TV, the only sound to accompany our daughter's slurps, cut from the lunchtime news, presented by Julia Summerville – discussing the change to trading legislation that would allow high street stores and supermarkets to open on Sundays – to a Dixon's advert for a JVC Camcorder. A new lightweight electronic gismo now at only £1,299. As the following advert rolled, depicting a very youthful Fry and Laurie comically advising about a new twenty-four-hour telephone banking service, I mused that any potential purchaser of that eye-watering-expensive camcorder would require the operator to train to Olympic levels in weightlifting just to be able to heft it to shoulder height. Also, the change to Sunday trading legislation was a relief because I'd lost count of how many times I'd driven into my local Tesco's car park on a Sunday morning wondering why they were shut. After a couple of Aussies had stated they wouldn't give a Castlemaine

4X for anything else, the local news bulletin caught my attention.

"Jen, turn it up."

"Breaking news this lunchtime. We have received unconfirmed reports of a disturbance on the Broxworth Estate in Fairfield following complaints from local residents to the town council regarding a foul smell emanating through the air vents from one of the flats. Police forced entry, where they discovered a woman's body. A statement from Hertfordshire Police confirms they are currently dealing with an incident involving a number of residents …"

"That's it!" I blurted, pointing at Beth. "See, the riots that I said would happen. It's in the book Mum showed you last night."

Beth apathetically raised an eyebrow as she slouched over her bowl, spooning in the milky sludge.

"Darling?" quizzed Jenny, turning down the volume on the TV.

The newsreader had moved to a report regarding the Local MP, Miles Rusher. Our incumbent representative for Fairfield appeared to be commenting on the government's *Back to Basics* campaign. Although future revelations would expose Mr Major and his dallying with an egg-obsessed minister, little did the Prime Minister know how much political sleaze was to follow. When the autumnal nights closed in, as the year Fred and Rosemary West were caught drew to a close, there would be the 'Cash for Questions' debacle for the failing government to deal with.

Our MP, spouting off about public decency – appearing to be taking the moral high ground and distancing himself from the Tim Yeo 'Love Child' incident from a couple of months back – continued the mantra that traditional family values were important. A bit rich, considering I knew Miles would be splashed across the headlines in a couple of years following some sordid affair with a Russian spy. In his defence, I suppose Miles wasn't aware he would fall for the young, leggy Russian blonde at this point in his life. From what I'd seen of him over the years, he seemed a decent sort, but as I'd learned over the past eighteen years, I couldn't bend time at will. So, giving him a bell and warning the poor man about a honey trap in the future would have been fairly pointless and ultimately lead to questions about me and who I was.

Sorry, Miles, enjoy your future sordid nights of passion with *'Onatopp'* because – akin to this decade's society's unstoppable clamour for the internet, no-frills air travel, coffee shops, alcopops, and rom-coms featuring Hugh Grant – your downfall is coming. Unfortunately for Miles, as the decade of 'Cool Britannia' gathered momentum, when 'SAS', those two footballing heroes, demolished the Dutch team at Wembley at the Euro 96 tournament, he would fall into political obscurity and prison.

So, back to the news item regarding the Broxworth Estate. Those 'yearbooks', which Jenny and I regularly updated, contained sketchy outlines of future events I could remember from my first life. However, I often would need to hear a news story on the radio or TV to trigger the memory regarding the finer details.

Although the Broxworth riots of '94 were easily remembered due to starting the day after my seventeenth birthday, my memory of the entire story was somewhat patchy. Some years ago, when Jenny had written that entry about the riots, I had no idea about the background story or the trigger that caused so much damage, injury, and loss of life for one poor police officer.

That said, to be fair to my memory, riots were commonplace on that odious estate. So, I could be forgiven for muddling up some of the details. After the community centre was trashed and burnt in 1981, following the copycat actions from the Brixton riots, marauding residents from that estate, causing mayhem and destruction, was almost a yearly event. So, much so, I wouldn't be surprised if the local card shops started producing 'Happy Riotday' cards to sit alongside the 'get well soon' and 'congratulations' selections. If they did, they'd make a killing with the residents of the Broxworth.

"Darling?" Jenny repeated as I waited for Beth to comment, which didn't appear forthcoming.

"That's the trigger for what's happening right now."

"The riots?"

"Yeah. I remember now. The spark for this riot was that dead woman. Some police officer made a derogatory comment about the woman just being a resident of the Broxworth Estate, which caused it all to kick off. I remember my brother making some snide remark about scum from the estate and Ivy berating him for his wicked thoughts."

"Beth, you remember what we showed you last night?" Jenny joined our daughter at the breakfast bar, peering at her, awaiting her reply.

Whilst continuing to munch, Beth offered a side-eyed look of disdain and, if I'm not mistaken, a contemptuous lip curl.

"Beth!" I barked, my annoyance a mixture of frustration with her refusal to believe the unbelievable and her rude attitude towards Jenny.

"What?" she fired back, offering a mouthful of mulched Alpen whilst allowing her raised, dripping spoon to shoot milk splatters across the worktop.

163

Jenny shot me a look of concern as I leaned across the breakfast bar and wagged a finger at her. "Don't be rude."

Beth waved her spoon at me, pausing a moment to swallow. "For God's sake! You accuse me of being rude whilst you, Mum, and Uncle George claim you're Marty-bloody-McFly! Come on, this is ridiculous."

She made a good point.

"And does Jess actually believe all this shite too?"

I nodded.

"Why?" Beth turned to Jenny. "Why would you believe?"

"Your father has proven it to all three of us."

Beth tutted before jabbing her spoon back at me. "And you want me to believe that you and I were supposedly besties in your first life?"

"Yeah, we were. You and I were very close from our school days."

"Oh, God, no! You're not suggesting we … y'know?"

"What?" I knitted my brows, wondering where she was going with this.

"You reckon we were close … so we didn't—"

"What?"

"Shag!"

"Beth!" Jenny slapped her hand to her chest in horror, either at the thought or the coarse word.

"No! No, no, nothing like that."

"Oh … good. 'Cos that makes me feel sick."

I pursed my lips and nodded. She made another good point.

"And what's that about your brother?"

"Sorry?"

"You said something about your brother and Ivy telling him off."

"Ah …"

"You don't have a brother."

"Yeah … tricky one, this," I glanced at Jenny for support.

"You might as well go all in. There's no point in holding back now."

"Right," I muttered, wondering how to inform Beth of the rest of my back story without her either lobbing the bowl and spoon at me, stomping off and leaving home for good, or both.

"Well?"

"When I was in my first life … before I time-travelled," I paused as Beth performed an exaggerated eye roll. "George was my grandfather. Stephen was my brother. After my parents died in a train crash, Stephen and I were brought up by George and Ivy."

"Their daughter, who died in a train crash in the '70s. You reckon she was your mother."

"Yeah … Joan and Neil Apsley. Joan's maiden name being Sutton."

"Hang on, your parents died before I was born."

"Yes, mine and the parents of the man I replaced."

"When you time-travelled," Beth sarcastically whined.

"Yeah. The reason Stephen and I have the same surname isn't a coincidence … he's my older brother—"

"Twenty-three-year-old Stephen, who's at uni in Durham and just happens to be twenty-seven years younger than you,"

Beth interrupted and raised an eyebrow, presumably thinking she was tearing seismic holes in my story. However, time-travel was at play.

I nodded.

"So, who d'you reckon you replaced, then?"

"I replaced the man who gave you a lift home last night."

Beth's jaw, akin to a ventriloquist dummy with a snapped wire, instantly dropped.

Jenny grabbed the 1994 'yearbook' and thrust the page in front of Beth, stabbing her finger on the entry she'd read last night.

"Look at the TV."

Beth and I swivelled our heads to see the portrait photograph of a police officer. I ramped up the volume.

"Police have confirmed that PC Darren Tomsett has died at the scene of the riots on the Broxworth Estate in Fairfield ..."

"Look at the book you read last night. Read what I wrote seven years ago," barked Jenny.

Still sporting that gaping jaw, Beth swivelled her eyes downwards and read aloud. *"31st March – Riots in Fairfield. A police officer called Thompson/Timpson/Tomsett is stabbed to death. No one is convicted of his murder,"* Beth mumbled as she read the paragraph Jenny had written many years ago.

"Beth, honey." Jenny grabbed our daughter's hand, waiting for her to swivel her head to look at her. "Your father is a time-traveller ... he's come from the future."

15

Rising Damp

"Brian?"

"Yes, Jason?" Brian stood to attention and grinned.

Brian's drooping, twitching left eyelid, an odd affliction that had significantly worsened over the years, performed a weird spasm, transforming his facial expression from one similar to that lazy, cynical tabby, Garfield, to that of Leonard Rossiter's Rigsby when nervously trying to impress Miss Jones.

"How long have I been coming in here?"

"Oh … don't you know?"

"Yes," I chuckled. "But I'm asking you."

"Oh, let's see." The twitch intensified as he rubbed his chin and glanced at the ceiling for inspiration. After an inordinate pregnant pause, he wagged a finger at me. "Twenty years, give or take a couple of decades."

"Two decades is twenty years."

"So?"

I puffed out my cheeks, wondering why I'd started down this road. Conversations with Brian, certainly in the last few years, were a baffling experience that left you pondering your own sanity.

"Well, without the give-or-take bit, you're close. Eighteen, to be precise. Now, apart from the first drink I purchased here in 1976 being a Coke, I've always stuck to the same tipple. Lager, varying varieties, from Skol to Harp, Fosters, and now Carling, and soon to be Peroni, I suspect. But always lager."

"Peroni? What's that when it's at home?"

"You'll find out. Now, we agree that I always drink lager?"

"Correct. I like to pride myself on knowing my customers."

"What's that then?" I nodded to the multi-coloured drink in a cocktail glass sporting a plastic flamingo-shaped straw and a pink umbrella Brian had just placed before me. A drink more suited to be served up in a Caribbean beach bar, not your local boozer. The decorated beverage appeared as much out of place here as it did in Mr Trotter's grip in the Nag's Head.

"Oh, that's the drink the lass was waiting for in the public bar. I wondered why she was still standing there." Brian leaned forward as he plucked up the glass, performing a quick, furtive, sideways glance. Not dissimilar to how Mrs Trosh, our retired school secretary, would have performed back in the day, before continuing. "I went on a course to learn how to make these. Thought they'd bring in a younger crowd." He nodded at the drink. "This one's called a Tequila Sunset." He tapped the side of his nose and performed that sideways glance again to check he wasn't being overheard. "Don't tell anyone, but I don't have any Grenadine, so I popped in a dollop of honey instead. Inspired, eh?" Brian winked, plucked up the drink, and disappeared through to the public bar.

"Usual, Jason?"

"Please, Rachel," I nodded at the barmaid as she grabbed a pint glass, still trying to determine if Brian was joking.

"Barmaid, my pint, if you don't mind," called out an elderly chap who'd shuffled into the lounge bar and plonked himself down at a table near the door. Cecil, who'd been coming here for a significantly longer period of time than I, give or take four decades to use Brian's calculations, called out again in a more belligerent tone. "Barmaid, my pint, if you please."

Rachel glanced up as she completed pouring my pint. "I'll be with you in a moment, Cecil," she boomed before glancing at me. "I don't mind offering waitress service to the old boy, but I wish he wouldn't shout."

"He's as deaf as a post, so he thinks everyone else is, too."

"Yeah, but I'm not," she chuckled.

"George reckons Cecil's got one of those hearing aids but doesn't like to wear it because ..." I held my hands aloft and performed the bunny ears. "And I quote, 'The damn thing spoils my looks and might scupper my chances with a nice bit of skirt'."

"Oh, charming. Though I'm not surprised. Cecil's nothing but a dirty old man," she chortled. "You know Alison? That new barmaid who started a couple of weeks ago."

I nodded.

Alison used to be one of my pupils and left the sixth form last year. It was one of those odd scenarios I'd often encountered now that I was teaching the age group I was in my first life. Then, when at a similar age, I'd known Alison and recall an awkward liaison at a party at a mate's house. Let's just say, as an inexperienced seventeen-year-old, I unexpectedly surprised the girl with my tongue as we kissed. Although an absolute lifetime ago, I winced at the memory of her shoving

169

me away and uttering a 'yuk'. A cringeworthy moment, to say the least. Due to my time-travelling, at least the poor girl wouldn't have to suffer my first failed attempt at a French kiss.

"Well, I had to have a word with her last week about the length of her skirt … or lack of, you might say. Cecil, the old git, would pretend to drop his stick and stoop to get it when Alison took his pint over to him."

I pulled a face. "Oh, hell. Sick, perverted bastard."

"That's a bit strong. Dirty old man, I agree."

Her comment confirmed that what I considered outrageous behaviour could still be regarded as comical in this era.

"Unacceptable, if you ask me. Young or old, not really how a man should behave."

"I know! The git must be eighty if he's a day!"

"Upskirting." I offered a knowing nod.

"Oh, good word," she chortled. "Upskirting, I've not heard that one before."

Of course, quoting Cecil's derogatory, outdated statement and politically incorrect term for a young lady was just that – a quote. However, that offensive term should have been left somewhere back in the '70s on something like the *Benny Hill Show*.

As for his barmaid comment, as opposed to barperson or server, which would be the terms used in my day, well, we were still in an era when the aggressive political correctness police were still in the process of cutting their teeth. In my first life, referring to a female server as a barmaid or waitress could land you in all sorts of bother. There would be cries of 'misogynistic tosser' or 'hang him' on social media. We weren't there yet, but I was fully aware that time was coming.

"There you go. One-fifty, please." Rachel placed my pint down on the beer towel.

Whilst dropping the coins in her outstretched hand, I pondered, as I often would, the cost of a pint. Seven quid at a bar in Soho back in 2019. I glanced at Cecil, gurning at the bar waiting for his pint of mild. State pension was about fifty-odd quid, which in my day wouldn't be enough to purchase the old boy's weekly beer intake.

"He's getting worse, you know."

"Cecil?"

"No, Brian," Rachel nodded through to the public bar. "As for this cocktail idea, I can't understand what's got into him."

"Not exactly the type of pub, is it?" I replied before taking a sip.

"No. Silly old fool. Ever since he watched that film, he thinks he's Tom Cruise."

"Brian, like Tom Cruise?" I chuckled. "That sounds like a mission impossible."

Rachel knitted her brow and shook her head at me. "Sorry?" she asked, presumably struggling to understand what the TV series from the late '60s and early '70s had to do with Brian or Tom Cruise.

"Oh … difficult to see Brian as the Lt. Pete Maverick Mitchel type, is what I meant."

I wasn't up to date with film releases. Beth and Chris would sometimes mention the films they were going to see, and I thought Tom Cruise had started his Mission Impossible films but, by the look on Rachel's face, probably not.

"Christ, Brian, in a fighter jet," she scoffed. "I think that would be a bit too complicated for him." She leaned forward and whispered as she pulled Cecil's pint of mild. "He's bought himself one of those new Nokia mobile phones. But listen to this. He said he won't take it out of the pub in case he loses it. I mean, what's the point? I said to him the whole idea of a mobile phone is so you can use it when you're not at home. It's in the name, as in mobile."

"Barmaid!"

"Cecil, I'm coming. My name is Rachel, not bloody barmaid," she boomed at the curmudgeonly old boy as she flipped up the bar flap and thumped his pint down on the table.

I checked my watch, expecting the members of the TTBC to arrive soon. We had a new, somewhat reluctant member who'd flatly refused to attend her first meeting. After the events at lunchtime, Beth, Jenny, and I had spent the afternoon discussing my first life and all things time-travel. After a few hours, our daughter retreated to her room to listen to music on her Discman. Whether she'd fully come around to the idea of a time-travelling father or she was biding her time to do a runner, neither Jenny nor I could ascertain. We'd asked her not to talk to Chris because convincing one child was about as much as we could take for the moment. However, Beth was like my old time-travelling pal, Martin, as in a bit of a loose cannon.

When Jenny nipped out to visit her parents, I'd suggested to Beth she should join us at our emergency meeting of the TTBC. A suggestion that received a dismissive shake of her head and that famous lip curl.

"Christ! What a bloody pervert," Rachel hissed as she stepped back to the bar.

I raised a questioning eyebrow at her.

"He said, and I quote, 'what's the point of coming in here if I wasn't going to wear a skirt and show a bit of leg?'."

"A good speech should be like a woman's skirt: long enough to cover the subject and short enough to create interest," Brian announced as he returned to the bar with the cocktail glass in hand before tipping the content into the sink after lobbing the umbrella and straw in the bin. I guess the young lass wasn't too impressed with her tequila sunset as Brian had renamed the cocktail, probably because the Grenadine replacement had rendered said cocktail anything but the appearance of a sunrise.

Rachel and I exchanged a confused glance.

"A famous quote from Sir Winston Churchill, no less."

"Brian," she hissed. "You're as bad as him!" Rachel nodded to the old boy, sipping his pint of mild.

"Leave it with me." I hopped off my stool to have a quick word.

Although previously a teenager in this era, I had the benefit of wisdom and the knowledge of the future. Throughout my second life, with a frightening amount of regularity, I had cause to intervene when hearing sexist, racist, and homophobic comments. To be fair, this had abated somewhat over the years as education prevailed. However, I'd become well-versed in setting quite a few tossers straight on the proper way to behave. When I returned to my stool, Rachel raised her hands questioningly.

"I told him his future," I grinned. "You and Alison will have no more incidents to deal with where Cecil is concerned."

"Sorry, lass, no offence." Cecil raised his pint as he called out to Rachel.

"Christ, what the hell did you say to him?"

"As I said, I informed the old boy about the future. Specifically, problems he will encounter when I report him for criminal activity."

"Is looking up someone's skirt an offence? That's news to me."

"It soon will be."

I felt the need to change the subject regarding my knowledge of the Sexual Offences Acts passed through parliament in the new millennium. The conversation I'd enjoyed with Cecil was similar to one I'd had with a young lad I'd dismissed when working at Waddington Steel in 2019. That particular pervert claimed innocence but had stupidly sent his upskirting pictures to his work email account. I didn't half employ some dippy gits back then.

I accept Cecil would presumably be pushing up daisies before the smartphone revolutionised society in about fifteen years from now. Still, I was able to sow the seed about what his future might look like if he persisted with his debauched behaviour. Before Rachel pushed me about my clairvoyant claims, I thought it prudent to change the subject. It was bad enough having to indoctrinate Beth into the TTBC, so I certainly wasn't going to be issuing application forms to Rachel or Brian.

"Did you hear the news about that police officer and the riots?"

"Oh, it's awful. Fairfield is such a lovely town, but it's always that bloody estate that hits the headlines. That poor policeman's family. I know someone who's a friend of a friend of the poor man's cousin twice removed. I can't imagine what they're going through."

"They've just said on the radio that the police have shot dead one of the rioters," announced Brian, whilst attempting to produce another cocktail as he squinted over the top of his specs at the ingredients card pinned to the back of the bar. "Apparently, they're drafting in riot police from the Met."

Brian's statement alerted my time-travel antenna. A part of my brain that subconsciously listened out for events or happenings at odds with history as I knew it to be.

"Brian, what was that?" I blurted, slamming my pint on the bar towel.

"Yeah, I just heard it," he replied before pulling a pained expression as he tried to twist the top of a gunked-up, probably pre-decimalisation, half-full bottle of Crème de Menthe. I presumed someone had opted for a Grasshopper but was unaware of Brian's lack of skill in the art of mixology, let alone how many Christmases had come and gone whilst that bottle of green-coloured liqueur cluttered up the nether regions of the shelving containing drinks that no one desired.

"You sure?"

"That's what they just reported. They're likening it to Blair Peach … you know that chap the police battered to death at that protest against the National Front?"

The Blair Peach incident happened around the time when my mother would be in the throes of potty training me. However, I became aware of the tragedy in my teenage years. Later, and like many attending university, I was at that age that thought we could change the world. I became quite the activist against the establishment, protesting against everything that seemed unjust. However, like the vast majority, I lost that desire when the realities of humdrum life, like the grunge of nine-to-five and mortgage payments, squashed my enthusiasm.

In this life, I was in my mid-forties when Blair Peach lost his life. As Ralph McTell so eloquently sang in *Water of Dreams*, I was aghast at how society wasn't more outraged about an innocent man's death when protesting against an ideology that millions had laid down their lives to fight against only thirty-odd years before during The Second World War. Despairingly, and when it suited, humans quickly chose to forget the unforgettable.

Although I wasn't aware of the facts, I doubted this incident was like the Blair Peach tragedy. A rioter on the Broxworth Estate was probably a member of a rent-a-mob intent on causing as much mayhem as possible. Also, a young police officer had just lost his life when trying to protect the people who killed him. However, as my time-travel inbuilt antenna in my brain had alerted me, my concern was regarding the potential occurrence of a time shift.

These were rare occurrences because time wasn't easily bent. What had gone before generally happens again. This was good for two reasons. Firstly, I knew the future, and although the TTBC had what you might call a hopelessly pathetic success rate in preventing unsavoury events such as serial killers and natural disasters, I could at least prevent my family from being in the wrong place at the wrong time. Stopping Chris, a massive Liverpool fan, from attending the FA Cup semifinal in 1989 being an example.

For many months, that particular event had been an agenda point at our TTBC meetings. We'd devised some frankly ridiculous hair-brained solutions to avoid the disaster. One being George and I attend the match, arrive early and somehow close the tunnel that led to the overcrowded pen. However, Jenny pointed out we would probably be arrested or, even worse, end up dead like the ninety-six. Like all disasters, watching the events unfold on TV was desperately sad.

Selfishly, the second reason I was pleased time didn't bend easily was due to being able to live a relatively luxurious lifestyle. Mine and George's betting spree had led to a comfortable and privileged existence.

The 1994 riots on the Broxworth Estate resulted in the death of a police officer. As I mentioned before, easily remembered due to it occurring the day after my seventeenth birthday and the death of that police officer hitting the national news. No armed response units were involved. No protesters were shot by a police marksman. Without any margin of doubt, time had bent.

The most likely explanation for a time shift was due to the intervention of a time-traveller. For example, my adopted children's lives changed because of my intervention. I could only assume the police had shot a rioter because of a small intervention from a time-traveller who'd caused a ripple effect.

As of last night, and as far as I knew, only four of us existed. Martin, the loose cannon that he was, still living in Spain, doing what he did best – inseminating the population. I was here, sipping my beer, and had not intervened in the riot. That left *other* Jason and a somewhat more disturbing explanation – Paul Colney.

"Alright, lad?" George nudged me, effectively hauling me from my reverie.

"What's up with Cecil? I just tried to exchange pleasantries with the old boy, and I can't say the silly old sod looks too chuffed. I said, what ho, Cecil. You look like you've lost a quid and found tuppence. And all I got in reply was one of his famous grunts."

"That's the problem. The old perv is … well, shall we say, a little too enthusiastic when it comes to tuppence."

George furrowed his brow and pursed his lips at me after confirming with a nod to Rachel as she waved an empty pint glass in his general direction.

"Sorry, lad. You've lost me."

"Oh, don't ask," I groaned, waving my hand to indicate that I had no intention of elaborating further.

George dropped the confused look in favour of a quizzically raised eyebrow.

"George, we have a problem."

16

Basic Engly Twenty Fido

"What, lad?"

"Paul Colney is here," I hissed.

"What? Where?" blurted George, as he spun around, ducking whilst furtively scanning around the bar. I presumed George's swift shift to a crouched position wasn't because of an acute bout of sciatica but rather an involuntary reaction when expecting Paul Colney to leap upon him.

"Not in here. In Fairfield," I hissed.

Whilst nestled into our favoured window seat, the command centre for the TTBC's top executives, I brought George up to speed with my musings regarding the death of a rioter and my thoughts about the intervention of another time-traveller, namely Paul Colney.

When Jenny and Jess arrived, somewhat frustratingly, I had to retrace my steps and repeat the entire story. I made a point about prompt start times for executive meetings, which both ladies dismissed with a tut, a pronounced lip curl, and a dismissive wave of the hand. Anyway, after bringing the session back to order, I concluded the story thus far. Although, similar to when bringing George up to speed, I left out the bit about Brian's foray into the world of cocktails and Cecil's upskirting antics.

Jenny had always said there was something creepy about the curmudgeonly old git, and I guess her womanly intuition had been correct. However, there was a time and place to discuss such matters. An urgent, albeit late-starting, emergency meeting of the TTBC wasn't the right time to discuss Cecil's perversions.

"Darling, where's Beth?" her tone chipper, so presumably she'd moved past my bark regarding the need for strict timekeeping to all meetings, whether pre-planned or emergency councils of war, as this could be described.

"Don't ask. Our daughter refused to leave the sanctuary of her bedroom, stating I could go forth and, well, you know what."

Jenny tutted. "That girl of ours is becoming unruly. My father would have taken the strap to Alan or me if we'd behaved the way she does."

"I'll talk to her if you like?" Jess suggested. "Colin rang earlier and said he'll probably not be back until late this evening, and Faith is out again tonight. I'll pop over yours after we've finished up here."

Jenny offered an acquiescent smile and nod. "I'll make you some supper. George, you too?" Jenny offered.

"Tidy, as my neighbour Owain Jones likes to say. Comes from the Valleys, you know?"

"No shit," I muttered.

"Oh, yes. Can't pronounce the name of the town he originated from. You know, all those consonants jumbled up together. You need a certain dexterity with the tongue to be able to do it justice."

"George, I'm well aware that Owain is Welsh," I rather exasperatedly threw back. "He and Marge have lived next to you for nigh on fifty years. If Vera on the other side was busy, he and Marge would babysit me … you know, when I was here the first time. He used to say 'tidy' back then, and I always thought he was having a pop at me for leaving my toys strewn across the carpet."

George pursed his lips at my retort.

"Supper then, George?" Jenny repeated.

"Yes, lass, that'll be grand. To quote Hamish from up at the Legion, Aye, that would be braw, lass. Never been too proficient in the kitchen, and Ivy will be at her sister's for a few more days."

"What about Paddy? What would he say?" I threw in, wondering if George intended to give examples from all corners of the United Kingdom.

Although I was chair of the TTBC, sometimes keeping the conversation on track was akin to holding a bunch of hormonal year elevens focused on the finer points of algebraic geometry. That said, most sixteen-year-old boys were keenly interested in curved surfaces, although that being more of the female breast variety than the curves of polynomial equations.

"Who's Paddy? Not sure I've met him."

"George, forget it." I turned to Jess, leaving George with a bemused expression that suggested he was in the process of raking through his acquaintances to identify an Irishman. "It's fair to say Beth isn't too chuffed with her mother and me at the moment. So, I think a word from you will help. It certainly can't harm, that's for sure."

"You sure you've got enough time? You say Colin will be late home."

"Yeah, it's fine. He's gone all the way up to Manchester for some meeting or other. I don't expect he'll be back much before nine."

Colin used to teach at the City School. However, he became disillusioned with trying to control the marauding delinquents who regularly attempted to disrupt classes. Although I loved my job, I accepted that teaching wasn't for the faint-hearted. To get through some days, you needed a stab vest, riot shield, and the dogged determination to prevail that would make Maximus Decimus Meridius's efforts to avenge the crucifixion of his family appear positively apathetic or even insipid. There were many classes where us teachers needed to take on a gladiatorial attitude to survive unscathed.

Anyway, Colin's new career in a startup computing company took him all over the country and thus afforded us regular opportunities to hold TTBC meetings without having to indoctrinate him into our rather exclusive club. I suspected Colin would need to look for alternative employment in the future because I'd never heard of the company he worked for. So, it was safe to assume the company fell by the wayside when Microsoft and Apple suffocated the tech market and took over the world. Well, I hope they still did because I'd purchased a healthy dollop of shares in both companies, which would mushroom into a nice little nest egg for Chris and Beth for their futures.

Despite a tough sell when persuading George to dabble in the stock market, he'd now become an avid trader to such an extent he could easily rival any budding hedge fund executive. In between protecting his crops from a rabid bunch of determined bunnies, George liked to dabble in a spot of trading. He'd caught the bug when Mrs Thatcher's government dismantled the public sector and dismembered the trade unions when selling off the nationalised industries. He'd made a killing with British Telecom and the likes, the profits going anonymously to the British Legion, which, after his exploits with Bert-Ballbuster-Bullard in Libya, he held close to his heart. George was forever grateful not to be a statistic in that list of four-hundred-thousand men who never returned to Blighty in 1945.

Tech companies stock formed an integral part of George's extensive portfolio. However, of late, he and I were a smidge concerned about our Apple stock. The company's recent less-than-successful innovations were a concern now they'd launched what appeared to be a few dead ducks. The Apple Newton PDA, with its hapless handwriting recognition program, being a perfect example. George had unearthed reports that the company was failing with the threat of bankruptcy looming. Although this was new news to me, not recalling this in my first life, I managed to convince George to hold his nerve and not bail on the collapsing stock. I had my fingers and toes crossed, hoping the company would sort itself out and still go on to produce the iPhone.

"What about *other* Jason, lad? It could have been his arrival that caused a shift in time." George threw into the conversation, raising his eyebrows to pose the question as he slugged a mouthful of beer.

"Darling, George could be right."

"What about the letter? Older me has written that a time-traveller returns, but also stated *other* Jason hadn't materialised," I whispered, leaning forward as we hunched over the table.

Although the early evening and the pub hadn't swelled to full capacity, we were always mindful that the subject of our conversation could give rise to awkward questions or, at the very least, a raised eyebrow if overheard.

"If it is Paul, how can he be back?" Jess hissed.

"What d'you mean, lass?"

"Well, he's dead. I know that because I witnessed his death when the evil git's body lay bleeding out across the bonnet of Dad's Cortina back in '77."

"Yes, lass, but you also had an encounter with him in Don's kitchen in '87, didn't you?"

"Yeah, don't remind me." Jess appeared to horripilate, shivering and rubbing both upper arms with crossed hands before continuing. "What I'm saying, apart from us, everyone believes him to be dead."

Jenny gently laid her hand on Jess's forearm, waiting momentarily until she had her attention. "The letter states a time-traveller under a pseudonym. I imagine Paul Colney has got himself a new identity."

All four club members took a moment to contemplate the hideous thought before Jess verbalised what had been bouncing around my head all day.

She raised a finger and narrowed her eyes. "So ... next Wednesday, something happens to me. If we stop that, whatever it is—"

"We will! Come hell or high water, we damn well will," interrupted Jenny in a low hiss.

"Hear, hear. I'll second that, lass."

Jess offered a tight smile to both and continued. "So, we heed the warning and stop whatever. But what happens to the future?"

"As in the future where older me reckons something *did* happen to you?" I chimed in.

"Yeah."

"It gets expunged."

"Do what, lad?"

"Look, this is 1994."

"I know that. I might be getting old, but I know what ruddy year it is," George baulked, appearing somewhat put out about the suggestion, as he saw it, that because of his senior years, he didn't know the date.

"Hang on, George. This is 1994. Events and happenings in the 1994 from my first life haven't happened."

"Sorry, lad, you've lost me. Events in history have pretty much repeated itself, according to you."

"Yes, they have," I hissed, before peeking up like an inquisitive meerkat to check our conversation was still private before continuing. "World events, stuff that's unrelated to us is all repeating itself. But, think of smaller happenings. In 1994, not that I know too much detail about this because Beth was always a smidge tight-lipped about it, but—"

"Beth, as in your friend, not your daughter?" quizzed Jess.

"Yeah. But, back then, or rather in the future, Beth's brother was serving a prison sentence for drug dealing and associated crimes—"

"Youth of today," George tutted and shook his head.

I side-eyed George, conveying my disapproval regarding his interruption. "Yes, as I was saying. In this 1994, that same man, Chris, isn't in prison; he's our son, who's a very different man and nothing short of an upstanding citizen."

"Apart from when he's cavorting in our bed with Lilo Lil and a harem of young hussies," muttered Jenny.

Jess raised an eyebrow at my wife. Fortunately, George missed her mutterings.

"Oh, I see, lad. We stop this thing happening to the lassie here." He prodded his half-consumed pint at Jess. "And what your older self knew in the future doesn't happen. Exorcised, as you say."

"Expunged, George." I corrected him. Although his misspeak segued nicely into the main crux of the problem. "Talking of evil spirits, we need a plan to stop Paul Colney."

"Hang on, Dad. As we stand today, you know you'll still be alive in 2015 because you wrote that letter. If we change history, that means you'll no longer be guaranteed to live that long."

"Nothing good comes from knowing when your time is up, lass. Mark my words." George offered a solemn nod before draining his glass.

Jenny and I nervously glanced at George. We knew he had less than three years left on this planet, assuming history would repeat itself.

George, clocking our furtive glances, shook his head at me. "No, lad, I told you before. I don't want to know. Just tell me this. One, will my Ivy outlive me? And two, have I got time to get that damn rabbit?"

"Yes, on both counts. I'm sure you've got time to outwit your broad-bean-ravaging Bugs Bunny."

"Good, I won't worry too much, then. Now, come on. I'll get the next round, and when I come back, I want to hear some sort of credible plan to save our lassie here."

Jess raised an eyebrow at me as George eased out of his chair before heading to the bar.

"Of course, you know, don't you?"

"Know what?" I quizzed, although I knew exactly what she meant.

"You know when George dies."

"February 1st 1997. I'm afraid he's got less than three years left."

Jess cupped her hands around her mouth. Her moist eyes suggested tears were welling up.

"Jess, sweety. Come on. Don't let George see you like this. He'll know what we've just told you. Anyway, your father not knowing when he dies is a positive thing. We only have one concern now which is stopping what will happen next Wednesday."

Jess nodded before wiping the end of her nose with her jumper sleeve. Jenny rummaged around in her handbag before producing a pen and notepad. Whilst twiddling the pen between her fingers, she looked at me expectantly. Presumably, this was the point I should verbalise our master plan.

However, despite the lack of any credible plan formulating, my eye was drawn to the pen. I presumed it was one she'd plucked from the kitchen drawer, you know, that drawer we all have which seems to magically fill with all the tat that you can't decide upon a proper home for. The pen, poised in an inverted position in my wife's hand, ready to note down the bullet points of my plan, I surmised had once been Chris's property. A novelty tip-and-reveal pen, now displaying a nude woman jauntily showing off her wares with hands on hips and a cheeky smile.

I nodded to the offending item and bulged my eyes.

Jenny glanced down and then back at me, shaking her head and looking bemused.

I nodded again.

"What, darling?"

"The pen," I mouthed.

"Oh, God!" she announced, dropping the offending item. "Where the hell has that come from?"

Now Jess had composed herself, she snorted a giggle and grabbed the pen before tipping it back and forth to watch the reveal. "I'd say this is quite old."

"Oh, Jess, get rid of it! Anyway, how d'you know it's old?"

"Au naturel in the nether regions. No woman these days would have that much hair … it looks like a bird's nest."

Jenny tutted as Jess laid the pen back on the table.

"I don't want it," Jenny protested, prodding it away.

"Err … let's get back on track, can we? I hate to pour petrol on the fire, but I don't believe locking Jess up for the day will solve the issue."

"If it is Paul Colney, and he intends to harm Jess, he'll strike another day if he fails on the sixth," she suggested, whilst warily glancing at the pen as if it were a spider, checking to make sure it didn't creep her way.

"Yeah, I had that thought, too."

"Oh, shit. What the hell do we do then? I can't go into hiding for the rest of my life. There's Colin and Faith to think about."

"Darling?" Jenny's voice raised a couple of octaves, presumably hoping I'd thought of a cunning plan.

However, no plan was forthcoming. To mimic Blackadder, I might as well stick my pants on my head and ram two pencils up my nostrils to feign madness before facing Paul Colney. Shaking thoughts of Rowan Atkinson from my mind, I grabbed the pen and used it as a pointer, alternating it between Jenny and Jess.

"I don't know. Well, I don't know the plan, as such. Although, first up, we need to find *other* Jason and see what he knows. Secondly, we will have to find Paul Colney and eliminate him."

My statement hung in the air like a cloud of ominous doom that cloaked and suffocated the air around the window seat as George shuffled back with a tray of precariously balanced drinks. Jess and Jenny knew what I'd said to be our only option. However, like me, probably harboured no idea of how to execute such a loose plan. Placing the arduous task of locating *other* Jason to one side, unearthing a psychotic nutter like Paul Colney, and then killing the bastard was a whole new level.

"Right, pint for you, lad, and a couple of G&Ts for the ladies." George passed around the drinks. "Brian's got the TV on in the public bar. The news is showing the riots on the Broxworth."

I solemnly nodded. Desperately sad news, especially as that poor young officer had lost his life. An event I knew would happen. Many years had passed since I stopped beating myself up about not preventing awful events. Yes, Jenny and I could have tried to warn that officer. Perhaps we could have persuaded him to throw a sickie or let his tyres down so he was late for work.

However, it didn't work like that. Time was a stubborn thing and refused to bend at will. We, at the TTBC, when attempting to alter the future, sported an extensive back catalogue of failed missions. A myriad of ignored anonymous letters to the authorities and individuals, not to mention the string of pointless disguised telephone calls, all of which were treated as crank calls.

Akin to the troubles in Northern Ireland and warning calls about an imminent bombing campaign, our warning calls from a variety of public payphones dotted across the Home Counties were treated as some crackpot trying to cause panic, hysteria and mayhem. With the regulation handkerchief over the mouthpiece, I'd made such a call to a local radio station warning of the Bradford City stadium fire in 1985.

However, it transpired that I'd mis-dialled and left a message on the answering machine of a pensioner who alerted the media and authorities after the fire. Although the fire was later purportedly started by a discarded cigarette butt and not arson, my call had piqued the interest of the authorities. Of course, I was only eight when this disaster struck in my first life, but could easily recall the date due to the disaster happening on what would have been my mother's fortieth birthday.

During a press briefing, the police had played my garbled message. To be fair, even if I had dialled the correct number, I doubted that anyone could have deciphered my warning due to my woeful attempt to change my accent and the muffling effect of the handkerchief. My gobbledegook mumblings had sounded like something the comedian Stanley Unwin might have uttered when using his Unwinese language.

"Right. What have you come up with? By the look of that, don't look as if you've thought of much." George nodded to Jenny's notepad before he sipped his beer after gingerly planting his backside in the chair.

"Not much, I'm afraid."

"Oh … can I borrow your pen, lad? I seemed to have misplaced mine." George whipped it from my hand and slotted it into his jacket pocket.

I wondered what Ivy would make of it when she discovered said item. She may harbour concerns about what her husband had been up to whilst away at her sister's and would probably deduce that George wasn't chasing rabbits up at his allotment but Bunny Girls in one of those debauched, seedy clubs full of libertine men with depraved minds, as she would put it.

"Okay, we're not getting very far. As I see it, we need to kill Colney and find *other* Jason. Which is all well and good, but I have no sodding idea where to start."

"Well, I do, lad. I was having a gander at the TV whilst Rachel poured the drinks. They were showing the riot police and a water cannon they'd used to disperse that murdering mob. When the camera panned around, I spotted you, or him, as it were, standing by the steps that lead up to Belfast House. I'm pretty sure, lad, that *other* Jason is holed up on the Broxworth."

17

The Hunt for the Red October

Leaving our drinks half finished, George and I bolted out of the pub. George's casual delivery of his revelation that he's spotted *other* Jason spurred us into action. Jenny and Jess readied themselves to scoot home, where Jess would attempt to convince Beth to believe in the ridiculous whilst Jenny prepared supper – tidy, to quote George's neighbour.

Akin to a car full of mindless teenagers, without the regulation booming beat of some hideous tune thumping from a set of souped-up speakers mounted on the parcel shelf, George and I cruised the streets that circumnavigated the Broxworth Estate, searching for a way in which hadn't already been barricaded by a line of heavily tooled-up riot police.

After two complete tours of the surrounding roads, we accepted defeat. George suggested we park up and try to walk onto the estate. However, although we harboured an urgent need to locate the man who I'd replaced back in '76, I feared dragging my eighty-two-year-old friend and former grandfather into a potential war zone might not be a super-sensible move.

A decision soon vindicated when attempting a desperate and somewhat panicked three-point turn. When boxed in and facing a posse of rioters, all brandishing the sorts of cocktails that even Brian wouldn't attempt concocting, as they broke through the line of riot police, I knew I'd made the correct judgment call. One rioter, spotting the opportunity to cause death and further mayhem, launched his flaming cocktail in our direction, only missing the boot lid as I floored the accelerator to increase the distance between us and a mob who wouldn't have looked out of place in some wretched dystopian zombie B-movie.

When caracoling through the desert whilst brandishing a fixed bayonet when giving Jerry and the Desert Fox what for, I expect George had witnessed significantly worse situations than the exploding fireball mixture of glass and burning petrol now strewn across the road behind us. That said, the grey-hue tint to his complexion would be an appearance generally reserved for those up at the morgue with a dead-pan expression sporting a toe tag.

After flouting the vast majority of rules in the Highway Code, my driving returned to something less like rally driving when I'd achieved a sufficient distance from the Broxworth. Rather than shoot back home, I made a detour to the Bowthorpe Estate, specifically my lock-up. George claimed he'd spotted my car last night in the High Street and, if my daughter was to be believed, Beth accepted a ride in my time-travelling Cortina only minutes before with a man who I presume must be *other* Jason.

"Lad."

George broke the silence after the Molotov cocktail incident as I swung into the road behind the row of shops. As I glanced left, his face lit up by the sodium-yellow light emanating from the line of street lamps suggested he'd recovered from the shock of the fireball near miss when I'd wheel spun onto Coldhams Lane.

"What?"

"How is it possible that your Cortina could still be parked up in the lock-up but also somewhere else at the same time?"

I side-eyed him but offered no reply as we crept along the road towards the alleyway. The row of flat garage units sported a variety of coloured up-and-over doors in varying states of dilapidation with either rust, dents, graffiti, or a combination of all three. The fifth one on the right, with the faded red door and *'Fuck the Poll Tax'* daubed in white paint jauntily sprayed at an angle across the upper section, being the one I rented to secure the Cortina and thus keep out of harm's way.

The Bowthorpe Estate, built in 1976 and now a sprawling suburb of Fairfield, was generally considered a decent area. It's where I purchased those two semi-detached houses, rented one to Don and later gifted the other to Jess and Colin when they married in '77.

However, as the years rolled by, the estate expanded southwards when gobbling up large swathes of the greenbelt. This part of the estate, with a myriad of rat-runs of social housing flanked by two high-rise tower blocks that ominously reared out of the ground, had colloquially become known as *'Little Dodge'*. Aptly named considering those tower blocks, positioned on the perimeter of the estate, attracted the likes of whom were searching for an escape from the hellish existence of the Broxworth.

The residents of the original northern area of the estate, which included Jess, were keen to distance themselves from the southern, less salubrious part. All referring to their little piece of real estate as the Thorpe Estate as opposed to Bowthorpe, which was associated with those ugly multicoloured-clad early '80s towers that played homage to their '60s counterparts on the Broxworth.

The garage I rented belonged to Hector, an elderly decent sort, who resided in one of those tower blocks, which I knew to become known as the 'Twin Towers' post 9/11 when townsfolk suggested it was a pity al-Qaeda hadn't rerouted their suicide planes to Fairfield and done the town a favour. A sick joke that a local councillor was overheard relaying at a function that ultimately led to a hasty retraction and swift resignation. I recall the chap being a complete knob-end, so I was more than happy for him to repeat the faux pas when that year flowed around again.

As chair of the TTBC, I had no intention of warning him about the consequences of an ill-judged comment that would destroy his career. Unfair? Maybe. However, some bell-ends deserved all they got.

Hector, with his jowly jaw and somewhat out-of-place pompous way about him, who could have played the stunt double for the puppet dog in the '70s TV children's programme, being one of the first to escape *Dodge City* when successfully cutting loose from the Broxworth a few years ago – a frying pan to the fire type scenario if the degeneration of the immediate area was anything to go by.

The graffiti daubed on my garage appeared almost four years to the day, one night in 1990. Fairfield joined in on the protests about the Community Charge replacing the 'Rates' on domestic properties. Amazingly, four years on, many *'Can't Pay Won't Pay'* stickers, although faded, were still evident across the town where protesters and campaigners had liberally slapped them on street furniture and shop façades.

Rather out of character and somewhat unusually, the residents of the Broxworth didn't feel the need to protest on this occasion. Probably because no one on the estate paid taxes, and the authorities were too intimidated to enter the hellish dump to enforce the law. Hence, *Dodge* being the rather apt moniker that the authorities, including Jenny's child protection team at the council, often referred to when discussing all things Broxworth Estate.

As I swung into the off-shoot alley, heading to my rented garage, the car's headlights illuminated a figure who raised his hands to protect his eyes as I flipped on the main beam.

"He's at your garage," blurted George, jabbing his finger at the windscreen.

When screeching to a halt and flinging open the driver's door, the figure took flight back along the dimly lit alley. Whilst attempting to give chase, and only twenty yards into my pursuit, I heard George call out.

"Lad, leave it. You won't catch him."

I halted, slapping my palms on my knees as my panting and heart rate demanded a rest. "Christ," I muttered, realising that now a man of sixty, my sprinting days were long gone despite indulging in a daily jog around the local park, which was performed at a more sedate, almost a serene, gazelle-like canter than a full-on sprint. With my hands still grasping my knees, I glanced up to spot the nebulous figure hightail away as he bounded over a chain-link fence before being swallowed up by the dark vista of the foreboding nether regions of the alley.

"Lad, you alright?"

I straightened up and nodded.

"Looks like the scoundrel was trying to break in."

George gingerly bent forward and retrieved the broken padlock, now pointing said broken lock at the jemmied-off hasp. A security measure I'd installed some years back after a previous attempt by some lowlife scum to gain entry had broken the lock situated in the centre of the twist handle.

"Kids, I suspect," I muttered, padding my way back to him.

George and I hauled up the garage door, fighting against the rusted and squeaking hinges, which emanated an abhorrent rasping squawk akin to nails screeching down a blackboard. With our arms aloft, both clasping the upturned base of the door, we peered into the dim light.

"It's still there, lad."

"Thank God," I mumbled whilst drinking in the vision of my yellow Cortina parked where it should be and safely out of harm's way.

However, George's question he'd posed a few minutes ago played on my mind. Assuming George wasn't hallucinating when spotting the Cortina on the High Street, that could only mean there were now two of them in the same time zone. This one and the one *other* Jason had travelled to 1994 from 2015.

"D'you reckon it's got a clone? Y'know, like that sheep called Dolly, you and Martin reckon some hair-brained scientists produce in the future?"

I puffed out my cheeks. "Christ, George, I have no bloody idea. I know I've made a study of time-travel, but this is ridiculous."

"Well, it was this car on the High Street last night; that I can tell you. My knees might be shot to pieces, and my frozen shoulder gives me jip more often than I'd like, but there's nowt wrong with my eyesight, lad."

"Yeah, I know. I just can't get my head around how there can be two of them."

"Popular car, lad. Why anyone would want a yellow one is beyond me. A chap at the Chronicle – Pipkins, or Perkins, something like that, head of accounts, he is, his name began with P, that much I do know – he bought his wife a beetroot-coloured little sports car. Ruddy awful thing if you ask me. Posh, it's called. That's a stupid name, too, and German." George uttered the last word as if a sour taste had filled his mouth.

Although most of the world had moved forward from his time in the desert, I understood how George struggled on that front. Like Don, who served in the First World War, it was difficult to forget. Although society must remember history to learn for the future, a generation must pass before attitudes change. Of course, many found Basil Fawlty's goose-stepping hilarious. However, the vast majority were missing the point of the script, which I knew with the benefit of the future that the scriptwriting was poking fun at the character and those who harbour similar attitudes, which should be buried in the past.

"I think you mean Porsche, not Posh."

"Maybe, lad. It's still German, whatever daft name they call it."

See my point?

"Right, I'd better fix that lock." I grabbed the torch off the shelf to illuminate the toolbox at the back of the garage. After the lock had previously been jemmied, I'd secured a few tools and spare locks for just this eventuality. After rummaging around for an appropriate screwdriver whilst George remained on sentry duty, I shot a look at the bonnet of the Cortina.

The sound of an exhaust pinging in older cars was a common occurrence. The contracting metal giving off that not-dissimilar sonar-type bleep from a submarine. As I gawped at the yellow bonnet with my screwdriver in hand, I held my breath and waited to rehear that auspicious sound. However, to quote Captain Ramius – only one ping.

Tentatively, I laid the palm of my left hand on the bonnet. As my skin touched metal, I realised that my 1974 Cortina XL didn't have a clone.

18

The Nixon Line

Whilst keeping my palm planted firmly on the warm metal of the car bonnet, my mind shot off in a myriad of tangents when throwing up bizarre possibilities. Had *other* Jason driven the car here and parked it in my lock-up after time-travelling from the future? And if that were to be the case, had my Cortina, unbeknown to me, been AWOL when scooting through time from 2015 to 1994 when it should have been tucked up nice and tight in this rented garage unit? Could this time machine, which doubled up as an old, not quite vintage, Ford saloon car, be simultaneously in two or even three places, time zones, years, or whatever?

"Shit," I muttered, pondering the other disturbing possibility that someone else had driven the car for some unexplained reason. Joyriders taking the car for a spin being one such possibility.

"George," I hissed, before swivelling my head and repeating my call loud enough to echo off the garage walls. "George." His eyesight might be bob-on, but my old friend's hearing was heading the same way as his knees. "George, did you hear me?"

"Oh, sorry, lad. I was just thinking about old Percy up at the allotment. He used to keep ferrets, y'know. Back in the day ... mid to late fifties probably ... although it could be the early sixties, for that matter. Anyway, that's irrelevant—"

"Correct. Irrelevant," I hissed. Although an audible comment, it wasn't meant to be uttered. Just an involuntary blurt from me when suspecting George was about to recount some shaggy-dog story. Although they were often amusing, this really wasn't the time or the place.

"So, back then, he and a few of the lads who used to drink in the Crossed Keys, you know that thatched pub which burnt down on Guy Fawkes Night sometime in the seventies ... although you young'uns now call it Fireworks Night these days."

"George, is there a point to this story?"

"Yes, lad, I'm getting there. Now look, I've lost my train of thought. Oh, where was I? That is annoying."

"You were discussing ferrets, a thatched pub and blowing up Parliament. Although I have to say, I'm struggling to grasp what the connection might be."

"Ah, yes, that was it. Well, lad, there is a connection, but I was just adding some background information to the point I was trying to make."

"Christ," I muttered under my breath.

"So, yes, that's it. Some of the lads who used to drink in that old pub would go cottontail hunting. Probably on the very land we're standing on right now."

"Sorry, am I missing something here?" I fired back, rolling my eyes.

"It was just an idea, that's all. I could ask old Percy if he still keeps ferrets. Perhaps I could use them to get that damn rabbit."

"Why not try dynamite or gunpowder?"

"No, ferrets would be cleaner. Anyway, lad, I'm not sure dynamite is legal."

"George!"

"Yes, lad."

"Christ, can you think of something else? We have a bit of an issue. As in the fact that some bastard, probably that time-travelling waster, Colney, intends to inflict harm upon my daughter in precisely six days from now."

"Sorry, lad. You were saying?" George padded around the Cortina as he shuffled into the garage.

"The engine," I nodded at my hand, still resting on the bonnet.

"What about it?"

"It's warm!"

"Gordon Bennett, you sure?"

Again, I nodded to where my hand still lay on the cooling metal. "Feel it."

George placed his hand beside mine before shooting me a look. "Hells bells, you're right, lad. Does that mean this car doesn't have a mechanical clone like Dolly the sheep?"

"I don't know. It's too complicated to think about. Hang on." I shimmied around George and yanked on the car door handle.

"It's not locked, lad."

"Clearly."

"Shouldn't you keep it locked? Bit careless that, considering what's gone before."

"Yes!" I exasperatedly fired back. "Of course, I keep it locked. And I'm fully aware of what this thing is capable of."

"Well, it ain't locked now, is it, lad?"

"No!" I rolled my eyes and huffed. "I think I can see that." I dramatically waved at the open door.

"Alright, alright. No need to get all mardy on me."

"Sorry, George."

"No need to apologise, lad."

"I'm worried what's going to happen, and ..." I let the sentence drift away, not wishing to verbalise my selfish thoughts.

"Apart from dealing with that scoundrel Colney, you're worried about this *other* Jason chap and how that's going to affect your relationship with the lassie? Am I right, or am I right?"

Ever the perceptive one, my wise counsel had burrowed, no pun intended, to the heart of my concern. A nagging worry, which aggressively tapped at my brain like a persistent randy woodpecker trying to call for a mate. Jess was *his* daughter, not mine. If he was here now, in 1994, was I about to lose a daughter, irrespective of what might happen next Wednesday?

"That woman is your daughter, my boy." George jabbed a finger at me. "You can forget biology and the fact that this *other* Jason fella might well be her natural father. She's only known you. Mark my words. Jess sees you as her father, and nothing will change that."

"I hope you're right. I really don't think I can—"

"No, lad. No more negative thoughts. Shooting off down a road paved in what ifs never done no one no good."

I shrugged and offered a wee nod before gesturing at the open door of my Cortina. "This doesn't make any sense."

"What doesn't?"

"This!" I wiggled the car door back and forth. "The keys to this bloody thing are at home in the kitchen drawer … or should be." As I slithered onto the driver's seat, the naked-lady-reveal pen secured in George's pocket popped into my mind.

George remained in position, his hand appearing super-glued to the bonnet as he leaned towards the windscreen. "Are the keys in there?"

"I'm looking."

"Well?"

"Hang on." I tutted, whilst flicking away the content of the glove box that someone, persons unknown, had seen fit to empty onto the passenger seat.

"Have you found them?"

"Sorry?" I barked, sticking my head through the gap of the open door.

"I said, have you found them?"

"No … George, why have you still got your hand on the bonnet?"

"Oh," he chuckled as he straightened up. "D'you want me to have a shufty?"

"Why?"

"See if I can't find the keys?"

"If I can't find them, I don't know how letting you look is going to help. Anyway, they're at home in the drawer."

"Unless someone hot-wired it, I'd suggest the keys are here."

I glanced up at George, who now held onto the top of the open door. "Yeah, you're right. Maybe *other* Jason or whoever took this thing for a spin has still got hold of them."

George reached in and flipped the sun visor down. We both gawped at my lap for a few seconds, where the key attached to a key fob containing a school photo of Chris and Beth now lay in the fold of my jeans.

"Boom boom! There you go, lad. As if by magic," he chuckled.

"What's boom boom got to do with the price of bread?"

"Your keys appearing as if by magic. David Nixon … *The Nixon Line.*"

My bemused look and shake of the head suggested to George that I needed enlightening regarding whatever left turn he was now shooting this conversation down.

"David Nixon, you know the magician with Basil Brush … the fox puppet in the cape with those fancy cravats and a big bushy tail."

"Yes, yes, I know who Basil bloody Brush is."

"Well, lad, there you go, then. Boom, boom."

I shook my head and rolled my eyes. Half bemused by how George managed to always take the conversation off-piste and half bemused by how the keyring with the attached car key had managed to magically transport itself from the kitchen drawer to my lock-up halfway across town.

"Gotta say, lad. I know you don't drive this thing, and clearly after what's happened before, I suggest you don't, but a couple of buckets over the bodywork wouldn't go amiss."

"Sorry?"

"The car. It's filthy. Looks to me like you've been indulging in a spot of rallying in the thing."

I peered out the door to where George was nodding to the rear door and wing. "Lovers' Lane, I muttered."

"Do what, lad?"

"He was down Lovers' Lane."

"Who was?"

"*Other* Jason."

"When?"

"Last night when he offered Beth a lift."

"Your lassie was in Lovers' Lane?"

I winced.

"Oh, dear. Oh, dear, oh dear," George tutted, shaking his head.

"Hmmm."

"What on earth was the lassie doing down there, for Lord's sake?"

"Well, she wasn't bird-watching, was she?"

"Oh … different generation, I suppose. I'm not sure that's information I'll divulge to my Ivy."

"I can't say I was too chuffed about it either. But you're right with one thing … different generation."

"Well, yes, take that Martin chap. He was born, what, ten years after Beth? The bloke's got no morals and seems quite

206

content to entertain all sorts of women. Many at the same time if my memory serves me correctly."

"Look, George, as I said, I'm not happy about it. When I was Beth's age, I was just as active. Well, maybe not, but that wasn't for the want of trying."

"Yes, lad … I suppose you were. But you're a lad; she's a young lassie."

"I'd be careful to keep that thought to yourself, old boy. You'll have the politically correct police arresting you and recommending stoning as a punishment."

"I'm not an old fuddy-duddy. But that sort of activity was frowned upon when I was courting my Ivy back in the thirties."

"I'm sure. But listen, this mud caked on the car confirms it was *other* Jason who took it out for a spin … or, no, hang on. That's not right. He must have travelled back in it and then thought he'd better park it back here."

"How would he know?"

"Know what?"

"Where you keep it. How would *other* Jason from 1976 know where you keep this thing in 1994?"

"Well, there can only be one answer."

"What?"

"*Other* Jason and older me must have enjoyed a long chinwag about 1994 in 2015. Because he was me, older me would know where to park the car."

"Good grief. Well, where is this *other* Jason chap now, then?"

"I have no idea. But like that rabbit of yours, we're running out of time to ferret him out."

"You don't reckon that scoundrel you chased off was him, do you?"

"Oh … what, you reckon he was just parking it back in the garage, not trying to break in?"

"Could be. That would explain why the engine's still warm."

"Bollocks, you're right."

George raised an eyebrow.

"Sorry." I held my palm up as an apology. "With what's going on, you may have to give me a free pass regarding obscenities for a few days."

"Lad."

"What?"

"Lad …" George nudged my arm.

I shot my head around and peered out of the garage opening to where George was now pointing. As if freeze-dried, my tongue clamped to my palate whilst my sagging jaw caused my anhydrous mouth to gape.

The silhouette of a man who filled the space uttered one word.

"Jason?"

19

The Laughing Gnome

Supper could be described as a somewhat Stygian affair. Jenny and I apathetically picked at our food due to our muted appetites being affected by the events of the last twenty-four hours, coupled with the lack of ideas on how to proceed with our hapless and ill-considered plan. A plan at this stage that heralded the prospect of success akin to Sinclair's C5, which launched not a decade ago.

One such futile machine languished in the back of the shed amongst the under-used garden implements, a rusting Swingball, a collapsed child's swing and a decapitated gnome who'd suffered his fate when involuntarily heading a leather football that Chris had launched at him a decade ago.

In this life, I'd purchased the pod-like machine in white. Simply because that was the only colour available and may have been one of the reasons for its failure. Well, no one wants a white car, do they? So, yes, I was one of the first ignoramuses to rush out and grab one, even though I knew the electric recumbent tricycle would soon become a technological flop of epic proportions. A damp squib that made the Betamax video-tape recorder, Colgate's foray into the frozen ready-meal market, and the smokeless cigarette of a decade ago appear like winners.

Anyway, in my first life, at the time of the C5's release in the mid-eighties, I was an eight-year-old lad obsessed with Star Wars, all things sci-fi, and thus completely mesmerised by the adverts for the futuristic electric tricycle. So, as the mid-eighties rolled around again, then being in my mid-fifties and reasonably well off, I took my chance to grab a C5 I'd longed for when a schoolboy dressed in short trousers.

I won't tell you what Jenny said about my impulse purchase because I think you can make an educated guess. However, what I will say, if the aspiring millionaire had asked my wife to critique the prototype, which the developers expected to revolutionise the way the great British public travelled, they might have backtracked after she'd pointed out the many and blatantly obvious flaws.

With nigh on fifty per cent of days enjoying some rainfall, the open cockpit was a sure-fire plan for failure – much like our fairly non-existent plan to eliminate Paul Colney and save Jess.

Of course, assuming that fiendish psychotic bastard had resurfaced and now skulked around town like some faceless Jack the Ripper planning to embark on a campaign of rape and murder that only he knew how. As I disinterestedly nudged a carrot around my plate, I pondered that my older self may have become confused. Perhaps I suffered from delusional thoughts in my old age and thus convinced myself that Jess's fate was down to Paul Colney and not an act of some other killer still to be identified.

The life path of a time-traveller is never smooth.

I'd read somewhere a serial killer is at large every three years. Also, an average of nearly two murders per day were committed somewhere in the UK. So, could we be putting all our efforts into protecting Jess from the ghost of the time-travelling nutter from over half a decade ago when we should be diversifying and considering other possibilities? Too many ifs and buts to ruminate about, which had the effect of repressing my appetite. Unlike George, who hoovered up his plate of Jenny's casserole with a display of fervent gusto that any speed-eating champion would be proud of.

The silhouetted man who'd appeared outside my lock-up earlier wasn't who George and I initially suspected him to be, as in *other* Jason. Instead, the pleasant chap had been Hector's neighbour who'd popped down to check on proceedings after Hector had spied activity in the alley from his position of the high ground. Namely, through the net curtains of the lounge window of his tenth-floor flat situated in the North Tower.

Before my wife had served supper, George and I had brought Jenny up to speed with our discoveries in my lock-up whilst I'd unceremoniously upended the contents of that kitchen drawer. Which, I hasten to add, yielded a plethora of useless tat, most of which was smothered in red ink from a leaking pen. Notwithstanding my ink-splattered hands, appearing like I'd embarked on a frenzied attempt at self-harm, the Cortina's key ring wasn't to be found. Well, obviously not because it was in my pocket. However, I felt the need to check if the key that fell from its hidey-hole above the sun visor was a clone of the one that should be in that kitchen drawer.

After a conversation with George, as he sipped his tea and Jenny, who prepared supper, about clones, time leaps, alternate timelines, Lovers' Lane, and our yellow TARDIS with a warm engine, my head thumped to a level that a handful of paracetamol tablets did little to abate.

211

Jenny nudged a carrot with her fork, similar to how I poked and prodded my food across the plate. A situation similar to when faced with one of my grandmother's liver and onion 'specials' that, unfortunately, I recall was most Wednesday's go-to position when my grandmother planned our evening meals. As a small lad living with my grandparents, I never looked forward to Wednesday's tea. When bored with pushing the carrot around her plate, Jenny dropped her fork and folded her arms.

"Not going to eat that, lass?"

"Help yourself." Jenny apathetically waved her hand at the plate.

"Champion." George grinned and tucked in.

"Nothing else for it, but we're going to have to bring Colin into the club."

I raised an eyebrow in reply. We were still in the throes of trying to initiate Beth's membership, so the thought of adding Colin didn't bear thinking about.

"We can't protect Jess if she keeps Colin in the dark."

"I know … but, Jen, we're in enough of a mess with Beth, let alone—"

"Jason … we don't have a choice, do we?"

"There's got to be another way?"

"Cracking bit of stewing beef this, lass. You get it from the butchers in the High Street?"

"Sainsbury's." Jenny shot at George before sitting forward and folding her arms on the edge of the table. "Darling, I know that would be a nightmare, but if it is Paul Colney coming after Jess, we have to hide her, Colin, and Faith away from their house. He knows where she lives, remember?"

"That butchers turns out a nice bit of brisket. You should try it sometime." George mumbled between chewing whilst playing head tennis between Jenny and me.

"What if I move in with Jess this week? We tell Colin we've had a bust-up."

"No! I'm not having Colin thinking that our marriage is on the rocks."

"Granted, it's not ideal. But at least I could be with her all day and every day until the 6th."

"And what about Chris? Hmm?"

"Those big out-of-town shops will be the death of the High Street, you know?"

Jenny and I both side-eyed George before continuing with our conversation.

"What's Chris got to do with this?"

"It's Good Friday tomorrow. Chris and Megan are joining us at Mum's and coming here for Sunday lunch. You missing in action will mean we'll also have to lie to him."

"Oh."

"What's he going to think if you're not here?"

"You should think about shopping at that butchers occasionally instead of lining the pockets of old man Sainsbury." George waved his knife in Jenny's direction, offering a knowing nod.

"What the hell would we say to Colin if we also attempted to induct him?"

Jenny shrugged. "Same as we have to Beth, I suppose."

"Based on our daughter's shun, how d'you think that's going at the moment?"

"Alright, I get your point. But listen, I'm not telling all and sundry that you and I have had a falling out—"

"It was on some documentary the other night," George interrupted. "Some bloke, economist chappie with a plum in his mouth. He reckoned in twenty years from now, the High Street will no longer exist," George offered whilst mopping up the gravy with a slice of wholemeal.

"And …" Jenny paused to check George wasn't about to cut in again with his wisdom on grocery shopping. "And, as we discussed the other night, protecting Jess up to or on the 6th won't work."

"I know, I know." I held my hand aloft, accepting Jenny's point.

"Time could bend, and Jess comes to harm on the 7th, 8th, the summer, Christmas Day, for all we know."

"I know," I repeated, trying to stop Jenny from sermonising and hammering home her point that disappointingly was perfectly valid.

"Oh, hang on, lad."

"What?" I shot at George, hoping he'd conjured up a solution to this impossible scenario.

"Well, you coming from 2019, you'd know whether that chap's predictions come through to fruition."

"Sorry?" I furrowed my brow at him.

"The High Street, lad. What that chappie on TV said. Has the High Street all but disappeared in the future?"

"Sorry, George, I haven't the foggiest idea what you're on about."

"I was saying about that TV show and that economist—"

"George!" barked Jenny, causing both George and me to shift awkwardly in our chairs.

"Alright, lass. Everyone's a bit mardy today. I know the boy's a bit of a pain, but at least that Martin fella could crack a smile."

"Well, in case it's escaped your attention, we only have a few days left to save Jess from some terrible catastrophe! So, forgive me for being a bit tetchy. And as for Martin, you've changed your damn tune!"

George nodded and patted my wife's hand. "Sorry, lass."

Jenny groaned and cupped her chin in both hands, propped up by her elbows. "No, George, I'm sorry. I've got one of those yoghurts in the fridge. You know, the ones with the pieces of mandarins that you like. Or how about a slice of Arctic roll?"

"No, I'd better not. Thanks all the same. Got my figure to think about." George glanced down and rubbed his satisfied belly. "Course, you know the simple answer to protecting Jess whilst we figure out how to find *other* Jason and hunt down that evil Colney bloke, don't you?"

I shot Jenny a look, who reciprocated as we waited for George to look up from where he continued to rub his stomach.

"Martin. That lad has always been a match for that ruffian, Colney. I suggest you stop all your bellyaching at each other and get the lad back here pronto, like."

Jenny and I held each other's stare.

"Darling, where is Martin, or whatever stupid name he goes by these days?"

"Last time we spoke, he was in Spain."

"What's that, lass? Is Martin no longer Martin?"

"He changed his name to appear hip," I threw in, thinking George made a good point.

"Hip?"

"Cool, on-trend, for the want of a better word. In true Martin style, he thought his name, Martin, was a bit grey ... dull, if you like, and didn't help attract the ladies."

"Well, the lad didn't have a problem on that front, if I recall."

"No, I know. He wanted to appear more ... cosmopolitan, appealing to the more discerning European lady, if I can remember what he said. To be honest, I wasn't really listening when he told me. To be fair, though, as he's dead and buried in Fairfield, it was probably a good idea to grab a new identity."

"Oh, well, he always was a bit strange that one. Anyway, I suggest you get hold of the cosmopolitan lad and book him on the next flight."

Although George's suggestion hadn't helped move the issue towards a satisfactory conclusion, Don's old house was currently unoccupied, so we could billet Martin in there. Thus, at the very least, we'd have a bodyguard for Jess.

When we spoke on the phone last week, Martin said he planned to spend the Easter break with a couple of Spanish señoritas. Two ladies he'd recently made acquaintance with at a nudist beach – nothing changed where my loose cannon was concerned. Jenny huddled close as I dialled the number, both of us praying Martin would pick up. Fortunately, he did, and when taking in my quick synopsis of our dilemma, he duly agreed to put the nude resurrection celebrations on ice, hot-foot his way to Alicante Airport, and catch the next flight.

George decamped back to his house just before my two daughters resurfaced from upstairs. Jess ferrying down their empty dinner plates, Beth appearing to carry the weight of the world in her arms.

When Jenny had earlier dished up supper, Jess had suggested she eat hers with Beth upstairs to continue their conversation. A chat, I hoped, involved Jess fitting the final pieces of the jigsaw puzzle that would reveal the picture of the truth to Beth regarding her father's time-travelling capabilities. A tough ask, I mused and suspected Jess had failed by the look of disdain on Beth's face as they entered the kitchen. That said, going by the fact that the dollops of casserole on both plates in Jess's hands appeared largely untouched, my seventeen-year-old's rather sour demeanour could be due to stew and dumplings not being her absolute favourite. Beef casserole for Beth was my liver and onions.

With an overflowing pedal-bin bag in one hand and the other poised to grab the backdoor's handle, I shot Jess a look, who offered a shrugged response. Fair enough. Despite predicting the riots and the death of that police officer, along with George's stack of mementoes in the form of winning betting slips, asking Beth to believe the unbelievable was a stretch.

Jenny made the teas, and the girls settled onto bar stools. There appeared to be a moment of muted reflection looming on the horizon, so I moseyed on out to dump the bag in the dustbin. Although facing catastrophe the likes of which most would never have to contemplate, domestic chores still needed to be completed.

When lifting the bin lid, I mused about the fact that we were still a few years from the wheelie bin becoming commonplace. Although nowhere near as exciting an invention as the C5, those multi-coloured plastic lumps on wheels would revolutionise waste disposal as the ever-increasing amount deemed necessary irrevocably changed the look of suburban front gardens. A point in time that would nudge the poor old garden gnome into history. As I said earlier, our lonely, headless specimen lay forlornly next to his head in the seat of my redundant C5.

Of course, in years gone by, this is the point when I would light up a cigarette. Then, as I puffed away, I would contemplate and cogitate the meaning of life or just think about tomorrow's lessons. The latter would involve praying none involved Band F students, who I'm convinced were all the demented, sadistic offspring or in some way related to Annie Wilkes and Damien Thorn.

Black BMW cars always caught my eye. Of course, today's models are outdated compared to my company car from my first life. When spotting a 3 series, it always reminded me of that not-so-happy life. Well, I died in one – I think?

The German car was becoming increasingly popular and often the brand of choice for Yuppies. So, spotting a black 3 series parked further along the road shouldn't have seemed odd. But it did. For the last week or so, I recall frequently seeing a similar car almost at every turn. As I squinted to read the licence plate, the driver flicked his main beam on before roaring away in the other direction.

"Don't start conjuring up conspiracy theories, Apsley," I muttered, shaking my head at my annoying ability to spot phantoms that weren't there.

As I was now a non-smoker, I stood on the drive and sucked in the night air. I closed my eyes, preparing for round three with Beth. A rematch, which a boxer promoter looking to whip up a bit of pre-fight hysteria, could bill as *'Bitchin' in the Kitchen'*. I accept, not the name of a fight that I could see Ali being involved in. However, I would need to be agile of mind, if not fleet of foot, to stand any chance of fending off my daughter's quit wit.

The unmistakable waft of cigarette smoke hauled me from my star-gazing pose, causing me to ping open my eyes.

The man not ten feet away narrowed his eyes at me as he pulled hard on his cigarette before uttering a single word.

"Jason?"

20

International Man of Mystery

For the preceding twenty-four-hours, none too surprisingly, our focus diverted away from my birthday celebrations to the trickier task of trying to work out how to protect Jess, the possibility of an attempted assassination of Paul Colney, assuming the nefarious bastard was back on the prowl, and discover the whereabouts of *other* Jason.

For the third task on this list, the presence of the man who stood before me suggested we could slap a metaphorical big tick beside it to indicate objective achieved.

Appearing a little dishevelled, clearly cold, going by the visible shivering, and sporting a look of mesmerised wonder, which I probably reciprocated, the man whom I'd pondered about his whereabouts for the past eighteen years now hovered awkwardly at the end of the driveway.

"You're Jason?" he repeated. "Jason Apsley?"

"Err … yeah," I muttered, furrowing my brow when bemused at how my voice appeared to have shot up a few octaves as if some thug had just grabbed hold and squeezed my nether regions.

"Yes," I repeated in a more normal timbre. "You must be Jason Apsley, no middle name." Why I felt the need to confirm that he, like me, had only been afforded one Christian name, I had no idea. However, this was a super unusual situation.

Perhaps I could be forgiven for my nervous spouting of pointless facts. Let's face it, it's not every day you meet another time-traveller who could act as your stunt double from twenty years ago and has been missing in action for a similar length of time.

So, this is how identical twins feel. However, the man who stood before me, eyeing me up and down, probably thinking my middle girth demonstrated a level of contentment, was eighteen years my junior. That said, due to time-travel, he was born forty-three years before me.

Time-travel – what a head fuck.

"You got time for a coffee?" I gestured with my thumb over my shoulder, indicating we should perhaps go inside. No sooner had I uttered those words, I realised how ridiculous and typically British they were. The man presumably had no fixed abode and had just enjoyed an unwanted time-travel whizz from 1976 to 2015, then back to 1994. And here I am, enquiring if he could shuffle his diary around to squeeze in a slot for a coffee and a catch-up.

"Yeah, I think I've got time to squeeze a cuppa in," he chuckled. "I'll drink coffee but prefer tea if you've got it."

"Course, you do," I chortled.

"Is that funny?"

"No … I'll explain. But I can't get over how much your voice sounds like mine. Not how it sounds in my head, of course, but when I've heard my voice on a recording, if you get my drift … if you know what I mean, sort of."

Other Jason snorted a laugh as he crushed his cigarette butt under the sole of his trainer, employing three or four twists of the foot more than was required. He appeared to be playing for time.

"Sorry … I babble when I'm nervous."

"You nervous?"

"Are you?"

"God knows … I've had a hell of a couple of days. I really don't think I've had time to get nervous."

"No, I can imagine."

"Yeah, I reckon you can. Your daughter said the same thing to me twice on the same day. Only, the odd thing, those observations were made twenty-two years apart."

"Jess?"

"No, Beth."

"Beth said she was nervous."

"No, Beth said I sounded like you. First time on the 12th of August 2016, when having a coffee together in my bank, and then a few hours later on the 30th March this year … yesterday, which I'm led to believe is 1994."

"Our birthday."

"Spot on, pal. I would imagine yours was better than mine."

"I wouldn't be so sure," I muttered, before what he'd just said battled its way through the fog of ridiculous information to wallop my brain. "Sorry, did you say you and Beth had a coffee in 2016 … in your bank?" I knitted my brow as I asked the question. Moronic as it sounded, I'm sure he'd just uttered that rather odd line.

Other Jason stepped forward. I stepped back. Not sure why, but I just felt the need to keep an acceptable distance between us in case something untoward happened. Not that I believed he would strike me. However, if we were somehow, sort of, the same person-ish, would standing in close proximity cause some weird time-travel effect like a temporal paradox or something or other? Perhaps sparks would fly, and both of us would vaporise in a puff of smoke? The narrowing of his eyes suggested he found my retreat somewhat oddish behaviour.

"I did … I think. We definitely had coffee in my bank, and I'm led to believe it was 2016." He puffed out his cheeks and shook his head.

I guess the poor chap was still attempting to rationalise and come to terms with time-travel. As I knew, not a straightforward phenomenon to get your head around.

"I must say, you don't seem overly surprised that I claim to have travelled through time?" He paused, jabbing his middle finger at me. "Which, I might point out, apart from being impossible, is also damn right ridiculous."

"After eighteen years of living in yesteryear? No, mate. That's not surprised me one iota."

"Yesteryear for you, not me."

"Fair point. But how come you met Beth in 2016? I take it you mean 2015?"

"Hell, I don't know. I was hoping you might come up with some answers. There I was, nipping out of my flat on my way out into town, and then it's suddenly not 1976 anymore, and I'm in 2016."

"Flat 121 on the Broxworth?"

"Yeah. That's temporary, though. A stop-gap until I move into the house I've purchased over on Homecroft Avenue."

"I know."

"You do?" He furrowed his brow.

"I know because I took your life, remember?"

He nodded and pursed his lips. "So you did."

"Can I just clarify? You said 2016, not 2015?"

"Yes … as I've just told you. 2016."

"Oh. And you just happened to bump into Beth and go for a coffee in your bank, you say?"

I accept a fair chunk of time had passed under the bridge since living in my old life, but I couldn't recall banks offering a coffee service. In that time, they were closing branches, not diversifying into dispensing hot beverages and cakes.

"It's a long and complicated story, pal. But, yes, my bank was no longer a bank. It's turned into a café called Star-something-or-other. Anyway, I'll come back to that. Soon after we left the cafe, I ended up here in 1994. Gotta say, she's a bit of a card that girl, isn't she?"

"Beth?"

"Yeah. Obviously, she was a woman in 2016. A real looker, you might say, but as wacky as that Beryl girl in *The Liver Birds*. Your daughter swears like a trooper. Never heard a woman utter so many obscenities."

My mind drifted to last night and that 'wanker' comment she'd levied at me. "I'm afraid Beth can utter the odd choice phrase from time to time. I take it you said the word 'amazeballs' to her?"

"Yeah," he scoffed, rolling his eyes. "I knew that would happen. Beth, in 2016, was obsessed with the stupid word. When I met younger Beth last night, I inadvertently repeated the word and she picked up on it. I can't say I've ever heard of it before."

"That's how I knew she'd met someone from the future. That word isn't from these times."

"Well, she's got an entire repertoire of bloody odd words in 2016."

"Why am I not surprised," I mumbled. "How was she? Y'know, in 2016."

"Annoying."

I raised an eyebrow. Many words could describe Beth when she was once my best friend, and I could attribute quite a few of those to her now she holds the position of my adopted daughter. Annoying would be in there somewhere for both versions, but not in the top ten. I wondered how time had affected her and if what's happened now would change her in the future.

"I take it you found the letter?"

"The one in your jacket pocket?"

"Yeah?" he nodded, crossing his arms and rubbing his biceps.

"Hell, yeah, I found that alright. Christ, I haven't been able to think of much else since reading it."

"You think it was written by you? Y'know, in 2015?"

"Err … sorry?" I stepped forward, no longer worried about the possibility of time-travel arcing and disappearing in clouds of smoke, bemused that he appeared not to know that my older self had written the letter. A letter which I'd assumed my older self had given him twenty-one years in the future.

"The letter … d'you think your older self wrote it? I mean if he … well, you … shit, this is confusing. What I mean, if what's in that letter is true, we've got a problem—"

"Hang on," I interrupted. "Didn't my older self give you the letter?"

"No … oh, sorry, mate, you were already dead when I landed in 2016."

"Dead! I'm frigging dead?" I detected a quivering tremor in my voice. "Oh, bollocks … you did just say I'm dead, yeah?"

"I'm afraid so, pal. Chris said you died in … ah, when was it—"

"Chris?" I blurted.

"Yeah, your son. Or adopted son, I should say. You adopted Carol Hall's little lad, right?"

I vacantly nodded, my thoughts drifting when contemplating my demise and the fact that this new information had effectively placed me back on death row after being reprieved not twenty-four hours ago. "Chris," I mumbled before shooting him a look when breaking my wool-gathering gaze of the driveway.

"He said you died in July 2016. I don't know the exact date, but we met on the 12th of August 2016, and he said you'd passed a couple of weeks before."

"Oh … bollocks."

"Sorry, mate. I'm only telling you what he said. Hey, if it's any consolation, Beth and Chris really missed you. You must have been a decent sort of bloke and a good father to them because they clearly both loved you very much."

"Did you meet Jenny? Did she give you the letter?"

That question seemed to stump him.

"No, sorry … I'm not sure who she is. Look, I was only in 2016 for an hour or so before—"

"She's my wife. Jenny's my wife."

"Oh, right. Ah, more bad news on that front, mate. I think Beth mentioned something about your wife dying a year or two before you."

"No. No way!" Shocked at hearing his unbelievable claim, I stumbled back a pace whilst rhythmically shaking my head as if that action would somehow expunge his statement. "No, that can't be right. Jenny's only in her bloody late forties now, so she can't have died before me! That's ridiculous—"

Other Jason shrugged. "Hey, I'm just telling you what they said. Don't shoot the messenger," he nonchalantly replied, raising his hand in a placating manner.

Shoving the hideous thought that Jenny wouldn't make her allotted three score years and ten to one side, I pushed him regarding the letter. "Who gave you the letter, then? I take it Beth or Chris must have? Do they know … well, more to the point, does Chris know?"

"Oh, no, sorry. Look, I need to explain. They didn't give me the letter. It was in—"

"Hang on. No, that can't be," I interrupted. "Of course, you didn't meet my older self because that letter states you hadn't shown up by then." I closed my eyes and raised my hand to stop him from attempting to interrupt my thoughts. "*Other* Jason still hasn't materialised," I muttered to myself, remembering the words penned on that page. I opened my eyes when hearing the click of a lighter and the crackle of burning tobacco. "Are you saying that Chris and Beth in 2016 still didn't know about my time-travelling?"

Other Jason nodded as he fired out a stream of smoke through his nostrils. He removed the cigarette from his lips and used it as a pointer as he waved his hand in my direction. "Well, they didn't know until—"

"No. Hang on," I thrust my hand up to interrupt him whilst I tried to get my head around this. Holding that position, I rubbed my chin and vacantly stared into the middle distance. That letter stated that I, in the future, didn't believe my children knew where I'd come from. But Beth must have known. I told her yesterday.

"Time has bent," I muttered, as I bowed my head, trying to slot the various pieces of information into some sort of chronological order.

"Sorry, what? Time's what?"

"Beth and Chris didn't know about time-travel when you met them. They didn't know I'm a time-traveller?"

"Err … Chris did. Then he told Beth."

"Chris?" I pulled a face, confused about how Chris knew and not Beth. In this timeline, it was the other way around.

"Look, as I understand it. You … well, your older self, told Chris you were a time-traveller just before you died. That's how we met in 2016."

"You met me in 2016 before I died? Oh, right, so that letter is dated 2015, but by 2016 we had met?"

"No, mate. I just told you. You were already dead. I met Chris, not you, in 2016—"

"But—"

"Hold up there. Stop interrupting and listen. You died in 2016. Just before you toddled off to meet our maker, you informed Chris about time-travel. Then, following up on your dying request, Chris came searching for me. You apparently were convinced that when you died, I would turn up after what seems to be a period of forty years of flying through time from 1976 when you replaced me."

I opened my mouth to speak but closed it again when he offered a shake of the head, indicating I shouldn't interrupt. I waited as he took another long drag on his cigarette.

Although I'd become one of those over-exaggerated moaning ex-smokers, at this somewhat stressful moment, the redolence from that bluish haze that hung in the evening air was nothing short of sublime.

Other Jason allowed the smoke to drift from his mouth as he continued. "That morning in '76—"

"When you time-travelled?"

"Yes—"

"12th of August 1976, the day I arrived from 2019."

"It appears so. Some spazo in a beaten-up rust-bucket of a Bedford van rear-ended my car, and then his accomplice mugged me … well, it was more of a carjacking if you like—"

"You crashed the Cortina and time-travelled?"

"Bob's your uncle. You've got it in one."

"Who did you get the letter from, then?"

"After you died, Chris moved the Cortina to his garage. Kept it in cold storage as per your dying instructions. After we left that café, Chris showed me the car, just so we could ascertain whether it was the same vehicle, which it was. Oh, whilst I think of it, did you find my cassette tapes?"

"Cassette tapes?"

"D'you always repeat questions?"

I shrugged.

"Bloody annoying. I can see Beth's your daughter. Like father, like daughter. She said she was a daddy's girl."

"Did she?"

"Yeah … look, my stash of cassette tapes. Did you find them? *Wish You Were Here* by Pink Floyd and *Disraeli Gears* by Cream. And a few others."

"No … there was nothing in the car apart from a packet of Marlboro, a few coins and a letter offering you a job as a teacher up at the City School."

"Ah, yes. The job you took."

"I did," I nodded. "But can we get back to the letter? Where did you get it from?"

"Where my cassette tapes should have been. In the glove box."

"In the frigging glove box!"

"Chris and Beth suggested that you'd popped it in there, presumably hoping it would travel through time."

"Really?" I somewhat sarcastically offered.

"I don't know, do I? That's what the three of us came up with to explain why it was in there." He waved an accusing finger at me. "It's you who placed it there."

"Older me."

"Yes. And assuming you hadn't lost your marbles, that letter states that something will happen to Jess in 1994. Which it did."

"Oh, Christ. You know, don't you? Of course, you do. What did happen to Jess?"

"Well, according to Beth and Chris, Jess disappeared without trace on the 6th of April 1994."

"Disappeared! Did you say disappeared?"

"Yes! That's what they said. Have you got hearing problems?"

"No! What d'you mean she disappeared? Where? How?"

Rather than take a drag, he moved the cigarette away from his mouth to answer. "She went to collect her daughter from college—"

"Faith?"

"Correct. Apparently, she never turned up. Jess and her car were never found."

"My God," I muttered.

"That letter you wrote in 2015 suggests, at that point, you'd discovered some information about this other time-traveller who's got something to do with her disappearance. What was it you wrote? A time-traveller returns under a different name and causes her disappearance?"

"Yeah … oh, shit!"

"What."

"The letter I wrote … older me reckoned a time-traveller returns under a pseudonym …" my sentence trailed away as my mind raced. Paul Colney had to be living with a false identity. He was dead, as was his brother, so still calling himself either of those names wouldn't be possible. Obviously, I'd assumed the letter was referring to Paul. However, in that attempt to appear hip and cool, Martin had ditched his name in preference for Tyler Powers in homage to two time-travelling characters, Sam Tyler and Austin Powers. Both of whom were still in the future, so as far as everyone else was

231

concerned, his name was original. When Martin informed me of his name change, I'd said it sounded like a stage name for some ageing porn star. Which, unsurprisingly, he'd liked and probably suited considering the myriad of female liaisons he enjoyed as he systematically shagged his way across the Continent.

Was it possible that older me was warning about Martin, not Paul? Had Martin become a demented serial killer? The effects of time-travel somehow skewing his brain? No, that's ridiculous; serial shagger, maybe, not a serial killer. However, could his return be the catalyst for what's about to happen?

It wasn't lost on me that, not an hour ago, I was the one who begged Martin Aka Tyler Powers to return. In my attempt to protect Jess, had I unwittingly set the wheels in motion, which would lead to her disappearance?

"Why hadn't my older self been more specific?" I mumbled.

Jason again blew a stream of smoke through his nostrils and waved his cigarette at me. "Ah, well, you see … apparently, according to Beth and Chris, by the time you wrote that letter, you'd gone completely gaga."

21

Turkish

"Jason? Darling? Where are … oh," Jenny called out from the back gate. When spotting I appeared to be chatting with a neighbour, she halted her calling and padded up the drive. However, she stopped short at twenty feet away, slapping one hand to her mouth and the other to her chest.

"Don't say anything about death. Mine or hers," I hissed out of the side of my mouth whilst offering Jenny my best it's-going-to-be-okay smile. I suspected, going by how I was feeling, probably radiated as a concerned grimace.

Jenny placed her hands on the side of her face as if to hold it from shaking as she footslogged another ten feet or so along the driveway towards us.

"Oh–my–giddy–aunt."

"Jen … this is—"

"*Other* Jason," she interrupted, now mesmerised by the man, who appeared just how I had that first day Jenny and I met in 1976. The day I opened the door to my flat on the Broxworth Estate to be greeted by her and Frenchie.

"Err … yeah," I nodded, wincing when trying to conjure up something to say. "Jen, this is *other* Jason. Jason, this is

233

Jenny, my wife." I waved my hand back and forth between them as if completing introductions at a dinner party and not presenting a stunt double time-traveller who's been missing for eighteen years.

"After all this time," she whispered, much more to herself than anyone else. Jenny allowed her sentence to drift away, presumably stumped by what else to say. Despite the infinite number of questions which fired around her brain, Jenny held her position as if her fluffy pink slippers were welded to the driveway.

"Jason Apsley, nice to meet you," he grinned, stepping forward and offering a hand to Jenny, who remained mesmerised by what stood before her.

With his hand thrust forward, Jenny holding that 'scream mask' pose, and me continuing to offer that odd grimace, time appeared to freeze. As if the movie director producing the film of my life decided this to be that seminal moment to grab the viewer's attention. No one moved. Similar to most opening scenes in a Guy Richie film, the likes of which I eagerly awaited their release later this decade, this could be the moment the background changes to a plain colour, and our character names flash up with some accompanying cool music. Perhaps *Freeze-frame,* that hit single by The J. Geils Band would be appropriate?

I imagined the names flashing up. *Other Jason*, with a picture of a grinning man, cigarette jauntily clamped between his lips, with his hand thrust out. *Jenny Jessica-Rabbit Apsley*, with long auburn hair, freeze-framed as the gentle breeze caught it whilst she held her hands slapped to her cheeks in mock horror. Me with a stupid grin. As for a name, well, it wouldn't be Turkish. However, in the same way that Jason Statham's character was named after a plane crash that killed his parents, perhaps I could be afforded a similar name. My parents died twice, I might add, along the train track near Finsbury Park. So, maybe I could be *Jason Finsbury Apsley*? As middle names go, it wasn't bad. It stole a march on *Jason Twat Apsley*, as I liked to refer to myself in a previous existence.

"Jenny Apsley," she whispered, her barely audible introduction metaphorically unpausing proceedings.

"You're aware that me and your husband have time-travelled, then?" he asked, retracting his hand when realising my wife was too stunned to peel hers away from her cheeks.

My wife offered the tiniest of nods in reply.

He glanced at me, then back at Jenny. "I take it you haven't, though?"

My wife side-eyed me before offering an almost robotic sideways head movement to confirm she hadn't dabbled.

"Right ... who else knows?" he asked, now addressing me. He took a final drag on his cigarette, lobbed the butt to the path and performed that trainer-shoe twisting movement before glancing up with a raised eyebrow, awaiting my answer. "Is time-travel what people do now? Are there loads of us roaming around?"

Jenny and I exchanged a look, but neither she nor I responded.

"Time-travel. Who else knows about time-travel? Is there some club or association I should join? You know, become a member so I can learn the ropes and get back to 1976."

"Not really, I'm afraid. We have a small group called the Time Travellers Believers' Club, or TTBC for short. But we're not what you would call an association, as such."

"No coach trips to Margate, then? Or an annual dinner and dance with an awards ceremony for the best time-traveller of the year?"

"No."

"No, I suppose not," he scoffed. "So, who else is in your believers' club?"

"My grandfather … well, he's not in this life, but was before. My time-travelling partner, Martin. Your daughter, Jess, and as of last night, Beth, who we're in the throes of trying to convince at the moment."

"Jess?"

"Oh, and of course, Paul Colney," I added as an afterthought, ignoring his question. "He's not in the club but has time-travelled."

"Who's he?"

"He, the bastard, is who I assumed my older self was referring to in that letter written in 2015. Now I'm not so sure."

Jenny shot me a worried look.

"I'll explain in a minute."

"Who's this bloke? You called him a bastard. Is he a problem?"

"Paul Colney. A psychotic megalomaniac with a penchant for rape and murder, amongst other nasty traits such as intimidation, drug running and causing general mayhem. He also just happens to be your half-nephew."

"Half nephew?"

"Absolutely. Shirley Colney, dead, was my adopted daughter's paternal grandmother, who is also your half-sister on your mother's side. That makes Paul Colney your half-nephew. Beth, my adopted daughter, whose father was David Colney, Paul's younger brother, is your great-half-niece."

His jaw sagged; I continued.

"Your mother, Mary, had a daughter out of wedlock. Her older sister, Evelyn, and her husband, William Curtis, your aunt and uncle, who both died in the war, adopted that child. Your mother then married Arthur Apsley, which is when you came along a year later."

Whilst gawking at me as if I had produced a second head, he lit another cigarette, never taking his eyes away from me as he continually puffed to ensure the tobacco caught.

I continued as Jenny stepped close, linking an arm around mine and resting her head on my biceps. "That older half-sibling was Janet Shirley Curtis, who married Paul Colney senior and produced four sons. Evil bastards, all of them. The youngest, Andy, now serving time for rape. David, Beth's father, is now dead following an accident back in '76. He, I believe, just happens to be the reason I time-travelled. Then there's the two eldest boys. Twins. Paul and Patrick. Paul murdered Patrick in 1987 after time-travelling following his death in that Cortina in 1977. That evil bastard, Paul, as far as the rest of humanity is concerned, is dead. However, the members of the TTBC know differently.

Other Jason appeared perplexed. Fair enough, it was a bit of a head spinner. He removed the cigarette from where it had been clamped tightly between his lips. "What the—"

"Your heinous half-sister produced four evil bastards. One of whom, I believe, has time-travelled and is coming for Jess."

"Colney ..." he clicked his fingers. "The Colneys from the Broxworth?"

"Yep."

237

"I'm related to them?"

"Yep." I uttered the 'p' with emphasis, accompanied by a nod.

"Christ. I've met the twins a few times … nasty bastards. And you reckon I'm related to them?" he repeated, probably wishing for a different answer.

"I'm afraid so. Because I'm you … well, I've been you since I arrived in '76, so by association, that sort of makes me related to them as well. Oh, just as a side issue, Patrick Colney is the father of Faith, who is technically your granddaughter. I might need to whizz you through the family tree; it's a pretty complicated affair," I chuckled, which morphed into a whine when clocking his bemused expression.

"Hang on, go back a few pages. You said Jess is in this club? She knows we're time-travellers and that I'm her father, not you?"

Jenny squeezed my biceps, now positioning herself a smidge behind me, causing her to peek around my arm to be part of the conversation.

Although, after last night's events, we needed to find *other* Jason, we feared the impact of discovering him may well affect our relationship with the woman who we regarded as our daughter. That disquiet regarding what might happen jostled for position as our number one concern as we both battled to work out how we would save Jess from whatever fate lay in her path just six days from now.

Jenny's grip tightened, causing me to glance at her. If eyes could speak, they'd scream the terror that oozed from that pained expression. When turning back to face him, I allowed the words, wise counsel, if you like, uttered by George earlier to roll around my head. Jess was our daughter, and biology had

238

nothing to do with who she regarded her father to be. Generally speaking, although harbouring a propensity to turn most statements into an elongated shaggy-dog story, George was usually right about most things. I hoped that statement about how Jess regarded Jenny and me was one such statement.

"So, Shirley Colney … who I think I've met. She's that witch who, along with her neighbour … what's her name?" He clicked his fingers. "Come on, what is it?" he mumbled. "Ah, yes, Susan something. She and her are the two women who sort of control the other women on the estate."

"They did."

"Where are they now, then?"

"Oh, I'm sorry. I thought I said. They're dead. Shirley was killed by Beth's maternal grandmother. Susan, Susan Kane, was murdered by Paul Colney ten years after he died, a couple of days before he battered his brother to death."

"Jesus, I'm lost."

"As I said, I need to take you through the family tree."

"I think you better. You said something about David Colney being the reason you time-travelled."

I whizzed through the life of the future David, as in the serial killer part, and the abuse of Beth when a child in my first life, before clarifying what happened to David in this life. Although I explained how he died, I was economical about the truth regarding my involvement. There was no need to shout from the rooftops that I'd intentionally allowed David to fall to his death, which, if it came to light, I suspected some clever barrister could twist to convince a jury of twelve that I'd committed murder.

After dispatching his cigarette butt in a similar fashion to the previous two, he pursed his lips and nodded.

"You came back to save your daughter."

"Beth was my best friend in my first life, not my daughter."

"She is now, though."

"She most certainly is."

"Well, apart from knowing it's scientifically impossible, not to mention full-on ridiculous, but I believe the reason I've time-travelled is to save mine."

22

American Beauty

My daughters, oblivious to Jenny and my arrival as we stealthily stepped through the back door, continued their conversation. With their backs to us, we hovered on the doormat for a moment, Jenny up on tiptoes as she peeked over my shoulder.

The portable TV, although on low volume, skipped through a plethora of ads for must-haves in this era, none of which would stand the test of time. The Graham Taylor 'Do I not like orange' advert for the Yellow Pages drowned out the noise of the back door's squeaky hinges. As I'd taken the lead, I waited in position to listen in on their conversation and see how far Jess had progressed with convincing Beth to join our rather exclusive club.

The newest member, the man Jenny and I just met, waited as instructed in the garden whilst we laid the groundwork to prepare for introducing him to Jess. Although she'd briefly seen him last night, this would be upping the stakes. Out of the corner of my eye, I spotted him casually lolling on the swing seat, smoking another cigarette.

Although in 1976, smoking was the norm, in fact, you were considered a bit of a strange one if you didn't partake, I mused that if he continued to smoke at the rate to which he'd demonstrated thus far, my double was nailed on to suffer a myriad of cancers before he reached my age.

"What did Dad say about my job in the future? I was some marketing executive, I think you said?" Beth probed Jess as they remained perched on the bar stools at the breakfast bar. Beth hooked her blonde hair around her left ear as she leaned towards Jess.

"Uh-huh, that's what Dad said. You apparently held down some sort of high-flying job and lived a few doors down from here." Jess wagged her finger towards the fridge, which, along with the wall it stood against, was positioned in the general direction Jess indicated to where Beth's house would have been situated further along Winchmore Drive.

"And I didn't have any children, no husband, and was a super-bitch?"

"Oh, well, yes to the first two," she chuckled. "As for being a super-bitch, remember what I told you about you and Dad being close friends? So you can't have been that bad."

Beth shifted closer still, causing the back legs of the stool to tip up. "Dad didn't say him and me … you know?" Beth jauntily nudged her head upwards. "When we were close friends?" With one elbow on the breakfast bar, she raised her hands and performed air quotes around the two words 'close friends' before continuing. "We didn't get it on? We weren't doing it?" Beth sniggered, then grimaced. "I mean far out, but can you imagine me and Dad being lovers in a different life? Gag fest or what!"

"No … he just said you were close. Dad mentioned something about him being the loner and you being the wild kid from the children's home. I remember him saying that because you were both different from the other kids in school, you got on well together."

242

"Dad, a loner?" Beth pulled a face. "I can think of a shitload of words to describe him, but not loner. Knob-head, gullible when I con him for money, lap dog when he panders to Mum. Oh, and he's a total prick when it comes to my mates. Well, the boys, that is."

"Oh, Beth. Come on—"

"Oh, and what about when he drones on about the school and the tossy kids he has to teach?"

"Like you," chuckled Jess.

"Thanks!"

"Oh, Beth, I'm only pulling your chain. Teaching kids is tough, and Dad's brilliant at his job. You know some of the kids he teaches can be difficult, to say the least."

"When I was their age, I had to do as I was damn well told," Beth parodied me in a deep voice, shaking her head from side to side.

"Remember, that's your father you're taking the piss out of. I know I only got to know him when I was pregnant with Faith, but I couldn't wish for a better Dad."

"Oh, yeah, I know. Don't get all mumsy on me. You're supposed to be on my side … we're sisters, you and me. We can't let the Gestapo grind us down."

"Mum and Dad aren't the Gestapo."

"Well, they act like it sometimes. Dad's like that Herr Flick from 'Allo 'Allo! He's always so serious."

"Beth! Come on, that's not fair. Think about what I've just told you about your real father. Now, that man was pure evil, so you should be grateful you have Mum and Dad."

"I know," Beth whined. "I'm just saying, that's all. It was a joke, alright? Course, I love him, but he's my Dad … so I don't love him like that."

"No, I know. But he's always been honest with me. When he said you and him weren't together in a different life, I believe him."

Beth nudged Jess's arm. "Hey, get this. Harriet, you know, that girl who was in my class. The one who collapsed pissed out of her head at the school prom."

Jess shrugged. "Not really, but go on."

"She confided in me and Faith that she calls her dildo, Jason." Beth let a wide cheeky grin emerge whilst Jess impassionedly stared back at her. "Are you going to ask me why?"

Jess tutted and shook her head. "I have a feeling I'm going to regret this … go on, why does Harriet call her dildo Jason?"

"Because she's always fantasised in lessons about boffing Dad." Beth sniggered again. "I mean, what sixteen-year-old fantasises about shagging a mate's dad who's sixty?"

"Don't get any ideas, Mr Apsley," Jenny whispered while playfully poking my ribs.

"Oh, Beth, d'you mind. Don't talk about Dad like that."

"Yeah, whatever, but you reckon he's not your real dad, don't you? Time-travel and all that shite. Hey, you got a dildo? Or is Colin all man enough for you?"

Jess raised an eyebrow.

"Come on, tell all. I've got two, but I don't give them pet names. So? Come on, does Colin keep you satisfied, or do you have a little play in the bathroom when he's got a headache?"

"We might be sisters, but I'm not answering that."

"Oh, God, Mum thought I was mucking around with Dad's electric shaver the other week. She banged on the bathroom door and asked me what I was doing," Beth sniggered. "Don't think Mum's got one, though. I've had a good old rummage through her bedside table a few times but never found anything that takes batteries. Hey, I've heard them, you know. Mum makes this odd squealing sound when—"

I cleared my throat, causing both daughters to swivel around. Jess offered a tight smile; Beth's jaw sagged.

"Oh, shit!"

"Quite," I announced, stepping in and leaning up against the sink whilst Jenny pushed the back door to a close, leaving it slightly ajar.

"Mum, I … I wasn't going to … I didn't mean anything."

Jenny stepped towards Beth, who leaned back against the breakfast bar, sporting a face of terror that wouldn't look out of place on any guest of the *Overlook Hotel*. Jenny never laid a finger on either of the children. However, when it came to discipline, that's where my wife verbally excelled.

"Mum?" Beth's rising inflexion and audible quiver as Jenny advanced suggested my daughter had misplaced all the bolshie attitude she'd displayed over the last twenty-four hours.

Jenny wrapped her arms around Beth and pulled her close, planting that trademark elongated kiss on her crown.

From her position, when nestled into my wife's bosom, Beth swivelled a questioning eye in my direction.

I offered an impassive non-verbal response before turning my attention to Jess. "Where have we got to with Beth? Have you managed to convince her?"

Jess puffed out her cheeks. "She's putting on a brave face … but, yeah, I think we're just about there."

"She believes in time-travel?"

Jess shot a look at Beth's squashed face as Jenny hugged her close.

"I think so. I've talked through everything. Taken her through the exercise books, you know the drill."

I offered a nod in reply. "Okay. So, we need to pull a plan together about you and what we need to do to stop what may happen."

Jenny stepped back a pace and cupped Beth's cheeks as our bemused daughter searched Jenny's eyes for answers.

"Where's my bollocking? Why aren't you angry with me? Shouldn't you be interrogating me, chastising me for what I said? At the very least, apply thumb screws."

"Sometimes, sweetheart, there are situations where there are more important things to worry about. This is one such situation." Jenny reached over and gently laid her hand on Jess's arm. Leaving Beth to continue flicking her eyes back and forth across her mother's face as she presumably tried to work out why she hadn't landed in a steaming heap of shite for comments about listening in on my wife's and my bedroom antics.

That's leaving to one side the discussion regarding dildos and Harriet. Not that this often happened, but I knew Beth's friend may have harboured unhealthy desires regarding me. About a year ago, she'd stayed behind when the bell sounded to ask me a question, closing her eyes as she did. When spotting the 'Love You' message penned on her eyelids, I stumbled through my words similar to Professor Indiana Jones. For sure, learning that she'd named her sex toy after me was somewhat odd. Something I thought was reserved for George's elusive broad-bean-ravaging bunny.

"Jess, you seem very calm about it all." Jenny raised a questioning eyebrow whilst rubbing her arm.

"I know we'll figure it out." Jess shot me a look and then back at Jenny. "You and Dad won't let anything happen to me."

"We won't," I chimed in.

"I don't know if it's time to tell Colin."

"Time-travel?" Jenny enquired.

Jess nodded, chewing her lip. Her oscillating glances between us were now on a two-second timer whilst we both contemplated that suggestion. A suggestion that Jenny had muted earlier over our evening meal. Of course, Jess wasn't aware of what was lurking in the garden, which would throw a whole sack of spanners into the works.

"Jess, I don't think so, not at the moment. Look, I've called Martin, and he's agreed to return from Spain. He's going to catch the first flight in the morning. The new tenant I have lined up isn't moving into Don's old house until after Easter. That gives us a week or so to come up with a better plan. Now, with Martin next door to you, that will offer some protection in the short term." I paused as I considered the possibility that older me was referring to Martin and not Paul when he mentioned a returning time-traveller. If that were to be the case, I'd be placing the fox in the henhouse.

"What about Colin?"

"Martin knows he'll have to pretend to be Leonardo, for Colin's sake."

"Who's Leonardo?" quizzed Beth.

247

"Sweetheart, you remember what we discussed yesterday? Leonardo, that man who stayed with us when you were ten. The man who is actually Martin … the other man who time-travelled with your father."

Although a little teary, Beth seemed to be just about holding it all together. "This is mega weird."

Jenny planted another crown kiss on Beth's head as our daughter pulled her mother close.

"Okay, so as I was saying, Martin will be here tomorrow. If anyone's capable of dealing with Paul Colney, it's Martin. There's a slight concern, though." I winced, trying to work out how to phrase the next line.

"Dad?" Jess blurted, presumably detecting my reticence to continue.

"So … what if older me was referring to Martin in that letter and not Paul Colney?"

"Martin, a killer? No," Jess attempted to chuckle but stopped herself as she considered that thought.

"No, I agree, but older me wasn't clear in the letter."

"I can't see that. You … older you, that is, must have been referring to Paul. Come on, we know Paul was alive again in 1987. It must be him. You and I saw him in Don's house. Seven years on, he's probably still out there, somewhere." Jess shivered, an involuntary reaction when thinking about Hertfordshire's most wanted ghost.

"Yeah, I know. It was just something that crossed my mind."

"Why d'you think older you was so vague? I mean, why didn't he … you, just spell it out?"

"Ah, well, there's a possibility that older me was not all there when I wrote the letter. I could have been deluded … a bit gaga."

Jenny furrowed her brow as she non-verbally questioned that statement.

I shrugged and widened my arms at her. "He said that Beth and Chris mentioned I might not have been in control of all my faculties."

"When… when did he say that?"

"When we were chatting, just before you came out."

Jess started that oscillating head routine again, gawking between Jenny and me. However, this time, she'd set the timer on a higher speed as her alternating head twists appeared to be on a half-second speed setting. After at least ten sideways rotations, she halted when looking at me.

"Who said? Who's he?"

Jenny nodded as I shot her a look.

"Jess—"

"Err … hang on," interrupted Beth. "When did Chris and I say you've gone gaga?"

"2016."

"What?" Beth's jaw sagged.

"The man who gave you a lift last night said he met you in 2016. That's when he got hold of the letter I wrote in 2015. A point at which apparently you and Chris reckoned I'd lost it."

"You've lost me," Beth muttered.

"And me."

"Me too. Darling, what are you on about?"

"Okay. As I understand it. *Other* Jason landed in 2016. He met Beth and Chris—"

"I thought we'd established he met you?" quizzed Jenny as she slowly uncoupled from Beth and stepped towards me.

I nervously hopped from one foot to the other, realising I would probably have to announce that I knew, to within a few weeks, when I would die.

"Darling?"

"Look, let me finish." I held my palms up. "He met Beth and Chris, got hold of the letter and travelled to 1994. As I said, older Beth and Chris reckoned I wasn't all there in 2015 and may have been imagining things when I penned that letter."

"So, I'm not in danger ... or maybe not?"

"No, you are. Beth and Chris, from 2016, say you disappear in 1994."

"Disappear?" Jess blurted.

"Darling," Jenny reached out and grabbed my hand. "He got the letter from Beth and Chris because you ..." her voice trailed away as if caught by a sudden breeze that whisked her words into the ether.

The look in her eyes suggested the penny had dropped. She vice-like gripped my hand as I replied with a nod.

"Err ... hello. Is someone going to tell me what the frig's going on?"

"You've found him, haven't you?" Jess muttered.

"Who?"

"Me ... sorry, I was earwigging at the door. It's a bit chilly out there. Mind if I come in?"

"You!" exclaimed Beth, sliding off her stool and scrambling backwards, coming to a halt as she collided with the fridge.

"Hello, Jessica. We briefly met last night. I'm your father."

23

The Twilight Zone

"Jesus, fuckerdefuck, fuck, fuck. This is fucking well weird. I mean, what the fuck? Fucking hell, what the fuck's going on?"

"I must say your daughter has an interesting vocabulary, Jason. When I met her thirty-nine-year-old version yesterday, she possessed a similar diction to now."

"Sorry, Mum, but fuck me!"

"Beth—"

"I know I just threw in about ten fucks," Beth interrupted her mother. "And I'll happily be grounded for at least five years for that, but fucking hell, this is seriously fucked up."

"Sweetheart—"

"Oh, fuck it. Why not go all out and make it ten fucking years? Someone tell me what the fuck is going on here. Living in this fucking nut house is like being in the fucking twilight zone. Dodo, do do, Dodo, do do," she sang, animatedly waving her hands.

I presumed my daughter was referring to the '80s film reworking of the '60s classic series due to being too young, as I should be, to remember the originals. Whilst picturing the presenter in that sharp suit smoking a cigarette, I considered

252

that Rod Serling could have easily written and narrated my life. The events of the past half hour, let alone the preceding eighteen years, would have made a good subject for one of those half-hour episodes.

Beth's string of expletives appeared to slap a bit of a dampener on the conversation. Well, to be fair to Beth, this was somewhat odd. Here we were, *other* Jason and me, with Jess, his daughter, who was also mine, whilst Jenny wrestled with the knowledge that she and I knew roughly the date when I'd kick the bucket, so to speak. To add to the mix, we had Beth, who appeared super-glued to the fridge, her splayed-out arms reminding me of that Solvite wallpaper paste advert, attempting to get her head around the fact that the man who'd given her a lift home last night she previously encountered twenty-two years in the future. Also, to add to this mess, Jess, after thirty-eight years, had finally come face to face and was now conversing with the man who walked out on her and her mother. Fair to say, not your average exchange of words, which took place on a Maundy Thursday evening in suburban kitchens up and down the country.

"Jessica?"

"No." Jess barked at the cuckoo who'd flown in. "My name is Jess. And just so you're abundantly clear, you're not my father." She shot her arm in my direction, jabbing a finger at me. "This is my father. He will always be my father, so don't get any ideas about worming your way into my life." Jess held her arm aloft whilst her piercing eyes bore laser-styled holes through *other* Jason.

If looks could kill.

My mind and I performed a fist bump. 'Get in there', that voice in my head joyfully announced whilst I suppressed a grin. It appeared my daughter had made it clear regarding who she

253

considered to have won the race to be her one true father. Also, I mused that George, as always, had predicted correctly. My old friend's ability to prognosticate the likely outcome was due to his wisdom. However, you could be forgiven for thinking *he* was the time-traveller when voicing his unwavering belief regarding how events would pan out.

Jess took a breath and continued. "And another thing. That woman who gave birth to me is also not part of my life, in case you're thinking of hooking back up with her and playing happy families."

I considered that unlikely based on the fact that her mother was a lady in her sixties, and due to time-travel, *other* Jason was still only forty-two. But hey, who am I to judge? I believe the Hungarian-American socialite Zsa Zsa Gabor enjoyed the attention of a few significantly younger husbands. That said, I'd met Jess's mother at her wedding. Although I spent the whole day trying to avoid her because she thought I was the man she hooked up with in the '50s, I don't recall her benefiting from a similar stunning bone structure as the pulchritudinous actress. Jess's angry, barking tones hauled me from my reverie.

"So, let me be clear. This man is my father. And this woman, as far as I'm concerned, is my mother. Got it?"

"Jess, I'm sorry for not being there for you—"

"Discarding me like chip paper, you mean?"

"You're right. I'm so sorry. I wasn't ready to be a father."

"Too late! You weren't ready then, and you're too pissing late now."

"Tea, anyone?" I asked, waving the kettle in the air.

"White, two sugars." Announced *other* Jason whilst holding Jess's death stare.

"My usual, please. Being my proper father, I don't need to stipulate how I like it, do I?" Jess barked, keeping her eyes glued to the man who'd sent Beth off on one.

"Beth?" I quizzed, shooting her a look as she attempted to melt into the fridge door.

"Tea! You're offering cups of tea like we're at the fucking village fête, and the bleeding vicar's just rocked up holding a tray of fondant fucking fancies. Has anyone realised what paranormal fucking nut shit crap is going on here?"

Jenny shot me a look. I knew it wasn't regarding our seventeen-year-old's continuing attempts to send the air a deep shade of blue.

"Jen, we still have at least twenty-one years together. That's pretty good," I whispered.

"But …" she paused.

I could see the pain in her eyes as they watered. Of course, *other* Jason had stated that Jenny would die before me, but that was not information to divulge at this point in proceedings. No, that titbit of unpalatable news needed to stay on the back burner or perhaps shoved deep inside a steel furnace. I just prayed time would bend again. If we saved Jess, would that ripple effect mean Jenny would outlive me? As always, in my somewhat bizarre life, a plethora of ifs, buts, and who the fuck knows whats, to coin a phrase that my daughter seemed intent on trotting out each time she opened her mouth, clouded the possibilities that lay ahead.

"Err … hello. Is someone going to explain what the fuck is going on?"

Jess blinked first, turning on her sister. "Beth, for pity sake, shove a sock in it! Sit down, shut up, and behave for once. Not to put too fine a point on it, but you're getting on my *fucking* tits."

All four of us, including the cuckoo, shot a look at Jess. For sure, never had I heard her speak like that to Beth. I guess Beth's constant hollering had stripped away Jess's steel-like persona she'd applied since hearing about the threats to her life. It appeared our potty-mouthed daughter was the unfortunate recipient of Jess's backlash.

Beth, sporting a gaping mouth, settled back onto her stool before bowing her head to pick at her nail polish. "Sorry," she whispered.

"Tea? Beth … tea?"

She nodded. "Sorry. Am I grounded … y'know, forever, like?"

Whilst clinging to my arm, Jenny nodded. "Until you're at least thirty."

Beth pursed her lips and nodded before returning to the task in hand. Namely, nail polish picking. "Not too bad then," she mumbled.

"O–kay," I announced whilst clapping my hands, schoolteacher style, to grab everyone's attention.

Apart from Jenny, they all complied. My wife – being the most accomplished tea maker north of the river, according to George that is, and, as we are discovering, George is always right – took over as chief tea maker whilst I prepared to set out the agenda for the next half hour.

"Jason, I think the best way forward is for you to give a quick recap for the benefit of all present and run-through of what's happened since you time-travelled. Perhaps keeping to the more salient points so as not to raise too many unnecessary questions." I surreptitiously nodded towards Jenny, who had her back turned while busying herself with hot beverage refreshment preparation.

Fortunately, his nod suggested he'd picked up on my point that I harboured no desire for my wife to learn about her premature demise. However, I knew the fact that I was dead when he time-travelled would inevitably come to light.

With teas in hand, we listened as the cuckoo relayed his story. When he reached the point in the story when Chris had apparently come looking for him after my older self had requested he do so when on my deathbed in 2016, Jess picked up on the fact that I must have passed.

"Dad?" she shot at me, interrupting the cuckoo's flow.

"It's okay. I would have been in my eighties by then. That's not a bad innings, is it?" It wasn't okay, but what else could I say? Unless time was prepared to bend, I was again on death row.

"I'm lost. What you on about?" Beth mumbled before offering a perfect emoji-styled frown when taking a break from pinging flakes of baby-pink nail varnish across the floor.

Jenny scooted around the breakfast bar. Expertly swerving between the cuckoo and me, she displayed the dexterity of an F1 driver negotiating the tricky chicanes on the Monaco circuit before grabbing hold of Beth in her trademark mothering-style cuddle.

"Mum?"

Jenny sucked in a lungful before puffing out her cheeks. "*Other* Jason, this man, who your father replaced in '76, could only re-materialise when your dad ... when your father dies."

Beth peered up at her mother before shooting a look at me. I bowed my head, not wishing to witness what I knew was coming. Although high-spirited, what some might label in the future as ADHD, Beth was an intelligent girl. Her concordat comment of the previous evening exemplifies her bright mind. Despite the fact we were holding a ridiculous conversation, she cottoned on to what Jenny was saying. Her chin wobbled a nanosecond before an avalanche of tears poured.

"Dad," hissed Jess, encouraging me to look up. Wiser and more worldly than Beth, she didn't blub but searched my eyes, hunting down the pain that beheld there, similar to what I recognised in hers.

Breaking eye contact, I glanced at *other* Jason, who appeared lost in this environment of three distressed women.

"You'd better continue."

As his education and degree-level qualifications suggested, he was an intelligent man. However, apparent differences between us were emerging. Like I'd been in my previous life, dealing with sensitive situations and knowing how to empathise with a fellow distressed human being appeared well outside his comfort zone. After awkwardly shuffling his feet and clearing his throat, two or three times more than necessary, unless he was suffering from an acute bout of consumption, he continued where he left off, describing the conversation he'd enjoyed with my grown-up children in 2016.

However, when we reached the point in his recounting of events regarding the discussion in the bank, which would morph into a branch of Starbucks in the future, that opened up the debate once again.

Of course, there were questions about what Starbucks was. Due to me being the only one in the room who'd ever ordered a Frappuccino with whipped cream and caramel sauce, it was down to yours truly to enlighten them all regarding the twenty-first-century phenomenon of High Street coffee chains. Those coffee shops that gobbled up every other retail unit and interspersed with a liberal sprinkling of charity shops. George's favoured butchers, that apparently produced a tasty bit of brisket slapped and wrapped in greaseproof paper by a jolly butcher, was, like me – on death row.

This was all reasonably easy to do, explaining that Starbucks was like one of the few Costa Coffee shops we'd visited in London a year ago. I thought it prudent to clarify these new coffee houses were a far cry from the café just off the High Street. Joe's Café, with its Formica tables and cigarette-stained net curtains, still offered instant coffee in chipped-white mugs served up by Joe and his wife, both of whom usually sported a rollie sticking out the side of their mouth and an off-white gingham tea towel slung over their shoulder.

Beth, still clutching her mother but now having control of her chin wobble, said my description sounded like the *Double R Diner* in *Twin Peaks*. Although I'd not watched the TV show in this life, I could just about recall it from my first. However, when I suggested it was more like Central Park's Coffee House in *Friends,* that received blank stares. Clearly, that hadn't hit our shores yet. I suggested Beth keep an eye out for it. I felt sure my daughter could resonate with Phoebe because of the similarity regarding offbeat and often ditzy behaviour.

However, moving away from American TV shows, we'd reached the point I feared would come. The reason *other* Jason was hell-bent on getting to his bank after landing in 2016 and the tricky subject of a bag of sparkly stones.

Midland Bank, where I'd discovered his safety deposit box in 1976, now traded as HSBC. It no longer offered a safety deposit box service. Also, I'd diversified that bag of solid-cut carbon into other financial holdings. The trouble is, those stones were never technically my property, a point that he made with an accusing finger.

"By my reckoning. And based on how much a packet of cigarettes has increased in price, you owe me about a quarter of a million quid."

24

Stand and Deliver

All eyes focused on me. Beth, again in a state of mesmerised wonder. Jess, wide-eyed with two raised thick pencilled-in eyebrows. Jenny, sporting an exaggerated grimace, which suggested her mind was screaming 'oh bugger'.

"Fuuuck," Beth whispered. "A quarter of a mill? Are we, like, super rich?"

"I'd take a cheque, but as the clerk in the bank repeatedly informed me this morning that I no longer hold an account there, that won't do. So, it better be cash."

"Ah." I shot Jenny a look, who shrugged a 'don't-ask-me' response.

"Okay, the diamonds were yours, not mine—"

"Damn right, they are, pal. So, if you can see your way clear to handing over a briefcase full of cash, I can start a new life when we've made sure Jess is not in danger. That's assuming you don't know how I can get back to 1976, that is?"

"Sorry, mate. No can do. Time-travel isn't what you call an exact science. That Cortina …" I paused when recalling the man skedaddling over the chain-link fence earlier that evening. "Oh, it was you. It was you up at my lock-up?"

"Ah ... so it was you in that motor that pulled up and blinded me with the main beam?"

"It was. You were putting the car back, I take it?"

"Yeah," he nodded. "I wasn't sure about the effect of me driving around in that thing. While I work out what's going on, I thought the safest thing to do was to pop it back in your lock-up."

"How did you know where ... ah, Beth and Chris in 2016?"

Other Jason glanced at Beth, who bowed her head.

"Beth, sweetheart?" Jenny probed our daughter, who'd restarted that nail-picking routine.

"It's not the girl's fault. I quizzed her last night after Beth and Chris let slip in 2016 that you used to keep it stored in a lock-up. When I met this younger Beth later that evening, I made out I knew the location of the lock-up. Which Beth here confirmed, along with Jess's address." He glanced at Jess. "I came to warn you." Due to Jess offering an impassive response, he turned back to me. "Course, I had to force entry into four other garages before I found yours."

"How did you know you'd got the right one?"

"There was a heap of service documents on the workbench with my name on them."

"Right."

"So, the cash, then. And on the subject that you owe me, I need a place to kip."

"Don's," piped up Jenny.

"Good idea. He can bunk up with Martin."

"What about Colin? He's gonna do a double take when he sees him!" fired out Jess, wagging that none-too-friendly digit at her biological father.

"Hmmm, yeah … could be tricky." I grimaced whilst rubbing my chin, contemplating that, as time moved forward, handing out an application form to Colin to join the TTBC would become inevitable. "I don't see any other solution, though. Colin's at work most of—"

"Who's Martin?" *Other* Jason interrupted. "You mentioned his name earlier."

I rattled through a quick précis of Martin's life from before time-travelling, through to why he was returning to Fairfield from sunnier climes, followed by an explanation regarding the details around Don's house. I omitted informing him about Martin's new name and my concern that he could be the reason Jess's life may be in danger. Of course, silently praying that Martin hadn't turned into some time-travelling murdering schizoid like a certain Mr Colney. Also, for the purpose of this conversation, I refrained from divulging any information regarding his penchant for entertaining the ladies.

Although Martin's impromptu return was expected to be on a temporary basis, before whizzing back to lie in the sun with his naked señoritas, it crossed my mind that I would need to impress upon him the need to focus on Jess's wellbeing rather than talent spotting in the local area. A tough ask for my thirty-eight-year-old gigolo, time-travelling companion, I mused.

You see, time-travel is super complicated. Although physically, and due to time-travelling twice, Martin was thirty-eight, he should be forty-eight. Or, maybe, only six. If he had time-travelled just the once, he would be forty-eight, perhaps not so virile and sporting a touch of middle-age spread, which would dampen his desire to wave his manhood around on an Iberian nudist beach. If he hadn't time-travelled at all, Martin would just be a little lad of six now, in short trousers. Even for

Martin, I suspect that age would not promote carnality to the level he now demonstrates. Still with me? No, I guess not — as I always say, time-travel is a head fuck.

Because of *other* Jason experiencing time-travel, the synopsis of my loose-cannon's life story was reasonably believable and easy to swallow.

"Okay, and you say this chap, Martin, will be here tomorrow?"

"Yes, he's flying into Luton Airport in the morning."

"And the cash you owe me?" *Other* Jason paused with his mug at his lips. "When will I see the cash?"

"Dad, have you really got a quarter of a mil of diamonds?"

I held out my palm, traffic-cop style, to halt Beth's enquiries into my financial status. "Can I come back to that?"

"Yeah, but—"

"Beth, not now—"

"But can I have a couple of diamonds for earrings?" She demonstrated the size with her thumb and forefinger, the gap between her digits, which she squinted through at least the size of a penny. "Mel's parents bought her a pair last year, and I've always wanted some. Don't need to be mega, you know, like something Boy George would wear, but real diamond earrings would be sick."

"Who's this George boy?"

"Don't ask." I shook my head, shutting down that avenue of the conversation with a dismissive wave of my hand. This wasn't the time to explain to a man who'd missed the last eighteen years the finer points of the *New Romantic* movement of the past decade, including the flamboyant, eccentric fashion. Going by the fact he missed his *Pink Floyd* and *Cream* cassette tapes, I somehow imagined he'd share a similar view of George about men wearing makeup. You should have heard George go off on one when Adam Ant hit the TV screens a decade ago when sporting that white stripe across his face and eye shadow.

"Dad, can I?" Beth tipped her head to one side and shot me that doe-eyed look. A tactic that, nine times out of ten, was a tried and tested method she employed to successfully persuade me to open my wallet. "The earrings?" she whined.

"Beth … can we just hold that thought for a moment?" I winced, wishing not to be dragged off on this particular tangent.

"And what d'you mean by sick?" other Jason curled his lip. "How could owning a pair of diamond earrings be described as sick?"

"It means wicked, cool. Jesus, even Mum and Dad know what that means," Beth scoffed before muttering an acerbic 'dinosaur' comment to finish off.

"Oh … one of your words, then?"

"Do what?"

"When we met in 2016, you had … how shall I put it? A way with words. Clusterfuck, fucktangle, fuckerdedoda, along with amazeballs."

"You said amazeballs yesterday … when you gave me a lift home. I'd never heard it before."

"That's because I sarcastically said it after listening to you constantly repeating the stupid word along with shamazing and all those ridiculous fuck words in 2016."

"Ehm … can we get back to what's important? I think you need to tell us what else Beth and Chris told you in the future, other than a string of unnecessary expletives. We need to know everything that happened to Jess in their time," Jenny cut in to sideswipe the conversation.

Other Jason pursed his lips, glanced at Jess and nodded. "Sure. We need to stop what's going to happen. I agree. After that, we talk finances," he raised an eyebrow at me, which I confirmed with a nod.

Although I'd built a nice little nest egg over the years, with healthy accounts for Chris, Beth, and Faith's futures, a portfolio for each growing steadily, laying my hands on a quarter of a million quid would be tricky. The obvious short-term answer would be to scale up my betting to a more industrial level. That would involve employing a strategy that George and I would need to pull together to enable me to amass the required cash to pay the man without courting unnecessary attention to my lucky streak Biff Tannen style.

Sticking that thought on the back burner, I focused on his story regarding Jess and his earlier point when standing on the drive regarding *my* daughter's disappearance next Wednesday. A day that was now racing towards us at warp factor ten, to quote Mr Chekov.

Although Beth hadn't successfully persuaded me to cough up for diamond earrings, she and the rest of us listened as Jason described how Beth of the future informed him about Jess disappearing on the 6th of April when driving across town to collect Faith from college.

"Hang on, let me get this straight. Beth, as in Beth in the future, said I left home to pick up Faith and just disappeared when driving out into the country?"

Other Jason shrugged. "Yeah. You were never found, apparently. She said something about a spiderweb thingy they set up … not sure I understood that bit, but something like a missing persons' database."

"Why was I driving into the country? Faith's college is in town?"

"No idea." He shrugged again, widening his palms as he continued. "I'm afraid your guess is as good as mine."

"And how come you ended up here, then? Y'know, in 1994?"

"Ah, well, we're back to that Cortina. See, I thought I'd take it as the car was technically mine. Course, Beth and Chris were somewhat distressed when I wheel spun out of the drive before accidentally reversing into a dustbin lorry."

"You crashed the Cortina, which pinged you through time to now?" I asked, before supping the dregs of my coffee.

"As batty as that all sounds, that's correct."

"How come you were in Lovers' Lane, then? You said you took a wrong turn when I asked you last night." Beth threw at him with an aporetic lilt to her question.

"You're right, I didn't. When I came to, I was just there." He raised his hands, suggesting the ridiculousness of that statement. "Chris's house, nice gaff, by the way, was built on the old Belton's electronics factory site. I can only assume where I crashed into that dustcart is the same place I woke up in twenty-two years in the past. Well, the past from where I'd been, but still the future for me, if you get my drift."

Jenny, Beth, and I focused on Jess, unable to find the appropriate words to fit the moment. The obvious answer was to persuade someone else to collect Faith next Wednesday. If Jess stayed at home, surely, she would be safe. However, I guess it wouldn't be that simple. If Colney had returned, then he'd just strike on another day. If the reason was something to

267

do with Martin's return, whatever that be, either a twist of fate or he'd taken murder as a hobby, then again, time would just repeat the event on another day. Either way, preventing Jess from driving next Wednesday wouldn't solve the issue.

Beth was the first to break the silence when looking up at *other* Jason. "This version of me you met … you say I was thirty-nine, then? Frigging ancient," she scoffed. "So, come on, what was I like?"

Other Jason seemed to ponder that thought momentarily before nodding to himself when conjuring up the appropriate phrase.

"Bloody annoying."

Beth blew a raspberry. "Thanks!"

"Also, stunningly beautiful, slim, a Hollywood-leading-lady look about you. Annoying, as I just said, married to a lawyer called Phil, who I could tell you love, along with your delicate, and by the sounds of it, slightly introverted ten-year-old son, Oliver."

Uncharacteristically, Beth didn't offer an instant reply. Instead, she just gawped at him with a faint hint of a Charlie-Bucket-finding-the-golden-Wonka-ticket-styled surprised smile before uttering good-old Scooby's favourite line. No, not *Ruh-roh*, when declining Fred Jones's suggestion that they should hunt ghosts, but—

"Yikes!"

"Darling, we're going to be grandparents again. In 2005, we'll have another grandchild." Jenny's glee was short-lived when remembering I would only know Oliver until he was nine or ten.

More worryingly, unless I could bend time, Jenny would only know her grandson until he was perhaps aged eight.

268

"Oh, Chris has a son, too. Can't remember what he said his name was, but he's at university. Chris is married to Megan if I remember correctly. To be honest with you, the last few days have been a bit of a blur."

"Did you meet Phil? My future husband. Is he tall? I hate short arses. He'd better be tall. Oh, God, he wasn't bald, was he? Please tell me he's got hair … dark, preferably. Presumably, we're rich, though? I mean … if he's a lawyer. And what about me—"

"No." he interrupted Beth's machine-gun flow of questions. "I didn't meet him. Just the way you … well, your older self, that is, talked about him, suggested that you were close."

Beth raised her hand, her mind appearing to whir at ten to the dozen as she swivelled around on the barstool to shift her attention to me.

"Err … Dad, I thought you said I was an unmarried, super-bitch marketing executive? How come I'm now a Hollywood actress married to Phil, the lawyer, with a son called Oliver?"

"I said you looked like one, not actually one. You had a Britt Ekland look about you. Tight jeans … you were wearing impossibly tight jeans."

Jenny curled her lip at him, that motherly disapproving expression that might be offered to some lech ogling her daughter.

"I don't think your comments about Beth's appearance are totally necessary."

He held his hands surrender-style to his chest. "Sorry, I meant nothing by it. It was just hard to get my head around the fashion. I had a chat with a lad on the street wearing a jacket which looked like it was made out of a shiny sleeping bag, would you believe? Not that I understood a ruddy word he said."

"Puffer Jacket," I chimed in.

Beth and Jess shot me a look.

"They were called puffer jackets in my day."

Jess and Beth raised an eyebrow at me whilst *other* Jason continued.

"He kept saying bounce and bro and telling me he ain't got no food, as he put it. You know, I met some right weirdos. This woman, who now lives in my flat, was covered almost head to toe in tattoos and had that many metal piercings I thought she'd come off second best in a wrestling bout with a rivet gun."

Intrigued by his description of the future, Beth pushed me for answers. "Well, Dad? What about what you said about me in the future?"

Before I could answer, *other* Jason cut in. "Alternate timelines. Timeline curves if you like. This would have sent my debating society at university into a frenzy," he chuckled.

"What you on about?"

"Time-travel changes the future. Well, scientifically, it's not possible. That's what I believed until a couple of days ago. Actions that we take now change the future."

"Get to the point," Beth barked.

My daughter had been blessed with many qualities. Stunning good looks were one. And considering her natural parents being David Colney and Carol Hall, I struggled to compute how their mix of genes could produce Beth. And not being too uncharitable about it, but you'd expect their female offspring to be any horror movie casting director's ecstasy.

Anyway, one quality that she wasn't blessed with was patience. In fact, you could say that Beth possessed similar forbearance to that of a line of passengers boarding an EasyJet flight when the announcer stated the gate had opened.

"Look, when your father time-travelled from 2019 to 1976, his future was wiped … a clean slate, if you like. Actions he took changed his future and those around him. In his first life, he didn't marry this lovely woman," Jenny bristled at the compliment. "Also, he didn't adopt you. Therefore, the woman you were in 2019 when he time-travelled is not the woman you will be in the future."

"Oh … will I still marry Phil?"

"Who knows?"

"Oh." Beth pushed out her bottom lip, appearing a smidge deflated at hearing this news.

"So … does that mean that what older Dad wrote in 2015 is not going to happen?" Jess quizzed. "Presumably, we're worrying about nothing."

The four of us pondered her statement as I reached to the windowsill and grabbed the letter. When tapping the held-out sheet of paper, I caught their attention.

"I've written that time has repeated. That news item on the radio when I drove to work was about a serial killer and the police appealing for information regarding the whereabouts of David Colney. As I've quite rightly written, time doesn't bend easily and tries to pull back to the laid down path that history demands." I glanced up from the page. It appeared I still held their attention, apart from Beth, who seemed to have dropped into some sort of catatonic state.

"Time is pulling back to reinstate the future. David Colney is dead. I know because I … well, I just know." I could detect my cheeks flush, although thankfully, I'd just stopped myself from admitting to murder. Something Jenny knew, but my daughters didn't. Relieved neither picked up on my near-miss faux pas, I continued. "However, there's still a serial killer at large. Now, in 1994, and presumably in 2015, when I wrote this letter." I glanced at Jess. "Although I agree that *other* Jason time-travelling may have now changed the future, we can't ignore the warning I sent from the grave."

"Fuckerdefuck," Beth mumbled, then shot me a look. "Dad, did you say that in the future, my real father was a frigging serial killer?"

25

Three White Rabbits

"Would you stop your incessant whingeing? You're like my Uncle Seamus, that you are," he delivered in a somewhat dodgy Irish accent, which sounded more Sean Connery than Frank Carson.

"I didn't know you had family in Ireland."

"I don't. Just hang on a moment. She'll be here any minute now," he fired out in his usual lilt.

"I'm not whingeing, as you put it. I'm just saying, time is of the essence."

"Don't get all schoolteacher with me, Apsley."

"Christ, come on," I huffed, checking my watch … again.

"Just give me a minute, alright. Jesus, you don't half whinge. Remember, I'm doing you a favour here."

"Five minutes. No more. Then I'll drag you out of here if I have to."

"Looking at the paunch you've developed …" he paused, patted my tummy, and smirked. "I reckon you couldn't drag on a fag, let alone attempt to manhandle me."

"Whatever," I barked, swatting his hand away. "Come on, we need to go," I spat back whilst sucking in my expanding girth.

"Jesus, Apsley, you don't half go on. I'm not one of your kids, you know."

"No, they're far more mature," I muttered, peering down and rubbing my hand over my stomach. Despite my regular jogs around the park – more of a shuffle compared to those fitness freaks, all of whom wouldn't look out of place as extras in *Fame* as they whizzed up in my slipstream and lapped me – there was no denying the evidence regarding the extra unwanted timber that stretched my polo shirt to the max. I wondered if it had shrunk after accidentally falling into the boil wash. "Wishful thinking there, my old son," I muttered.

"Oh, shut it. Nothing changes, I see. You're still a pain in the frigging arse."

"Thanks!"

"You're welcome. Hey, talking of kids, How's Beth? What is she, eighteen, now? Bet she's a right handful." He jiggled his eyebrows and grinned. "You know, I met her a few times in our old life. Me and her—"

"When? I don't recall you two meeting," I interrupted, choosing to ignore his rude put-down that I was, apparently, a pain in the arse. Martin smirked before turning away to focus on the marauds of bustling commuters.

"I tried it on once." He glanced at me again. I presume, trying to solicit some kind of reaction. "She turned me down … missed out there, she did. Hey, can't understand why you didn't go for her back then. She was better than your ex. What was it? Don't tell me … you tried it on, but the ice maiden gave you the cold shoulder?"

274

"Beth and I were friends. We weren't like that."

"I bet you tried, though. Didn't you?" He nudged my arm and winked.

I tutted and shook my head at him.

"See, you did," he chuckled. "Beth turned you down like she did me. That woman was so cold, I reckon your knob would drop off with frostbite if it got anywhere near her."

"Jesus, Martin. Have you completely transgressed?"

"Woah, what d'you mean?" he shot his head back, appearing hurt by my comment.

"Look, I know we've both been living in yesteryear for a couple of decades, but you've turned into a misogynistic old pervert."

"Hey, d'you mind? I tell you what, though. This era is so much better than our old life. You can call a bird a bird, don't get slapped for throwing out the odd wolf whistle, and no one can track your movements because smartphones haven't been invented. I've got to get as much action in before bloody Google Maps rocks up and ruins my life."

"Has it ever occurred to you that these women you wolf whistle at might not find your outdated attitude offensive?"

He shrugged. "They don't seem to mind."

"Yes, mate, because that's how society is, was, is, if you get my drift. They didn't give you a slap because that's how things were back in the bloody seventies and eighties. It's the bloody nineties, mate. We're heading towards the millennium. So, unless you aspire to be labelled as some lecherous old git, I suggest you change your ways."

Martin shrugged. "Blimey … you gone all women's lib?"

"No, I'm talking about equality. I really don't know what's happened to you. Okay, I know you've always liked the ladies, but you weren't like this in 2019."

"Different era, mate. I've been enjoying the sun, booze, and birds in the Costas." Martin raised an eyebrow at me before turning away to scan the crowds of commuters.

I rechecked my watch. Although Jess was safe with Colin, Faith, and the rest of my family over at Jenny's parents, I needed to get Martin ensconced in position at Don's old house. Hence, he was ready to perform his protection-detail duties when she returned. Worryingly, I considered the few minutes together demonstrated that my old loose-cannon time-travelling colleague seemed to have changed his character, and not for the better, I hasten to add. Perhaps my ridiculous fears that he'd morphed into some misogynistic rapist strangler weren't too far off the mark. Hmmm.

"Come on. We need to get going," I muttered.

"One more minute."

I rechecked my watch. "Anyway, when d'you reckon you propositioned Beth? I think she'd have told me if you had."

"It was at one of those awful summer barbies you and Lisa used to throw. I didn't know she was the ice queen then. She's a lot older than me, but boy, she's one fit bird, that woman."

"Was that before or after you knobbed my wife?"

"Lisa or Jenny."

My jaw sagged.

"Frig, what's the matter with you? A joke, alright? April fool," he chuckled. "Look, stop catching flies and close your mouth. Despite your missus being pretty hot, I know she would never stray from you. God knows what she sees in you, mind. I mean, what is it? She got a fetish for moaning old gits? I know it's not down to the size of your truncheon because Lisa reckoned you didn't fare too well in that department."

"Did she really?" I sarcastically batted back.

"Yes, mate. Sorry, but I can't help it that your ex was none too impressed with your tackle, can I?"

Again, lost for words, I just gawped back at him.

"Anyway, you're well shot. Bit of a starchy cow, that one, and not exactly adventurous in the bedroom department, either."

"Well, you didn't seem to mind her lack of adventure."

"Hey, any port in a storm, as they say. Me and Caroline were arguing a lot at the time. Although Lisa was a bit prudish …" he paused and turned to face me. "Missionary only, and liked to keep her bra on, if I recall correctly." He yawned and stretched his arms up. "She was okay-ish, I suppose."

My mind drifted to Beth's claims about her brother and the three young ladies cavorting in our bed. Whatever the reason, presumably caused by some time-travel ripple, Lisa Crowther, in this life, clearly felt more comfortable experimenting in the bedroom than the last.

"Right, well, whatever. Lisa is from another life, so who cares?"

"Yeah, you're right, mate. Sorry, I didn't mean to piss on your strawberries. So, your Beth, is she just as fit and horny looking now as she was then?"

"Jesus, that's my daughter you're talking about. She's only seventeen, for Christ sake."

"Alright. Jesus, Apsley, don't be so tetchy. I was only enquiring about her well-being."

"Yes, well, I know what you're like. You're a thirty-eight-year-old man, and Beth, in this life, is an innocent seventeen-year-old … not a forty-something woman you can try to woo."

Although my daughter *was* seventeen, innocent, she wasn't. However, as always, with Martin's track record in that department, I wouldn't put it past him to have another crack at wooing Beth twenty years before he made his first attempt to swoon the ice maiden, as he put it. I imagine being turned down wasn't a situation he was accustomed to experiencing.

"Keep your knickers on, old man. I have no intention of wooing your daughter. We're waiting here because I've already landed myself an Easter bunny to keep me warm over the festivities."

"And who is this little bunny, as you call her?"

"I told you. This woman I met on the plane. Christ, nothing changes, does it?"

"What?"

"You! Apsley, you don't listen. You're always in your own little world."

"Err … sorry, but we have a bit of a crisis on our hands. And all you can think about is hanging around outside Thomas Cook's Bureau de Change, waiting to hand over Don's old address to some woman. We should be focusing on getting you over to Don's to keep an eye on Jess."

"Apsley, I'm aware of the crisis, alright?" he hissed out of the side of his mouth whilst continuing to scan the crowds. "A few extra minutes won't matter."

"Why didn't you give it to her on the plane?"

"I did," he sniggered, turning around and offering me a lascivious grin. "Although, I couldn't give her the address

278

because I'd forgotten where Don used to live. That's why I asked you to write it on the back of my ticket, which I'll give to Sally when she turns up. Which, if you show a bit of patience, will be any moment now."

"You've lost me. You did give it to her on the plane, or you didn't?"

"Oh, keep up, Apsley. I didn't give her the address. I gave her something else … in the toilet."

"You didn't?"

"Mile high club, mate. Nothing better than shooting your load with a trolley dolly at thirty-three thousand feet."

"My God." I puffed out my cheeks and shook my head whilst checking my watch, which still displayed the same time as it had ten seconds ago, the last time I checked.

"I take it you're not in the club, then?" Martin muttered, as he stood on tiptoe and waved at someone in the crowd of commuters, all bustling through the airport returning for the Easter break.

"Presumably, you're not asking if I'm pregnant—"

"Well, with your gut, I wouldn't be surprised. No, I mean, you haven't partaken in mile-high nookie."

"No … not had that pleasure." I glanced south again and sucked in my stomach.

"Not surprised. You're sixty now. I reckon your chance has gone, my old mucker. Here she comes. Fit as fuck and goes like a rabbit."

"Jesus," I muttered. "She's not into broad beans, is she?"

"Do what?"

"Oh, forget it." I gestured my hand at him, dismissing his question.

279

Martin waved again, this time with both hands aloft while shaking his ticket, Neville Chamberlain style. That said, the Prime Minister of the day triumphantly waved the Munich Agreement, stating the Disraeli quote 'peace for our time' and not a budget airline ticket with Don's address scrawled across. Information to be supplied to the woman, whom he'd made the acquaintance in the toilet on the plane, so she would know where he could be located to enable them to continue their merrymaking in a more spacious environment than an aeroplane toilet cubical.

As Martin had correctly surmised, I wasn't in that club. I imagine both parties involved would need to demonstrate a certain level of dexterity in order to make a successful initiation in such a cramped space.

When on the flight to Turkey for our honeymoon, I'd suggested to Lisa that we could give it a go. Just a throwaway comment whilst tucking into my inflight meal that didn't go down particularly well – the meal or the comment – and caused the elderly gent sitting between us to become hot under the collar. I'd booked the seats on the plane and inadvertently booked seats A and C. The chap in B, who flatly refused to swap places, stating that statistically his seat was the safest if we crashed, spent the rest of the flight praying and twiddling his worry beads whilst shooting me filthy looks. I guess I could have explained that Lisa and I were newlyweds and I wasn't just some random bloke propositioning a young lady.

"Here she comes. What d'you reckon, Apsley? I've hit the jackpot with this one."

Two women headed our way. An elderly lady jabbing her stick on the floor every six inches as she shuffled along, clutching a tatty carpet bag, and a young air hostess tottering along in impossibly high black stilettoes, wearing an excited grin and half of Boots' makeup counter. All tits and teeth, as Jenny would say.

Although fully aware Martin wasn't overly fussy where he inserted his manhood, I had the tall, young woman, dressed in the short, hot-red skirt, pegged as the most likely to be Sally, as opposed to the carpet-bag lady.

"Jesus, Martin. How old is she?" I hissed out of the side of my mouth as she skipped over and flung her arms around him.

"Alright, babe?"

"Babe," I muttered, tutted, and rolled my eyes.

"Sorry, I had to see my supervisor about our schedule after Easter."

"No worries, babe. So, this is where I'm staying." Martin handed over his ticket with the address scrawled across.

"Cool. Oh, sorry," she giggled, shooting me a look whilst pawing at Martin's chest. "You must be Mr Powers."

"Sorry?" I furrowed my brow at her suggestion whilst the girl stepped up her Martin manhandling to the next level, now almost fully draped over him.

Ignoring me, she peered up at my loose cannon with doe eyes. "You didn't say your dad was picking you up."

"Oh, no," Martin chuckled, grinning at me. "This is … this is an old friend. Old being the operative word." Martin continued to smirk as he introduced me by way of an outstretched hand.

"Jason." I offered a toothless, tight smile.

"Hmm," she squeaked out, running her eyes up and down me before turning her attention back to Martin. "I'll nip over to Mum's and be at your place by three."

"Sounds like a plan."

"You don't have a brother, do you?"

"No. You got a friend who's looking for some company, too?"

"Oh, no. It's just that I nearly kissed some bloke over at the car rental place. He looked just like you."

"Lucky bloke."

"Sorry?"

"Lucky bloke, if he looks like me."

"Oh, you!" Sally playfully slapped his arm before rubbing her nose on Martin's whilst childishly giggling.

After a quick glance in my direction, she tiptoed up and whispered in Martin's ear before openly rubbing the front of his jeans. Then, swivelling around, she tottered off in the direction from which she'd just come whilst exaggeratingly swishing her bum and checking over her shoulder that she still had his full attention. Which, of course, she did.

"Dirty cow," Martin sniggered.

"Look, mate. I'm not one to be the party pooper, but you have a job to do. Rather than entertaining your new conquest, you're supposed to be on lookout duty, protecting Jess."

"Hey, no problem. This *other* Jason bloke, the poor sod that looks like you, can take turns with me to keep watch. Whilst he takes his shift, Sally and me can relax."

"Relax?" I threw at him with a raised eyebrow as we headed for the exit.

"Yes, Apsley. You should relax more, you're always too uptight. Always have been … always will be. Here, hold on to these," he said, handing me his rucksack and case. "I need a slash before we get going."

After we'd waited around for Sally, I guess another few minutes wouldn't make much difference. Whilst Martin shot off to relieve himself, my mind drifted to the events of the previous evening.

After Beth had questioned my statement about her biological father's future serial killing spree, now expunged due to me killing him, our daughter retired to her room. A headache stated as the reason, although I suspect she needed time to compute the events of the last two days.

Fair enough.

Discovering your adopted father's a time-traveller, who used to be your best mate from school, the person to whom in her other life she'd divulged all her teenage secrets to, was a lot to take in. Also, I presume the knowledge imparted upon her by *other* Jason regarding who she may or may not be destined to marry – perhaps a lawyer called Phil, who, at the stage, no one could confirm if he slotted into the tall, dark and handsome category – must have been somewhat difficult to take. I guess, for the next however many years, for every man she met with the name Phil, the poor girl would wonder if he was to be the man for her.

Similar to that journey I made with Martin in 1977, I'd ferried *other* Jason across to Don's house. I'd needed to get him in there and under wraps before Colin returned from his trip to Manchester and my granddaughter, Faith, arrived home. Timing was key. I'd stayed with Jess until Colin arrived, making out I was just visiting rather than not leaving her alone because a time-travelling ghost may be planning to inflict harm upon her. At this stage, I didn't know if that ghost was Paul or Martin. Clearly, my older self assumed I could read between the lines better than I could. Or, I, in 2015, had lost my marbles, and this whole charade was a fuss about nothing now the future had probably been expunged due to *other* Jason's time-travel flit.

Pinch punch or white rabbits. April the 1st. April Fool's Day, and only five days from Jess's potential disappearing act.

"April fool … you numpty," I muttered.

"Thanks!" exclaimed Martin as he grabbed his bags, leaving me to gawp vacantly into the middle distance. However, my mind had flown out of the traps, now hurtling towards oblivion.

"Apsley … you alright? Jason, you having a stroke or something?" Martin shook my arm, peering down at me.

Breaking my trance with a shake of my head, I shot him a look. "What did Sally just say to you?"

"Well, that's kind of private, mate, if you get my drift." Martin offered an embarrassed smile. Whatever the girl had whispered, it was enough to make Martin turn the colour of his trolley-dolly's skirt.

"No, not that. I'm not referring to the sweet nothings she whispered in your ear. Presumably a cornucopia of sordid sexual acts she plans to perform. I'm referring to when she said about you having a brother?"

Martin frowned. "Sorry?"

"She said she just met a man who could be your brother."

"Yes, but, as I told her, I don't have a brother."

"That book," I muttered.

"Apsley, you're not well, mate. You forgotten your medication this morning?"

"I'm not on any medication."

"What's the matter with you, then? What book?"

"The book … the first page," I mumbled before grappling for his arm. "You remember Carlton King?"

"No. Should I?"

"The kid at school, who your mum went out with."

"Oh, course, yeah. The bloke who used to play golf with Dad in my old life."

"That's him. He's written a book claiming Paul Colney is still alive."

"Well, yes, we know. Well, we don't, but it's a possibility. That's why I'm back for a few days in case it's him who's come back to harm Jess."

"No, you're not getting it. The first page in that book has one line … *The irrefutable evidence that Paul Colney is alive'*."

"Okay, so this Carlton King has tracked the evil bastard down. So what?"

"So what? What d'you frigging mean, so what?"

"Precisely that. So what?"

"Paul Colney, if he wants his liberty to stay intact, can't afford to be tracked down, agreed?"

Martin nodded.

"So, if someone claims to know where he is, as Carlton has stated in his book, the bastard will have a bit of a problem."

"Apsley, you're talking in riddles."

"Look, Colney, apart from being a nutter, isn't stupid."

"Debatable, but go on."

"Only two people on this earth can positively ID the man without any question of doubt that he is Paul and not his twin, Patrick."

Martin nodded, so I continued.

"If Paul is alive and kicking, he will either call himself Patrick Colney or live under a pseudonym. If this Carlton bloke, who's now an investigative journo, has been sniffing around digging the dirt, it stands to reason that Paul won't be too chuffed."

"Well, no, I guess so, but—"

"Paul will want to ensure the two people on this planet that can identify him as the dead Paul Colney don't corroborate Carlton's claim. One being Andy, his brother, who's in prison and likely to stay there for the foreseeable future and—"

"Jess," he interrupted me.

"Precisely. Colney knows about the book and knows he has to silence those who can corroborate Carlton's claims."

"Okay, but we suspected this. We've always known that there's a possibility Paul Colney might still be alive and would resurface one day."

"Yes, but your lovely trolley dolly just confirmed it when she nearly kissed a man at the car rental stand."

"Shit! Because, in my first life, Andy Colney raped my mother. Hence, I look like the Colney boys."

"Spot on. Your girl, Sally, spotted him not half an hour ago."

"Bollocks."

"That's my line. But yes, bollocks."

Part 3

26

September 2015

Keeping up Appearances

"Brandon, ye little shit, sit the feck down. I've had enough of your bleeding pissing about, so I have."

Although the statement could be construed as a smidge on the coarse side, the woman's strong Irish lilt reminded me of the man I put in hospital after crushing his knee on Carol Hall's doorstep, the day after I'd met my Jenny all those years ago.

"Fin Booth," I muttered, barely audible above the indecipherable chatter filling the over-crowded room, which competed for space with the unpleasant stench of expelled stale breath.

Despite the unpleasant odour, I offered myself the tiniest of smiles, pleased that I'd managed to remember the big lump's name. Since losing Jenny, it's fair to say that me and my memory weren't getting along too well – past any reconciliation point and were heading for the divorce courts, so to speak – because basically, I couldn't remember bugger all. See, there was me, wanting to reflect on the wonderful times my wife and I had enjoyed, and then there was my memory, a useless wobbling pink blancmange refusing to play ball. Life had become a daily battle. I was in full retreat, my pink blancmange advancing, leaving me with only a smattering of minor victories to celebrate, like remembering Fin Booth.

"Brandon! I'll not tell ye again. Sit ye wee arse on the fecking chair, or, so help me God, I'll fecking brain you, that I will."

"I'm bored," he whined, elongating the second word of his statement to emphasise his displeasure. The boy, who I presumed to be a year or so younger than my nine-year-old grandson, Oliver, continued to practise his helicopter impression, which involved spinning around with his arms stretched out wide.

The continued rotations, causing lights to flash from the soles of his trainers as he stomped around, resulted in him colliding with the other visitors as we all congregated in the airless reception area, waiting to be processed.

"I'll give ye fecking bored, ye wee gobshite."

The woman, who I presumed to be his mother, grabbed one spinning hand, thus curtailing the rotations of his rotary arms. Because of a combination of his mother's grappling and the centrifugal force produced by his pinwheeling motion, the lad hit the deck after unceremoniously being knocked off balance. This manoeuvre resulted in his head enjoying an altercation with the edge of a robust, uncomfortable, bolted-to-the-floor plastic chair. The ominous cracking sound and instant wailing suggested the chair emerged victorious from the duel.

"Oi, shut him up, or I will," announced a thug of a man to my right, who leaned forward in his chair whilst sporting an unpleasant grimace. He rhythmically cracked his knuckles and offered a repeated annoying sniff whilst swirling gum around his mouth. "Oi, you tart. I said, shut the little twat up."

After she'd finished grappling with her wailing child, I felt sure the woman would offer her opinion regarding the sniffing goon's threat. However, for the moment, she seemed intent on coaching her child how to be a little shit.

"Jaysus, Brandon, I'll be telling ye daddy what a bad boy ye are if ye don't fecking shut the feck up."

The knuckle cracker's green padded bomber jacket and eight-hole Doc Martens, along with the swastika tattoo on his neck and the four-letter 'C' word amateurishly tattooed across the digits of his right hand, suggested he wasn't someone who I could probably strike up any sort of decent conversation with. That said, as I scanned the room, I doubted many occupants were likely to fit into my social circles. Not that I had any, mind. However, you get my drift.

"Oi, you deaf, bitch?"

"Feck off, twat. Don't ye fecking tell me what to do, ye gobshite motherfucker." The boy's mother fired back whilst expertly tossing her long peroxide-blonde hair over her shoulder with one hand and repeatedly slapping her wailing son with the other.

I presumed her take on parenting was to dish out physical violence to her offspring, whether they required discipline or comfort. One action to cover all bases sort of thing.

I figured the young, bored helicopter pilot, in, say, ten years from now, would probably end up here on a permanent basis as opposed to 'just visiting', à la Monopoly style. With the combination of his mother's parenting and the role-model guidance from whoever they were here to see, I felt sure the lad was destined for a career that involved regular, if not prolonged, stays at Her Majesty's pleasure and not as a Sea King helicopter pilot.

"Who the fuck d'you think you are, you slag—"

"Sinéad Penn," she fired at him, a raised hand held in mid-air, traffic policeman style, to halt the gorilla's advance. "And if ye want to hang on to your droopy bollocks, I suggest ye sit down and shut the feck up."

Although I doubted the petite woman's hand, held in a halting action, could stop his advance, the name she uttered appeared to have the desired effect. Frozen in time, bum in the air and knees bent, the goon hovered, appearing to turn a smidge green around the gills.

"I take it ye not aware that I be Kurt's missus," she spat, simultaneously landing a forceful smack on Brandon's head with her free hand.

Brandon scurried away from his mother's flaying arm to locate suitable space to continue his rotations out of his mother's reach.

"Oi, get back here, ye fecking shithead," she barked.

The goon offered an over-exaggerated apologetic grin. "Hey, sorry, love. I-I d-didn't mean anything by it." When shifting his focus to the chewing-gum-stained carpet tiled flooring, seemingly a good six inches shorter than when he'd risen a moment ago, the Nazi-styled thug slithered back to his seat.

Sinéad fired back an icy stare. If the look couldn't kill him, I had the petite, blonde Irish woman pegged as more than capable of finishing the job.

The name Sinéad Penn rang a bell. However, unlike her fellow countryman, Fin, I couldn't place it. Pink blancmange had won that battle.

A middle-aged woman holding one of those 'benefits-conning' walking aids, presumably forgetting herself when feeling the need to vacate the vicinity of Sinéad, hopped out of her chair. While employing a surprisingly able gait, she whizzed across to the other side of the room before being closely followed by two elderly gents. I say elderly, but in reality, they were probably a good few years my junior. Besides Brandon, who'd added engine noises to his spinning routine by way of spluttering globules of spit that arced across his landing area, the room took on a deathly hush.

Two women, perched on the seats behind me, chatted in hushed tones. Whilst trying to block out Brandon's sound effects, I closed my eyes, tipped my head back to feign the appearance of an old boy dozing, and thus took the opportunity to listen in to their conversation.

"Who's that Kurt Penn, then?"

"Shit me. Don't you know?"

"Nah, should I?"

"I can't believe you ain't 'eard of him. Right nasty bastard, that one. My Tom, doing a ten stretch for burglary, reckons he's the hardest bastard in 'ere."

"Tariq never said anyfink about him."

"That your old fella?"

"Yeah … he's good to me, but he's a bit of a dippy twat."

"What's your Tariq in for, then?"

"Oh, he didn't do it."

293

"None of them did, sweetheart," came the somewhat sarcastic reply. "My Tom pleaded not guilty. But, being as the back bedroom was full of the hooky gear he'd nicked, and the silly sod dropped his balaclava at the house he burgled, the jury thought otherwise."

"Oh. That's a bugger. Well, my man's on remand, ain't he. Holding up the building society with our littlun's Nerf gun."

"Aren't they orange? Wiv foam bullets?"

"Yeah. As I said, Tariq's a bit of a tit. When he threatened to shoot if they didn't 'and over the money, he machine-gunned a whole cartridge of yellow foam pellets at the glass screen. Course, security disarmed him before he had the chance to reload. He went tooled-up, you know. Six cartridges in all. My littlun's well pissed 'cos the gun's now been seized as evidence."

"Didn't he know the gun was a toy?"

"Yeah, but Tariq's never been the sharpest hammer in the toolbox, if you get my drift."

"Chisel."

"Do what?"

"It's the sharpest chisel, not hammer."

"You're shittin' me?"

"No … deffo, chisel."

"Oh, well, I never knew that."

"How long before his trial?"

"Bleedin' months, I reckon. Frig knows what he thought he was doing. I said to him, why didn't you cover your face? There's those bleedin' spy cameras all over the place."

"Or use a proper gun that wasn't orange?"

"Yeah. He said he didn't fink anyone would notice the difference."

"Well, at least he had a go. Can't knock him for that, can you? Some men just sit on their arses watching the racing all day long. At least my Tom and your Tariq tried to put food on the table."

"S'pose. My old mum reckons Tariq's a few tins short of a six-pack. Not sure what she's on about, really. I mean, Tariq's a muslin, so he don't drink."

"I think your mum is saying … oh, forget it. I take it you mean Muslim?"

"That's what I said. Tariq's one of those muslins."

"No … oh, forget it."

"So, what's wiv this blonde Scotch woman then? That Sinéad … she some sort of mafia bird, is she?"

"You mean Scottish?"

"Yeah, that's what I said."

"No … you said … oh, it don't matter. Look, she's Irish, but that's beside the point—"

"How can you tell?"

"What?"

"That she's Irish."

When there was a pause, I presumed the slightly more educated of the two was considering if the conversation was worth continuing. For pure entertainment value on my part, fortunately, she did.

"Look, as I was saying, Sinéad's old man, Kurt Penn, is a lifer. He's doing life for chopping up a rival gang member. Apparently, the word on the street, they found the victim's head nestled amongst the little kiddy's fish fingers below a tub of Ben and Jerry's Cookie Dough ice cream."

"Where?"

"What d'you mean where?"

"Where was the head and fish fingers?"

"In the freezer, of course."

"You're shittin' me?"

"No … where else d'you keep ice cream?"

"Oh, yeah, see your point," she giggled. "And they reckon I'm the clever one. D'oh!"

"Look at the poor sod, spinning around like a loony. Must have given him a hell of a shock to discover a severed head when delving in for an ice pop."

"That kid found the head? You're shittin' me?"

"No. And get this. I 'eard the little nipper took it out and stood it on the kitchen worktop next to the kettle. Sinéad came home wiv a few mates after a drinking session to find it there staring at her."

"You're shittin' me?"

"I ain't. Her, the missus, lives on the Broxworth in Fairfield. Runs the damn place."

"You're shittin' me?"

"I ain't. Whatever you do, don't make the same mistake as Nosher Nesbitt."

"Who's that?"

"The skinhead with the tattoos behind us who looks like he's cacked his combats."

"Shit. 'Ere, you seem a friendly sort. D'you reckon your old man can keep an eye on my Tariq? He's not really enjoying himself much in 'ere."

The sound of a cacophony of buzzers and clanging gates hauled me away from the entertaining conversation drifting over my right shoulder. Two prison officers, each wearing stab vests and a disinterested grimace, waved the masses through to be processed, which I was led to believe would involve airport-styled security checks.

Needless to say, I didn't know anyone incarcerated in Havervalley Prison, or any other prison for that matter. However, two weeks ago, a chap called me out of the blue, claiming to be a prison chaplain.

Of course, I'd informed him that, although he sounded like a decent sort, I wasn't interested in his religion. I'd assumed that religious types had progressed from knocking on your door in an effort to convert the masses to a tactic of cold calling via the phone. However, when we'd got past me rudely telling him it was all bollocks, the persistent, surprisingly cheery fellow made a rather intriguing request.

After listening to his story, I agreed to the visit. Following a spot of detective work when silver surfing, I discovered the man who'd requested an audience with a retired schoolteacher, namely yours truly, was a certain Mr John Curtis. To quote the woman behind me – nasty bastard.

My delving and digging had thrown up that this particular individual was guilty of raping and murdering three women in Spain around the time when Tony Blair swept New Labour to power in a landslide victory. All heralded as the dawn of the new political era. The final banishment of the militant faction, with Derek Hatton and the Liverpool council consigned to history, along with sweeping aside the sleaze that dominated politics in the early nineties.

New Labour radically altered Clause IV – enough to cause members of the Fabian Society to turn in their graves – in favour of synthesis between capitalism and social justice, which promised the earth. I suppose we got the minimum wage, The Good Friday Agreement, along with the Iraq War and a big white tent on the Greenwich Peninsula. Like Mr Major before him, and akin to Tom and Tariq, they had a go instead of slouching in their vests drinking beer whilst watching the racing Onslow-style. Of course, like successive governments before them and the ones to come in the future, they fell short of their promises. It seemed in both my lives, despite their genuine desire to do good, all politicians failed to deliver. Or perhaps society's expectations were too high – who knew?

Anyway, this individual, who I could only glean the sketchiest information about, had requested an audience with me. The carrot for me to attend being that he claimed to know the whereabouts of Paul Colney. Now, I certainly didn't want to meet that man again. Also, I'd rather hoped he died at the hands of some other reprobate. Alas, if this John Curtis were to be believed, it appeared Paul Colney was still out there. Fair to say, the lifer who was looking to convert to Christianity before he died had piqued my interest enough for me to show up at Thursday visiting hour behind the oppressive walls and razor wire that befitted Havervalley Prison.

"Mr Apsley."

As I stood impersonating a scarecrow, an officer with an impressive lack of humour that befitted the building we were in, inspected my mouth. Whilst he peered inside, sporting a scowl similar to that of my dentist before informing me about

298

opportunities to improve my oral hygiene routine, I glanced through the door-shaped portal of the metal detector. The young chap, who'd called my name, enthusiastically waved whilst showing off a set of Hollywood teeth. He certainly wouldn't receive a disapproving glower from his dental hygienist.

"You can put your arms down, sir," the officer informed me in a tone most people employ when addressing an octogenarian. I wasn't deaf, but I guess my wispy hair and wrinkles seem to suggest that I should be.

"Mr Apsley," Hollywood's leading man repeated as he stepped forward and thrust out a hand. "Simon … the prison chaplain here at Havervalley. Havervalley is happy valley when God is in your heart," he chuckled. "A little morale booster, I like to say to the men to keep their spirits up."

As we shook hands, he clamped his left over mine, sandwiching it between his, before leaning in and offering me another close-up of his pearly whites. I wondered how Kurt Penn responded to his happy valley ditty. Although Nosher Nesbitt was a powder puff in comparison to Sinéad, I imagined he would knock the chaplain's teeth down his throat so hard the poor bloke would have to chew through his sphincter.

"We spoke on the phone, you remember?" he raised a perfectly trimmed, regularly plucked eyebrow at me.

See, there it was again. Yes, I accept my memory had kicked itself into the long grass, but his tone, although amiable, suggested my appearance would indicate I was senile and needed a reminder about who he was and why I was here.

Growing old sucked.

"Yes, of course. I can't imagine what he wants to say to me, but I'm here now."

299

Whilst the stragglers filed past, those who entered whilst displaying the enthusiasm of a slave when entering the Colosseum, Simon corralled me to one side. The only visitors remaining in the security tunnel being me, Sinéad, and the helicopter pilot, who appeared to have landed and was now focused on completing his final checks by way of picking his nose.

"As I say. You don't have to see him. Even now, you can back out."

"No, it's fine. I'll see him."

"Okay."

"When we spoke, you said something about this John chap is looking to repent and find God before he dies."

Simon glanced at Sinéad, who slouched against the wall, arms folded, rolling her gum around whilst offering a rhythmic slurping sound as an audible accompaniment. Shifting his stance to place his back to her, Simon leaned close and whispered.

"I shouldn't say, but John is quite unwell. Although he looks fine, the man is riddled with cancer. I'm hoping to help him face his demons, repent before our Lord, and seek salvation."

"Fine. As I said, I'm not a believer in any shape or form, so I'm not sure why he wants to see me."

"No, quite. This man he mentioned. Paul Colney. I take it he's someone you knew, perhaps … a lost acquaintance?"

That wasn't a question I'd been prepared for. Of course, stating Paul Colney was a murdering psycho, rapist nutter, who was dead at least once, probably wasn't the best route to take. After performing a reasonable impression of a fish on the river bank, I pursed my lips to grab a moment to collect my thoughts.

"Mr Apsley?"

"Oi, gobshite." Sinéad walloped the sole of her trainer against the wall with enough oomph to cause it to shake. "How much fecking longer ye gonna make me and me boy stand here?"

"Err … not much longer, Mrs Penn." The officer rubbed his hands together as if balling Plasticine.

Like Shirley Colney, similar in stature, a twenty-first-century version of the matriarchal mafia queen, Sinéad appeared to be able to make any man feel the urgent need to nip off to the bogs.

After being distracted by Cruella de Vil's daughter, Simon swivelled his head around to face me, raising that eyebrow again.

"Oh, yes. I knew of Paul Colney many years ago. Look, I'm happy to see this chap. No problem."

"Okay. Category A prisoners' visitors' room is separate from the main area. The lady here and yourself will be taken through to the room by Frazer." He nodded to the officer, still moulding Morph. "There will be a few more officers in that room … I'm sure you understand. Once you're there, the prisoners will be escorted through." Simon nodded to Frazer, who waved his hand to Sinead and Brandon to enter the first gate.

I nodded a thank you before shimmying into the slipstream of the Penns. Before we stepped through, Simon grabbed my elbow.

"Don't let him intimidate you. Although he displays no violent tendencies, almost a model prisoner, John Curtis has a

301

history of coercion and control without feeling or thought for others."

"He's a psychopath, then?"

Simon offered a tight smile.

"Don't worry, I've met one before."

27

1994

Two-Ton-Ted from Teddington

"Erm ... what the hell are all these?"

Martin shrugged and offered his usual boyish grin in response as I dramatically waved my hand back and forth across the half dozen or so passports. After unceremoniously lobbing his bags in the boot of my car, the contents of his rucksack had spilt out. I flicked away a dog-eared paperback copy of a Frederick Forsyth thriller – a publication which I'd be surprised received much attention during his flight after Sally had gone above and beyond with her duties – and grabbed the navy-blue passport sporting the Great Seal on the cover before flicking through to the picture page.

The photo of a frowning Martin stared back at me.

"Ethan Hunt! From Wisconsin. Are you taking the piss?"

"I thought it would be cool."

"These are illegal!"

"So?" He offered that petulant shrug. "You can get hold of anything if you have the right contacts."

I grabbed another, this one issued by France with the cover in that familiar European Union burgundy. As I raked through to the picture page, I detected Martin shuffling his feet. That nervous act was presumably born out of his concern about my reaction.

"Oh, you've got to be kidding me!"

Martin grinned.

"Thierry Henry!"

"One of the best ever. He scored one-hundred and seventy-four goals in two-hundred and fifty-four appearances for the Gunners." Martin tapped the open page, which I'd jabbed at him. "He achieved the all-time top strike rate in the Premier League, you know. Well, he will do over the next decade. I've got a twenty-thousand plata on that stat … gonna make a killing on that bet." He added a knowing nod as if to add gravitas to his point.

"Plata?"

"Peseta," he announced in a Spanish accent, which sounded more Sean Connery than Julio Iglesias.

"Oh … but, err … isn't it going to appear a smidge odd when Mr Henry becomes famous? And as for Ethan Hunt, that's just full-on ridiculous."

"Well, you see, my forger—"

"What d'you mean, my forger?" I interrupted. "You say it like you're talking about the bloody postman."

Martin opened his palms and shrugged. "I need a forger, don't I? So, Ernie reckoned—"

"Ernie?"

"Yeah. My forger's name is Ernie. He's Brazilian with one leg. Course, I don't think that's his real name. Forging documents for a living is against the law ... even in Spain."

"No shit."

"Funny, though, it took me ages to understand his nickname."

"Nickname?"

"Ernie ... known as the *Milkman* ... he drove the fastest milk float in the west."

"Cart. Not float. Cart."

"Oh, for shitting hell's sake. You know what I mean. You've always been a knob, Apsley. You know that?"

"You have a way of bringing the worst out of me."

"Huh."

"Anyway, why on earth have you picked these ridiculous names? I mean, talk about bringing attention to yourself."

"Ernie—"

"Your Brazilian, Long-John-Silver impersonating forger?"

"The very same ... he kinda caught me a bit on the hop ... no pun intended."

I offered an over-exaggerated eye-roll.

"He needed names, so I just went for whatever popped into my head."

I wagged my finger at another blue passport sporting the Canadian Royal Coat of Arms. "Christ, don't tell me you chose Michael J. Fox or Ben Johnson for that one?"

Martin offered a girlish giggle. "Dion Morrisette. As I said, I was on the spot and could only think of Alanis Morissette and Celine Dion."

"So you amalgamated the names and came up with that?"

"Inspired, don't you think?"

"You blow my brain, you know. Anyway, why d'you need them?"

"I can't be Martin Bretton, can I? I'm dead."

"I know, but you're Tyler Powers. And that's a bloody stupid name, too. And remember, while you're here, you're gonna have to be Leonardo Bretton again. Which, I might add, is almost as bad as Tyler Powers. I really don't know why you didn't call yourself Keith. At least that was reasonably believable."

"I just didn't like Keith, okay? Anyway, Sally likes the name Tyler. I had to cover her mouth to stop her screaming my name when we were—"

"Yes, alright, I don't need a diagram."

"She's rampant, that one."

I rolled my eyes … again. He sniggered … again.

"Anyway, when Ernie knocked up my Tyler Powers passport, I thought I'd bag a few backups just in case I needed to change my name again."

With my hand poised on the boot lid, ready to ping it closed, I contumeliously shook my head. Martin, although thirty-eight, and apart from when it came to his involvement with the fairer sex, displayed the maturity of a schoolboy.

"And when exactly d'you think you might need one of these fake passports, then?"

"Who knows? But if I fancy a trip to the States, you know, take in a bit of Muscle Beach." He flexed his biceps before swishing his legs back and forth. "Or rollerblading down Venice Beach Boulevard. I won't need to apply for a visa."

306

Whilst Martin continued to inform me of his plans to conquer the United States, I became distracted by a black BMW 3 series that appeared to be idling near the car park entrance. As my focus shifted from my time-travelling loose cannon, the Beemer shot off up the ramp to the next level. I was doing it again, seeing phantoms that weren't there.

"Apsley? You alright?"

"Sorry, yeah. What were you saying?"

"Forget it. Off in your own little world again, I see."

"Look, Martin, you are being careful, aren't you?"

"Are you enquiring if Sally and me practise safe sex? Don't be silly, protect your willy … that sort of thing?"

I raised an eyebrow.

"Personally, my favourite is … if you think she's spunky, cover your monkey."

"My God. You're unbelievable."

Ignoring my statement, he grinned and excitedly wagged his finger at me. "This is a good one. You'll like this … cloak your joker before you poke her. Classic one that, eh?"

See what I mean? A thirty-eight-year-old man with the brain of a thirteen-year-old.

"Oh, and—"

"No!" I shot my free hand towards his face. "No more. We need to get going. Standing in Luton Airport's short-stay car park while you rattle off your all-time favourite immature mucky ditties about safe sex is not how I intend to spend my Good Friday afternoon. And regards to being careful, I'm talking about the way you earn a living."

"You mean betting?"

307

"Yes. If you're planning on gallivanting around California, that takes serious cash. So please, convince me you're not making outrageous bets that are going to bring attention upon yourself."

"Chill, old man. I have a strategy."

"That's what worries me."

"You're a whittler, Apsley. Live a bit, man. Do something spontaneous and wild."

"Like shagging in the cubical on a plane?"

"Nooo … that's everyday stuff. Be adventurous. I dunno … start small and build up. Surprise Jenny and whisk her off for a weekend away at some nudist beach. I reckon she'd love that … a chance to get away from it all and let it all hang out. You must remember that 'Free the Nipple Campaign' back in our day. Caroline and two of her friends participated in that topless march in Brighton. Of course, I supported my wife, so joined in the protest to show moral support."

"Martin, what the fuck are you talking about?"

"It was, I dunno, about a couple of years before we time-travelled. There was that campaign about women having the same rights as men and being able to freely walk around with no top on during hot weather. Of course, I was all for it … thought it was a very valid claim for equal rights. I mean, it's not fair, is it? I'm passionate about it, you could say. If women want to strip off in public, I think that's more than acceptable."

"Yeah, I'm sure you do. Did you protest about equal pay, too?"

"No," he frowned, appearing confused. "Why would I do that?"

"Exactly. Anyway, two things. One, Jenny would not enjoy getting her kit off at some nudist beach—"

"Shame. Your missus has got a nice set … well, from what I can remember." He shot his hands up. "Oh, I haven't seen them … y'know, in the flesh if you know what I mean. Through her t-shirt … they looked …" he paused and cupped his hands on his chest, peering down at them. "Well, I guess, well-proportioned and per—"

"Martin!"

"Sorry."

"Yeah, I should think so! Christ," I tutted, taking a lungful before continuing. "So, as I was saying, apart from Jenny not feeling comfortable about whipping her breasts out in public, and whilst we stand here discussing your passionate belief in the campaign to free the nipple, we have a psycho nutter in the shape of Paul Colney driving out of Luton Airport in a rental car, current location, and intended destination unknown."

"Mr Apsley. Hello, Mr Apsley."

Martin and I shot a look towards the stairwell that led into our level of the multistorey car park. The precise location where we'd wasted ten minutes discussing speedy dairy deliveries and the right and wrongs of the liberation of women's nipples. Difficult to see how those two subjects could fit into the same conversation, although Benny Hill segued from one to other with ease.

With a Jason-Bourne-styled stash of travel documents lying exposed in the boot, I flung the lid closed as the chap hot-footed towards us.

"Who's this geezer?" Martin hissed out of the side of his mouth.

"God knows. Let me do the talking. Just keep schtum."

"Yes, Dad. Course, Dad. Whatever you say, Dad." His unwelcome sarcasm oozing like the pus from a stage-four decubitus ulcer.

"Jason, hi. I thought it was you. I was just coming down the stairwell and recognised the back of your head."

Although I had no idea who he was, we politely shook hands as the new arrival glanced at Martin.

"Have we met? You look familiar."

"I'm not sure." Martin crinkled his brow, presumably trying to work out, as I was, the man's identity and, thus, which name to select from his extensive repertoire before introducing himself.

"Oh, I tell you who you look like, but obviously, it can't be," the enigma paused and turned to me as we released our handshake. "You remember that caretaker at the school when I was there? Ah, what was his name …"

I shot Martin a look. The tiniest nod in reply suggested he and I were on the same page. Although I still couldn't place this chap, I figured he must have been a pupil of mine. Also, due to recognising Martin, and that I had him pegged for being a chap in his early thirties, that placed him at the school during Martin's short tenure as the caretaker when wielding his screwdriver, oiling the boiler, and chatting up the fifth and sixth-form girls, including his mother – not necessarily in that order.

"Martin, that was it. You remember him, surely?"

I offered a tight smile.

"Yeah, we used to call him Timmy … y'know, that bloke always chasing women in the *Confessions of a* series of films. What was that actor's name?"

"Robin Askwith," I piped up, allowing him to continue and affording me a few precious seconds to think. I'd worked out his identity. Along with concern about what he knew and whether he was playing this situation, I needed a moment to plan what to say.

"That's it. Because that Martin bloke was always sniffing around the girls, we called him Timmy the Tinker. I have no idea what happened to him. I guess he'd be a guy in his early fifties by now."

"I'm his younger brother. Leonardo." Martin offered his hand.

"Oh … hell, that's embarrassing. I'm so sorry. I didn't want to appear rude. How is your brother?" he asked, taking Martin's hand.

"Just the same," I chimed in. "Still chasing women." I side-eyed Martin, who glowered his non-verbal response.

"Oh, right. Well, fair play to him. Anyway, you remember me?"

"I do."

"So, what did you think of my book?"

311

28

A Few Good Men

"I have to confess, I've not read it," I offhandedly replied, whilst folding my arms. An unconscious act screaming defensive body language, which Carlton made a point of noticing as he drifted his eyes to my chest. I suspected all that guff about 'Timmy the Tinker' when describing 'Martin the Caretaker' from back in '77 being a break-the-ice type of conversation that any well-tuned journo would employ to wheedle their way under your skin hoping to break down barriers and thus nabbing a juicy story.

Carlton knew his trade. Although I'd skipped through the book since it arrived two days ago, I'd been somewhat preoccupied with other events like convincing my daughter I was a time-traveller and dealing with *other* Jason. All regular everyday activities … not.

From what I'd gleaned with that perfunctory flick-through of his sensational account of the events seven years ago, it appeared to be as Jenny suggested. A collection of known facts about the murders in '87 spun into a new story by a canny journalist with a few catchy lines like *'the irrefutable evidence that Paul Colney is alive'*.

That said, canny was not a word I would have used to describe Carlton when a pupil of mine. Back then, Carlton King had perfected the ability of acting the complete knob. So, I guess he must have got his head down after scraping into university. If I recall correctly, I think he sneaked through the clearing process and went on to study a pile of utterly useless crap, similar to my degree. Namely, the calamitous decline of the Indigenous population of Mexico and the seventeenth-century culture of Central America. Gripping stuff, which has had a similar effect on both my lives to that of a mild case of hives. The latter being a particularly unpleasant experience I'd suffered after contact with latex a few years back. Gloves applied to clear a blocked drain, not any kind of black fetish get-up that Martin might be more used to wearing. Anyway, both my degree course and the hives were irritating.

The trouble is, after what had just nearly transpired with Martin's new Easter bunny at the car-rental desk, coupled with the fact that the TTBC's members knew the high probability of Paul Colney still breathing air, Carlton's book held more truths than I suspected the author knew himself.

"Oh, I'm surprised you haven't read it … what with all your connections to the Colney family. I'd have thought you'd have dived straight into it, wanting to discover what I've unearthed. It's a good read, even if I do say so myself."

He sported that smug journalist look. An appearance of unwavering confidence, which was a marked difference from the day I forced him, as a sixteen-year-old fifth former whilst donning a fetching pair of marigolds, to clean the boys' toilets.

"What about you, Mr Bretton? Is that why you're here … back in the UK? Mr Apsley here gave you the heads up about what I know, and you thought you'd better fly in for an urgent tête-à-tête?"

313

See what I mean? All that codswallop earlier when pretending to be unable to remember Martin's name. Carlton had been reeling us in before striking out and digging for information.

Before Martin came up with some stupid reply, I jumped in. "I'm sorry, but what d'you mean my connections to the Colneys?"

"You were arrested and investigated in '87 along with your good self," he nodded at Martin, a knowing smirk slowly blossoming on his lips and up that smug face. "Perverting the course of justice, I believe."

"So? No charges were brought."

"No, luckily for you both—"

"Err … excuse me—"

"You were on that bridge the day Shirley Colney died." He interrupted my interruption. "I've also discovered you took a few days off work to attend Patrick Colney's trial in '77. That's unusual for a teacher to take time off during term to attend a trial of a man you apparently have no connection with, wouldn't you say?"

Carlton, appearing all pleased with himself as he rattled off his list, closed the gap between us as he took half a pace forward, giving off the demeanour of a man going for the kill. Annoyingly, he entered my personal space, leaving me no option but to lean back against the boot of my car as he prepared to deliver the dénouement to his narrative regarding the Colney family and me.

"And, according to one of my reliable sources, you were present and questioned by the police the day David Colney died when falling off the flats back in '76. So, as I just said, Mr Apsley, you've a close connection to the Colneys."

Martin slapped his hand on Carlton's sternum. The inquisitive journalist, that old student of mine, narrowed his eyes at me before slowly glancing down at Martin's hand.

"Please remove your hand."

"I will if you step back. If you don't, I'll rip your bollocks off." Martin, in his element, offered Carlton a thin smile as the now not-so-confident journalist shot him a sideways look.

Martin's intervention vindicated George's suggestion to bring my time-travelling loose cannon back to protect Jess. For the first time since this conversation started, Carlton appeared ruffled.

I peeled myself off the boot lid. Although relieved Martin had stepped in, I couldn't help thinking that Paul Colney would offer a whole different level compared to Carlton.

With Martin looking all menacing, affording me the opportunity to reestablish my stance, I tugged my polo shirt down and dusted off the back of my jeans.

"Look, Carlton, I'm pleased you've done well for yourself. I mean, you were a bloody pain in the arse when at school." After detecting a twitch of annoyance regarding my reference to his school report, I continued. "So, with your prospects, forging the career that you have is admirable. But listen, you're chasing ghosts, looking for phantoms that aren't there."

"Who mentioned ghosts?"

"You did. Your claim that Paul Colney is alive and kicking. I'm afraid your journalistic nose is sniffing in the wrong sewer on this one."

"No, I don't think so, and I think you know that. People have a right to know the truth."

I know journalists have an open mind, which is part of the job requirement when delving into a story. However, I suspected Carlton, or anyone outside our exclusive club, couldn't handle the truth.

"The Colney twins are dead, and that's the end of it."

As I uttered those words, I wished that to be the truth. I held his stare, resolute in my efforts not to blink or look away. I needed Carlton to halt his digging. Otherwise, we were in danger of becoming embroiled in a conversation about time-travel. As for the public having the right to know the truth, unless Martin, *other* Jason, and I wanted to become the centre of a world media frenzy, that was one truth that needed never to see the light of day.

With a wary eye on Martin, Carlton raised an accusing finger at me. "You seem a little too keen for that to be so."

"It's the truth."

"Hmmm. I don't think it is—"

"Apsley, shall I just hit him?"

Carlton hopped back a pace as Martin offered his best Vinny-Jones-styled menacing glower.

"No … not yet," I muttered, not peeling my eyes from Carlton, who, going by his pained expression, appeared ready to defecate in his jeans.

"You can threaten me all you like. But I know you're involved. You were both arrested when they released Patrick Colney, who subsequently died before going on a rampage of murder and arson. I suggest you know more than you're saying." After flicking a couple of looks at Martin, warily checking for raised fists, Carlton jutted his chin at me, moving his statement to a question.

"Sounds to me like you've done your research. You don't need my opinion on the matter."

"I have, but I wondered what your take on it was?"

"Take on what?"

"Paul and Patrick Colney. I believe one of those two men is still alive."

"One?"

"Both, perhaps."

"They identified Patrick through dental records."

"Did they?"

"That's what I was told."

"Who's the man who entered the bail hostel a few hours after his death, then? And who was the man identified as Patrick Colney entering Susan Kane's flat two days prior?"

"I have no idea."

"Paul Colney?"

"He died in 1977."

"Yeah, weird one, that." Carlton glanced down and rubbed his chin before shooting me a look accompanied by his favoured wagging-finger action. "From the records that a source has slipped me, Paul Colney died in a road traffic accident … in a car that just happened to be previously owned by your good self. Also, another man, who was reported as the driver of that vehicle but was never identified, died too."

"Really? Sorry, Carlton, it's nice to see you … I think. But I haven't got time for this," I nonchalantly replied, feigning disinterest. In an attempt to give off the appearance of boredom, I exaggeratedly yawned and checked my watch. However, in reality, I was squirming. My stomach performing

317

an energetic floor routine that could have spanked Nadia Comăneci's perfect ten.

Sensing he'd already backed me into a corner, Carlton switched his interrogation to Martin. However, due to earlier threats of violence, he kept his distance and didn't offer a raised finger. "How is your brother? I heard he left the UK in '77 and went to South Africa. That's where you live, is it?"

"Yes, mate. And Martin's fine, thanks."

"Oh, good. So, are you … what, just visiting for Easter?"

"Something like that."

"You've not come in from South Africa, though. Flights from there don't land at Luton."

"No." Martin barked his one-word answer before shooting me a look that suggested he needed help.

"Leonardo has just come from Spain. He's been holidaying there. Anyway, Carlton, we must let you get on. I expect you're busy. I imagine you're here to pick up a member of your family, not just trawling around the short-stay car parks looking for a story?"

"I was just in the area," he shrugged.

"An airport?"

Carlton shot Martin a look, then nodded at me.

"Are you following me?"

"No, course not!"

A blatant lie if I ever heard one. Carlton might have forged a career in journalism. However, he hadn't perfected his lying skills, which were still on par with his pathetic excuses for failing to complete his homework.

"You've been following me, haven't you?"

Carlton shrugged. "Always knew you were too intelligent to be a schoolteacher." He backed up a pace when clocking Martin's clenched fists. "Look, you know something about Paul Colney, and seeing you pick up Mr Bretton this morning confirms that."

"No, it doesn't. I've told you … you're chasing phantoms."

"But I'm not, am I? Paul Colney is alive, and I think you also believe that to be the case. There's something going on with you, Mr Bretton here, and Paul Colney, who I believe now lives in Spain. Funnily enough, the very place you arrived from this morning."

"Leonardo came in from Alicante after holidaying there. He lives in South Africa." I chimed in, worried that Martin might blurt out something stupid. At this stage, I'd prefer Martin to get arrested for assault than fall into any trap Carlton had planned.

"There's a British national who I've been investigating. It all links to my book … which apparently, Mr Apsley, you haven't read. Phantom is a pretty apt description because I can't pin him down. But, as I said, I reckon he could well be one half of the evil Colney twins."

Martin and I exchanged a glance.

"The other odd thing is the family resemblance. The pictures I've seen of him show an uncanny likeness to you and your brother." He raised his eyebrow at Martin.

"What's his name?" I fired out before inwardly wincing and regretting the desperate tone of my question. Clearly, the man Sally spotted at the car-rental desk was the same person who Carlton was chasing. It didn't take a giant leap to suggest he was Paul Colney. Also, I presumed Carlton wasn't aware that Martin's look-alike had visited the car-rental desk earlier.

However, if he knew the name that evil bastard was now going by, that information could very well save my daughter's life.

"I thought you weren't interested?" he quipped.

"Just out of interest … making conversation. You seem hell-bent on believing Paul Colney is alive."

"As you said, that's a bit ridiculous, isn't it? Moments ago, you reminded me that he died over fifteen years back."

"The first page of your book … the irrefutable evidence that Paul Colney is still alive," I quoted from memory. "You think he's still out there … now living in Spain?"

"Come on, Apsley, let's go before I smack him."

With hands defensively held against his chest, Carlton continued in a more conciliatory tone, less smug, if you like. "Look, maybe we got off on the wrong foot."

"Probably because you're a dick," Martin threw in.

"Okay, okay, there's no need for hostilities."

Despite the activity of commuters rolling their cases back and forth to and from cars, our conversation remained reasonably private. However, after a furtive glance around, covering all points of the compass, Carlton stepped half a pace forward and lowered his voice to a conspiratory tone.

"Paul Colney, despite being questioned about several sexual assaults and a string of other misdemeanours back in the early seventies, never had his collar felt. At no point had he been processed through the system, and his fingerprints weren't captured on any police records. His mother, Shirley Colney, identified his body after his death. However, as you well know, Shirley died in 1987 when your adopted daughter's grandmother played skittles on Carrow Bridge, killing Fairfield's mafia matriarch, some Australian gorilla enforcer type, and her husband." Carlton paused as he awaited my nod. "So, the lovely Shirley could have been lying about the man she identified, but we'll never know. Now, here's the thing. I do believe Paul Colney is alive. Some other poor bastard was in that car that day, not Colney. And for whatever reason, Shirley chose to claim the body was that of her son, Paul."

Martin and I exchanged a glance; Carlton continued.

"In 1987, I'm convinced Paul murdered his brother, Patrick, Susan Kane, and was also responsible for the arson attack on that bail hostel. Then, he disappeared … until I tracked down a man living in Spain who I believe to be him. My book, which, if you'd have read it, you'd know, poses questions about the events of 1987 and the failed police investigation, which the Fairfield Constabulary seem keen to keep buried. I sent you the book because I thought you might be interested in what I've discovered."

I narrowed my eyes at him. "You mean you wanted to see my reaction after reading it?" I jabbed a finger at him, causing my old student to hop back a pace. "You didn't talk to me about the book beforehand because you thought you'd glean more information from my reactions."

"And I've been proven right," he smirked. "Two days after you receive my book, one half of the Bretton brothers suddenly returns to the UK. Funny that, don't you think?"

"As I just told you, Leonardo's returned for a visit that's been planned for some months," I lied.

Martin vigorously nodded. That act as good as confirming my lie.

"And what about your brother, Martin? Why hasn't he accompanied you?"

321

Martin offered a bemused look and stuck out his bottom lip.

"Martin was going to join us but unfortunately couldn't secure time away from work," I threw in, thinking on my feet.

"I'm going to prove that Paul Colney isn't dead and was responsible for those murders in 1987. At the moment, I don't know why, but you two and possibly the police are covering up what happened."

"You're chasing phantoms."

"No … I'm chasing a murderer. And, Mr Apsley, I think you're involved."

"I'm not involved in anything. Anyway, this bloke you're investigating, what's his name?"

"I was hoping you could enlighten me. I know everything about this man, apart from the name he's now using. As I said, he's a phantom."

"Why the hell do you suppose I would know the name of some bloke you're investigating who you reckon is the dead Paul Colney?"

"Because he's your nephew …" Carlton paused as my chin sagged. "See, Mr Apsley, I have turned out well, and I'm a talented journalist. I've discovered that Shirley Colney was your half-sister, which makes Paul Colney your nephew. So, I suggest you start talking."

Unsurprisingly, I'd become a smidge lost for words. Martin, in his usual timbre, stepped in to fill the void.

"I suggest I stick my fist down your throat."

29

Sex, Breakfast of Champions

"Bloody hell, the poor sod looks just like you," chuckled Martin as he unceremoniously lobbed his bags in the hall.

"Martin, this is Jason. Jason, meet Martin. Three time-travellers in one place and in one timeline." I waved my hands between them as a way of introduction.

"Martin," politely stated *other* Jason, offering his hand, which Martin accepted.

"Course, you're a lot younger than my pain in the arse mate here." Martin raised his eyebrows at me. "Also, you haven't succumbed to middle age spread yet, either. Apsley, you need to get down the gym. Start pounding the treadmill before Jenny trades you in for a newer model."

Other Jason raised his eyebrow at me.

I huffed and shook my head. "Martin's an acquired taste. You'll get used to him … eventually."

"Hey, I don't plan on being here that long," Martin chortled. "As soon as we've sorted out that bastard, I'm off. I have some unfinished business in the shape of two lovely señoritas waiting for me back at my villa. Gotta say, old Don's house is a bit decrepit. I'm surprised you haven't pulled the decorators in by now."

I side-eyed Martin whilst waving the way forward for the three time-travellers to move through to the kitchen.

"Right, let's have a coffee. Then I need to get going over to Jenny's parents." After filling the kettle and flicking the switch, I leaned back against the sink as Martin and *other* Jason flopped onto their chairs. "No issues last night, I take it?"

"No … although, if I'm stuck in this place for the next however many days, I'm liable to go stir crazy."

"Hey, what's it like time-travelling into the future?"

"A complete pain in the bloody arse!"

Martin shot his hand at me. "Hey, Apsley, that would be like us travelling to, say, 2037-ish. I wonder how we would have fared in that time."

"God knows—"

"Hey," Martin nudged *other* Jason's arm. "Gotta say, mate, this era is way better than the time we came from. 1977 was a real craic; loads of fit birds … had a whale of a time. Obviously, I missed out on a decade when I died, but since 1987, I've had the time of my life. I mean, I don't have to work for him, for starters." Martin nodded his head in my direction before continuing. "I hope you're different, you know, not a bell-end like Apsley. God, he really was a top-drawer tosser back then—"

"Martin!"

"Hey, no offence, Apsley. Come on, though, you admit yourself what a total twat you were."

"Yeah, I get that, but I'm not sure you recounting our lives from 2019 is particularly helpful."

"Okay. Fair play, old man."

"Right, we have some developments. There's a possibility that Paul Colney is living under a pseudonym. And ... that evil bastard might have just arrived in the UK from where he's been hiding out in Spain."

"And to think, I've been living in the same place as that tosser."

"You don't think Ernie provided services to him, too, do you?"

Martin shrugged. "Who knows? I reckon the *Milkman* keeps his client base pretty close to his chest."

"Yeah, probably."

"The Milkman?" *Other* Jason chimed in, shooting looks between the two of us.

"He's a forger, apparently. Services you might need if you're hanging around in 1994."

"I'm not sure I've got much choice in the matter."

"Well, after we've dealt with you-know-who, you're welcome to take the Cortina out for a head-on and see where you end up." I paused and puffed out my cheeks. "To be honest with you, I'll be glad to see the back of it ... I know Jenny will."

"Bit risky, though, ain't it? I mean, you could end up in anytime ... anyplace, anywhere."

"That sounds like a Martini advert." That was *other* Jason. Presumably, now pondering the idea of ramming the Cortina at fifty miles per hour-plus into a tree or an unsuspecting bus stop.

"That's what I said to Sally at thirty-thousand feet." Martin offered that foot-wide grin again.

"Martini?"

"No, Apsley, keep up. Anytime, anyplace, anywhere."

"Course, silly me."

"If I crash that car again, it's possible I could just end up dead?"

"I'd say so. Who knows?"

"Look, I've had a night to sleep on things. Apart from this time-travel being a bit of a difficult issue to get my head around, I reckon it might all be for the better. As long as you come through as discussed." He paused until I nodded. "I can make a fresh start in this time … leave all my baggage behind."

"Come through with what?" Martin shot looks between us.

"Quarter of a million quid."

"Quarter of a mil!"

"Today's value of those diamonds that were in my safety deposit box."

"*My* safety deposit box," somewhat sarcastically chimed in *other* Jason.

"You got that sort of cash, old man?"

"Not in my back pocket, no. Jason knows I need a bit of time on this one. I'll have to pull together a betting plan. Up the ante, so to speak."

"What about … you know, as you accused me earlier?"

"Sorry?"

"Being careful!"

"Well, yes, I know! Christ, you don't need to question me about being careful."

"Okay, but that's going to take a bit of time to pull that sort of cash together … you need some help?"

I knitted my brows, concerned about what he might be suggesting.

"Jesus, Apsley, don't look so bleeding worried. I've got a bit stashed away and can sub you a few quid if you like."

"What does a few quid look like?" I asked, turning to make the drinks now the kettle had boiled, thinking it was kind of him to offer, but a few tenners weren't really going to make much difference.

"Well, I dunno … I could bung you a hundred … probably could stretch it out to a ton-fifty without too much difficulty."

I chuckled as I poured the water. "Well, every little helps, as they say."

"Grand."

I spun around with the kettle poised at forty-five degrees, thus shooting boiling water across Don's old lino floor. To offer symmetry with the angle of the kettle, my mouth slewed to one side.

"Hey, old man, you wanna be careful. If you can't use a kettle without spilling boiling water, you're gonna have to go in one of those homes."

"Grand! One hundred and fifty grand?"

"Yeah, should be fairly easy to lay my hands on that."

"How?"

"Look, Apsley, for the past seven years, I haven't just been shagging my way around the Costas, soaking up the sun, guzzling sangria. I've made investments. I'm a property tycoon now. Plenty of easy cash to be made in Spain, mate. I know where the resorts will be built. Caroline and I visited a fab place in 2014. Five-star jobby … you know, all-flash, spa, private pools, the works. Of course, it wasn't built when I landed in

Spain a few years ago. So, I made a few strategically placed bets. That way, I managed to build up a fair whack of spondoolies, dibbed in early with developers, and made a killing."

"Bloody hell."

"Now, look," Martin paused to wave his hand over his torso. "I keep in shape, and this alone can pull the women. However, owning a few Ferraris and the benefit of a healthy bank balance helps reel the fit birds in. The girls love the yacht I've got moored in Marbella."

"A yacht?"

Martin leapt up and took the kettle from my hand. "Give it here. You're gonna scald yourself."

"How big?"

"Oh, nothing flash. Seventy-footer. I get invited to all the parties by the rich and famous. Had drinks on this two-hundred-footer a month or so back. The owner, Juan, a South American banking tycoon, reckoned he bought the little dinghy off your hero, James Hunt."

"Really?"

"Nah, I doubt it. I think that was just a made-up story to spice up his parties. Hey, but Juan knows the right girls to invite. All the sort that Mr Hunt would have liked if you know what I mean." Martin offered a salacious wink.

"Bloody tragedy, the world losing that man last year. Sex, breakfast of champions," I muttered.

"Hunt?" quizzed *other* Jason.

"Yeah, died last year."

"Blimey, I'm surprised he was still racing."

"Oh, he wasn't. Heart attack, I'm afraid."

"Heart gave in when knobbing a few birds, I imagine," chuckled Martin. "Didn't he have that slogan on his racing overalls?"

"Yeah, but I don't think he was doing that at the time. James had settled down with his new girlfriend. Anyway, I take it you're attempting to surpass his alleged bedded-women totaliser, are you? What was it, five thousand, give or take the odd one here and there?"

"Sounds about right. And, yes, I'm trying. The last party Juan threw, I had hordes of beauties all over me. I didn't come up for air for days." Martin made the drinks, passed a tea to *other* Jason and settled back in his seat. "What? You look shocked."

"I ... I am."

"Well, sorry, mate, but when you got five Miss Worlds in your ten-foot circular water bed, you're not surfacing too soon, I can tell you."

"Not the collection of Miss Worlds ... the money, the cars, the fortune."

"Oh, well, I've been busy."

"Jesus, I thought I'd done well with pulling together enough for Chris and Beth. Oh, shit! You've been careful, haven't you?"

"Yes! Money goes to money, old man. Betting is now just a little side hobby."

"You never said anything about this during our calls."

"You know me. Not one to brag."

"Jesus ... well, yeah, if you could sub me that cash, that would be a big help."

329

"Gents, I don't want to be accused of putting you on the spot, but that is my money."

"No, you're right. The diamonds were originally yours. I will pay you. Fair's fair."

"Hey, look, I'll just give you the quarter of a mill. Then it's done."

Other Jason and I shot each other a look.

"Martin, can you really lay your hands on that sort of cash?"

"Course ... that's just loose change. Call it a thank you for killing me in 2019. Best bloody thing that ever happened."

"Wow ... I don't know ..." I paused. "Well, I s'pose—"

"A thanks will do, old man."

Other Jason offered a thumbs up. "Great. I'll need it in cash 'cos I'm struggling on the identification front at the moment. I don't even have a bank account."

"Ah, yes, I know that feeling. Look, we'll deal with Colney, then I'll put you in touch with the *Milkman* and get you all set up."

Other Jason nodded and raised his eyebrows. Like me, presumably struggling to get his head around it all.

"I take it that watch is the real thing, then?"

Martin swivelled his wrist around and tapped his Rolex. "Sure is. Three grands' worth of Swiss finest. A bloody steal. That would be nearly fifteen back in our day."

The three of us slurped our drinks. Although still in a state of shock about Martin's financial situation, and not forgetting the issue of Paul Colney, I felt relieved the quarter-of-a-million situation was resolved. The thought of George and me trawling around betting shops across the south of England for the next God knows how many weeks, trying to amass a fortune to pay *other* Jason, just didn't appeal.

Other Jason placed his mug on Don's old kitchen table. Martin made a valid point; the furniture and décor were somewhat dated.

"That's settled. I think I might stay in 1994."

"And leave that baggage back in the good old '70s, eh?" I said, pointing my mug at him.

"Yeah, it's a better idea than risking another crash in that car. Best I forget the past. Also, I won't have to look over my shoulder in case anyone comes looking for those diamonds."

"Shit … are they—"

"Don't ask, and I won't have to lie."

"Jesus," I muttered. For many years, I harboured a nagging concern about the provenance of that stash of sparkly stones I'd discovered in *his* safety deposit box and whether they were less than kosher. The diamond in Jenny's engagement ring, expertly arranged by old man Maypole, was probably illegally acquired. Information I would probably not divulge to my wife. When clocking my worried expression, *other* Jason attempted to calm the waters.

"Look, too much time has passed, and you don't need to worry now."

"I hope you're right. Shit!"

"I am. As I said, don't ask, but the acquisition wasn't full-on illegal. As I said, best leave that all in the past."

"Including Annie?"

"Oh, you met her?"

"I did … she thought I was you, of course."

"When?"

"Back in '76. I'd only been there, I dunno, it wasn't long. She just rocked up at the flat one day."

"Rocked up?"

"Arrived. Turned up."

"Oh … what, she came over from South Africa?"

"Yeah, she just turned up. She came to apologise and practically begged me to get back with her. I met her again a week later when she lured me to her hotel—"

"Get in! Did you do her? Slip her the sausage, Apsley?" From a seated position, Martin pumped his hips and clenched his fist.

Other Jason shot Martin a look, then raised his palms in the air when glancing in my direction.

I shrugged a response whilst Martin continued his smutty schoolboy antics.

"Well, come on, did you do her? Bash her booty, take her up in the lift? Come on, spill the beans," he growled, allowing a salacious sneer to creep across his face. "I bet you banged her a good'un, eh?"

"Is this bloke alright?" *other* Jason asked, frowning at Martin's Lord Flashheart impression.

"Not really. He has the mental age of a pubescent fifteen-year-old with raging hormones, but his heart's in the right place."

"Wha … oh, well, that's fucking charming. You soon give me a call when you need a bit of muscle, don't you? And we're soon forgetting my offer of cash, I see. I was merely asking if you boffed his missus, that's all."

"No, I didn't. I turned her down. I'd just started dating Jenny. So, the last thing I was going to do was nip up to her hotel suite, pretend to be him, and play a game of hide the sausage, as you so eloquently put it."

"Well, I would have."

"Martin, you would do anything with a pulse."

"Hey—"

Other Jason grabbed Martin's arm. "I appreciate you helping him out with the cash, but stick a sock in it, pal."

"Jason, I wouldn't have gone to her room even if I hadn't met Jenny. Your Annie thought I was you. That just wouldn't have been right. It was you who she wanted, not me."

Other Jason offered a nod, conveying he understood my reasoning. "How was she? What did she—"

"From what I can remember," I interrupted as he paused. "Totally stunning."

"What? A fit bird begs you to do her, and you decide not to slip her one? Fuck me, Apsley, what's the matter with—"

Other Jason's arm shot out, balling the neck of Martin's t-shirt before hauling him across the table. "Shut it! You're starting to fucking annoy me."

"Woah! Hold up there," I blurted.

Martin, fist poised in mid-air, *other* Jason still white-knuckle gripping Martin's t-shirt, froze in position for a second before glancing at me. Concerned this was going pear-shaped, I stepped forward with my palms open.

"Gents, please, can we take a breath? We have Paul Colney to deal with and Jess's life to save. Knocking seven shades of shit out of each other isn't going to help."

Akin to a couple of heavyweights at the pre-fight weigh-in, both men held their positions before Martin opened his palm. *Other* Jason, clocking the offer of diplomacy, released the t-shirt from his grip.

Martin retook his seat whilst performing a number of 'I see you' gestures.

The whole purpose of these two on a stakeout in Don's old gaff was to protect Jess. The way things were panning out, I feared they might kill each other instead.

"Shake?" *other* Jason offered his hand to Martin.

Although a welcome cooling of hostilities, *other* Jason's choice of word and accompanying actions confirmed the different eras we came from. Like a public schoolboy, the one man in the room who was actually born in 1934 employed an action you might see in a monochrome movie when two cowboys shake hands after a saloon brawl. Okay, some Westerns ended up with a gunfight, so I hoped this one would fall into the first category.

Martin, appearing a little wary of the offer, extended his hand, which *other* Jason grabbed and gave a hearty squeeze.

"I've dealt with all sorts in South Africa, and I mean all sorts. Mention my Annie in that tone again, and I'll split your head open."

I sucked in a breath, awaiting Martin's reaction. Going by the sincere nod in reply, perhaps my time-travelling loose cannon was finally showing some maturity. Better late than never, I suppose.

"Fair play. Your Annie is off the agenda. But, hey, wait 'til you see this trolley dolly I banged. Legs up to her armpits, fabulous tits, and nipples the size of dinner plates you could serve up a full English on."

Maybe I was a little premature in that maturity assessment.

"Right, can we get back on track? Paul Colney," I announced, clapping my hands in an attempt to break the tension.

"So, you reckon he's here? Back in Fairfield?" chimed in *other* Jason.

While performing a double act, me as the straight man, Martin taking on the role of the clown, which kinda suited him, we brought *other* Jason up to speed with this morning's events. When touching on the subject of Paul, our performance morphed from *Alas Smith and Jones* to more *Derek and Clive*, purely based on the choice of language that Martin liberally threw about when making it clear what he thought about Mr Colney. Fair enough, Martin had encountered two previous altercations with the man, so his rather low opinion of the bastard was to be expected. I offered a fleeting mention of Carlton, and Martin described how he made the journalist whimper when threatening to rearrange the man's face.

"I still don't see how knowing that he might be back helps us. We know he plans to strike on the 6th of April, but other than that, we're in the dark."

I placed my cup on the draining board before scrubbing my hands over my face, parting my fingers as I spoke. "I know, but it's a start. If Martin's young lady spotted Paul, we know older me was referring to him."

"What if I see if Sally knows anyone at that car rental place?"

"And do what?"

"Well, she might be able to get a list of who rented a car this morning. Then, we could narrow it down and might get lucky with an address as well. You have to provide contact details when you hire a car."

"Who's Sally?"

"Ah," Martin offered a foot-wide grin. "That fit little trolley dolly with the legs I made friends with—"

"Oh, yeah. Dinner plate nipples. How could I forget?" *Other* Jason sarcastically replied.

"That's the girl."

"Friends? You bashed her brains out at thirty-three-thousand feet. Is that what you call being friendly?"

Other Jason shot Martin a look. "Err … you did what to this woman?"

"Checked out her undercarriage whilst she hopped on the beef bus."

"Christ," I muttered.

"Foxtrot. Uniform. Charlie. Kilo. We hopped on the lurve train." To be fair, his attempt at a deep Barry-White-type voice was a significant improvement on his Irish or Spanish accents from earlier. "And what a journey that was. Quite possibly the fuck of the century, to quote Mr Douglas."

"What the hell is this bloke on about?"

"Ah, welcome to the world according to Martin Bretton."

"And who is Mr Douglas?"

"Kirk's son."

"Streets of San Francisco?"

"The very same."

"Okay, but what's he got to do with Barry White here, knobbing some bird on a plane, or beef bus, whatever that is, whilst checking the landing gear and mouthing the NATO phonetic alphabet?"

"That's a fair question. Let me translate from Martin-speak to plain English. As he's already alluded to earlier, regarding the full English nipple comment, Martin's made an acquaintance today. A *young* lady with whom he has struck up a relationship. I say relationship, but probably more akin to what James Hunt might have enjoyed back in the day. Anyway, said young lady is coming around later to continue that relationship. So, what Martin is alluding to … his new acquaintance might have contacts at the car-rental desk who could be persuaded to divulge confidential information."

"The names of who rented a car and any temporary address?"

"Precisely. If we can narrow it down, we might discover the name he's using. If we can just get ahead of Paul and blindside him, remove Jess from his line of sight, we can thwart the bastard's plans."

"The crusade to blind the bastard!" announced Martin with a thrust of his arm in the air, leaving us two confused as we gawped at him. "What?" he exclaimed when clocking our bemused expressions.

"Martin, what the blue blazes … what the fuck are you on about?"

"Really? God blinded Paul on the road to Damascus for his persecution of Christians and for generally being a badass."

Other Jason and I exchanged a shrug.

"The New Testament. Hey, there's more to me than bird-boffing and titty-sucking, you know."

337

30

Overpaid, Oversexed, and Over Here

After consuming the delights of the extensive fare on offer during our Good Friday luncheon at Jenny's parents, Chris cornered me, raising concerns about his little sister. To be fair to my son, Beth had crawled into her shell since the revelations about her natural father's killing spree, which can't now happen. Plus, the fact the members of the TTBC all knew I would die in 2015 and the issue that Beth might marry a lawyer called Phil at some point in the future.

Chris said he'd probed Beth regarding her rather unusual moroseness, only to receive a shrugged response. As my son correctly pointed out, Beth would typically reply with a volley of expletives, not a nonchalant, non-committal-type shrug.

Taking a leaf out of my daughter's book, I'd shrugged a response before suggesting her unaccustomed state of serenity could probably be put down to her just being a teenager with mood swings. With Jess and my wife also sporting a somewhat peevish expression throughout the muted get-together, something Frances also picked up on, Chris didn't buy it – fair enough. However, this wasn't the time to issue an application for our rather exclusive club to my son and future daughter-in-law.

Fortunately, Frances, as per usual, held court when becoming loud and flirtatious after managing to see off a bottle of her favourite Chablis, which had the required effect of distracting everyone else away from Beth's, Jess's, and my wife's mardiness.

Of course, to exacerbate Jenny's state of irascibility, today also happened to be the first meeting of mother and son since Beth had let slip about Chris and three young ladies cavorting in our bed, one being my ex-wife. Apart from a few cutting remarks thrown his way when somehow the conversation came around to David Koresh, the Waco siege last year, his many wives, and the general subject of polygamy, Jenny hadn't openly taken Chris to task about his four-way tryst.

With the Easter celebrations a smidge muted, Chris and Megan left early. Presumably, to do what the young and in love do. Frances, before reaching the bottom of her second bottle, chose to retire to her room for a nap. When Jenny's father, John, said he'd join her, we made our excuses to leave. Not that I thought Frances would be up to much after glugging the best part of ten glasses of wine. However, the glint in John's eye suggested those thoughts were not solely for the young but also for the young at heart.

After Jess assured me she would be alright, employing her well-practised stoic persona before suggesting I should stop fussing, the Pooles set off home. With *other* Jason and Martin – if the latter wasn't too distracted by Sally – keeping an eye out for Jess when performing their stake-out duties, I felt sure my daughter would be safe tonight. Still with a face on, Beth agreed to join Jenny and me at the pub where we'd earlier agreed to meet George.

Although the vast majority of future history repeated itself, every time someone travelled back through time, the future for those closest to them alters. Yesterday evening, after returning from depositing my lookalike at Don's, Jenny and I invested an hour perched on the end of Beth's bed whilst attempting to explain these phenomena to our confused daughter – a tricky conversation involving a fair swathe of palaver – and, to say the least, it panned out to be a bloody tough sell.

Jenny, choosing not to admonish Beth for her outbursts and torrents of invectives, coupled with her decision to lift the twenty-year grounding order levied earlier that evening, appeared to have the effect of calming the waters. However, as this situation had for George, Jenny and Jess, accepting time-travel was a thing would require time and further evidence until Beth could confidently accept her parents weren't complete loonies. That said, and, despite the somewhat odd conversation, along with having her parents in a vulnerable position, Beth grabbed the opportunity to push for the diamond earrings – can't knock the girl for trying, can you?

Of course, the thirty-nine-year-old, apparently annoying Beth, who *other* Jason had the pleasure of meeting in 2016, harboured no knowledge of my time-travelling. This Beth, the seventeen-year-old version, now knew that information more than two decades before her older self didn't. That altering of time could lead to changes in her life. Whether Beth would still meet and marry a tall, dark, handsome lawyer, who knew? However, whether this Phil chap still gets down on bended knee or not, the woman who *other* Jason enjoyed a coffee with in 2016 no longer exists in the future – time-travel had expunged that event.

Although that feeling of being on death row remained, twisting my intestines into a Gordian knot any self-respecting sea scout would be proud of, I employed this argument to suggest that I may not die in 2015. Whatever happened over the next few days, I would be wheeling Jenny in for a full MOT to ascertain if any underlying health conditions festered.

Other Jason's claim that Jenny died in 2014-ish, meant my wife passed at sixty-eight. That was one timeline change that needed some work and, to quote George, come hell or high water, I was determined that part of future history would not repeat.

As part of my hobby, that anorak status regarding the study of time-travel and the effects on the human body – not that any of the 'eminent' scientists could have the foggiest of what they purported in their thesis – I'd previously invested time delving into predictions about my life expectancy. The reason for my ferret-like digging was due to the perceived life expectancy of someone born in 1934 as opposed to 1977. So, the act of time-travelling could have cheated me out of thirteen years of life. That's assuming I was now on *other* Jason's timeline as opposed to mine when taking into account that my mother, in this timeline, no longer gave birth in 1977 due to dying a year before.

By association, I knew that Jenny – if classed as average, which my wife most certainly wasn't – should live to eighty-four-ish. Therefore, something, presumably a disease, had cheated my wife of at least sixteen years of life. My task, when I'd got us out of this mess, would be to ensure I investigated and hopefully stop said reason for her early demise.

We'd brought George up to speed with the events of last night and my encounter with Carlton this morning. As always, my wise counsel didn't offer much in the way of any meaningful solutions. Just a few 'ye gods and little cod fishes' and the occasional 'Gordon Bennett' randomly lobbed into the conversation.

341

Whilst George squeezed through the packed bar to secure a second round of drinks, I swirled around the dregs of my pint. I peered into the glass as an act of divination, perhaps hoping the whirl-pooling liquid would somehow reveal the future.

If Martin's new young lady friend could somehow glean the required information, that could afford us the upper hand, the element of surprise if you like, which we sorely needed to thwart the nefarious Colney's heinous plans. I felt sure if we failed to locate Colney's hideout before the 6th rolled around, it would be a case of 'Goodnight Vienna'.

Beth slurped at the last quarter-inch of her Coke, chasing the ice cubes around with her straw as she noisily sucked up the remnants of her drink whilst glowering at Jenny in response to my wife's flat refusal to allow me to slip in a cheeky shot of Malibu. Like me with my pint, Jenny swirled her Gordon's and tonic.

George attempted to weave through the crowded bar whilst balancing a tray of drinks. I hopped up to help when noticing both pints slopping over the sides, fearing a re-run of Julie Walters' 'Two Soups' sketch, and thus would end up having to sup my pint from the tray with Beth's chewed straw.

"There you go, young lass. A Coke," announced George, placing Beth's drink before her. He nudged her arm, causing her to look up. "I got Brian to plant one of those fancy little umbrellas in the top. Make it more … Caribbean if you see my point." I noticed George offer Beth a wink as he flicked the pink umbrella, an action which my daughter picked up on. After taking a sip, her mood immediately brightened.

"Thanks, Uncle George."

"I hope there's no alcohol in that!" Jenny belligerently barked.

"Jenny lass … this girl, who I might add, is as close to a granddaughter that I'm ever going to get, has had a difficult few days of it. She's kept her promise about keeping schtum and toed the line. Now, I respect your wishes, but perhaps we can give the young lassie here a bit of latitude, eh? Don't think a couple of drinks are going to do her no harm, is it?"

"Mum?" Beth hovered with her mouth over the straw. "I'll behave. Promise I won't swear. I'll do as I'm told, and I won't tell the world Dad's really Doctor Who—"

"Alright, alright. Don't become all obsequious. It doesn't become you."

"All what?" I chimed in, knitting my brows and shooting a look in my wife's direction. Although flummoxed by her word choice, I was relieved that Jenny hadn't got the hump with George. Also, I was delighted to see Beth crack a smile for the first time in nearly twenty-four hours. Clearly, the act of defying the law, as in drinking a double Malibu and Coke when underage, was all that was required to drag my daughter from her melancholy state.

"Obsequious … means eager to please or obey, lad."

"Dad, can I remind you, you're supposed to be the schoolteacher," Beth smirked. "Oh, what was the job you had in the future? You were some poncy executive knob in marketing or something or other?"

"Beth!" hissed Jenny.

"Oh, Mum, knob's not a rude word. Look, even Uncle George didn't mind that one."

"Sweetheart, I'm not referring to the word knob. I'm reminding you to keep your voice down when discussing the future."

"Ah, yeah. Oops!" she giggled.

George leaned forward to be heard above the chatter emanating from those around us. "I don't think anyone can hear themselves think in here. I'm damn sure I can't remember the place being so packed. It reminds me of the NAAFI. Too many blokes, all bellowing at each other before a brawl."

"Easter … like Christmas, brings everyone out," I replied, wiping the bottom of my glass on a beer mat before carefully placing the swimming beer tray onto the windowsill behind me.

The group of young lads, whom George had attempted to shimmy through a moment ago when impersonating Julie Walters' waitress character, appeared to be upping the ante. Their alcohol-induced exaggerated laughter now drowning out the jukebox.

George tapped the arm of the lad closest to him. "Hey, lads, keep it down. No need for all your shenanigans, d'you hear?" After two hearty taps to his arm, the lad swivelled around, holding his palm up.

"Ah, sorry, I didn't …" he paused as he locked eyes with Beth. "Beth? Beth Apsley?" he inquired, ignoring George and nervously smiling whilst his flawless olive-skinned complexion morphed to mirror the colour of Martin's latest conquest's uniform.

I wasn't close enough to tell, but I suspected his pupils had dilated to that of the circumference of beer trays. If the hubbub in the pub was a few decibels lower, I think we could hear his heart thump to a high-tempo rhythm.

With her right hand, Beth lifted her long blonde hair around her ear before coyly nodding a reply.

"You … you, remember me?" he stammered. Although nervous and clearly trying to think of something engaging and

344

funny to say to my daughter, I guess it didn't help when having George, Jenny, and me playing head tennis as we watched the exchange.

Going by my daughter's expression, the coy little smile, coupled with the repeated ear-hooking of her hair, Beth liked what she saw.

"Um, should I?" she nonchalantly replied. My daughter, even at the tender age of seventeen, knew how to play it cool.

"Fil," the lad tapped his pint glass against his chest. "I was a couple of years above you at school. Fil De Roberto."

"Oh, yes. Hi ... err, hi..." Beth replied. Although I couldn't tell if Beth remembered him, she appeared mesmerised. He was – as required to tick her boxes – tall, dark, and handsome. Despite his appearance, enhanced by a coiffed shock of black hair, George Michael style, I assumed his name had also caught her attention. I remembered him from school and knew him to be called Filippo, not Philip. That said, *other* Jason hadn't stipulated either and probably didn't know.

"I'm at uni in Nottingham and just back for Easter. I thought that was you ... you look," he paused as he glanced at the three of us. "Mr Apsley, hello," he nervously grinned. "I'm studying law."

"Law? What like ... the law? As in *the* law ... to become a lawyer?" Beth blurted.

"Yeah," Fil swivelled around to flash his best smile. "Err ... don't suppose you fancy going to the flicks tomorrow? We could see *Wayne's World 2*, or *Free Willy*." When detecting my daughter's skewed-lipped expression, suggesting his film choices hadn't quite cut the mustard and sealed the date, Fil plumped for something more educational. "Or ... *Schindler's List*, if you like?"

"A date? Like a kinda date, you and me?"

Fil made a weird noise in his throat, appearing to find it difficult to swallow. He lost eye contact, now appearing to talk to a space about a foot above Beth's head. "Um, yeah," he stammered, shooting a look at me. Whether that was through embarrassment or asking for permission, I couldn't tell. "Yeah," he repeated, coyly shooting my daughter a look. The lad's relief floodgates opened when Beth grinned and nodded.

"Yeah, okay. Cool."

"Great ... that's great! That's really ... great."

Clearly, his uni course majored on the ins and outs of the British legal system and not the vast array of words available in the English language to express pleasure. Jenny, George, and I glanced back and forth between them as the two teenagers beamed at each other.

"I take it you have honourable intentions where my daughter is concerned?" I raised an eyebrow at him. When shooting his head my way, a look of pure terror appeared etched in every nook and cranny of his furrowed forehead.

"Oh ... yes, sir. I ..."

"Lad, he's pulling your chain," George chortled.

"Oh, ha." Fil grinned at me before turning to Beth. "Pick you up at seven?"

Beth nodded. "Oh, d'you know where I live?"

"Oi, Fil, come on, we're going into town," another lad announced, grabbing Fil's arm. "Oh, hi." He nodded at Beth before nudging Fil again. "Come on, we're going."

"Yeah, alright. Phil, give me a minute; I'll meet you outside."

Fil waited a second for his mate to disappear. "Sorry, that's Phil. We were at school together … he's studying law, too. Although the clever git's at Cambridge. You remember him?"

Beth offered a crinkled nose. Unlike Fil, Phil was anything but tall, dark, and handsome, and I suspect wouldn't receive any ticks in his boxes. The only tick my daughter would award that boy would be the sort that carries Lyme disease. I could detect by her expression that Beth's mind whirred when considering the two possibilities – two Phils – two potential lawyers.

"Anyway, I'd better get going. See you tomorrow."

"You know where I live?" Beth repeated. I detected a hint of desperation in her voice. Fil clearly had her smitten.

"Yeah, don't you remember? I had private maths lessons with your dad, here. I'm not as clever as Phil. Mr Apsley," he paused to nod in my direction before continuing. "Your dad tutored me on Saturday mornings. I was about sixteen, just before my GCSEs … I remember you."

"Oh, okay," Beth beamed.

"You were fourteen … I remember you playing your records upstairs in your bedroom. You said hello to me once."

"Did I?"

Fil nodded, offering that best smile he'd mustered up.

Beth blushed and dropped her eyes. Her reddening could be described as only slight pinking compared to the poor lad, who again unconsciously conveyed he'd held a torch for my daughter – and, it appeared – for some years.

"Oi, Fil, you coming?" bellowed Phil, hovering by the pub entrance. Fil nodded, then turned back to Beth. "See you tomorrow," he blurted, a smidge too enthusiastically, before disappearing through the throng of drinkers.

"That was Phil," hissed Beth. "Am I going to marry him?"

"There were two of them," I pointed out.

As if she'd bitten into a sour cherry, Beth grimaced. "Oh, per-lease. The other one is horrible. I wouldn't go out with that little munchkin if he was the last man on earth. He looked like an Oompa-Loompa."

"Beth!"

"Oh, Mum, he was all …" Beth screwed her nose up. "Short and spotty."

"If you don't have anything nice to say, then don't say it. I'm sure he's a lovely lad, too. And at Cambridge, no less."

"Well, he can stay there. But Philip, who asked me out," Beth paused to temper her enthusiasm. Being too gushy in front of your parents could be considered bad form. "Well, he seemed alright, I s'pose."

I smirked at her as I leaned across the table and spelt it out for her. "Phil number one is F. I. L. short for Filippo. Italian, as his surname suggests."

"Oh, that explains it. I thought he had that swarthy look about him. The bloody Eyeties … I fought that lot in the war, you know. We had that Marshal Graziani and his bunch of reprobates on the run, that we did."

"Yes, thanks, George," I sarcastically batted back. "I seem to remember you having a thing about Sophia Loren, and she's Italian. Also, you and Ivy like that little Italian restaurant in town and a bottle of Chianti." I raised my eyebrows at him, leaving George to wriggle uncomfortably in his seat. "Also, a couple of years before your time, back in the eighteenth century, we were at war with the Yanks. Now, I don't hear you offering derogatory opinions about them, do I?"

"Overpaid, oversexed, and over here." George nodded and gulped his beer.

I clicked my tongue and offered a disapproving shake of the head.

"Alright, lad, you've made your point."

I tutted and turned back to Beth.

"So, as I was saying, the young man taking you to the cinema tomorrow is called Filippo."

"Well, that bloke who met me in 2016 didn't say if my husband was Filippo or Philip, did he?"

"Oh, Beth. You're only seventeen. You're not getting married anytime soon. As we said to you last night, you might not marry a Phil this time," Jenny threw in.

"Well, it won't be that weasel, Philip. I can tell you."

"Philip Baker … really nice lad, if I remember."

"Wow, looky here, haven't you all grown up?" We all shot our heads up to look at the man who'd called out to Beth. "Amy Elisabeth Apsley, a delectable vision of beauty!"

31

Elementary, My Dear Watson

Beth swivelled around to find Martin sporting that foot-wide grin of his as he shimmied around a group of gents who'd blocked our view of the door.

"Martin?" I hissed.

"Jenny ..." he pursed his lips as he paused. "Looking as gorgeous and ravishing as ever, I must say." Martin, ignoring my hiss, nodded at my wife, who did her best to offer a tight smile. A sardonic grimace would probably cover it.

Although Jenny could not be described as one of Martin's super fans, I guess she realised she would have to bury the hatchet for a few days based on the fact Martin had returned to assist in the TTBC members' moment of crisis. To say Jenny was shocked and surprised when I informed her about his millionaire status could be described as an understatement. What she actually said was, 'You're fucking joking! That bloody idiot, a ruddy millionaire', and believe you me, that was not a usual statement uttered by my wife.

"George, good to see you, old fella. Still as strong as an ox, I see."

"Hello, lad. Less of the old, mind. Good to see you again. What you doing here, though? I thought you were—"

"Yes, my point exactly," I interrupted. "Martin, you should be watching Jess."

With a guiding arm, Martin moved through the gents blocking his path. "Your double is taking the first shift, and I can report that it was all quiet on the Western Front when I left." He mock-saluted me before tapping Beth on the shoulder. "So, you remember me?"

"Yeah, think so. You were here when Shirley tried to kidnap me and Faith."

"That's it."

"Leonardo, but you're really Martin, the time-travelling ghost. And, if I've got my head around this time-travel shit, you're also my cousin. Both of us have a Colney as a biological father."

"Beth, honey, remember what I said," Jenny hissed as she leaned across the table.

"Oh, Mum, you can hardly hear yourself think in here. No one's going to overhear us."

Jenny tutted and rolled her eyes.

"Yeah, that's me. Shame about the family tree, though."

"Yeah, well, I try not to think about where I come from." Beth's expression suggested she took another bite of a sour cherry.

"Gotta say, girl, you've turned out pretty well. There's certainly no puppy fat on you anymore. What do they say? Blossomed," chuckled Martin before offering that lascivious grin he'd perfected, which just managed to stay on the right side of acceptable – millimetres from being pervy. "You're a

351

right stunner, now, aren't you? Bet you've got the boys salivating and nursing a box of Kleenex when thinking about you."

"Martin!"

Now he'd nudged over the line.

Beth started her braying donkey routine. George looked on in horror. In one swift movement, Jenny reached up and caught Martin across the face with a slap. The sound of my wife's well-timed whack was loud enough to be heard above the chatter and the Pet Shop Boys banging out *Go West*, which thumped out of the ageing jukebox.

Apart from the synth pop duo, and to be fair, they weren't actually in the room, a hush descended as most punters swivelled to witness Jenny glowering at Martin, who still sported a smirk despite his glowing cheek. Just at the point when the Pet Shop Boys started to precursor every line with *Together,* the door swung open, and a young woman sashayed her way into the bar heading our way.

"Hi, it's nice to meet you all. I'm Sally. Oh … did I say something? It's weirdly quiet in here, isn't it?" The young woman I'd met earlier performed that routine of clambering over Martin, her hand on his chest, a jean-clad leg rubbing his thigh before continuing. "Sorry, did I miss something? I needed the ladies."

Wide-eyed, unblinking, Sally peered around the bar whilst all occupants continued to hold their mannequin pose. Some, marionette style, raised their hands to take a sip without taking their eyes off my wife and Martin, who continued to hold centre stage.

Although I doubted a bucket of pig's blood were to be discovered finely balanced above her head, and this being a backstreet pub in an unremarkable Hertfordshire town, not a school prom in Maine, the poor girl's exophthalmic expression could be juxtaposed to that of Stephen King's *Carrie*.

Fortunately, whilst the pop duo repeated the song title as the tune faded away, the chatter restarted as if by a flick of a switch, and not the telekinetically sealing of exits, trapping us all in a raging inferno.

After Martin apologised to both Jenny and Beth, he introduced Sally to the group. Now out of her air-stewardess uniform, I thought the girl looked exactly that, a girl. I guess in her mid-twenties, wearing the other half of Boots' make-up counter, a cheetah-patterned crop top, matching scrunchie entangled in her messy hair, which I think was by design, hooped earrings and a black choker to complete the ensemble, the girl was dressed to impress. Martin's reapplied foot-wide grin suggested Sally had achieved her goal.

Beth threw a confused look when Sally called him Tyler, but fortunately, she remained schtum whilst George nipped to the bar to grab the new arrivals a drink. I say nipped, but George, although active, rarely nipped anywhere these days. However, woe betide anyone who treated him as an old man.

Whilst Jenny glowered and Beth inspected Sally, either capturing style ideas or, like me, thinking the girl was probably too young for Martin, I pushed my loose cannon for answers.

"So, come on, have you managed to glean any intel?"

Martin wrapped his arm around Sally's waist, pulling her close. "We did indeed. Sally pulled a blinder, didn't you, girl?"

Sally beamed, delighted she'd pleased her man. Whether, at this point, Martin was just employing his natural charm or he'd made the girl aware of his business portfolio, yacht, fast cars, and fortune to woo her, who could tell? However, by the way the young Sally cooed over him, there was no denying that if Martin planned to return to the bosom of his cavorting naked señoritas and leave the girl behind, he would break her heart.

"Well?"

Martin extracted a sheet of green-bar-dot-matrix-printer paper from his jacket pocket before unfolding it, swivelling it around, and laying it in front of me.

"What am I looking at?"

"D'oh! It's computer paper!" announced Beth, rolling her eyes. "Schoolteacher, God help us."

That 'D'oh' phrase from Laurel and Hardy, not Homer, because we were still a few years from that immature, obese, doughnut-swilling, yellow cartoon man from reaching our shores.

"Beth!" hissed Jenny.

"Here we go. Pint for you, lad. White wine spritzer for the lassie, here." George placed the drinks down before nestling back into his seat. "What did I miss?"

"Dad being a thicko!"

Ignoring my daughter's put-down, I grabbed the sheet whilst Jenny pursed her lips at Beth. Martin explained how he and Sally had come by the information, which appeared to be a printout of names and addresses.

"So, as I said. Sally pulled a blinder. After she came around, and we'd finished enjoying some time relaxing—"

Sally rubbed his thigh and giggled, causing Martin to pause.

"Relaxing?" I raised an eyebrow.

"Yeah, you know. Just enjoying each other's company, as you do."

"Is that what they call it these days?" scoffed Jenny, folding her arms and raising her chin.

"Sorry, Jenny, lass. Call what? You've lost me."

"What you would call having a roll in the hay, and I would call shagging. Or boning, as that dick, Craig, calls it."

"Beth!"

"Oh, right, hmmm," George cleared his throat. "Err … best you carry on, lad." George nodded at Martin before plucking up his pint.

"So, Sally knows a bloke at the car-rental desk—"

"He's been chatting me up for months. Not my type, of course. He's only in his twenties and really immature." Sally interrupted Martin before rubbing his biceps and looking up at him doe-eyed. Martin grinned at her, both lost in each other's gaze.

"You two need to do a bit more relaxing," sniggered Beth, before seductively licking her straw.

Jenny tutted before prodding my arm with a stiff finger. "It's your fault. You're not tough enough on her," she muttered, directing her disapproval regarding our daughter's smut in my direction.

Rather than respond, I cleared my throat as an indication for Martin to continue.

"Yeah, reckon we do," chuckled Martin, salaciously raising his eyebrows at his girl. "Sally gave this bloke the come-on. You know, a bit of flirting, showing some cleavage," Martin paused whilst clocking George's bulging eyes. "All standard stuff, if you know what I mean?"

George coughed and thumped his chest when glancing away from Sally, who'd puffed out her chest as if to add visuals to Martin's account.

"So, course, this prat goes all gooey-eyed, and Sally goes for the kill. She casually enquired if she could have a printout of the details of today's rentals, and he complied, unable to resist her. By that point, the bloke was putty in her hands and, I wouldn't have been surprised if he'd offered his bank account details." In true Martin style, he paused to feast his eyes on the girl's visuals before continuing. "When Sally draped across the counter and sucked her finger, I thought the bloke was going to shoot—"

"Don't!" Jenny whacked out her palm, causing Martin to flinch. "We get the picture, thank you."

"Easy, Jenny. You need to relax more."

Beth snorted Coke through her nose before slapping her hand to her mouth to contain her guffawing when clocking my wife's acerbic glare. Regarding the Coke snort, that was the liquid variety, not a line of white powder. Just thought it best to clarify.

As I scanned the sheet, one name jumped off the page.

"Found him?" Martin enquired.

"That one?" I suggested, stabbing my finger on the sheet.

"Got to be."

"Tony Lencoy," I muttered.

"Do what, lad?"

"George, there's ten names on here. Four women, and I doubt they're him. Of the six men who rented a car this morning, Mr Lencoy—"

"Is an anagram of Colney," blurted Jenny.

"Precisely."

"Could that just be a coincidence, lad? What about the other names?"

"Nah, look at the address that Mr Lencoy has given." Martin pointed at the sheet, specifically the addresses.

I glanced down, tracing my eyes across to the address. "Bloody hell, he can't be up there, can he?" I glanced up at Martin. "Well, if it is him, we need a plan to deal with the git."

"Yeah, but there's more. Look across to the other side," Martin nodded at the page whilst extracting a second sheet from his pocket.

"Return and collection … why would he return a car and change it?" I muttered, peering at the printout. "He returned a Mondeo and rented a Cavalier."

"Look at this." Martin slapped the second sheet on the table. "Two weeks ago, Tony Lencoy rented that Mondeo after arriving from Málaga."

"Spain!"

"It's him, Apsley. The dick has used an anagram of his name."

Sally furrowed her forehead at Martin but said nothing. I wondered what backstory he'd spun when persuading her to help. Worryingly, whatever bull he'd conjured up, this conversation was starting to unravel that lie.

"Darling, why, if it is him, would he give that place as his address?"

"That's what's printed there, so it must be him. Unless the psycho bastard's given a false address, which he may have, I s'pose." Martin tapped his finger on the computer paper. "You know, it's been years since I've seen these damn great sheets.

Back in the '90s, when I was a kid, Mum used to bring home boxes of these for me to draw on," he chuckled, which quickly morphed into a whine when Sally shot him a look.

"It is the '90s."

"Well, yeah, I know," he shrugged.

"What you on about, then? You were a kid in the '60s."

"Huh." Martin offered Sally a Wallace-type grin whilst swivelling his eyes in my direction, appearing desperate for a rescuing explanation to cover his time-travel cock-up.

"Martin's little joke," I shrugged, struggling to come up with anything better when put on the spot.

"Who's Martin?"

Her question hung in the air. The five members of the TTBC in attendance at this impromptu meeting all glanced at each other, waiting for someone to explain.

"Err ... I meant Tyler."

"Who's Tyler, lad?"

"George!"

"Oh, hell. Yes, sorry, I forgot. He's called Tyler now, ain't you, lad? Although, presumably, you should be Leonardo this week?"

I groaned.

Sally shifted an inch away from Martin as her expression morphed from lustful desire to concern. "Hang on, who's Leonardo?"

"Sally," Jenny butted in. "Martin ... err, Tyler, has a few middle names he occasionally prefers to use."

"No, he doesn't! I've seen your passport."

"Which one?" I muttered under my breath.

"Oh, I just use them as a joke … sort of," Martin grimaced, presumably realising that wasn't going to cut the mustard.

"What joke? I don't get it?"

"Err—"

"No, hang on. You said this bloke you were trying to find was an old schoolmate." She turned to me and wagged a finger. "You just said that you need to deal with him."

"Oh, well, not quite deal with. More, sort of …"

"What?" She turned to Martin. "Tyler? You'd better explain. I've stuck my neck out by getting this information. I could land in all sorts—"

"Oh, fuckerdedoda, this is frigging ridiculous. Look, miss bimbo, trolley-dolly. You, all tits and teeth, as my mum would say. His real name is Martin, not Tyler, Leonardo, or anything else for that matter, alright?"

Sally's jaw dropped, and the rest of us followed suit like a domino effect.

"Martin is a time-traveller from the next century, as is my dad. Well, in fact, Dad and I were apparently best mates in the future. Not in a relaxing way, if you know what I mean." Beth animatedly waved her arms as if that action would clear up any misunderstanding. "Anyway, what I'm saying, Dad and Martin time-travelled, and so did this other bloke who they are trying to find." Beth shifted forward in her seat to lean around Martin as she continued. "You see, this bastard who Dad is hunting is planning on hurting my sister, who is actually the daughter of a man who Dad replaced when he time-travelled from 1976." Beth glanced around at me. "How'm I doing, Dad? On track so far?"

My jaw sagged a smidge further towards the table.

Jenny buried her head in her hands.

George glugged his pint.

Martin maintained that exaggerated Wallace-type grin, which had started to morph into more of a grimace as he contemplated the disappointing thought that there would be no more relaxing time with Sally anytime soon.

Sally, sporting that Carrie-type stunned stare, shifted away from her man.

"Yeah, so, as I was saying. The geezer Dad replaced showed up in 2016 after he'd travelled from 1976. He gave me a lift home and said I was going to marry Phil."

"Who's Phil?" Sally stammered, as she rose from her seat, shooting worried looks around the table.

"Oh, Phil … good question! I don't know. Apparently, he's a lawyer, and I love him. I just hope he's not a bald, short-arse. Can't stand short men. Nothing attractive about a vertically challenged bloke, especially bald ones." Beth held a placating hand up to George, whose hair had thinned. "No offence, Uncle George. I mean men my age with no hair. I prefer the George Michael look. You know, from Wham! Maybe his name is Filippo, not Philip. I s'pose I'll see if we get on tomorrow when we free his willy."

Only Beth laughed. To be fair, her Freudian slip was quite funny.

"I mean, *Free Willy*, or maybe *Schindler's List*, we'll see."

"Sally?" Martin whispered as Beth took a breath.

Beth dived in again, not allowing Sally to speak. "I'm now part of the Time Travellers Believers' Club, as is everyone here, and also Jess, my sister. My brother doesn't know yet, so you'll have to keep it to yourself for now."

"What the … you're mad! I don't find this at all funny."

"You don't? Jesus, what d'you think it's like for me? I mean, fuckerdedoda, I'm now scrutinising every man called Phil, wondering if I'm going to fall in love with him. I mean, when someone chats me up, now I have to ask them their ruddy name to check if he's the one."

Sally wagged a finger at Martin. "You can walk home! And don't call me."

"Sally," Martin pleaded, leaping from his chair. But she was gone. No sashaying out as she had entered, more of a stomping and door-slamming exit, closely followed by Martin as he scooted after her.

Although since 1977, I'd referred to him as my loose cannon, my daughter appeared to have stolen that title in the space of ten seconds.

"What? I only said it how it is. All that tiptoeing around you lot were doing was ridiculous." When clocking our shocked expressions, Beth felt the need to clarify after an exasperated roll of her eyes. "Alright, alright, the bimbo and tits and teeth comments were probably a bit rude, but come on, it had to be said."

I raised my palms skywards. "Beth, we can't spout off to just anyone about—"

"Well, she was annoying me. Come on, the girl was just some thicko tart, and I'm damn sure Martin can do better than her. Anyway, that's got rid of her, so we can crack on." Beth snatched the printed sheet. "Where's this git, Tony, hiding then? Oh, fuckerdedoda, not the bloody Broxworth."

"Lad," George tapped my shoulder.

"George, I'm sorry about Beth's language—"

"No matter, lad," he interrupted. "Now listen. The young lassie they found on the Broxworth on Thursday night. You know, the body of that sex worker that sparked the riots."

"What about it?"

"It's coming back to me now. When I still worked at the Chronicle, back in the '70s, when the Colney family were terrorising the estate and you found Jess. She was seeing Patrick at the time—"

"Yes! George, please don't turn this into *War And Peace*. Get to the point."

"Alright, lad. I'm getting there."

Jenny squeezed my arm to remind me to be patient. "Go on, George."

"Thanks, lass. Well, as it so happens, I can remember Jess talking about Paul and the girl he was seeing." George raised a finger to halt my interruption that I knew and he suspected was coming. "Now, I remember the name of Paul's girlfriend for one simple reason. Sherlock Holmes." He nodded to conclude his statement.

I shot a look at Jenny, my expression suggesting George was either three sheets to the wind after two pints of mild or he'd started to lose his mind. Using that arm grip squeeze technique to suggest I should hold my tongue, Jenny probed George for more information.

"George, what does Sherlock Holmes have to do with this situation?"

"Well, lassie, that's my point. You see, the Yanks produced a set of Sherlock Holmes films during the war to promote anti-Nazi rhetoric. They starred two British actors."

"Christ," I muttered.

George, failing to hear me, continued. "Nigel Bruce played Doctor Watson, and Basil Rathbone played Holmes. In my book, Rathbone was the true Holmes, not like these half-baked awful remakes they keep churning out for television."

"George, I'm gonna have to say, but I have no idea what you're rabbiting on about. How much have you had to drink tonight?"

"Lad, if I'm right in what I'm thinking, not enough. So, the young lassie discovered last week was called—"

"Rathbone!" I exclaimed. "Sandy Rathbone."

"You got it in one, lad. Elementary, my dear Apsley."

"Shit," I hissed, glancing down at the sheet and checking the date Tony Lencoy entered the UK. "Bugger … he *has* gone back to the Broxworth. Sandy Rathbone must have recognised him, so he murdered her."

32

The Brittas Empire

"Darling, I'm not happy about this. It's far too dangerous." With her hands clamped to her cheeks, Jenny pleaded with her eyes.

"Mum, I'm going with them, end of."

"Not if I say you're not. I'm not happy about any of you embarking on this fool's errand. We know what that man is capable of. What if—"

"Mum, we need to show strength in numbers," Beth interrupted as her head appeared through the opening at the top of her pink mohair jumper she'd just fought her way into, strands of her blonde hair flying at all angles caused by static charge, which befitted her gung-ho attitude. "If we're going to do this shithead, then we need to significantly outnumber him and be fully tooled up."

"Tooled up! What the hell d'you mean tooled up?" My wife shot me another look whilst now holding her trademark hands-on-hips pose.

"Jen, we're just going on a reconnaissance mission, that's all. We don't actually know if this Tony Lencoy is Colney." As my hand emerged from my coat sleeve, I jabbed a finger at

Beth. "We're not going tooled up, as you say, and at no point are we engaging with the enemy."

"Well, I think we should be armed. Hey, why don't we take a golf club each? At least we can defend ourselves if we have to engage."

"Engage?" shrieked Jenny.

"Jen, she's joking. We're just going to take a look around and see if we can spot him."

"Why don't we put a set of clubs in the boot, just in case? We could take a baseball bat, too." Beth stuck her tongue in her cheek as she smirked at me.

"Don't." I wagged a finger at her.

"What?" she shot back, feigning innocence, before popping her hair scrunchie between her teeth whilst stretching her hair back with both hands.

"You know full well what. You're purposely winding your mother up."

Beth snatched her scrunchie from her teeth and tied her hair, preparing for action. "Oh, I don't know what you mean. You've got me all wrong, Dad."

"Beth, lass, I think you should listen to your mother. I know this is only a trip for a quick recce, see the lie of the land, so to speak, but it's no place for a young lady."

"Uncle George, I'll be fine. Martin and him, that other bloke, are meeting us there, but Dad needs someone to ride shotgun with him."

"Lad?" George questioned. I knew he was suggesting he should take Beth's place.

Although I'd just about convinced my wife this fool's errand was only a recce mission, if we encountered the enemy close up and the afternoon went south, thus requiring a quick getaway, George could slow us down. I couldn't afford to put my old friend in a position where he was left with no choice but to do a 'Captain Oates' to save the rest of us. In terms of 'taking one for the team', that would be taking it too far.

"George, it will be fine. We'll just have a spin around the estate, park up and watch for a bit and see if we get lucky and spot him."

"Why do you all need to go? Surely Martin and you-know-who could do it on their own?"

"Look, Beth has a point. We need to be mob-handed. Them two can cover the bottom of the estate, and Beth and I can cover the Coldhams Lane end. That way, if he ventures out or returns, we'll spot him and know that the address he's given is kosher. All we need is to spot the Cavalier he's rented, maybe see him as well, and then we know where he is. We'll have the upper hand."

"Then what?"

"I don't know. But at least we'll know for certain—"

"We take him out. Do him one and dump his body in the river."

Jenny and I shot a look at Beth, who seemed convinced her suggestion to be the right path.

"Jenny, don't worry." Jess padded through from the kitchen, nursing her mug of tea. "There's no way Paul Colney will be back in his old flat. He probably just gave that address to the car rental place because the idiot couldn't come up with anything else."

"I know, but—"

"Anyway, there'll be someone else living there now."

"It's worth checking, though?" I chimed in.

"Yeah, course, it would be silly not to," Jess nodded. "Remember, you must be back by eight, so I'll be home when Faith and Colin get back."

"And, young lady, you have a date with Filippo tonight. You don't want to let the boy down. He seemed … well, he appeared to be well-turned out." Jenny added whilst plucking a stray hair from Beth's shoulder. "Perhaps you should stay here because he's picking you up at seven."

"Good try, Mum. I'm joining Dad on the mission. If I'm a bit late back, you, Jess and George can keep him entertained. Bore him shitless with baby pictures of me and probe him about what baby boys' names he likes."

Jess, about to sip her tea, lowered her mug. "Why? What an odd question to ask a young man."

"Because …" Beth leaned forward and shook her head, her pose suggesting a 'D'oh' comment would come next, but it didn't. "Because, my lovely thicko sister, I need to know if he is the one I'm going to marry, don't I? You-know-who, Dad's big-eared lookalike, reckons I will have a son called Oliver.

"Oh, Beth. Why can't you be—"

"More like my perfect brother?" Beth interrupted. "More like Chris, the wonder boy, who's doing everything right and making Mummy so proud?"

"No, I mean … less—"

"Annoying?"

"Yes, if you like, annoying."

"Huh," she grinned. "Well, Mother, dearest. Newsflash, I am annoying, and according to Big Ears, I stay that way right through until I'm nearly forty."

367

Jenny tutted before being rocked back on her heels when Beth threw her arms around her neck.

"I love you, Mummy. If I don't make it back. You can chuck all my stuff, but I want to be buried with George."

"Oh, Beth."

"Err … sorry, lass, nice thought, but I have no intention of popping my clogs anytime soon, thank you."

Beth swivelled her head, keeping her face tight to her mother's cheek. "Oh, not you, Uncle George. I mean my George Michael CDs."

"Right, come on. We need to get going."

Jenny kissed her daughter's cheek before Beth excitedly skipped through the open front door. As far as father and daughter outings go, and based on Beth's enthusiasm, this stakeout mission to locate a time-travelling ghost appeared to be up there with her first ride on a carousel horse at the local fair and the Bananarama gig in the late '80s. I might just add that I recall the first experience in these two examples being significantly more pleasurable than the second. A hideous excursion that involved me acting as chaperone to six twelve-year-old girls.

"Darling, it will be alright, won't it? You won't do anything silly?"

"Jen, it will be fine." I glanced at George. "Your job, keep these two ladies safe. Ring my car phone if anything happens, and we can be back in minutes."

"Don't worry, lad. I have my old service revolver here in my pocket." George patted his jacket and winked at me. "That evil scoundrel comes around here, and he'll be chewing lead."

"You haven't? Surely you haven't brought a gun into the house!"

"Jen, George is pulling your leg."

"Oh, George. You're as bad as Beth!"

~

"Breaker one-nine. Do you copy? Over." Beth giggled while fiddling with a walkie-talkie as we headed over to the Broxworth Estate.

"My God, why have you brought those old things?"

"I dug them out of a box from the garage. You remember we used them on our holidays in France? We kept one in the caravan, and the other we took to the beach. You and Chris would go down early and then call Mum and me in the caravan. Chris used to do that call sign 'Rubber Duck', d'you remember?" she giggled before holding the radio to her lips. "Breaker one-nine, this here is Rubber Duck. Over," she parodied her brother's deep voice.

"What you intending to do with them?"

"Martin and Big Ears can have one, and we'll have the other. That way, we can keep in contact."

"Really?" I raised my eyebrows as I pulled up to the lights at the top of the High Street.

"You've got to have all the right gear for a stakeout. Still think we should have tooled up … you never know what might go down, and anything's possible where my dead uncle is concerned."

"Hmmm. You do know we're not getting out of the car, don't you?"

369

"Yeah … but what if we spot the nutter, and there's an opportunity to take him down—"

"Beth, we're not taking anyone down. This isn't a vigilante mission where I'm John Wick, and you're Uma Thurman wielding a samurai sword."

Beth shot me her trademark gaping-jaw look. "The model? What's the Vogue model got to do with samurai swords and being a vigilante?"

I side-eyed her as I negotiated a roundabout. "Time-travel."

"Do what?"

"Uma Thurman plays a vigilante in a yellow jumpsuit, chopping people up in a series of films that haven't been released yet. You know," I chuckled. "I think you would be perfect in the role of the bride."

"Fuckerdedoda, Dad, what are you drivelling on about?"

"Time-travel. I likened your suggestion that we're on a vigilante mission to a couple of films in the future."

"What like Death Wish?"

"Well, sort of. I seem to remember you loved the *Kill Bill* films. We watched them at the cinema together … not sure if Lisa and I were married at that point, but she hated anything like that … y'know, blood and gore."

"Lisa?"

I side-eyed her again. "Sh–it." I grimaced.

"Dad, who the hell is Lisa?"

"My wife … my wife from my first life."

"Woah! What the frig!"

"Beth!"

"Hang on, you were married before you time-travelled? Oh shit! Have you got—"

"What?"

"Fuckerdedoda … have you got kids?"

"Yes, you and Chris."

"No kids … you know."

"No."

"But you were married to this Lisa, though?"

"Yeah, well, actually, we'd just got divorced when I … y'know."

"Oh … so where is she now? Like, now, as in this time?"

I grimaced again, shooting her repeated looks as my head oscillated from the windscreen to Beth, waiting for the penny to drop.

"Noooo … no frigging way!"

"Yes, frigging way."

"You were married to that little slut that Chris was knobbing?" Beth roared. "Oh, this is … well … fucking amazeballs! Oh, shit me, does Mum know?"

"Course, she knows."

"Oh … right. Does Mum mind?"

"Mind what?"

"That you were married to that little slut?"

"Beth! Time-travel. Your mum doesn't have any choice whether or not she minds."

"Oh, yeah. Hey, I can now see why Mum wasn't overly keen on her. I just thought Mum didn't like it that Chris was seeing her because Lisa was so young. Course, I couldn't stand the silly cow."

"Nor could I."

"You married her!"

"Yes, but that was in a different life."

"Oh, frig. Lisa was one of those three girls that Chris—"

"I know!"

"Oh, this is brilliant. My God, who else did you know? Know again from your first life?"

"Oh, hell, I don't know. There's loads of people."

"Like?"

"Like … like you want me to name them. Like actually come up with a name?"

"Yeah," she giggled. "And don't say Cinder-fucker-rella."

"Your language is atrocious. I don't know where you get it from."

"You!"

"Fair point."

"Am I the same as you remember? You know when we were both seventeen?" I detected a serious lilt to her question. All the bombastic humour from her earlier questioning now fading away.

"Yeah, pretty much. Although you're happier in this life. Remember, when I knew you in our first life, you were raised in that children's home along with Chris."

Beth turned away to gaze through the side window.

"Beth? You okay?"

"What about Chris?"

"In my first life?"

"Yeah."

"I never met him … you never spoke about him, either. He was in and out of borstal, ending up in prison. Drugs, I think."

Beth shot her head around. "Shit."

"I know."

"Are we going to tell him?"

"About me?"

"No, what happened in the last episode of Emmerdale Farm and Gordon Brittas's latest disaster in the last episode of the Brittas Empire, just in case he forgot to set his video recorder. Christ, Dad, course I mean frigging time-travel!"

"You were the queen of sarcasm when I knew you before," I smirked. "Also, Emmerdale Farm changed its name to Emmerdale. Can't remember when. Probably in the next century."

"Christ, is that still on TV then?"

"Yeah."

"Brookside?"

I ran my finger across my throat.

"Oh, I like that. Well, are we telling Chris?"

"I guess we will, but not right at the moment." I shot her a look as I swung the motor into Coldhams Lane. "You must keep this to yourself. As you're discovering, believing time-travel is real isn't a straightforward thing to get your head around, and we can't afford another episode like last night's debacle with that Sally."

"Yeah, okay." Beth shrugged.

"To say Martin isn't best pleased with your performance is a bit of an understatement. I think Sally probably just thought we were all weirdos in some obsessive fan club for Red Dwarf."

"Thanks, Dad."

"For what?"

"Adopting me and Chris."

"You're welcome. What about your mother?"

"What about Mum?"

"Can you be a bit less … well, can you—"

"Annoying?"

"Just remember she loves you as if you were her own. More probably."

"I love her too."

"Can you show her, then?" I asked, turning to see her nod. A nod of sincerity that didn't often come from Beth. I nudged through the lights, heading towards *Dodge City*, as my wife called it.

"Dad—"

"Hang on!" I braked when swerving towards the kerb, causing the dickhead behind to thump on his horn and give me the finger. "Oh, bollocks, look!"

33

The Professionals

"Dad? What's the matter? Why have we stopped?" Beth alternated her head swivels from where I appeared to be gawping through the windscreen and the driver of the car who'd halted beside us, who now blocked the carriageway, causing a tailback.

"Oi, dickhead. What the hell d'you think you're doing?" he hollered, as the passenger window glided down.

Dumbstruck by the scene in the car park, not a hundred yards ahead, I ignored the pillock who continued to verbalise his displeasure regarding my driving techniques. Now adding repeated thumps of his horn to accompany his rant, presumably somewhat disgruntled that his string of expletives were failing to gain my attention when feeling the need to vent his spleen about my impromptu emergency-stop manoeuvre. However, I couldn't peel my eyes off the events in the Beehive Pub's car park.

"Learn to drive, you frigging knob. I nearly rear-ended you."

"Dad, what you staring at?" hissed Beth, before leaning across me to offer a middle-finger gesture to the chap who still felt the need to thump his horn. "Rear-end on that! Swivel, you twat. Go on, naff off!"

After a torrent of equally impolite suggestions, interspersed with a stream of unpleasant invectives in reply, he complied with Beth's request. After excessively revving his engine, the driver shot up the road, leaving a cloud of tyre burnout and engine-oil-infused fumes in his wake. After Beth had offered a similar gesture to a few more drivers who felt the need to hoot as they sped past, she shook my arm.

"Dad, what's the matter?"

I pointed towards the pub's car park. "Look."

Beth followed my line of sight. "Oh … they're here already. That is Martin and Big Ears, isn't it?" she questioned, squinting through the windscreen at the two men chatting whilst leaning on the roof of a car.

Yesterday evening, when Martin returned to the bar after failing to placate Sally, we'd pulled together our sketchy plan for today. Earlier that afternoon, when he and Sally had returned to the car rental desk, so Sally could pull her flirting routine to gather the required intel on Paul Colney, Martin had rented a car for himself. We'd agreed he would drive to the Beehive Pub, where we would meet before enacting our stakeout.

"Come on, then." Beth nudged my arm again.

"Beth, look at the bloody car they're leaning against."

"Oh … that looks like yours, or one just like it."

"It damn well is," I muttered, checking my mirror and slamming my foot on the accelerator.

"Thought Martin said he'd hired a car?"

"That's what he said," I mumbled, just about containing my fury whilst performing driving skills similar to the man Beth had enjoyed a none-too-civil verbal exchange.

"Why have they come in your car, then?"

Instead of answering, in true American movie style, I screeched the tyres to a halt after I shot into the car park. I jumped out, leaving my door open, and scooted over to where Martin and Big Ears, as Beth called him, now gawped in our direction. Behind me, I could hear Beth in hot pursuit.

"Bloody hell, it's Bodie and Doyle," chuckled Martin. "Didn't you bring Major George Cowley along for the ride?"

"Shut up!" I bellowed with all the indignant bluster of Windsor Davies's screaming Battery Sergeant Major character.

"Christ, fallen out the wrong side of the bed this morning, have we, Apsley?"

"What the hell is *that* doing here?" I halted a few feet from my yellow Mk3 Cortina.

"That's down to me," butted in my lookalike. "I suggested we came in this because I thought if Colney sees it, it might flush him out."

"Flush him out!"

"Yeah. Hey, Apsley, calm yourself. You're liable to have a bleeding coronary. I thought your man here had a good idea."

Exasperated by their stupidity, I flung my arms in the air. "So, you thought, I know, let's take the time-travelling machine for a spin, and maybe we'll get lucky and flush out Fairfield's most wanted ghost!"

"Well, when you put it like that—"

"And … and, if you were really lucky, I mean, really, really frigging lucky, you might spin off the road, hit a tree, and end up whizzing through time to God knows when."

"Hang on," *other* Jason nodded to two lads who'd paused by the car park entrance, taking in the scene, and perhaps had heard my rant about a time machine. Either that, or they'd spotted my car with the doors open and were contemplating the opportunity for an Easter Saturday joy ride. Well, we were near *Dodge City*, so a fair assumption to make.

With the four of us turning our attention to them, the lads moved on. I scrubbed my hands up and down my face before holding up a hand to stop Martin, who appeared ready to add further thoughts on the situation. "Okay … as far as I know that car operates as a normal vehicle when not getting its bumper wrapped around a tree—"

"Or rear-ended into a dustcart," added *other* Jason.

"Yes, or rear-ended into a dustbin lorry. And I get Colney must know something odd happened to him in that car in '77—"

"There you go, then," interrupted Martin. "With me and your double, here." Martin thumbed at *other* Jason. "Parked up on the estate in this old heap of shite, the knob-head might want to pop out of his flat and check it out."

"Then we can do him," Beth punched into the conversation. She continued as the three of us glanced her way. "Flush the tosser out of hiding, and then we can pounce," she leapt forward, sporting a grimace and clawed hands.

"Ehm … Beth?"

"Yes, Dad."

"We're not pouncing on anyone."

378

"Apsley, she's got a point."

Whilst dismissively shaking my head at my grinning daughter, thinking Jenny had made a good argument that this excursion was a particularly shite idea, I swivelled around and huffed at Martin. "Please don't back her up. It's bad enough having to listen to Beth's crazy ideas."

Martin nodded at *other* Jason, who, with a lit cigarette clamped between his lips, opened up the back door of the Cortina. A second later, he produced a cricket bat, holding it aloft with as much enthusiasm as Goochie's muted celebration when hitting the three-hundredth run in the test against India a couple of years back. Unfortunately for the England captain, the perceived lucky number of three threes wasn't so fortunate when the Indian bowler took out his middle stump. However, remembering his run total being the highest achieved in Test history since the war made it an easy bet to place, thus securing me a nice little earner, to quote a certain Arthur Daley.

"See, I said we should be tooled up."

"What the hell are you intending to do with that?"

"A bit of insurance in case today goes belly up … found it in your lock-up." *Other* Jason twizzled it around as he held it aloft.

"And how exactly did you get into my lock-up?"

"Ah, sorry about that. We had to smash the padlock."

"Again? Jesus, that was a new lock after you bust the original one yesterday."

"Oh dear, how sad, never mind." Martin mockingly rocked his head from side to side. "Bloody hell, Apsley. I think we have bigger fish to fry than a bleeding padlock. I'll add a quid to the quarter of a mil I'm subbing you, and you can get a new one."

"Quarter of a mill!" blurted Beth.

I shot my hand up at Beth. "Not now."

"Come on then, Apsley. We need to get into position."

"Yeah, okay. You're gonna take the bottom end, with eyes on Dublin House, and Beth and I will park up at the shops. It's all pointless because this Tony Lencoy, if that is Colney, will have given a false address. He couldn't risk coming back here."

Other Jason air shot a ball to deep-extra-cover. "If you reckon he murdered that woman that sparked the riots, he's returned to the estate even if the bastard's not living there."

"Jess confirmed that Sandy Rathbone was associated with Paul back in the day. Of course, that's not conclusive evidence that he murdered her. Also, although the rioting has finished, there's going to be some police presence there, so I imagine Colney will be keeping a low profile."

"Anyway, Apsley, Paul Colney died in '77. As far as anyone on the estate is concerned, that's seventeen years ago. Most residents will have moved on or won't remember him."

"Or me," muttered *other* Jason, whilst feigning a straight drive for six. "I left my flat a couple of days ago, landed forty years in the future, and now I'm going back ..." he held the bat in the air and paused. "Or forward, eighteen years."

"Martin, take this." Beth handed over one of the walkie-talkies.

"Really?" he chuckled.

"Now listen. Your call sign is Big Ears—"

"Big Ears?" chuckled Martin, waving the radio at *other* Jason, who shrugged a nonchalant, disinterested, non-verbal reply. "And what are you, Noddy?"

"No, Dad and me will be Orange."

"Orange? Why orange?"

"D'oh, Take That."

"Take what?" That was *other* Jason, now leaning on his bat as if waiting for the bowler change at the end of the over.

"No, *Take That*, as in Jason Orange."

"Jason and an orange … I don't get it?"

"James And The Giant Peach. What about that, instead?" chortled Martin, I suspected, knowing he was sending the conversation into chaos.

"Oh, Christ, does it matter?" I blurted.

"I was going to call us George, but I thought that might get confused with Uncle George—"

"Why George?"

"George Michael, you dumb arse, big-eared knob. Jason Orange, because he's gorgeous, like George, and Dad's called Jason."

"They're pop stars," chimed in Martin. "*Take That* is a boy band … all a bit before my time. Well, my first life, if you see. I was born in '88, so never really got into *Take That*, although I didn't mind a bit of Robbie—"

"Christ, does it matter?" I hissed.

"Well, it could get confusing … y'know, if we say Jason instead of orange when calling you because there are two Jasons." Martin offered a cheesy grin, feeding off my frustration.

"Oh, fuckerdedoda. Kylie, then. Me and Dad are Kylie. Got it?"

Martin wagged a finger at me. "You should be so lucky."

I offered an eye roll in response.

"Right, then," Martin announced. "Let's spin around because I can't get this out of my head. On a night like this, we should crack on."

Beth and other Jason shot him a look.

"Martin, that was shocking."

"They're Kylie songs from the future," Martin informed Beth.

"Crack on? Kylie has a hit with a song called, crack on?"

"No … not that bit—"

"Can we go, please?" I interrupted. "Standing in the Beehive Pub's car park discussing Kylie Minogue songs of the future is not getting us very far, is it?"

Martin laid his hand on his heart. "My heart beats especially for you. Lead the way, Kylie. Big Ears will follow."

34

Battle of Britain

"Big Ears, do you copy? Ehm … this is Kylie. Over."

"Kylie, this is Big Ears. We're in position. Eyes on Dublin. Over."

"Big Ears, this is Kylie. Please confirm rozzer status. Over."

"Rozzers?" I hissed at Beth, who shrugged back.

Although my daughter appeared to be playing it cool, the panache she demonstrated with the walkie-talkie, coupled with the way she wriggled in her seat, suggested a heightened level of excitement.

For the umpteenth time, I rechecked the door locks. When parked in and around the Broxworth Estate area, it was prudent to keep your doors locked. However, with Beth's heightened state of exuberance, I feared if we spotted Colney, she might leap out of the car, intent on enacting her desire to do him, as she put it. Deciding to play it safe, I kept my hand poised, ready to grab her just on the off chance my gung-ho daughter made a lunge for the door lever.

"Big Ears to Kylie. Over."

"Receiving. Go ahead, Big Ears. Over."

"Rozzers status all clear. Over."

"Ten-four. Over."

I rolled my eyes.

"Big Ears, are you receiving? Over."

"Go ahead, Kylie. Over."

"Maintain radio silence unless bogie spotted. We need to maintain hot brick status. Over."

"Received. Ten-four. Over."

"Hot brick?"

"Maintain battery life."

"Oh."

"And radio silence. Really? Who d'you think you are? Hans Gruber? Christ, what next? Car fifty-four, where are you?"

Beth shot me a look, sporting a furrowed brow. "Another film from the future?"

"No … this one is well before your time, and mine, for that matter. That's more of an era for Big Ears. Look, all I'm saying … we're not a couple of Spitfires buzzing over the English Channel calling out bogies at eleven o'clock."

"Goose, shall we buzz the tower?" she giggled.

"Hmmm … Maverick suits the persona. Let's just sit tight and see if we spot anything."

"Okay, cool." Beth lifted her walkie-talkie, took a breath, paused, and then lowered it to her lap, remembering the instruction given to Big Ears.

Twenty-four hours post the uprising, the death of a rioter and a police officer, the estate appeared to be tranquil – well, tranquil for the Broxworth. Apart from a few lengths of blue-and-white police tape flapping in the breeze down by the bin storage near Shannon House, a collection of broken and boarded-over windows, and a light covering of rocks, bricks, and broken bottles strewn across the whole area, you could say the Broxworth looked none the worse for the maelstrom.

With the passing of less than a minute of muted surveillance, Beth and I both jumped in surprise when the ringtone of my car phone hauled us both from our reverie. Although now an outdated item, I'd purchased one for myself and one for Jenny as soon as they became widely available. With no desire to race to the era when mobile phones would become all-consuming, as they had in my first life, I'd resisted upgrading to one of the newer half-brick-shaped alternatives now available, as per my son's great lump. I guess I would succumb when the damn things became small enough to fit comfortably in your pocket. If I'm honest, I was quite looking forward to playing 'Snake' on a Nokia, which I felt sure couldn't be too far away from release.

Beth and I exchanged a glance as I snatched up the receiver.

"Jen, is everything alright?" I blurted. For a brief panic-fuelled moment, I became concerned that Colney had outmanoeuvred us and was now in a position to strike at my house. For sure, although he was up for the fight, George would be no match for that psycho.

Beth leaned across to earwig the conversation.

"Yes, darling. We're all fine. I just wondered how you're getting on."

"All quiet on the Western Front, to quote Martin."

"They're there then? Martin and him."

I raised a finger to my lips, encouraging Beth to keep schtum and not blurt out anything daft like the fact they'd turned up in the Cortina. As far as Jenny was concerned, that car should be crushed into a small yellow cube, not too dissimilar in size to the carry case of my car phone.

"Yeah, them two are parked down by Dublin House. We're just sitting here near that row of shops. As you said, I think it's a waste of time."

"What's *Dodge* look like."

"Pretty normal, to be honest. Apart from the mess, you wouldn't know World War Three has just concluded."

"Is Beth behaving herself?"

Beth pursed her lips and narrowed her eyes at me. That expression which Tom often displays when outwitted by Jerry the mouse.

"Yes, she's fine. Getting bored, I think."

Beth clicked her fingers and waved through the windscreen.

As I glanced up, I spotted a white Vauxhall Cavalier shoot past the parking area near the fenced-off, burnt-out community centre.

"Jen, better go. This will be expensive."

Beth clicked her walkie-talkie button. "Big Ears. This is Kylie. Are you receiving? Over," she hissed, presumably keeping her voice low, knowing the histrionics that could follow if Jenny overheard. At this point, I didn't fancy explaining the walkie-talkies, the call signs, or that Beth was now indicating that the mission had elevated from surveillance to a go-go-go status.

Unfortunately, Martin came back loud and clear.

"Kylie, this is Big Ears. Receiving. We have eyes on target vehicle. Holding position to confirm positive ID. Will not engage at this point. Over."

"Jason? What was that?"

"Oh, sorry, just the radio. I'll turn it down." Keeping my voice light, I animatedly waved my hand at the walkie-talkie, which Beth frantically attempted to quieten. Before I knew it, Beth's hand had grabbed the door lever, and she was out, striding towards Big Ears' position with the walkie-talkie held to her lips.

"Sh–it," I hissed.

"Jason … darling, what's going on?"

"Nothing. Look, gotta go, I need to move the car. I'll call you back." Before Jenny could counter, I disconnected the line and flung open my door.

"Beth," I hollered, giving chase before skidding to a halt to trot back and lock the car. An unlocked vehicle parked on this estate would be stripped down to the engine block within minutes. The undesirable lowlife who inhabited this hellhole could make the highly trained, slick Formula One constructor's pit-lane teams look positively lethargic.

Although I needed to catch up with Beth, I figured the chances of the driver of that Cavalier actually being Colney were low. So, although comforted by that thought, that didn't negate the fact that we were on the Broxworth Estate. Placing the riots to one side, even on a typical day, this was a stab vest and riot shields kind of place that you only visited in emergency situations, and you hunted in packs. With the car secured, giving it a slightly higher chance of being in one piece when we returned, I hot-footed in the direction of where Beth had shot off to.

With Beth nowhere in sight, spinning me into a state of panic, I threw caution to the wind by breaking cover into open ground as I belted across the central square towards the community centre. Despite being aware I was heading for the place where I presumed the white Cavalier would be parked and thus may, unfortunately, come face to face with Tony Lencoy, who could be Paul Colney, I continued to call out my daughter's name as I scooted around the corner of the building.

Fortunately, as I skidded to a halt, I spotted Beth crouched beside a two-tone Fiesta. Not a colour by design or a colour depicted in a Ford brochure, but more of a washed-out, muted orange body with a faded royal-blue driver's door. Whilst catching my breath, realising my heart didn't overly appreciate the hundred-yard dash, I wearily padded the last few steps to join her.

"Jesus, Dad, get down!" Beth hissed, grabbing a handful of my bootleg jeans and aggressively tugging.

"Beth, what the frig?" I hissed, as I crouched beside her.

"Big Ears, this is Kylie. Over."

"Receiving Kylie. Over."

"Do you still have visual? Over."

"Affirmative. Driver still in position. Over."

I nudged her arm. "Beth, what the shitting hell are you doing?"

Beth glared at me as she raised a finger to her lips.

"Big Ears, can you confirm the index number of suspect's vehicle? Over."

"Negative. Over."

"Big Ears. This is Kylie. I'll break cover to check the licence plate. Over."

Before I could stop her, my gung-ho daughter, in a crouched position, commando style, dashed across to another Fiesta. This one, a casualty of the riots, in a none-too-fetching charred-metal grey. Wisps of smoke still rose from its scorched interior, a stark reminder of the events two nights prior.

On my hands and knees, I peered around the two-tone hatchback to grab a better view of the vehicle in question. I felt sure when Beth clocked the number plate, this charade would come to an end. Vauxhall had produced millions of Cavaliers over the past few decades. The latest model hitting the dizzy heights of achieving second in car sales charts for the past couple of years, and only being pipped to the top spot by the Ford Fiesta, two of which rather sad specimens afforded Beth and myself cover.

"Big Ears. Index Number. Lollypop. Nine. Three. Four. Fiddlesticks. Chegwin, Lollypop. Over."

"Big Ears to Kylie. Chegwin? Over."

"It's all I could think of. Over."

"You need to learn the radio code. Over."

"Fuckerdedoda. Is that it? Over."

"Affirmative. That is the registration of the suspect's hire car. Over."

"Dad! It's him," hissed Beth.

"Beth." I hopped into a crouched position and waved both hands to get her attention. "Beth, we need to go back to the car."

My daughter shook her head as she raised the walkie-talkie to her lips. "Big Ears. Can you identify the driver? Over."

"Kylie. That's a negative. Suspect is an IC1 male. No other details. Over. Oh shit, hang on. Suspect is exiting the vehicle. I now have full visual ... holy shit!"

Part 4

35

September 2015

The Outcasts' Outcast

"Please keep your hands above the table, and at no point touch the prisoner."

I nodded to confirm his boomed instructions. Like the rest of his colleagues, he'd opted for the slow, high-volume tone they all deemed necessary when addressing an old boy like me. Either that, or they thought I might be a foreigner, and the only effective way to communicate was to shout.

Sinéad and Brandon appeared to know the form and didn't need to be instructed on the correct protocol. Or perhaps none of the six officers had the stomach to engage with her.

Kurt Penn's aura entered the room a good few seconds before he did.

Some men have a look, an appearance that suggests a wide berth being the sensible course of action. Nosher Nesbit being a case in point. Any decent human being would consider

Nosher, simply going by his appearance, as someone to avoid, like a Gary Glitter gig or a particularly prevalent bout of herpes.

In contrast, Kurt Penn appeared to be a thirty-something, clean-cut type, who you'd instantly trust like the consultant reassuringly talking you through planned open-heart surgery. No visible tattoos, a set of gnashers to rival the chaplains, and a George Clooney smile that harmonised with his lips in perfect symmetry.

However, that aura and the invisible but somehow apparent aureole, a halation if you like, encircled the man to suggest, although radiating trust, like hemlock was beautiful but deadly. Kurt Penn was the walking definition of wynorrific. Well, apparently – and according to the wife of Tom, the bungling burglar with a propensity to drop his balaclava – the man had hacked off another's head before casually storing said severed body parts amongst Aunt Bessie's and Captain Bird's Eye's finest.

Whilst patiently waiting for my 'dinner date', obeying the rules with my palms on the table, I surreptitiously watched as Kurt kissed his wife and cuddled the helicopter pilot. Although the officers had forbidden physical contact, I presumed there'd be a separate rulebook for the Penn family.

Whilst focusing on his family, Kurt didn't offer me a second look. However, I could tell the man had made a full assessment of me with his one fleeting glance. Like any trained spy, assassin, or Jason Bourne type, that one-second eyeball at my withering frame confirmed my threat level to be on the low side. Okay, it's pretty easy to ascertain that I, at the ripe old age of eighty-one, posed little or no hazard. However, I figured he knew my weight, height, inside-leg measurement and how many hairs stubbornly protruded from my right ear.

Notwithstanding his statistical assessment of me, and like the man I was waiting to see, he couldn't know I was a time-traveller.

That last unknown piece of information gave me the upper hand because I knew something that Mr Cool didn't. Events and news items from the future were becoming harder to recall as each year passed, and my brain degraded to the consistency of pink blancmange.

As had always been the case, I would need a memory jogger like a news report to remind me of what was about to happen. Seeing Mr Penn and linking the name to the face brought back those memories from my first life. In 2017, I'm reasonably certain, with the aid of two officers on his payroll, the notorious criminal escaped prison. He then embarked on a killing spree, which made Raoul Moat's rampage in Northumberland appear like a game of hide and seek at a five-year-old's birthday party.

Now I could remember the manhunt, the regular news flashes and blow-by-blow accounts of his break-out clogging up the national news. A day after scaling the walls, Kurt emptied his pump-action shotgun into his wife's head. Punishment meted out for breaking her marriage vows after the 'lovely' Sinéad stupidly chose to up sticks and run off with another man. If my memory serves me correctly, Kurt Penn's lawyer being the man keeping Sinéad warm at night.

Unfortunately for Kurt's legal representative, who'd foolishly decided wooing Sinéad would be a good idea – and they say lawyers are clever – didn't fare so well as the young Irish blonde who died instantly with a brain full of lead. When they discovered his body, the newsreader covering the story omitted some details because they were deemed too distressing to report. However, they confirmed the man had suffered a sustained attack involving many hours of torture before Kurt separated the man's head with the application of a buzzing electric carving knife.

I guess Kurt was what you might call the jealous type. Anyway, in less than two years, Kurt would blow his head off when turning his shotgun on himself to avoid recapture. I glanced around at the six officers, wondering if any of these were the two involved. If they were, both men would soon enjoy a stay in Havervalley Prison on a permanent basis, not dressed in dark uniforms and definitely not holding the keys.

Kurt Penn, an angelic-looking nasty bastard, if ever there was one. On that subject, another officer appeared, leading a second prisoner into the visitor room. Presumably, this man, and by no means sporting the clean-cut appearance of Kurt, would be the other nasty bastard with whom I'd have the pleasure of his company for the following thirty minutes.

As he settled into the chair opposite me, I assessed his age as around sixty-ish. His unkempt, salt-and-pepper beard, making an accurate stab at age difficult. Also, Simon had stated the man was a walking advert for cancer, so I guess that may have accelerated the ageing process.

I cleared my throat, waiting for him to look up at me. "You asked to see me."

After what seemed an age, enough time for me to watch Kurt throw five or six playful punches at Brandon, John Curtis raised his head and nodded.

"You know how to time-travel?"

As if Kurt had landed a not-so-playful punch in my direction, my head snapped back enough for the officer closest to us to glance in our direction. Plus, my reaction also afforded me the uncomfortable feeling of whiplash.

"Sorry?"

"You heard me the first time, Apsley."

Something about the way he said my name caused bile to rise in my throat. There was threat, hate, at the very least, a layer of contempt in his tone. Presumably, as he claimed to know Paul Colney, that idiot must have mouthed off to John Curtis about time-travel, the Cortina, and me. Most sensible individuals would dismiss such claims. However, it appeared John Curtis had chosen to believe the psycho bastard from my past.

"You've been listening to fantasy stories, I think."

John repeatedly flexed his right fist. His clenching jaw visible as his beard pendulated to the rhythm of his grinding teeth. Coupled with his heavy snorting, it all added up to suggest the chaplain had made a valid point regarding his character. John Curtis, the serial killer, appeared to go to great lengths to control the hate and evil that lurked beneath.

After shooting a surreptitious side glance to his left, presumably assessing the distance between us and the officer, he nudged his head an inch closer.

"Don't come the bollocks with me, Apsley. You and Martin Bretton time-travelled. I want to know how," his cadence whisper hissed across the table like a slithering viper preparing to strike.

My options were limited. I could continue to deny, thus leading him to lose his shit, presumably bringing this visit to an abrupt end. That would prevent me from discovering what happened to Paul Colney. Did that matter? Maybe not. Or I could play along and see where this was leading to. Admitting I'd time-travelled was obviously not a route I took lightly. However, divulging or confirming to John Curtis was low risk.

397

He was a man of dubious character with a limited lifespan. No one would believe him if he relayed this conversation to all and sundry.

"Let's say, for argument's sake, I have. What's it to you? Why d'you want to know?"

"I'm dying. Cancer of the liver, lungs ..." he paused and waved his right hand up and down his torso. "My whole body. If I can time-travel, I can start my life again without the cancer and not in this dump."

"You're a murderer."

He shrugged. A twitch of the lips suggested he revelled in the label.

"Well, I can't. But let's say I could. Why would I tell you how to time-travel?"

"You want to know about Paul Colney?"

"So, I help you time-travel, and you tell me about Colney. That's the deal, is it?"

He rhythmically nodded to confirm.

"Look, a part of me is intrigued to know what happened to that psychotic nutter. But, in reality, it's no more than a passing interest. Fortunately, I haven't seen or heard anything about him for the best part of thirty years. Hopefully, the twisted git's dead. And luckily for me, because of my failing memory, I can't even remember what the bastard looks like."

His lips twitched again, not as a smirk, but radiating anger, annoyance, and the evil that behold beneath the surface.

"And anyway, I can't help you. Time-travel, as far as I know, can only take place when dying in one particular car ... a 1974 yellow Mk3 Ford Cortina. You're in here and, by my understanding, will die here."

John shrugged. "We'll see …" he paused as the officer approached our table. John rotated his head to watch the regulation, standard issue, black boots circle around us before continuing. "You must know how that works. You know, don't you? If time-travel in a shitty Cortina is possible, there must be other ways."

Like a child denying guilt, I swayed my head from side to side.

"Pity. Unless you try harder, I'm gonna change my mind about telling you what I did to your daughter." He twitched his lips again. Definitely a smirk this time.

My eyes widened, not because of the uncomfortable lump forming in my throat, but because of the mention of Jess, who disappeared without trace on the 6th of April 1994. The day that ripped my family apart, stole Colin of his wife, Faith of her mother, and broke Jenny's and my heart. Although not our daughter, Jess had been part of our life as much as Chris and Beth.

Twenty years had passed, and our lives had moved on. Still, the hole she left created a vacuum that could compete with anything the Large Hadron Collider buried near the France-Switzerland border could conjure up.

We'd spent years searching for Jess. When following up on reported sightings as far-flung as Hong Kong, I'd notched up enough air-mile points to grab a free business-class flight to Mars. Not to mention the fortune shelled out on private investigator's fees and an office full of box files stuffed with reports and emails. Now, here I was, sitting opposite the man who claimed he'd played a part in her disappearance.

The energy between us fizzed and banged; a kaleidoscope of fulgurating strobe lights appeared, and bolts of lightning bounced between us. Either that, the generator was on the blink, or I'd succumbed to the early stages of a stroke.

"Oi, Apple, you old git. You worked out who I am yet?"

The bolted-down chair negated the opportunity to push away from the table. Instead, and based on the fact that my legs had taken on a consistency of that useless pink stuff sloshing around in my brain, I pushed my back against the chair to increase the distance from him.

He called me Apple.

The eyes.

It didn't matter how many years had passed, how grey the hair had become, skin sagged and wrinkled, the eyes and the evil that behold there couldn't be disguised by his ageing features which attempted to belie the hideous truth.

John Curtis was Paul Colney.

I'd been an idiot. I hadn't seen it because I didn't want to. Colney had taken his mother's maiden name – Curtis. Despite his attempts to disappear, continuing his hobby of rape and murder whilst hiding out in Spain had led to his capture.

Although he'd lived under that pseudonym for twenty years. Stating when apprehended that he was really the dead Paul Colney wouldn't have helped his cause. Instead of a lengthy spell in *Happyvalley*, as Simon liked to call it, John Curtis claiming to be the time-travelling ghost of Paul Colney would have resulted in being permanently incarcerated in Broadmoor. If cancer hadn't got him, he'd banked on securing parole at some point. Perhaps he's hoped to con a Lord Longford-type character who could be duped into believing Paul could be rehabilitated, thus eventually securing release for good behaviour and seeing out his years whilst continuing to dabble in his hobby.

"Jess," I whispered.

The delight, power, if you like, radiated like a beam of light as he revelled in my pain. "Strangled her. She begged me not to … whimpered right to the last moment."

Unable to respond, my desert mouth and failing mind steadfastly refused to comply.

Paul continued. "Help me time-travel, and I'll tell you where she is … let you dig her up and bury her … have a funeral with flowers, sherry, tears and hymns, stuff like that."

"I don't … I don't believe you."

Paul curled his lip. "I hated the little slag since the day she took up with Patrick … wasn't a bad-looking tart back then, but when I saw her again in '94, she'd gone all mumsy." Paul peered up at the ceiling, appearing lost in his thoughts. "I'd made a life in Spain. Got meself a new identity, had a bit of fun, that sort of thing. Back then, I called myself Tony. Tony Lencoy." Whilst keeping his chin raised, he swivelled his eyes down and grinned. "You get it? Lencoy … that's an angiogram of Colney."

I didn't respond. I presumed he meant anagram, not some sort of X-ray.

"Then there was a bit of heat when my name got banded about on the news in Spain. See, I went on a bender in … '95 or '96, can't remember exactly. Not drink … rape and murder. I'd notched up six in less than a year, and the Spanish filth were getting close. So, I changed my name again. Chose John after my old gramps and Curtis after Ma … that being her name before she married that twat of a father of mine. Good riddance to the bastard. Anyway, back in '94, when my Tony identity was solid, I came back over Easter, didn't I. Had a poke around, see what was going on." He sniffed and wiped

401

the sleeve of his sweatshirt across his nose. "I heard some journo at the Chronicle was doing a bit of digging into the family, running a piece in the paper ... thought I'd check it out. See what crap he was digging up."

I remember my old student Carlton King, destined to become the newspaper's editor, had run some articles around that time. They were just editorial pieces about speculation linking to the failed investigation of the murders in '87. However, only Martin and I, the last two surviving members of the Time Travellers Believers' Club, knew those murders were committed by the then-vanished, previously dead Paul Colney.

Paul leaned back in his chair, allowing the plastic back to rock him back and forth as he reestablished eye contact. "It was ..." he paused and shrugged. "I dunno, a whim, if you like. Spotted this bird in town, didn't I? She stood out of the crowd ... wearing an Afghan coat ... kinda reminded me of Jess. So, done a bit of digging and found out her married name, where her daughter went to college, where her old man worked, that sort of thing. Easy really. Gave her a call and told her I was a mate of Faith's. I knew she'd come when I said her daughter was doing drugs with a load of kids from college out near Fairfield Woods." He grinned, holding that nefarious look as he wallowed in my pain. "No one goes to that layby until it's dark ... bunk-ups on the back seats, blow jobs with a stranger, that sort of thing. I knew it'd give me a chance to hide in the woods and take her when she turned up."

"No ... you didn't. This is a story to get me to tell you how to time-travel."

Paul rubbed his bottom lip with his thumb and forefinger, appearing to contemplate what to say next. The fact he didn't have a response confirmed his lies. Although I wanted to know

402

the truth regarding my daughter's disappearance, Paul Colney was using this as an angle to glean information that he stupidly thought would help him time-travel.

Paul had always been the unhinged, half-witted twin. I imagine as equally insane as Ronnie, the one half of the Krays, whom I presumed Paul modelled himself upon. When he time-travelled from 1977 to 1987, he should have realised that he hadn't aged. He was twenty-three in '77 and still the same age in '87. Like Martin and I, when we travelled back in time, we hadn't become younger or not even born. Although he couldn't, but if he travelled again, the evil bastard would still be a haggard, middle-aged man riddled with cancer.

Paul raised his hand away from his lips, leaving his index finger pointing skywards. "She begged me … telling me all sorts of stuff just to stop me killing her."

I shook my head.

Paul repeatedly nodded as if to counter my continued disbelieving gesture.

"See … your daughter reckoned you weren't really her father. She said you time-travelled from 2019 back to 1976." Paul expanded his arms out wide. "I mean, what bollocks, eh? But I knew the silly slag was telling the truth because of what happened to me the night that twat Bretton crashed your motor."

I detected my lips part, not a full-on sagging jaw, as such, but well on the way. There were only five people on this planet who knew that information: Jenny, Jess, George, Martin and me. None of us had told Paul Colney – unless.

"Now, course, I thought that all a bit odd. I knew you from the estate when you moved into that flat next to Carol Hall. But your Jess … just before she turned a funny colour as my hands throttled the life out of her ..." He paused to demonstrate a strangling action with his hands. "Like this, it was ... the thumbs pushing into her throat nice and firm. So, where was I? Ah, yeah, your Jess reckoned you replaced her real father. Other Jason, she called him. Now, I get she was light-headed, probably a bit deluded at that point, so she might have been spouting a load of old bollocks—"

"Where is she? What did you do with her?" I interrupted. I had no desire to hear further details of how he'd murdered my daughter. And, with the information supplied, I knew he was telling the truth. Twenty-one years ago, Paul Colney murdered Jess.

"Ah, no, see, it don't work like that, Apple. I need to know how to time-travel. Then, and only then, I get to tell you where I dumped her. Oh, and in case you're thinking about telling this lot about my confession, I wouldn't bother 'cos I'll either be dead or out of here Doctor Who style."

I could have crumpled to the floor and wailed with pain with the knowledge of finally knowing the truth, but I didn't. The last thing I intended to do was offer this bastard the satisfaction and the opportunity to feed off my pain. Although, at this point, I had no idea how, but I would stop him. I mean, stop him from killing Jess twenty-one years in the past.

"No. Oh, no." As I leaned forward, surprised by the strength and fortitude in my voice, Colney pushed back in his chair. "You're going to die in here ... in pain ... hopefully, bucket-loads of pain. If there's any kind of justice in this world, you'll suffer right to the very end ... your—last—stinking—breath."

Colney's jaw muscles pulsed as he restarted that teeth-grinding routine.

"At least when you're gone, the taxpayer won't be forking out to keep scum like you fed and watered." I raised my hand, intent on offering him a finger-wagging warning, instantly lowering it when clocking the officer's glare. After dropping my palms to the table as previously instructed, I continued. "So, you parasitical, murdering piece of shit, this is how it's going to play out. I'll time-travel back to 1994. I'll warn Jess about you, and the police can capture you hiding in the woods." Whilst offering my best grin, my confidence steadily built as I fed off the anger radiating from the beaten man.

Of course, there was a myriad of obvious problems with my plan. The only way to time-travel was to crash and die in the Cortina. I guess an eighty-one-year-old version of me rocking up on Jess's doorstep in 1994 could add some rather tricky complications. Add in that the Cortina didn't have a time destination clock, as in the ability to set one's desired year of arrival, it'd be just my luck I'd die in a high-speed head-on with a piece of street furniture and end up in the '50s. Then, I'd be dead before 1994 came around again. Or even worse, I could end up landing in the Victorian era. I imagine the decent folk of Fairfield living in the nineteenth century might find it somewhat bemusing to discover a disorientated elderly gent climbing out of a yellow spacecraft. As time bends go, that would be pretty seismic and could scupper H. G. Wells's plans for original works of science fiction. Perhaps he'd have to major in other genres or branch out into something like erotic, steamy romance. Hmmm, perhaps not. That said, I had no idea if the Cortina could time-travel to a year before its manufacture.

Of course, I'd contemplated attempting to travel back to 1994 on many occasions. Apart from the list of obvious issues, I'd wrangled with the problem that if I did, Chris's and Beth's timelines could change. Also, would the sixty-year-old version of me just disappear when I rocked up? My children were happy, both with families, so could I go back in time and expunge what had gone before? However, now that I knew Colney had murdered Jess, I knew I had to act. Also, I'd lived alone for the past eight months after losing Jenny to breast cancer. If I returned to 1994, could I ensure she sought treatment and thus save her from leaving this world so early?

All that aside, I now had the upper hand over the seething halfwit who appeared about ready to lose his shit. I'd always feared that Colney had something to do with Jess's disappearance. Even if I couldn't get back to 1994, at least I knew the truth. Also, although the detectives on that case were probably all retired, I felt sure I could have a word in someone's shell-like about searching in Fairfield Woods near that layby.

Colney leapt forward, grabbing my shirt collar and, with surprising strength, hauled my withering frame over the bolted-down table. As his face contorted into something resembling the full-moon look sported by David Kessler, three officers pounced and dragged him, kicking, snarling, and screaming, away from me.

That's when the afternoon took an unexpected turn.

Sinéad, not someone I had pegged as a Mary Poppins or Edith Cavell type, placing nursing at the bottom of her list of suitable professions to consider, sprang into action.

"Mary, mother of Jaysus," she shrieked. Her mass of peroxide-blonde hair flew at all angles as she scooted over to me before supporting my weight when assisting me up from my prone position on the table. "Come on, wee man, sit yourself down. Ah, the gobshite hasn't hurt ye, has he?"

As I plonked back onto my seat, with the angel of death tending to me, checking my pulse and generally fussing, my attention became distracted by the lack of noise. For some reason, Colney appeared to have put a halt to his bellyaching.

Two officers stood by the exit, the other four in a semi-circle, corralling Colney into the far corner of the room. The smiling assassin, in the shape of Kurt Penn, rather intimidatingly hovered millimetres from a petrified-looking Paul Colney.

Our ability to communicate, show empathy, and uphold the laws that societies form are part of what makes us human. Without them, we're merely wild animals. Two of such who didn't fit into the human-being mould held centre stage. Kurt Penn, the nasty bastard, pinned his hand around Colney's throat and squeezed whilst the officers looked on.

Before he sucked in his last breath, Colney and I briefly locked eyes. Then, the murdering nefarious bastard's body limply slithered to the floor.

36

1994

Mockingbird Heights

Beth peered over the bonnet of the burnt-out car and raised her walkie-talkie to her mouth while keeping a wary eye out. She held it there as she bobbed her head around, trying to spot the man Martin and *other* Jason had eyes on.

"Beth, stay where you are," I barked, probably too loudly, because my daughter dropped to a squat position and raised a shush finger to her lips whilst frantically waving her other hand for me to keep quiet.

"Big Ears. This is Kylie. Update please. What's happening? Over."

"Kylie, this is Big Ears. Sorry, I got distracted. Frigging hell, I think it's him! He looked my way before opening the boot. I can't see his face at the moment … oh, no … frigging hell …"

Beth and I shot each other a look, locking eyes as she raised her walkie-talkie and clicked the button.

"Big Ears, come back. What's happening? Over."

"He's got a gun … err, over."

"Fuckerdedoda! Over."

Breaking cover, I scooted in a low crouch over to Beth. As I skidded to a halt, my shoe caught an empty beer bottle, causing it to clang as it bounced under the burnt-out Fiesta.

"Ehm, Kylie, you there? Over."

"Yeah. Sorry, Dad's just … well, being Dad-ish. Over."

"Kylie. Listen up. The nutters got a sawn-off, and he's now looking your way. Jason, I think he heard you when you dashed across to Beth's position. Over."

"Shit!" I hissed. "We gonna have to make a run for it."

Beth nodded as I took her free hand and prepared to peek over the car's bonnet. I shot my daughter a look as she held her breath when the unmistakable sound of boots scraping on the tarmac halted just a few feet away.

After bobbing down to take cover and copying Beth's action from earlier when slowly raising my finger to my lips, my wide-eyed daughter clamped her hand over her mouth. Over the background hum of the estate's activities – a mixture of bellowed vulgar exchanges, radios thumping out some hideous bass beat, and two women on the second-floor balcony of Belfast House hurling salvos of abuse at each other – I detected the sound of those boots scrape on the ground when walking away from our position.

Although I wasn't aware I'd been holding my breath, I exhaled and scrubbed my hands over my face. "Beth," I hissed. "We need to get back to the car."

Beth shook her head.

"Yes! The bastard's got a ruddy sawn-off. He's walking around here like Jesse James in the bleeding Wild West!"

"Kylie. This is Big Ears. Everything okay your end? Over."

409

As Beth raised her radio to respond, I made a grab for it, but my daughter held on tight as we grappled for control.

"Beth, give it here."

"Get off! It's mine."

"Beth, for Christ sake … shit, that hurt," I hissed, after she'd bent my finger back and prised the walkie-talkie out of my grip.

"Ehm … Kylie. Please respond. Over."

"Kylie here. Go ahead. Over."

"Big Ears is now tailing the suspect on foot. Over."

Beth and I scrambled to a kneeling position and peered over the bonnet. After a quick scan around, I spotted a man carrying a rucksack and what I presumed to be the sawn-off wrapped in a jacket as he headed for Belfast House. Thirty yards behind, I could make out *other* Jason sneaking along, hugging the building whilst keeping his head down.

"Dad, is it him?"

"I have no idea," I muttered whilst shaking my finger, trying to relieve the pain from Beth's assault. "Christ, that hurt, y'know."

"Oh, don't be a pussy." Beth dismissed me with a wave of her free hand as she raised the walkie-talkie to her lips and clicked the button.

"Don't consider a career in medicine. Your bedside manner is a bit wanting."

Beth raised her eyebrow at me whilst clicking off the button. "Dad, don't be a wuss. We're on an important mission. Man up and grow a pair." She nodded at my shocked expression and then clicked the button. "Big Ears. This is Kylie. Do you copy? Over."

"Go ahead, Kylie. Over."

"Can you confirm a positive ID of the suspect? Over."

"Fucking too right, I can. I've been in a couple of skirmishes with that wanker. Not a face I'm likely to forget anytime soon. Remember, the tosser looks like me and is a bleeding blood relative. That evil piece of shit is my ruddy uncle." The radio clicked again. "So that's a big frigging ten-four. Over."

"Join the club, Big Ears. Remember, we're cousins. Over."

"Welcome to the family, Kylie. You're playing the part of Marilyn in The Munsters. Over."

"Do what?" Beth pulled a face. "Oh. Over."

"The Munsters. Marilyn being the only normal one in a family of monsters. Over."

"D'oh, yeah, get it. Over."

Without giving a second thought about potentially suffering more finger-bending torture, I snatched the walkie-talkie from Beth's grip.

"Martin, what the hell is he doing? This is supposed to be just a reconnaissance mission."

"Kylie, your voice ain't half got deep."

"Martin!"

"Kylie, this is Big Ears. Can I remind you of our agreed protocols? No use of real names, and confirm when you have finished speaking by applying the suffix over to your sentences. Over."

"Is he for real?" I fired at Beth, who offered a shrugged response.

"Martin, for frig sake. What is he doing? And don't tell me about radio fucking protocols. Over!"

"Big Ears is tailing him to find out where he's going. I thought we wanted to find that out. Over!"

Beth tutted and snatched the radio. "Big Ears. This is Kylie. We're going to follow. Over." Beth stood and rammed the radio in her jeans pocket. "Err … Dad, come on."

"What the frig d'you mean, come on? You're suggesting we tail a psycho, murdering serial killer like we're off for a walk around the fucking park feeding the sodding ducks!"

Beth smirked. "And you had the gall to ask where I get my potty mouth from."

"You know what I mean," I huffed. Although I had to admit, she had a point. "Your mum will go ballistic if we follow him."

"I won't tell her if you don't."

"I … err, Beth!"

Whilst re-securing her hair in her scrunchie, she leaned forward, peering down at my crouched position. "Dad, we're going to finish this once and for all."

"Well said. You can tell her bloodline."

I swivelled around to find Martin standing behind me.

"The girl's right. We're never going to be free until we finish this. Look, Colney is going up the steps to Belfast House."

Although I harboured no intentions regarding 'finishing it' as my daughter and Martin had suggested, my time-travelling loose cannon made a good point.

In a few days, if history were to repeat itself, my daughter's life would be in danger. It wasn't difficult to assume that Paul Colney would obviously play a starring role in whatever would happen to her. My older self had given me the heads up, expecting me to act. Whether we confronted the git now or waited for him to strike, a reckoning loomed ominously on the horizon.

"Dad, I thought you said his old flat was in Dublin House?"

"It was. Colney lived up there." I nodded to the building closest to our position. The other side of the central square to where Colney, closely followed by *other* Jason, had disappeared into the stairwell.

"What's the bastard doing over there then?" Martin questioned, pointing to Belfast House.

"Mum said that his old flat would now be rented by someone else. Shirley died seven years ago so that flat wouldn't still be empty, would it?"

"I don't know. But someone must be helping him. Although the whole world knows he's dead, he must have a friend who is giving him somewhere to stay."

"Who?"

I glanced at Martin and shrugged. "I don't know. But whoever it is, do they know it's him?"

"What … like someone else who knows he's a time-traveller? Could there be another person who knows about all this crazy shit?"

"Dad?" Beth chewed her lip, waiting for me to answer Martin's impossible question.

"I don't know. Right, come on, we can't leave Big Ears on his own to deal with Colney. We'd better offer some backup."

413

"Yessss!" hissed Beth, clenching her fist.

I pointed at her, pausing for effect. "You stay behind me at all times. You hear?"

"Yes, sir." she saluted. "Now, can we go get this fucker?"

37

Death Becomes Her

Despite Beth's youthful eagerness to rush in – and, as Elvis so poetically informed us with his aching sincerity of a soulful voice, that was what wise men suggested only fools do – I laid down the plan of attack. With discretion being the better part of valour, I persuaded the team to follow my plan. Firstly, we would take a leaf from *other* Jason by way of a cautious approach of using the cover of Shannon House rather than chaotically bolting across the central square towards a man brandishing a sawn-off.

The second part of my cunning plan, as in when we reached Belfast House, was slightly looser. Basically, I had no idea, and we would just wing it. As for my lookalike and what might be going through his head, that was anyone's guess.

This morning, we'd all agreed to try to locate Tony Lencoy, then decamp back to my house and formulate a plan for the next five days. Notwithstanding *other* Jason's bravery or foolhardiness, whichever you prefer, to pursue the man waving a shooter, that action had escalated the mission way beyond a situation in which my seventeen-year-old daughter should be involved.

Although, as Beth suggested, we could keep the finer points of today's mission on a strictly need-to-know basis, I knew Jenny would wheedle it out of me. My wife, quite rightly, was going to go ballistic. However, could I leave *other* Jason up there to face that psycho alone? Probably not. This was our fight, not his.

Less than a minute into the first part of the plan, after hauling Beth back, who'd repeatedly ignored my earlier instruction to remain behind me, I called the advance to a halt by way of a raised hand.

"Frig sake, Apsley, why have we stopped? At this rate, we'll miss Match of the Day and Des Lynam's witty remarks about how shit Spurs are."

"We stopped because of that." I waved my hand towards Belfast House. "And I think we have slightly more important things to worry about than seeing Match of the Day."

Martin broke cover and leaned forward to peer at the monolithic, brutal grey concrete tower. "Who have your lot got today?"

"My lot? West Ham?"

"Yeah, bubble boys."

"Ehm … home to Ipswich, I think. They should win that easily."

"Yeah, reckon so. Gunners have—"

"Fuckerdedoda, what the bollocks are you two drivelling on about? We have a dire situation on our hands, and you're discussing sodding football!"

"Fair point."

I pointed to the second level of Belfast House, where Martin now focussed, his hand placed above his eyes as he squinted to block out the rays from the sinking spring sun.

Beth and I joined Martin, all three standing in a tight huddle. To the left of the landing, the two women I'd spotted earlier were still exchanging their views, one now with the upper hand as she escalated the disagreement from a vulgar verbal exchange to slapping and hair-pulling. To the right, our target man bounded along the landing towards the catfight. A couple of seconds later, we all spotted *other* Jason, who'd reached the same level and now appeared to hover at the top of the stairwell, peering at Colney's progress from the cover of a concrete post.

Beth's gung-ho bravado, as in preparing to hot-foot towards the 'situation', came to an abrupt halt when I slammed my arm across her chest.

"Hang on! You need to stay behind me."

"Come on then, what are we hanging around for? Dad, we can't leave Big Ears to face the enemy alone."

"Apsley … look. That bastard's entering one of the flats."

"Jesus, of all the …" I paused, allowing my thoughts to wisp away on the breeze.

With the front door pushed ajar, the bloke with the sawn-off paused on the doorstep as he glanced along the landing and took in the scene of the two women fighting. It appeared both ladies – I use that term loosely – had moved to more violent tactics to resolve their disagreement, now duelling with improvised weapons presumably left over from the riots interspersed with high kicks and a spot of eye gouging. Although unpleasant, not a particularly unusual sight to witness on the Broxworth, where most inhabitants resorted to employing a caveman, or cavewoman in this instance, type persona to resolve differences of opinion.

"Dad?"

"Isn't that your old flat? You lived on the second level, didn't you?"

"Yup ... whoever that man is—"

"I'm telling you," interrupted Martin. "It's definitely Colney. You're forgetting that me and him have been close and personal on a couple of occasions, and I don't mean a dinner date and a cuddle on the sofa."

Beth nudged Martin's arm and winked. "Never had you down as someone who'd bat for the other side."

"Beth ... how many times have I got to tell you? Comments like that are ..."

"What?"

"Rude ... outdated."

Beth tutted and rolled her eyes. "I wasn't being, you know. I was just saying that Martin prefers the ladies."

"Yes, and I might remind you, I had no choice but to pleasure myself last night after your little escapade that sent Sally off in a huff."

"Oh, nice. Do I really need to know you had a wank?"

"Jesus, you two. Shut it!"

"Alright, Captain Apsley, don't get your Y-fronts in a twist. So, come on, what's the plan, then?"

"Hilarious," I fired back with a grimace. "Let's just hang on here and see if we can catch Big Ears' attention. Now we know where Colney's hiding, we can regroup and plan what we do next."

"Dad! We're not planning next week's lessons' timetable. This is a crisis situation that requires immediate, decisive, and direct action."

"She's right."

"No, she's not."

"She is. We need to act."

"She's—"

"Ehm … who's she?" Beth copied her mother's preferred stance of thumping hands on her hips, accompanied by a raised eyebrow.

"Sorry." I held my palm aloft. "I'm just saying, I think—"

"Oh shite," Martin interrupted, as he pointed and followed with his finger my lookalike's progress when storming down the landing and rugby-tackling Colney.

Before I could register what was occurring, Beth broke into a sprint, closely followed by Martin.

"Bollocks," I muttered, when scooting after them. My ageing knees, coupled with still recovering from my earlier flit across the square, reminded me I'd passed my sixtieth birthday. Before reaching Belfast House, I glanced up at the second-floor landing. It appeared, somewhere in the stairwell, Martin had managed to slip past Beth and now hurtled towards the two men who seemed to be locked together in some odd martial-arts-styled headlock.

Twenty or so feet to the left of the grappling men, the two women, who were long past complying with the Marquess of Queensbury Rules, appeared to be upping their game. I suspected they'd either knock each other out or would require the judge's decision to resolve their differences. As I hovered, catching my breath, Beth appeared on the landing.

419

"Beth! Beth, don't you dare move."

My daughter glanced down and nodded.

Based on the fact that she'd ignored every instruction so far, I waited to see if she would comply before making a bolt for the stairs.

With screaming calf muscles and a heaving chest, I leaned on the railing after clambering up the last few steps when reaching the second-level landing. Beth, Martin, *other* Jason, and Colney were nowhere to be seen. Acidic bile rose in my throat, caused by the fear of what I might see as I peered over the balcony. I prayed my daughter hadn't gotten involved and, in the ensuing melee, all four had tumbled over the railings. Of course, Colney lying splat on the tarmac below would resolve our issue. However, as you can imagine, I was relieved to see the walkway below clear of any prone bodies.

The two women, who continued to duel with their improvised weapons, one appearing to be a broken broom handle, the other a metal pipe, failed to notice me as I hurried towards them.

Like a scene from *Death Becomes Her,* they crouched and circled around, striking with their weapons while hissing obscenities. Wielding the metal pipe, *Goldie Hawn* landed a headshot on *Meryl Streep*, knocking her to the ground. With the advantage and *Meryl* lying in the foetal position, *Goldie* went for the kill with a few well-timed trainer kicks to the head. To say it was a shocking sight would be an understatement. The only saving grace to this hideous event, despite the level of violence, I presumed they wouldn't end up dismembered at the bottom of a flight of steps as were the two characters in the film.

In any other circumstance, anyone with an ounce of humanity would intervene. However, unfortunately for *Meryl*, who appeared to be on the losing side, protecting Beth was a smidge higher up my list of priorities. And on that subject, my daughter had once again failed to comply with the given directive.

When just a few feet from my old flat door, just at the point *Goldie* halted her assault, presumably satisfied she'd made her point, the unmistakable boom of gunshot assaulted my eardrums. That auspicious sound echoed off the surrounding buildings, closely followed by a woman's scream.

The adrenaline rush caused by the terror, which ripped a hole in my heart at the prospect of Beth being the wrong end of that gun, propelled me through the door towards the kitchen. As I reached the doorway, grabbing the doorframe to slow my speed, my mouth flopped open. My daughter, fortunately, hadn't been at the wrong end of that sawn-off – she was at the other end.

38

Scorpio

"Oh, bollocks," I muttered, drinking in the scene. The smoking gun held limply in my daughter's hands; a blood splatter arced up the wall; the equally shocked faces of Martin and *other* Jason and the nefarious grin of Paul Colney.

At that moment when the world seemed to halt its rotation, when no one moved, I realised *other* Jason's shocked expression wasn't due to Beth pulling the trigger but because his arm had been in the way of the flying shot. The fact he was still standing suggested a flesh wound.

"Apple, you wanker."

Before I could respond, Colney leapt forward and snatched the sawn-off from Beth's grip, turning it around and firing a second shot at *other* Jason. This second discharge resulted in a direct hit, and I suspected it wouldn't be classed as a flesh wound. Also, going by the unhealthy appearance of my lookalike, and not that I'm any kind of expert on such matters, I'm reasonably sure Martin had just saved himself a quarter of a million quid.

Beth appeared to be the first to jolt out of her trance, scrambling back to the door, grabbing my arm and hauling me down the hallway with Martin close behind. As we scooted out of the flat, I presumed Colney would be reloading and, therefore, not too far behind.

"Fuckerdefuck. Come on," Beth hollered, as she hurtled down the landing towards the stairwell. She halted for a nanosecond when spotting a group of menacing-looking hoodie-clad youths loitering and thus blocking her path down. She didn't hesitate, grabbing the stair rail and, two at a time, bounded up to the next level.

I'd been here before.

1976, the day David Colney made that fatal decision to go up, not down, when being chased by yours truly. As I followed my daughter, I prayed she hadn't made the same mistake.

"Beth," I panted. "Go across the next landing and down the other stairwell." Because of my laboured prattle, coupled with the fact that Beth's younger lungs and legs had propelled her at least one flight ahead, she didn't hear my plea.

When staggering through the roof service door at the top of the flats, Beth stood reeling around, realising that going up wasn't a particularly terrific idea. Colney would be joining us at any moment. Presumably, carrying a reloaded gun.

We were sitting ducks.

"Dad!" Beth's shriek suggested she needed her father to come up with an idea, and quickly with it.

As Martin barrelled through the door, he turned and slammed it shut, only to be knocked clear as Colney threw his weight against it.

Colney raised the gun as he warily stepped through the doorway. Both he and I shot a fleeting glance at Martin before locking eyes. That nefarious grin which emerged confirmed what I already knew. Martin remained motionless as he lay in a prone position, now holding a pose more akin to a man who'd just leapt out of a plane while enjoying a spot of skydiving. My time-travelling loose cannon appeared to have been knocked out cold, and Beth and I were moments from death.

Feeling the need to protect my daughter, I grabbed a handful of her mohair jumper and hauled her to my side. Unusually, Beth complied and buried her head in my chest. Despite our closeness making a bigger target, which, from this distance, Colney couldn't fail to miss, I wrapped my arms around her whilst waiting for the inevitable. Colney stepped a few paces forward and pointed the shotgun at our midriffs. My trembling daughter needed her father's reassurance. Which, at this precise moment, I struggled to see how I could provide.

"Well, looky here. Apple and my little brother's girl." He stepped forward, past Martin's prone body, while keeping the gun pointed in our direction. "Y'know, I can't see how that slapper, Carol Hall, and my ugly brother, David, could have produced something as fit as you," he chuckled. "Why don't I fill Apple with lead, then you and me go back to the flat."

"You sick fuck," Beth snarled.

Keeping my daughter close, I encouraged her to shimmy behind me as I pondered the thought that Colney may not have reloaded the gun. Did he have time? Were there any cartridges to hand? Could the sound of gunfire mean the armed police officers would come barrelling through the roof service door at any moment? If I could keep him talking, I might buy enough time to save our lives.

"The cavalry ain't on their way, Apple. You're forgetting, this is the Broxworth. Sure, everyone heard the shots, but no one on this estate will be ringing the filth."

The git made a valid point. Talking to the police, in any capacity, would be a death sentence for any resident of this odious estate.

"Guess you're also thinking, did he have time to reload?" he chuckled, stepping one pace forward, which Beth and I reciprocated with one pace back.

"Well, I guess in all the excitement, I kinda lost track myself. That was a good one, eh, Apple?"

Beth and I reversed another step.

"Hey, Apple," Colney grinned as he raised the sawn-off, now with his head cocked, looking down the barrel as he took aim at our heads. "Bang," he chortled. "This is the best fun I've had in years."

Beth's rhythmical tremble juddered when hearing Colney say bang, returning to its idling tempo when realising he hadn't discharged his weapon.

"Step behind me."

Beth declined my instruction with a shake of her head. No shock there, then. Even in a life-and-death situation, probably more death, I still seemed incapable of persuading my daughter to comply with a simple instruction.

"So, Apple, did I reload? Do you feel lucky?"

"Why are you back?"

"Bit of business to attend to."

"What? Murdering Sandy Rathbone?"

"Nah … that slag just got in the way. The silly cow was so high on nose candy she thought I was a ghost." Colney frowned, cocking his head as he pondered that statement. "S'pose I am, really."

"You murdered her?"

"Yup, just like I'm going to do to you. Although I strangled her, whereas, for you, I'm going to fill you with lead." Colney lowered the gun about an inch. "Or, I could make you jump to your deaths … just like your papa, hey girl?"

Beth's eyes swivelled up at me, pleading for me to do something.

"Hey, a funny thing happened today. There I was, wandering around in that shithole of a town, and I sees this bird, white boots, long Afghan coat. Got me thinking about Jess. How is the silly bitch?"

"She …" I paused as my mind raced for a diversion tactic. "Jess moved away years ago. I've lost touch with her."

"Frigging hell, Apple, what d'you take me for? The little slag's living with that weedy schoolteacher friend of yours in the same house she was back in '87. Gotta say, that Faith, my other niece, ain't bad looking either. Reckon I might take her after I kill Jess."

That didn't work, then – so much for diversion tactics.

Beth and I took another pace backwards as Colney stepped forward again. Despite his statement that no one would have called the police, I knew I had to keep him talking just on the off chance that one upstanding citizen lived on the estate, they'd heard the gunshots, and dared to call it in.

"How come you're in my old flat?"

"Yeah, funny that, don't you think? See, I couldn't stay in Sandy's flat … she started to stink. Not much fun watching the telly with a corpse slumped in the armchair beside you."

Beth's trembling notched up to more of a full-on shake with an Elvis-type 'rubber legs' movement as she attempted to remain upright. I hugged her tight, biting my tongue to create saliva due to my mouth desiccating.

426

"You remember that old slag's mate, Claire?"

I didn't respond, just taking another pace back.

"Sure, you do. Big jugs. Not bad looking, if not a bit tubby. You could say the girl had a couple of sturdy love handles. Well, back in '77, that is. Now she's just a big fat ugly slob … or was, I should say. I spotted her on the landing going into your old gaff. Seemed the perfect solution."

"Where is she?"

"Oh, what, like now? Where is she now?"

I nodded as Beth and I took another pace backwards.

"Fertilising the trees up at Fairfield Woods. Jesus, I built up a sweat when lugging that old boiler into a hole. And, I can tell you, I had to dig a bloody big trench to get her fat, bloated carcass in."

"Dad," Beth whimpered.

"Hey, pretty thing, don't worry. I'm only going to blow this twat's head off. Then, you and me can have a bit of fun." Colney took two paces forward and leaned towards Beth. "If you behave yourself, I might let you live. If not, I'll bury you with that bitch, Jess. Patrick's ex is next on my list."

"You know you're a time-traveller," I blurted, dragging Beth away from him as we backed up close to the low wall that circumnavigated the roof's edge. The very same place that David Colney had fallen from eighteen years ago.

"Nah, really," Colney chuckled in mock horror. "Well, I thought something odd had happened. I mean, we had that crash in your Cortina and poof, ten years just disappeared. Me and that twat over there … both of us time-travelled."

427

Colney glanced at Martin, who remained prone on the floor. The altercation with the hefty steel door had afforded him more than just a slight concussion.

"So did I."

"So did I what?"

"Time-travel."

"When?"

"2019 … Martin and I travelled from 2019 to 1976."

"Fuck off, did you?"

"We did … in that car. The Cortina is a time machine. Look, you can have it and then time-travel to whatever year you want … use it to escape."

"Why would I want to time-travel again?"

"Think about it. If the police are on to you, you can just hop in the time machine and disappear." I could tell by the narrowing of the eyes and the slight dipping of the barrels, which disappointingly now pointed at my groin, I'd piqued his interest.

"How does it work?"

"It's like the DeLorean. You just program it to where you want to go."

"Where is it?"

"Let Beth go, and I'll tell you."

Beth shot me a look, pleading with her eyes for me not to go through with this less-than-well-thought-through plan. It was a crap idea. However, when facing the two barrels of a sawn-off, suggesting the Cortina sported all the necessary equipment to move through time at will, seemed like the best option. Trying to conjure up imaginative ideas when a psycho nutter is aiming a loaded sawn-off at your knackers is quite tricky to do.

"Frig sake, you twat. I ain't that stupid."

"I have the car stashed in a safe place, and only I know where it is. Kill me, and you'll never find it."

"Give me the keys."

"I don't have them on me."

"Where is it? Where's the car and the keys?"

Colney stepped sideways, blocking my view of Martin as he swivelled the barrels around to point at Beth's head. "Tell me, or I'll blow the little bitch's head off."

Slowly and deliberately, I peeled Beth's hand from my chest and tried to encourage her to step behind me.

"No … don't move. I want the keys."

A hand appeared from behind Colney and tapped him on the shoulder.

"They're here, mate."

39

Buffy the Vampire Slayer

Colney spun on his heels, coming face to face with a grinning Martin, who held up and jauntily shook the car keys in his left hand. Before Colney could register what was happening, Martin planted his right fist dead centre of Colney's face. The force employed by my loose cannon resulted in Colney's nose exploding, causing a spurt of blood to fire upwards in a fan formation over his head. Taking the opportunity, I grabbed the sawn-off from his grip before he hit the deck.

Whilst Colney attempted to scramble to his feet, Martin walloped his trainer, *Goldie Hawn* style, into his midriff. Coughing and spitting blood, Colney wheezed as he rolled over when attempting to catch his breath.

"Get up!" I ordered, as Colney pulled himself to a kneeling position with his hands up in surrender. "Stand up."

Colney didn't move.

"Dad … shoot him!"

"Apsley, blow the fucker's bloody brains out."

Did he reload? Was I capable of pulling the trigger?

The pleading expression he sported suggested the answer to question one to be an affirmative. As for question two, that was on a whole different level. Yes, okay, I'd killed before when allowing his brother to drop to his death. Could I do it again? That would make two. If I ever landed in a situation where I needed to take someone else's life, that would make three. Then, I could claim serial killer status.

That wasn't the label I desired and not the type of man I wanted to become.

"Martin, find something to tie his hands."

"Apsley, just finish it!"

"No. I'm not him. He will stand trial for what he's done. We're going to do the right thing, put this man in front of a jury and a judge so that society can have their justice for the crimes this evil git's committed. I'm not stooping down to this evil scum's level. We're better than that. We take the high road, do the right thing … it's about morals."

"Oh, fuckerdedoda, can we just drop all the psychobabble and just blow the fucker's head off?"

"She makes a valid point, Apsley."

"No, she doesn't."

"She does."

"Ehm … I am here, you know! And, yes, Martin's correct. I make a valid frigging point. Dad …" Beth thumped her hands on her hips, Jenny style. "Just blow the psycho's brain's out."

"No, Beth. I'm not a killer."

"You are, Apple. You killed David. I know you were right here in this very same spot when my little brother fell. You and that old git, Nears."

"Maybe I was … but I didn't kill him. David tripped and fell."

431

"Dad?" Out of the corner of my eye, I could see Beth narrow her eyes at me, presumably trying to compute what I'd almost confessed to. "What's he talking about?"

"Ah, she doesn't know. Well, girly, Apple killed your *real* father. Not such the upstanding citizen you thought, is he?"

"Beth … David tripped and fell. It wasn't my fault."

"You and Grampa Don were there … here, oh, whatever, when *he* died?"

"Looks like your girl ain't too happy about this news, Apple."

"Unless you want another kick, I suggest you shut it." Martin, adopting a stance akin to Jonny Wilkinson before sending the ball between the posts, appeared ready to follow through with his threat.

Whilst keeping the fiendish scumbag in my sights, I held my left hand out to Martin, thus halting his penalty kick follow-through before answering my daughter's question.

"Beth … I chased David up to the roof after he daubed graffiti on Carol's front door the day she died. David just fell … I could have saved him …" I paused before continuing when she failed to respond. "Beth, sweetheart … I knew he would become a murderer in the next century, so I let him drop to his death … I'm sorry." I kept the gun trained on the kneeling scumbag, frightened to look away in case he took the opportunity. Also, if I'm honest, now a smidge concerned about my daughter's reaction to this revelation. Notwithstanding that she'd had to wrangle with the news that her biological father was a serial killer, Beth had to compute that Don and I'd aided and abetted David's demise.

432

Although Beth knew the type of family she came from and the fact that her natural father was an undesirable, I suspected hearing this news could be tough to take.

"I knew it, you fucker," snarled Colney, who appeared ready to scramble to his feet, only having second thoughts when clocking Martin in position to score a drop goal with his head.

"Amazeballs! Wow, Dad, I didn't know you had it in you." Beth leaned forward towards the kneeling Colney. "Jason is my real father. Not that serial killing knob of a brother of yours," Beth spat, her retort punctuated with globules of spit that fired into his face.

"What you on about, you silly bitch? David hadn't killed—"

"But he would have," I interrupted. "As I just said, your brother followed in your footsteps to become a serial killer in the next century—"

"How the fuck—"

"Time-travel. I told you a moment ago, you prick. I've come from 2019."

"Bollocks," scoffed Colney, as he started to lower his hands.

"Keep your hands in the air. And whilst we're on the subject, I know you murdered Carol Hall. You pumped the poor girl full of heroin to make it look like suicide."

"He murdered my real mother? Oh, fuckerdedoda, just shoot the fucker, or God help me, I will." I stepped sideways as Beth made a lunge for the gun.

"Beth! No. We're not killers." I jabbed the shotgun towards Colney. "Lay on your front with your hands behind your back." I shot Martin a look. "Get something to tie him up with," I hissed.

In that moment of distraction, Colney jumped up and made a dash for the stairs, failing when colliding with Martin, who again ended up on his backside. Colney panicked and scooted away towards the roof's edge, skidding to a halt and peering down at the five-storey drop.

Keeping the gun aimed at his chest, the biggest target area, in case my non-existent sharp-shooting skills were a bit off today, I calmly stepped towards the man who seemed to be calculating if he could survive the drop.

"Do us all a favour and jump," suggested Martin, as he scrambled to his feet.

Colney glanced at the three of us before looking down again.

"You won't survive, Colney. Do as I say. Get off the ledge and lie flat on your stomach."

Martin entered my peripheral vision when leaping forward with his hands raised. "I'll just push him off and be done with it."

"No."

Martin, ignoring my barked response, lunged forward.

With my left eye shut when taking aim, I didn't see it happen. As Colney glanced at the advancing Martin, Beth lunged forward and slapped her hand on his chest.

"Goodbye, Uncle."

Paul Colney disappeared over the ledge, along with Beth, whose hand he'd grabbed hold of.

Paralysed, allowing the gun to slip from my grip and clatter to the ground, my body followed suit as if my skeleton had suddenly ground to dust. My mouth flapped open to wail, but nothing came out.

Although coming second in the Colney-shoving race, Martin's torso lay over the low wall, his legs dangling precariously up in the air, appearing mid-dive.

"Fuck sake, Apsley, I could do with a hand if you've got a moment to spare," he blurted.

I scrambled to the edge on all fours and peered over to see Beth dangling with Martin's hand wrapped around her right calf. Copying my time-travelling mate's position, I grabbed her other flailing leg and, between us, using the low wall to gain purchase for our knees, we hauled my somewhat shocked daughter back to safety.

Whilst remaining in a knelt position, and like cradling a newborn, I cuddled her as I rocked back and forth, shushing her sobs.

"What a frigging mess," announced Martin as he peered down.

"Is … is he dead?" whispered Beth.

"Well, if he ain't, I reckon his headache will be a lot worse than mine, and I've got a head splitter."

"What?" I blurted. "He … must be—"

Martin turned and faced us, sporting a grin. "Course, the fucker's dead." He crouched by us and held his palm up to Beth.

"High five."

Beth slapped his hand and offered a teary smile.

"Whatever your dad here was wittering on about earlier," he shot me a look before returning his attention to my daughter. "Y'know, all that psychobabble about trials and doing the right thing, that fucker deserved to die. He's gone, and the wanker can never hurt Jess, you, your dad, or anyone. No more women in any timeline are ever going to have to fear that monster again. Not that anyone will ever know about your heroic act, but you deserve a bleeding medal. You're a regular Buffy Summers, that you are." For reasons only known to himself, Martin delivered the last line in that odd Irish accent that sounded more like Sean Connery.

"I'm prettier than Kirsten Swanson."

"That you are, but I be thinking of Sarah Michelle Gellar, 'twas her that played Buffy in the TV series."

"Who's she?"

"You'll find out."

"Future?"

"Spot on, girl."

Beth swivelled her eyes up at me. I guess she was searching for confirmation that the girl had done good.

I guess she had.

"You're prettier than Gellar, whatever he says."

40

Our Survey Said

Despite that nefarious bastard's claim about the police not attending after gunshots rang out, I felt it prudent to make our getaway. However, two things needed checking. Martin whizzed down to the back of the flats to confirm that Colney wasn't just suffering a migraine and was actually dead. Beth and I returned to my old flat, praying that by some miracle *other* Jason was still alive.

Just like the day when David fell to his death, we didn't encounter anyone in the stairwell. Of course, that day, back in '76, Don had to guide me back due to being in a state of shock. Today, there was no shilly-shallying about because we needed to get a lick on. The two ladies, previously acting out the rerun of the duelling *Goldie Hawn* and *Meryl Streep*, appeared to have concluded their spat and moved on. Despite Beth's younger legs, I made it through the open front door to my old flat moments before her.

Beth buried her head in my chest as we glanced into the kitchen, where my lookalike stared lifelessly back at us. The streak of rouge on the wall behind him, where he'd slithered to a sitting position after Colney had pumped a cartridge full of pellets through his abdomen, now appeared to be drying.

As we hovered for a second, another two gunshots rang out. Beth lifted her head, her expression suggesting we harboured similar concerns. Had Colney survived the fall, and now he and Martin were involved in a tussle? The question in both our eyes – who pulled the trigger?

Although racked with guilt regarding my lookalike, we hot-footed along the landing before hurtling down the stairwell towards the central square. Despite not believing the possibility that Colney survived the fall, I struggled to shake away the image that somehow the scumbag was still alive. Perhaps he'd shot Martin and, akin to some contorted monster created by Mary Shelley, now performed the Frankenstein walk as the miscreation methodically pounded towards us. Despite recognising my overactive imagination had probably elevated my fear, it was enough to spur me on to keep ahead of my daughter. I'd nearly lost her once today; I wasn't going to place her in the firing line if my daft hypotheses about the walking dead came to fruition. As we dashed out of the stairwell, Martin appeared from the alley leading to the rear of the flats.

"Apsley. That's four shots. Someone's bound to call the old Bill. We need to get out of here," Martin blurted through his panting.

"What happened? Was he still alive?"

"Nah, his head was cracked open like a rotten egg."

"What were the gunshots we heard, then?" questioned Beth.

"Someone is going to find his body. Too many awkward questions will be asked, and someone in the police is bound to recognise him as one of the dead Colney twins. That could be tricky because he's already been cremated nearly twenty years ago."

My mind caught up with what he was saying. However, my daughter's expression suggested she was still bemused as to why two more shots had been fired.

"I … I don't get it?"

"You blasted the git's face off?" I asked, just to gain clarification but also to bring Beth up to speed.

"Yup, two shots, point blank range. Pretty much took the tosser's head clean off. There's no way he's coming back from that. There won't be any dental records to compare either 'cos I reckon those pellets have ground his teeth into a fine powder."

Beth gagged, her head dipping forward before slapping her hand over her mouth as she attempted to avoid chundering across the tarmac.

"Big Ears?" questioned Martin.

I offered a slight shake of my head to indicate he didn't make it, then focused on Beth, who appeared to have turned a rather odd shade of green.

"Shit," hissed Martin. "Poor bastard."

"I know. I feel as guilty as hell. This wasn't his fight." I raised my eyebrows at Beth as she tucked her hair behind her ear and side-eyed me from her bent-over position. "You alright, sweetheart?"

Beth lifted her head, nodded, and puffed out her cheeks.

"Gotta give it to the man. He didn't hesitate to tackle that bastard up there." Martin raised his eyes towards the second-floor landing of Belfast House.

"What happened in the flat?"

"I didn't mean to shoot him … I didn't," Beth blurted. "The gun was on the floor. I just grabbed it, and it went off."

439

"Hey, hey, you. Back up there." Martin laid his hand on Beth's forearm. "You only nicked him. Colney killed Big Ears, not you."

Wrapping my arm around her, I pulled Beth close. "It's not your fault."

"Gotta say, Apsley, it's always exciting when I'm with you, and there's never a dull moment," chuckled Martin. "And, although a bit callous to say at this delicate moment, I just saved myself a quarter of a mil. Also, you no longer have to worry about *other* Jason mucking up your life. A win-win situation," he grinned.

I raised my eyebrow.

Martin cleared his throat and awkwardly shuffled his feet. "Hmmm, some things are best left unsaid, I guess."

"I think so. What about Big Ears' body—"

"What about it?"

"Well—"

"Hey, he don't exist, does he? He left that flat a couple of days ago in 1976. Now, here in 1994, he'll be just like my body was in 1977."

"What d'you mean?"

"The police won't be able to identify him. He's a ghost, a phantom … the unknown soldier."

"I guess you're right."

"I am. That DI, what was her name?

"French."

"That's it, good old Frenchie. She's gonna go loopy when she discovers she's got another two unidentified dead men on her hands."

"Yeah, and I have a feeling she'll come knocking on my door again."

"On that note, we better skedaddle. Come on, let's get Buffy home."

"Christ, Jenny, she's probably doing backflips, wondering what's going on. As for Jess, I'm gonna have to tell her that her father's dead, which I'm not looking forward to."

"You're her father, mate. Not him. From what I've seen, you're pretty good at it, too."

I offered a tight smile at his compliment. Considering Martin had always held a somewhat low opinion of me, I can't deny being surprised by the sincerity in his voice.

"Bring the Cortina back to my house. I want that damn thing stored in my garage from now on. Oh, and I'm gonna have to conjure up a different version of events for Jenny. Beth dangling off the roof after sending Colney sprawling is probably best left unsaid. Just agree with anything I come up with, alright?"

"Yes, sir." Martin saluted.

"And try not to crash the car on the way … you know what will happen."

"Hey, I'll drive like a nun who's two hours early for vespers."

"I seem to remember you saying that once before about my driving skills."

"Well, Apsley, you're no Lewis Hamilton."

"As he's only about eight years old, I reckon even I could beat him. Come on, let's go."

Martin jogged away whilst I helped an unsteady Beth as we attempted to hot-foot across the central square back to my car.

I just prayed both motors were still in situ and hadn't been hot-wired by some delinquent youths, of which this estate provided a home for more than its fair share.

A few yards into my jog, I turned and called out to the hero of the hour. "Martin … Martin."

My old time-travelling buddy glanced back, halted, and raised his palms. "What?"

"Thank you."

"For what?"

"Saving my daughter's life."

"You're welcome." He stepped back towards me, pointing and grinning. "How many years did I work for you back in our old life?"

"Oh," I pulled a face, wondering where this conversation was heading. "Oh, I dunno, about five, six, maybe?"

"Yeah, about that. And do you know how many times during those five or six years you said thank you, or well done, to me?"

"Ehm … probably not enough … say ten … yeah, let's go for ten."

Martin produced that *Family Fortunes'* wrong answer sound. "The survey says … none."

"Oh, you sure? I must have—"

"One hundred per cent zero times, mate," he interrupted. "None, zip, never, not bloody once."

"Maybe you didn't do anything that warranted a well done or a thank you?"

Martin raised an eyebrow.

"Or …" I paused and grinned. "There is, of course, another explanation."

"Which is?"

"Maybe I was just an ungrateful wanker."

Martin winked and pointed at me. "There you go … see, you *are* becoming a better person in your old age."

I snorted a laugh.

"Dad, can we go?"

Martin and I exchanged a nod before heading in different directions. Throughout our lives, Martin and I must have nodded at each other a million times. However, the one we just exchanged felt different from anything in our past. That nod was mutual respect and even, maybe, friendship.

Whatever it was, my time-travelling loose cannon, general pain-in-the-bloody-arse companion, had just saved my daughter's life.

I owed him.

41

If I Were a Rich Man

"And then he snatched the gun from me and just pulled the trigger! It was mad. The twisted, evil git shot Big Ears at point-blank range … no hesitation. And then—"

"Beth … Beth!" I hissed.

With her arms animatedly and enthusiastically assisting her, Beth recounted this afternoon's events. My daughter, along with the members of the TTBC, all shot me a look when I growled at her whilst surreptitiously nodding towards Jess.

"Dad, it's okay." Jess nonchalantly shrugged. Although I'd already informed her about the events in my old flat, Jess appeared undemonstrative when hearing Beth's version regarding the circumstances of her father's demise. "As sad as it is, I never knew him. As I told you yesterday, you're my father, not him. Although, I think we will all have to be grateful to the man."

"Darling, I don't understand. How did he come to just fall off the roof?"

Beth shot me a look, an action my wife picked up on. Beth was a lot of things, with many qualities. However, after that

444

look, I made a mental note to advise her never to play poker for money.

"Darling?" Jenny quizzed, whilst shooting looks back and forth between me and a red-faced Beth.

"Ha, well, it was odd, I guess you could say," I grimaced and rubbed the back of my neck. "You see, after we'd bolted up the stairwell, we hid behind the service door when Colney came barrelling through. I think it just must have been his momentum that took him over the edge."

"Stroke of luck, lad. Just as it was with that bugger, David, all those years ago."

"I think it was fate, George."

Jenny narrowed her eyes at me but chose to say nothing. How David died was information I'd decided to never divulge to George. My wife's silence suggested Jenny didn't plan to take this moment to enlighten my old friend. However, I harboured the distinct impression that as soon as we were alone, I would face the third degree.

"And where is Martin?"

I glanced at my watch. Not that I needed to, but just that involuntary action to Jenny's question. "Yeah, good question. Where the hell is he?" I muttered. "He did say he was going to drive slowly, but he should have been back here over half an hour ago."

"Oh, well, like the proverbial bad penny, I'm sure he'll turn up at any moment. Darling, do we have to keep that damn thing in our garage? Can't we just scrap it?" Jenny bristled at the thought before waving her mug at me. "No one is ever going to drive it again. Just call one of those scrap merchants and have them tow it away."

"No, lass. They do … they must do." George raised a finger and pursed his lips. "Lad, I'm a bit confused. *Other* Jason, God rest his sole, drove that Cortina out of Chris's garage in 2016 …" I took a sip of tea and nodded whilst waiting for George to continue. "So, what Jenny is suggesting can't happen. If that car is crushed, how will he drive it in the future? And, in the future, he's already dead, so how will he return to 1994 and help you rid the world of that evil git Colney?"

"George, to be honest with you, I have no idea. Timeline curves, alternative timelines, or something or other. What's happened in the future won't happen again. Older me won't now write that letter because what happened to Jess at the hands of Colney won't now happen."

"Oh … so, if in the future, you know, the future *other* Jason came from, I caught that damn rabbit which is systematically ravaging my allotment, then I've got to snare it again. Is that what you're saying?"

"Yes … I think so."

"And I probably won't marry a Phil or Filippo?"

"Who knows?"

"Oh, I was sort of coming around to the idea. I s'pose—"

"Hang on there, lad," George interrupted Beth with another raised finger. "Does that mean the alternate universe where your older self is, was, or whatever …" George paused and furrowed his brow before continuing. "Does that mean that scoundrel is alive and continuing his campaign of murder?"

All the members of the TTBC shot me a look, probably thinking George posed a good question and were expecting I could furnish a decent answer.

"I don't know. Older me, in 2015, presumably discovered what Paul Colney had done to Jess in 1994. Because *other* Jason said that older Beth and Chris didn't know about time-travel until I died, I can only assume that Colney in 2015 couldn't have been a threat then. Maybe he died years back … years back from 2015, I mean. Maybe he was caught, and another prisoner killed him. You know rapists don't fare well in the criminal world."

"What about those two women … that Sandy Rathbone and the woman who was in your old flat? They will never receive justice. A time-travelling ghost murdered them, and no one will be caught," Jess stated, pondering the tea dregs in the bottom of her mug.

"Darling, that poor girl. Her body can't be left in a shallow grave in the woods …" Jenny paused and pursed her lips before holding me in position with a lie-busting stare. "When exactly did Colney say that? You said earlier he told you that when you were all on the top of the flats. Was that something he shouted when tumbling off the roof?"

Bollocks.

My wife's last sentence harboured more than a hint of sarcasm.

"He said it in the flat," blurted Beth.

I clicked my fingers at Beth. "Yes, that must have been when he told us." I offered a tiny shake of my head at Jenny, willing her not to probe. Clearly, the story we'd concocted when driving home wasn't well thought through.

Our account of the events appeared to be riddled with holes large enough to pass a flotilla of oil tankers through, with my inquisitive wife at the helm of the lead ship. Although I'd intended to keep the exact circumstances of how Paul Colney died under wraps, hoping this new version would almost expunge the reality of Beth's actions, my wife's expression suggested I would have to come clean.

Beth had the presence of mind to button her lip, now sipping her tea with her head bowed.

"Dad," Jess mumbled as she glanced up from her tea-staring. "Can't you make an anonymous call to the police, saying that girl is buried in the woods?"

"Yeah, probably. The poor girl's family need to lay her to—"

I paused as Martin burst through the back door, appearing a smidge out of breath. His expression suggested I didn't need to bother asking him if something hadn't entirely gone to plan.

"Shit," I muttered. "I'm not going to like this, am I?"

"Not a lot." He nervously grinned.

"You crashed the Cortina?"

"No … not exactly."

I detected there would be a but coming. Martin closed the back door and glanced around the room before settling his eyes upon me.

"We do have a slight problem, though."

"How slight?"

"Huge probably covers it," he winced.

"What kind of a huge problem?"

"See, after I left you and Beth, I nipped around the back of the community centre to get the Cortina, but—"

"But what?"

"That reporter who's been following us—"

"King … Carlton King?"

448

"Yeah. See, in all the excitement, I may have forgotten to lock the Cortina when we went after Colney." Martin winced again.

"Martin, Jesus, get to the point. What the hell happened?"

"Okay, when I returned to the Cortina, I noticed some bloke rummaging around in the car. I hauled his arse out and punched him, thinking it was some scrote from the estate—"

"It was him … King?"

"Yeah. He's been following us. He said he'd seen what had happened. You know, the gunshots, Colney on the roof."

I shot Beth a look, all her bluster and excitement draining away.

"He threatened to go to the police unless I explained what was going on and how your Cortina, which he knew was involved in that altercation with a tree in 1977, was now parked up on the Broxworth."

"Holy shit."

Jenny grabbed my arm. "Darling, what the hell are we going to do? If he starts blabbing—"

"I've sorted it," blurted Martin, as he scanned around the room at the faces gawping back at him. "He won't say anything. I can guarantee he won't utter a word."

"How?" I barked. "Christ, Martin, threatening him won't work. The man's a snivelling gobshite journalist. He'll sing that loud from the bloody rooftops, I reckon even Topol couldn't compete."

"Apsley, he won't be singing anything, but I've gotta be on the next flight back to Spain."

42

Two weeks later

Games Without Frontiers

"Adam,"

"Uh-huh," he mumbled, as he dragged on his cigarette whilst vacantly watching the misty rain slowly obscure the windscreen.

"We could visit St Albans tomorrow. Look, it's not far from here." Verity raised the dogeared 1982 version of her A-to-Z map from her lap and showed the distance with splayed-out fingers mimicking a set of compass callipers. "There's the Verulamium museum, the old city walls, and the Roman Theatre. What d'you think?" Verity sipped the coffee she'd previously poured into the plastic cup from the flask borrowed from her mother before propping her bare feet on the dashboard and glancing at her boyfriend. "Shall we?"

Adam flicked the ash from his cigarette through the half-inch gap of the driver's side window. "Yeah, okay, sounds good," he mumbled, checking his watch and scratching his beard before offering his girlfriend a cheeky grin. "We'll stay here tonight, though?"

"Yeah, here's as good a place as any."

"Shall we have an early night?" Adam raised an alluring eyebrow at Verity as he pinged the butt through the gap.

"Mr Adam Waller, are you suggesting you want your wicked way with me?"

"I am, and I do."

"Oh, if I must," she giggled.

"Right, I'm going for a pee." Adam hopped out of their camper van and hot-footed into the trees, fumbling with his fly.

"Adam, d'you want me to hold it for you?" Verity playfully called out as she cranked down her window.

"I think you'll have a job. It's that bleeding cold out here, I can hardly find it," he chuckled, skipping along with his hand rummaging around in his underpants before stopping by the first tree. Adam leaned back and peered up, scanning the dusky clouds as he sighed in relief when relieving himself.

Adam and Verity, long-time sweethearts from way back when in their last year of primary school, had embarked on this trip around the British Isles while taking a gap year from university. Their planned trip had been delayed because of a broken drive shaft on the dilapidated second-hand van borrowed from one of Adam's father's mates. The repairs had taken two weeks, setting them back on their adventure. Although annoying, they were now on the open road and looked forward to the summer together. They'd planned to attend Glastonbury with Adam looking forward to Peter Gabriel, Paul Weller, and Van Morrison, but apart from that, they were free to do whatever took their fancy.

After completing one of those forever-type pees, Adam shook his appendage before thrusting his hips back to tuck himself in. Hoping Verity had made herself comfortable, he scooted back to the camper van.

As Adam and Verity enjoyed their carnal pleasure, causing the van's suspension to squeak, they were unaware of what might have happened in an alternative timeline. However, the next day, after an unexpected detour to Fairfield Police Station, they visited the old Roman city of Verulamium before continuing their journey.

No one can really understand or verify the existence of alternate universes or timeline curves … they're just theories about time-travel.

Or are they?

Of course, if the drive shaft on their van hadn't broken, the young couple would have made it to the outskirts of Fairfield a few weeks ago. They probably would have parked in the same layby on the 6th of April, a couple of days after Easter. If they had, they might have encountered Tony Lencoy, who'd just murdered and buried Jessica Poole.

However, time had bent from its laid down path. In this timeline, their borrowed van suffered a broken drive shaft. Tony Lencoy died on Easter Saturday, four days before murdering Jessica Poole. These subtle changes resulted in the young travelling couple avoiding an encounter with evil. A man in the woods with a spade, a blood-dripping Bowie knife, a menacing glower, and murderous intentions.

Unfortunately for Claire Bragg, the nefarious murderer still visited the wooded area adjoining the layby on Good Friday. Where, in both timelines, he dug a sizable hole and buried the poor woman's body.

The following day, before setting off for their trip to take in the sights of the ruins of the Roman City, Adam nipped back to the woods for the same reason he had the previous night. That morning, due to being daylight and not wishing to be spotted waving his todger around, Adam jogged to the end of the layby and stepped into the bushes.

As he gingerly pushed his way into the undergrowth and hooked out his appendage, that's the point when he spotted the burnt-out car. He couldn't ascertain the make and model. However, the splash of paintwork below the offside rear wheel arch suggested it may have originally been yellow.

43

Love is Like a Butterfly

Detective Inspector Adele Megson accepted the call on her mobile phone after applying the handbrake and killing the engine. She listened for half a minute while her boss, DCI French, raised an inquisitive eyebrow before folding her arms across her chest. That telltale action the DCI employed when she didn't want to be kept waiting.

"Yeah, course I remember that case. I was a DC back in the late '80s." Adele paused whilst the caller continued.

Two weeks after the riots, DCI French and her team had made scant little progress towards apprehending the perpetrator of Sandy Rathbone's murder or locating the missing woman who rented the flat where Jason Apsley had once lived. Also, if that wasn't enough to send her and the team into a spin, they'd discovered two more bodies three days after the riot. Both male and believed to be drug dealers.

Coincidentally – that word not in the DCI's vocabulary – one body was discovered in that very same flat rented by the missing woman, and the other with his face shot off at the rear of Belfast House. Furthermore, neither body could be identified. The local snouts informed her team that the *underworld* were as mystified to the identities of the bodies as were the police.

To add pressure to her already stretched resources, her team had another case to add to an already impossible workload. A call from a Mrs King, stating she hadn't seen or heard from her son for over a week, which was apparently unusual, suggested her team had another misper to investigate. Was it all just a coincidence? Was it a quirk of fate that the reporter who knew Jason Apsley, who'd suggested at that press briefing that Paul Colney was alive and kicking years after his death, just happened to be a misper?

Heather didn't believe in coincidence, and for that very reason, she and her DI were now parked outside number eleven Winchmore Drive.

On their way back to the station, following a relatively pointless excursion to interview a potential eyewitness regarding the murder of Sandy Rathbone, DCI French had suggested they swing by Jason Apsley's place.

Despite being the lead detective in Fairfield, and because of the national interest, a task force from the Met were drafted in to investigate the murder of PC Tomsett, along with the death of Gary O'Rourke, the lowlife rioter, who died when a trigger-happy police firearms marksman sent a slug through the man's heart. Although the DCI wasn't chuffed about having the Met crawling over her patch, she accepted that the workload was almost unmanageable.

"Right, okay." DI Megson paused and nodded. "Secure the vehicle, and we'll be there in about an hour." The DI ended the call and glanced up at her boss. "I know this is a case we don't enjoy discussing. But you remember the Cortina that reappeared in 1987 wedged between a tree and a bus stop along Coldhams Lane?"

DCI Heather French raised an eyebrow. "Not something I'm likely to forget, is it? I get the distinct impression I'm not going to like this."

"No, Guv, not much. It appears a couple of student types in an old VW camper van parked up in a layby on the Haverhill Road reported a burnt-out car with a body in the driver's seat. One of the Traffic boys, first on the scene, stated that it's an old Mk3 Cortina … index number Kilo, Delta, Papa, Four, Seven, Two, November."

"Christ!" The DCI puffed out her cheeks before glancing at Jason Apsley's house. "The body?"

DI Megson scrunched her nose and shook her head. "You remember that sitcom, Butterflies? Wendy Craig played the wife who couldn't cook."

DCI French raised that eyebrow again as she side-eyed her DI.

"My husband is blessed with similar culinary skills, as in everything is a tad overdone."

"The body's burnt to a crisp?"

"Got it in one, Guv."

"Right, come on. Let's see what this meddling schoolteacher has to say for himself. I think today could be the second time in your career you'll arrest Jason Apsley."

The DI's pager bleeped as the two officers approached the drive. DCI French nodded to her DI, confirming she could return to the vehicle and call the station, before planting her finger on the doorbell.

44

Naked Gun

"So, do you see the issue, Mr Apsley?"

"Of course, Chief Inspector. But as I said, my car was stolen from my lock up. I only discovered it was missing a couple of days ago. To be honest, I didn't report it because I suspect a missing old car that some joyrider took for a spin would presumably be deemed a low priority for your lot." I trotted out my well-practised lie. With my 'butter wouldn't melt' performance in full flow, I continued. "Have you apprehended the culprit?" I glanced at Jenny, who remained po-faced. Just as we planned, my wife saying nothing.

DCI French carefully placed her mug on top of the Easter copy of the Radio Times, depicting a farcical picture of Leslie Nielsen on a motorbike with a six-foot Easter chick, advertising the film *Naked Gun 2½ The Smell of Fear*. For sure, I reckoned the ever-sharp-minded detective could see, let alone smell, the fear radiating from my pale, quiescent wife.

"Mr Apsley—"

"Jason," I interrupted. "Please call me Jason."

Frenchie nodded. "Jason. Do you remember a student of yours from the late '70s?"

"Oh, well, that would be testing my brain. There are thousands of kids at the school every year," I nervously chuckled after jumping in when the DCI paused her deliberate cadenced questioning.

"The one I'm specifically referring to became a freelance journalist," Frenchie uttered the last word as if it tasted bitter. "Carlton King. That name ring any bells?"

"More tea?" Jenny leapt from her chair, snatching the mug from the Welsh officer who'd arrested me seven years ago, before reaching for Frenchie's cup.

"No, Mrs Apsley. My Inspector and I are both suitably refreshed, thank you."

Jenny, hand poised by the copy of the Radio Times, glanced past Frenchie into the middle distance. The DCI moved her head to gain my wife's attention.

"Carlton King. That name mean anything to you, Mrs Apsley?"

Jenny offered a thin smile as she grabbed Frenchie's mug. "No, no, I don't think so. I'll just take these through to the kitchen."

"Perhaps the mugs could stay on the table for the moment if you don't mind. I'd like to speak with both you and your husband."

Jenny shot me a nervous glance before returning to her seat as instructed.

"A couple of weeks ago, early on Easter Saturday, I held a press briefing. Usual form, updating the local reporters on our progress with catching the perpetrator of the murder of Sandy Rathbone … a nasty case that I'm sure both of you have heard about on the news." Frenchie paused, awaiting both my wife and me to nod. "Carlton King, now freelancing for the News

458

of the World, who was a previous student of yours, attended that briefing and posed a question."

"Not sure I can remember him if I'm honest. As I said, thousands of kids go through that school every year."

"Oh, that's disappointing. I felt sure you would remember him, especially as he used to work at the Chronicle. Your close friend, Mr Sutton, worked there for many years, and I expect he would definitely remember Mr King." Frenchie nodded at her DI. "Disappointing, wouldn't you say, DI Megson?"

"Yes, Guv. Disappointing."

I knitted my brows and feigned concentration. "Well, George may have, but sorry, that name isn't one I remember."

"Hmmm. Are you certain?" Frenchie glanced at Jenny before raising expectant eyebrows in my direction.

As always seemed to be the case when questioned by this particular officer, my surging hot flush suggested I wasn't being wholly truthful. Who needed a lie detector when I had my own built-in version, which presumably had now morphed the skin on my neck to resemble that of a freshly boiled lobster?

"Would you like a moment to rethink your answer?"

I vigorously shook my head, choosing to keep my mouth shut for fear of uttering something in a voice more befitting a choirboy.

"How strange, DI Megson."

"Very strange, Guv."

"My officers are also investigating the death of a man with multiple gunshot wounds, who appeared to have fallen from the top of Belfast House. Similar to the circumstances of the death of David Colney." Frenchie raised an eyebrow at her DI. "Similar, wasn't it, DI Megson?"

"Very similar, Guv."

"I presume you've also heard about that incident? The local press could be called all sorts, but efficient, they are."

Jenny and I nodded.

"We believe that death is related to the murder of another man with gunshot wounds discovered in your old flat. Along with the disappearance of Claire Bragg, the woman who resides there."

"Yes, all shocking stuff, isn't it?" I babbled, clearing my throat before continuing. "The reports on the news suggested it was all to do with rival drug gangs."

"Maybe. As I said, we're investigating."

"Of course. But … apart from my stolen car and a reporter I can't remember, how does this involve me and my wife?"

Jenny shot me a look.

"Mrs Apsley, are you alright? You don't look yourself. Would you like DI Megson to fetch you a glass of water?"

Jenny cleared her throat as she nervously wiggled her bum in her chair. "No, I'm fine. Just a bit of a headache, that's all. And please, call me Jenny." My wife bulged her eyes at me, then shot a glance to a side table where Carlton's book lay half hidden by a newspaper.

I offered an involuntary nervous giggle before clearing my throat and stepping sideways to ensure when Frenchie looked at me, the book wasn't in her line of sight. "I'm sorry we can't help you. But thank you for letting me know about my car. I'll arrange to have it towed and scrapped. You know, it just so happens, I was going to get rid of the old thing, anyway."

"No, sorry, Mr Apsley, but your vehicle is now part of our investigations."

"Oh, really? I'd have thought a stolen, burnt-out car would be rather low on your priority list."

"Well, you'd think so, wouldn't you? However, a week ago, we discovered a rental car parked on the Broxworth Estate. Well, I'd suggest it was more abandoned than parked. See, Mr Apsley, when we investigated, it appeared a Mr Tony Lencoy, who's now disappeared, rented that vehicle from Luton Airport."

"Oh."

"Yes, oh. My officers spent many hours, far too many, I might add, trawling through the airport's CCTV video tapes and just by chance happened to land on some footage in the short stay car park which shows *you*, I believe your friend Leonardo Bretton, and Mr King having a heated discussion."

Again, I offered that nervous schoolgirl giggle, followed by a defeatist-type whine. Jenny bowed her head, her knuckles white where she gripped her hands together.

"So, as that meeting occurred two weeks ago yesterday, on Good Friday, I'm a little surprised you can't remember Mr King."

Apart from the Welsh DI removing a Yorkie Bar wrapper from her suit jacket and noisily scrunching it into a ball, silence ominously hovered between the four of us.

"Oh, that." I clicked my fingers. "Ah … so that's who he was. This chap approached me and said he recognised me from school but didn't actually introduce himself."

Frenchie raised a disbelieving eyebrow. "And Mr Bretton?"

461

"Ah, no, I picked up an old friend that day. Tyler … Tyler Powers. Come to think of it, now you mention it, you know, he does look a bit like Leonardo. Funny that."

"Hilarious, Mr Apsley. Hilarious."

My vocal cords gave a nervous, childish murmur before I continued. "Sorry, but apart from teaching the lad, what has Carlton King got to do with me?"

"Mr and Mrs Apsley …" Frenchie glanced between us during that pregnant pause she'd perfected. That annoying technique game shows and reality TV programmes would infuriatingly adopt in the near future. "It has an awful lot to do with you because a few moments ago, my colleagues discovered the body of Mr King in your burnt-out Cortina."

We'd been expecting a visit from the local constabulary for the last two weeks. When Carlton had threatened to go to the police on the afternoon of that Easter Saturday, Martin reacted without thinking. He'd punched Carlton for a second time, knocking him out cold, killing him stone dead when the investigative reporter cracked his head against the car's roof.

Then, according to my time-travelling loose cannon, he'd panicked. With limited options at his disposal, Martin had driven to a secluded layby on the Haverhill Road, where he torched the time machine with a dead reporter inside. I was amazed it had taken the police this long to discover it.

Frenchie nodded at her DI, then bowed her head.

Like the condemned prisoner in the dock when the judge donned the black cap upon his wig, a cloak of doom descended when I considered what would happen next.

"Mr Apsley," calmly stated the Welsh detective. "I'm arresting you on suspicion of perverting the course of justice. You do not have to say …"

"Bollocks," I muttered.

"Quite. As I was saying. Mr Apsley, I'm arresting you …"

45

2015 … Again.

Calling Time

That day, over twenty years ago, when Martin torched the Cortina, effectively called time on any further time-travelling escapades. As Jenny had pestered me to do for many years, Martin's actions put the kibosh on that mass-produced saloon car's special powers – what a relief.

After managing to get myself arrested again, just as I had in 1987, I endured a lengthy interrogation when interviewed under caution by Frenchie and her chocolate-bar-obsessed DI. Of course, I stuck to my story and was duly released without charge some five hours later. The two 'drug dealers' were never identified. Well, of course they weren't. One being a dead Paul Colney, and the other a man who disappeared in 1976 – Big Ears, as my daughter called him.

However, apart from the members of the TTBC, no one knew that. Similarly, the police failed to charge anyone for the murder of Sandy Rathbone, and Claire Bragg remains, to this day, a missing person. Jenny and I, for many years, every Good Friday, would lay a small posy of flowers in the woods up at that layby to keep her memory alive.

How Carlton King ended up in my old car, as far as the police are concerned, also remained a mystery. During my interrogation, I learned that Carlton's burnt-out car, a black BMW 3 Series, had been discovered on a piece of waste ground near the Broxworth. Joyriders, I suspect. However, that at least confirmed I hadn't been seeing phantoms. That snivelling weasel of a reporter had been following me.

An appeal that showed a grainy CCTV camera shot of two figures in a yellow car came to nothing. We never issued Chris, Megan, or Colin an application form – ignorance is bliss, as they say. However, as you can imagine, we faced tricky questions from both men when the news of Jill Dando's death hit the headlines a few years later.

As was in my first life, the person or persons responsible for the death of PC Tomsett were never identified. I heard the firearms officer who took down a rioter, Gary O'Rourke, in this life left the force in 1995 after a period of suspension from duty. Of course, in my first life, he never pulled the trigger. I often mused that perhaps the intervention of Paul Colney or *other* Jason during that night of rioting on the Broxworth had in some way caused him to squeeze his trigger finger. Small changes can have huge effects – I guess I'll never know.

So, here I was, in my ninth decade, struggling with the onset of dementia. Time didn't bend easily. The suggestion *other* Jason mooted back in 1994, that I may have gone gaga in my later life, appeared to be coming to fruition. During regular visits to the GP practice, my fresh-faced doctor, who reckoned I was his best customer, always chuckled and thought it somewhat remarkable I wasn't already six feet under. Apart from needing to invest in a catering-sized pot of spot cream and work on improving his bedside manner, I guess he was a decent sort.

That version of 2016, where *other* Jason had come from, always played on my mind. My health was failing, and like those prisoners awaiting a lethal injection, death row couldn't be cheated. However, in this version, timeline, alternate world, whatever, as opposed to the version older me experienced when writing that letter, Jess remained alive and well. Now a retired fifty-nine-year-old respectable lady, living with her husband Colin, enjoying weekends with their grandchildren, my great-grandchildren, events that couldn't have existed in that alternate world.

You remember that nice Italian boy, Filippo? The one with whom Beth enjoyed a date on the day she murdered her uncle. Well, Beth didn't marry him. Yes, they dated for a few months, maybe through to the summer of '95 – again, that pink blancmange wallowing between my ears, hampering my ability to remember. Insipid, like a wet weekend in our now scrapped caravan, was the only polite word Beth used to describe the well-turned-out Filippo with the winning smile. Yes, he was tall, and dark, and I guess handsome. However, it would take one hell of a man to light my daughter's fire.

As had been the case in my first life, so far, no man had matched up to her high expectations. That aside, Beth in this life appeared to be a far more contented person than my 'super-bitch' bestie from my first life. *Other* Jason had stated that Beth was happily married in 2016. So, I guess the changes caused by Jess being saved rippled out and altered the future. Of course, I didn't feel guilty about those changes because we'd successfully saved Jess and rid the world of Paul Colney. And anyway, Beth made her choices. She forged her path through life, which was down to her, not anyone else.

"Jason, darling. We have a visitor," Jenny called from the bottom of the stairs.

"Oh, on my way, love," I replied, wondering why I'd traipsed up to the bedroom in the first place. As I said, pink blancmange is how I described that rapidly declining organ sloshing around between my ears.

Other Jason's statement about Jenny dying in 2014 had given me the heads up for both of us to regularly endure yearly MOTs. Those checkups discovered Jenny's cancer early and, after a few rounds of treatment, the oncologist – who benefited from a significantly better bedside manner and physiognomy than my GP – advised us that Jenny was now in full remission. Thankfully for me, Jenny would probably now outlive me.

As for my dementia, that was an unstoppable force. I'd accepted it would win the battle to accelerate my second death. Medical science hadn't found a cure for pink-blancmange-brain syndrome, as I called it – a term that amused my GP so much he said he might use it when discussing the condition with other patients. I think the man should have majored in stand-up comedy rather than medical training.

So, I was dying again. A chronic decline as opposed to that acute death experience in my old Beemer in Cockfosters' High Street. According to *other* Jason, Beth and Chris had previously stated that my final couple of years were spent alone. However, in this version of 2015, Jenny was still with me. No medical science can prove this, but we humans, the pack animals that we are, possess an uncanny way of surviving when sharing the love of another. I just had the feeling with Jenny still alive and kicking, I'd battle on for a few more years. As far as I was concerned, Jenny's extended life had offered me a reprieve, and I was no longer at the head of the line on death row.

As I padded into the kitchen, presuming one of the neighbours had popped in for a coffee, I stopped short when noticing a rotund middle-aged lady squashing the life out of the padded seat of a bar stool.

"Hello, Mr Apsley."

Although greying, with a few extra lines sullying her forehead, Frenchie didn't appear any different from the last time we'd spoken twenty-odd years ago.

"DCI French, hello. To what do we owe the pleasure?"

"Oh, please, it's retired DCI these days," she chuckled. Although still good-old Frenchie, those few spoken words served to convey that the redoubtable retired officer had mellowed significantly. "How're you keeping? Jenny tells me you're having a few struggles with your health. I'm sorry to hear that."

I batted her statement away with a waft of my hand. "Oh, just a bit of bother with forgetfulness, that's all. Apart from sometimes struggling to remember who I am, I couldn't be better," I chuckled.

Jenny placed three coffees on the breakfast bar and grabbed the seat opposite Frenchie. I remained standing. Not that for one moment did I consider I may be arrested, and although it was only my mind waning, not my body, being ready to run seemed like the best tactic.

"As you're retired, I presume you haven't come to arrest me?" I offered an exaggerated grin to hide my concern regarding the reason for her visit.

"Oh, no … Mr Apsley, I no longer have those powers."

"No, I s'pose you don't. Anyway, please call me Jason. So, if you still held a warrant card, would you be arresting me?" I shot Jenny a concerned glance, which she reciprocated along with chewing her lip.

"No … I just thought I'd pop around and update you on a … well, I suppose you'd call it a strange development."

"Development?" questioned Jenny.

"Strange, you say," I chimed in, holding my mug to my lips.

"Peculiar beyond the pale is how I would describe it."

"Go on. You have us intrigued." I feigned a grin as my stomach performed those Nadia Comăneci styled somersaults. Either my guts were in a state of panic, or I was late for my regular bathroom mid-morning turn-out.

"Yes, so we have to go way back to 1987. As you will no doubt recall that Cortina of yours appeared on Coldhams Lane ten years after crashing into a tree, killing Paul Colney and another man who we never managed to identify."

I nodded and inwardly winced, doing my level best not to show my concern. Despite my pink-blancmange syndrome, I couldn't forget the events of 1987.

"Do you remember that man was blessed with some rather odd tattoos? Something I will never forget. One of which was the football emblem of Manchester United with the words 'twenty league titles' penned in ink below. I'm not really a football fan. My father liked to follow the Arsenal in the sixties and seventies. Charlie George was his favourite player, I think."

"Outstanding player," I mumbled.

"Yes, I'm sure. That would be your era of football, too, I suspect."

I offered a thin smile. Truth be known, although not a Gooner, the *Invincibles* were more my era, being in my twenties when they achieved their unbeaten run in my first life.

"You see, Mr Apsley, that dead man's Manchester United tattoo also states they would win their twentieth league title in 2013 ... which they did." Frenchie, although retired, still knew when to employ that well-practised pregnant pause. "Almost as if he was a man from the future ... time-travel, perhaps."

Oh bollocks.

"As if," I chuckled. "That's the stuff of films."

"Yes, of course. I'm sure you're right. Still, very odd, don't you think?"

I side-eyed Jenny, who appeared to be feigning heartburn, rubbing her sternum, wincing, and avoiding eye contact with our guest.

"I have a protégé in the force. Super lad, who I arrested some years back and then persuaded to come over to the dark side. Detective Sergeant Nelson Richards, although I know he prefers to be called Viv ... silly station names—"

"I'm sure," interrupted Jenny, seemingly relieved we'd moved past talking about tattoos. "Did you have a station name, Heather?"

"I did. Not that anyone ever dared say it in my earshot. I was a bit of an old battleaxe back in the day—"

"Oh, Heather, I'm sure you weren't. You've done very well for yourself. We used to say, didn't we, darling?" Jenny patted the back of my hand. "We used to comment about Heather's successful career and what a role model she was for young girls."

I nodded, offering a tight smile. Although Jenny appeared to have perked up, now the conversation had moved on, I feared she was forgetting Frenchie hadn't revealed the punchline regarding the 'peculiar beyond the pale' statement uttered not two minutes ago.

"Bristols. That was the stupid name. Bristols. For the life of me, I can't imagine how they conjured up that one. I mean, I don't think I've ever been to Bristol, or Avon and Somerset, for that matter." Heather chuckled to herself, not something I'd witnessed before, and a far cry from her more usual undemonstrative demeanour. "The closest I've come to that county was when the Avon lady came calling." Heather sighed and plucked up her coffee.

"I think that doesn't exist anymore. I'm not entirely sure when, but they abolished that county some years ago."

"Oh, I didn't know that." Frenchie licked her lips after taking a sip of her coffee. "I'll bow to your greater knowledge. You know, with you being a schoolteacher."

"Retired."

"Aren't we both? Anyway, that's the silly name they called me. Bristols," she tutted again. "I really don't know where the idiots conjure up such rubbish."

Jenny and I both glanced at her chest. Frenchie had always sported a buxom bosom that could easily support a tray of twenty full beer steins with room to spare. As the years rolled by, her significant frontage appeared to have maintained its beer-carrying properties.

"You were saying about a friend in the force. Viv, I think you called him?" I quizzed, whilst Frenchie drained her coffee.

"Oh, so I was. I tell you, these days, I can't remember a damn thing."

"You and me both," I muttered.

"Yes, so, I was having a chinwag with Viv this morning … he's a lovely lad, you know. He's always coming around to see me. I think he likes to run the details of cases past me to get my take on things."

"You're a regular Miss Marple."

"I suppose I am." Heather pondered that statement as she gazed into the middle distance. "He's a bit like the son I never had. West Indian, he is. His parents came over here in the '70s, I think. Anyway, listen to me prattling on."

Jenny and I exchanged a glance as we all sipped our coffee.

"Lovely coffee, Jenny. Is it percolated? I do so like percolated coffee."

"Nespresso ... Jason likes his coffee, don't you, love?"

"I do." I nodded at Frenchie, pushing her to continue. Whether she was purposefully playing the little old lady routine or she had mellowed to such an extent that she now liked to discuss the ins and outs of brewing coffee, I couldn't tell. Notwithstanding the dread of what 'peculiar beyond the pale' might mean, I needed to hear it.

"Yes, sorry, I digress. So, Viv casually dropped into the conversation that his colleagues discovered an old 1974 Mk3 Cortina abandoned in the bushes near that layby on the Haverhill Road. Bright yellow paintwork, apparently."

"Oh ... like my old one?" I could detect my throat tightening as if an invisible pair of hands constricted my airways.

"Yes, like yours from way back when."

"They're classic ..." I paused and cleared my throat. "I think they would be classed as a classic car these days. It's a real shame it's been abandoned." I could feel my core temperature rising to a level that I presumed my supercilious GP would class as feverish.

"Yes, I suppose they would be now. Odd that we, the police, discovered it after yours was found there over twenty years ago. Of course, I was intrigued, so I enquired about the index number."

I felt my knees starting to wobble.

"That's what made me prick up my ears, I can tell you. Kilo, Delta, Papa, Four, Seven, Two, November."

I white-knuckle-gripped the worktop.

Jenny's mouth flapped open, then abruptly snapped shut when Frenchie moved past her second pregnant pause.

"Yes, how strange? Your old car had the very same licence plate, did it not?" The retired DCI rotated her head between Jenny and me as we both winced.

For the past twenty years, I'd assumed we were free from that bloody mass-produced saloon car. However, like a lost puppy pining for its mother, it just annoyingly seemed to find its way home.

"Ehm … more coffee, Heather?" I offered, keen to fill the void caused by neither Jenny nor me knowing how to respond.

"Oliver! For God sake, slow down. You'll give Nanna and Grandad a ruddy heart attack!"

My nine-year-old grandson burst through the backdoor, hurtling towards Jenny before flinging his arms around my wife. "Nanna," he sang in that choir-boys soprano voice.

"Hello, my cherub. This is a lovely surprise." Jenny planted a kiss on Oliver's crown as they hugged.

"I tell you, Phil. That trip to the soft-play centre was a complete clusterfuck! How can our nine-year-old be banned for abusive and violent behaviour? You need to sue the arse off that bloody place. God love him, but our boy is doing my effing head in. I mean, we need to get him checked to see if he's got that ruddy ADHD thingy. Fuckerdefuck, if he has,

473

that comes from your side because, spoiler alert, I'm completely fucking normal!" my daughter hissed at Oliver's father before stepping through the open back door.

Although not by any stretch of the imagination tall, dark, or handsome, and could be labelled as vertically and follicly challenged, Phil Baker, Filippo's old drinking buddy, and Beth had enjoyed a fling. The product of that brief liaison from ten years ago now cuddled his grandmother. Beth and Phil stayed close for Oliver's sake. However, due to both possessing vibrant and charismatic characters, neither could tolerate each other's company for much longer than it took to suck a wine gum.

In the interest of détente and to also enjoy time with our grandson, Jenny and I always accompanied them on their summer holidays. Although not living together, I guess you could say Beth and Phil enjoyed a 'modern' relationship where they held joint custody of Oliver and satisfied each other in the bedroom on a 'friends with benefits' kind of basis when they both felt the urge.

My once grandfather, then close friend George, who departed this world on the same day as in my first life, would have struggled to understand my daughter's and Phil's relationship. However, and rather oddly, it seemed to work.

"Hi, Mum, hi, Dad. We thought we'd pop in … oh, shit, you've got company. Shit, sorry!"

"Jason, Jenny, I'll leave you to it. It was lovely to see you both again. Perhaps we could catch up another day and discuss …"

"Cars?" I mumbled, still trying to digest the information about that bloody yellow thing and how it had made it back.

"Yes, cars. Perhaps films, too. Books maybe? I like H. G. Wells. How about you?" Frenchie raised that inquisitive eyebrow at me.

"My favourites," I grinned.

"I imagine they would be."

"DCI French, this is my grandson Oliver, my daughter Beth, and … Phil."

"Hello, nice to meet you all. I was just leaving, so won't encroach on your family time."

Beth's mouth flapped a few times before Jenny shot her a look, encouraging her to shut it. Keen to encourage Frenchie to leave, I waved my hand forward and escorted the retired officer to the front door. As I opened it, a dishevelled thirty-something man hovered with his finger poised about to ding the doorbell.

"Oh, can I help you?" I grumbled; there was nothing worse than wanky cold callers.

"I don't know. I'm looking for Jason Apsley."

"Well, sir, you're in luck. He is him." Frenchie tapped my arm. "See you soon, Jason. Perhaps you and Jenny can come around for afternoon tea? You could meet my friend Viv."

Frenchie affirmed her suggestion with an exaggerated nod before striding purposefully up the drive, waving back at me as she sunk into her car seat. I watched her drive off before reassessing the man in front of me.

"Sorry, can I help?" Quite a polite greeting for me, considering I treated most cold callers with the contempt of a Jehovah's Witness suffering from a particularly prevalent case of leprosy.

"You're Jason Apsley?"

"I am, and who are you?"

"My name is Carlton King."

"Oh, bollocks."

~

What's next?

So, after four books, I'm calling time on Jason's adventures and leaving him to see out the remaining years of his second life. However, fear not … there's more to come. Beth, now operations manager of the Time Travellers Believers' Club, takes up the story in the next adventure in that unremarkable Hertfordshire town of Fairfield.

Our girl may have her work cut out dealing with that investigative journalist who now finds himself living twenty years in the future. Plus, there's the tricky issue of what to do with a certain yellow car.

I hope you get the chance to read Beth's adventure in *Borrowed Time,* due to be published in 2024. In the meantime, perhaps check out my other books too!

Can you help?

I hope you enjoyed this book. Could I ask for a small favour? Can I invite you to leave a rating or review on Amazon? Just a few words will help other readers discover my books. Probably the best way to help authors you like, and I'll hugely appreciate it

Free eBook for you

For more information and to sign-up for updates about new releases, please drop onto my website, where you'll get instant access to your FREE book – Beyond his Time.

When you sign up, you get a no-spam promise from Adrian, and you can unsubscribe at any time.

You can also find my Facebook page and follow me on Amazon – or, hey, why not all three.

Adrian Cousins.co.uk

Facebook.com/AdrianCousinsAuthor

Books by Adrian Cousins

The Jason Apsley Series

Jason Apsley's Second Chance

Ahead of his Time

Force of Time

Beyond his Time

Calling Time

Borrowed Time

Acknowledgements

Thank you to my Beta readers – your input and feedback is invaluable.

Adele Walpole

Brenda Bennett

Tracy Fisher

Patrick Walpole

And, of course, Sian Phillips, who makes everything come together – I'm so grateful.

Printed in Great Britain
by Amazon

47522236R00272